The
JOHNSTOWN GIRLS

THE JOHNSTOWN GIRLS

Kathleen George

University of Pittsburgh Press

DISCLAIMER

This is a work of fiction. References to the men in the Bosses Club
and to other historical figures of 1889 are as accurate as I could make
them, but all other characters are works of my imagination. Alice
Quinn's ride on a mattress in 1889 is an actual event, which has in-
spired not only me but also Sharon Sheehe Stark and probably others
I don't know of. The places I use are often based on real ones, but
details are mine. The Pirates' 1989 season has been slightly altered
to fit my purposes. The photographs included are not intended to
be read as illustrations of characters in the book but are instead a
chronicle of real lives, other lives, of the times—I find these lost lives
very moving.

Published by the University of Pittsburgh Press, Pittsburgh, Pa., 15260
Copyright © 2014, Kathleen George
All rights reserved
Manufactured in the United States of America
Printed on acid-free paper
10 9 8 7 6 5 4 3 2 1

Library of Congress Cataloging-in-Publication Data

George, Kathleen, 1943–
The Johnstown Girls / Kathleen George
pages cm
ISBN 978-0-8229-4431-7 (hardback)
1. Twins—Fiction. 2. Sisters—Fiction. 3. Floods—Pennsylvania—
Johnstown (Cambria County) —History—19th century—Fiction. I. Title.
PS3557.E487J74 2014
813'.54—dc23   2014001173

For Vivian, Janet, Jenny, and Robin

Acknowledgments

I have so many people to thank that I hesitate to begin for fear of missing someone along the way. Any errors in the manuscript are mine. Any omissions here are my fault—and I hope I don't make any. Let me start with the late Monty Culver who read my first pass at a Johnstown flood novel and encouraged me. And to the Pirates' Alley Faulkner Foundation who named that early pass a finalist in their fiction contest years ago, another great encouragement. My husband Hilary Masters, a tireless supporter, read my other books in draft and so many versions of this novel in particular that I can't count them. *The Johnstown Girls* has benefitted greatly from the wisdom of the retired detective Ronald B. Freeman, from the research work of Meredith Conti, Susan Wiedel, and Ariel Nereson, from the war history expertise of Niles Laughner and Michael Kraus (curator of Soldiers and Sailors Museum), from the cooperation of Marylynne Pitz of the *Pittsburgh Post-Gazette*, Mary Ware of St. Claire Hospital, and Mary Robb Jackson and her husband Michael Challik of KDKA news, and from the incredible generosity of Richard Burkert, the president of the Johnstown Area Heritage Association (JAHA). I continue to be overwhelmed by Richard's willingness to share his time and his encyclopedic knowledge of Johnstown and its floods. One of our first contacts was a several-hour car ride along the path of the flood. Not to be forgotten are the staff members of JAHA who helped enormously: Kaytlin Sumner, Shelley Johanssen, and Marcia Kelly. I would like to thank classmates Nancy Hilbocky Rovansek and Lana Custer for answering questions about Johnstown and Shirley Small Lane for sharing her grandfather's diary with me. Financial support came from the Richard D. and Mary Jane Edwards Endowed Publication Fund at the University of Pittsburgh. Then of course this book would not have been possible without the wonderful staff at the University of Pittsburgh Press: Peter Kracht, the director of the press, and staff members Kelley Johovic, Maria Sticco, Lowell Britson, Alex Wolfe, and Joel W. Coggins. Gratitude, too, goes to "The Seven," my writing group, for humor and advice in our mutual endeavors.

The
JOHNSTOWN GIRLS

A Louis Semple Clarke photograph of a group at the South Fork Fishing and Hunting Club. Virginia Anthony Soule collection, courtesy of Johnstown Area Heritage Association.

Nina

Saturday, April 15, 1989

■ NINA FEELS AN UNEASINESS that borders on guilt. She is in her hometown. Her mother still lives here in Johnstown, but Nina never told her mother she would be here today, pretended instead that she's hitching a ride in tomorrow. She hasn't yet told her mother about Ben.

Ben's reservation specified that they wouldn't be able to get into their room at the Holiday Inn until three, but they came by at noon and the guy at the desk said blithely, "Oh, sure, you can go up now."

The room has that motel tang of cleaning fluid and air-conditioning, but it's spacious, the drapery and bedspread fabrics are pink and green, and the whole is not horrible.

Ben is on assignment. Nina is the tagalong, the paramour, the other woman—not true, only it's likely to look that way. He's not divorced yet. She came into his life after the separation.

Ben has to interview a hundred-and-three-year-old woman tomorrow. It was Nina's story idea, her tip. Since she comes from here, she knew about the woman. After a search in which she discovered Ellen Emerson was *still alive*, she pressed Ben to get the story assignment. And not just because she's in love with him.

Other journalists cut corners—crib earlier articles, juice them up, send in a photographer, and add a jazzy paragraph at the end about the

1

last couple of years. But Ben, who doesn't paste or recycle, pitched a whole series of stories, at Nina's suggestion, to their editor, Hal, who said, "Okay then, but get me something new. I want something new."

Good old Hal. *New* is the business they're in all right, but new is not that easy to get.

Mrs. Emerson is going to be the jewel of the series because of her age.

Ben frowns now. "I'm not used to really old people. In my family we die politely at fifty."

"Don't say that."

"It's only a slight exaggeration. I can't imagine her."

He's pulling plastic wrap off plastic glasses, looking forlornly at the bottle of Scotch he's brought along. "Not for now—I know it's a bit early in the day, but won't this be sweet tonight? I wish there were real glass glasses. Scotch out of a plastic cup just doesn't do it."

"I saw real glasses." She moves across the room and unearths them from a tiny tray almost hidden by the card that lists TV stations.

He puts the plastic glasses aside.

She sits on the edge of the bed and says, "You have to live way past fifty. I'll need you. In my life." What she wants to talk about this weekend in between his self-imposed work schedule is their relationship, where they are, how his divorce is progressing, when they will publicly become a couple, and what happens after that.

They plan to see a good bit today, three of the crucial historic sites so that he will feel grounded before his interview with Mrs. Emerson tomorrow morning. It was Nina's idea to stash their things in the room, to unearth combs and toothbrushes and freshen up and get something quick for lunch. They need to get out to the National Park site at 1:30.

The woman Ben will see tomorrow, Ellen Emerson, née Ellen Burrell, is the last survivor of the Johnstown Flood of 1889. Of course she was little more than a toddler at the time, so she's a hundred and three now, almost one hundred and four. And she has a hell of a story to tell. The only trouble is, in journalistic terms, it's yesterday's news, been told before. Still, survival is an appealing lure.

The assignment is a big deal. Ben, lucky Ben, gets to do up to six articles over the next month in a buildup to the centennial of the flood. It's the kind of assignment Nina wishes she got, but Hal would never give it to a newbie.

Ben gets that look on his face, that thing that men do when they're about to make a move, raised eyebrows, that look of appealing, even pleasant, evil. "I think . . . I think I'm going to tell Hal I need many visits to Johnstown and the old lady, oh, say, eight times over the next few weeks. What do you say?"

She laughs agreeably, knowing what he's agitating about. He hates going to her place.

She's told him she can't break a lease just like that. Plus she likes her place. And that, like old news, is an old argument between them.

Now he says, "Isn't this great—not having to worry about who is going to be tapping on the door, watching out the front window?"

But the sad fact is he can't afford multiple "overnight assignments" at Holiday Inns. He's paying for today out of his own pocket because Hal Carson would surely point out that the trip could be made back and forth in a day and would not necessitate an overnight stay. The overnight excuse is really for Ben's estranged wife, who doesn't want him but wants to keep tabs on him.

If you'd asked Nina two years ago if she could handle all this mess, she would have said a definite *no*. But every day she's still with him. She wants a future with Ben, that's the only thing she's certain of. Today is meant to be special—just time away from their usual grind.

He leans forward to kiss her.

Then he begins lowering her to the bed.

Oh, he is so gorgeous. He's exactly who she wants, the man she has always dreamed of. Earthy, not overly neat or buttoned up. Dark hair, a great smile. A sturdy six-foot, olive-skinned, highly intelligent hard worker. With good sense. With a heart.

"Oh, man," he says. "I dream about this, you know. You. Just hours and hours with you."

His hands caress her body—waist, hips.

"Now? Are you sure?" She's a pretty game girl, but they haven't had any lunch and they need to be up the road some fifteen miles for a 1:30 appointment at the flood site and it's already—

His head goes under her skirt. Soon her underwear is off. She gasps at the suddenness of his move, but his groan is so happy. She doesn't really like it when he goes straight for the goods, but she usually gives up any resistance after a few minutes and simply enjoys it.

She likes best when they have kissed and kissed and then he climbs up and props himself over her.

His jeans come off, then his underwear. He wants the whole ball of wax, so she opens herself to him. She loves to watch him work—whether for a story or for her pleasure or his. He's bent on his own pleasure now, paying attention to sensation, timing himself, thrusting slowly, then fast. She pulls him toward her and kisses him. Someday soon she will have a future with him, with his existing kids, then their own, blended it's called, maybe four children for her to fuss over—and in her imagination these kids keep having his hair and eyes and she can't stop hugging and kissing them. She wants a family. Kids. Chaos. Ballgames. All that.

After he comes—she doesn't today though she does most times—they lie there. He holds onto her tight as if he's drowning.

Ah, how will they support those four gorgeous children? Let alone buy tickets to sports events. Is that what he's thinking when he holds on tight? They're too old to have the problems they have. She is twenty-seven but lived jobless for two years trying to be a writer and now has plenty of pressure to pay off her college loans. He's thirty-six and doesn't make a huge salary at the paper even though he's really, really good at what he does. His two boys, eight and six, are always needing something. And his wife will need alimony. He can't fit in a second job though he has contemplated it. As it is, he works long hours at the paper, for the paper. Between her debts and her low-level position at the paper, she's not sure how they will manage when they finally live together, only that they will.

The first problem with her apartment is that it's small. Revise that. Tiny. The second problem is that another low-level employee at the *Post-Gazette*, Michelle, another general assignment reporter, has the apartment on the first floor of the house Nina rents in. Michelle is the one who told Nina about the place being available, which was good. But Michelle badly needs a friend; she's a bit nosy; she doesn't observe boundaries—pokes her head into the hallway when Nina goes out or comes in, often comes up to tap on her door. Michelle doesn't know about the relationship between Nina and Ben. Or . . . if she does, she is circumspect enough not to say anything. They both got speeches when they were hired from the woman in personnel, a mean old thing, about not getting romantically involved with colleagues.

Who can uphold such a rule? People are people. And the job is about the only place a hard worker can meet anybody else.

There are other awkwardnesses, though. Their fellow workers think of Ben as a married man and he's very private. He doesn't talk to his colleagues about the fact that he and Amanda are separated. It's one of those things—he and Nina started in secrecy and somehow it seems to continue that way. And it feels sort of icky.

Her stomach growls. She shakes him. "I love you but I have to eat something."

"Errrrr."

"What?"

"I don't want to move."

"Come on. We have to."

"I don't want you to move."

She kisses him a few times until he props himself on an elbow and then slowly gets up. There's that smile she loves as he pulls on his clothes. "I like motel rooms," he says.

"Oh, sure," she teases. "They give you those free tissues and an ice bucket and everything. Glasses, too, plastic and otherwise."

He starts to laugh and shake his head. "See, you understand me." Meaning Amanda doesn't. Then he's back on the bed, an arm around her, trying to tug her back down.

ON THIS SATURDAY, Ellen Emerson makes her way to the dining table where there is a BLT all ready and well presented, including the toothpick. On most days lunches at her apartment are huge, warm meals: meat loaf, chicken, pork chops. Today is different, a sandwich—because she was telling Ruth how good BLTs were in the Penn Traffic restaurant years ago and Ruth said, "I can make you one good as that!"

What a funny notion Ellen has that she is independent at all. It's not true. Without Ruth, what would she bother to eat? Applesauce and cottage cheese and perhaps ice cream. Soft things, right out of the jar or cup. Because she's old, ancient, the fact that her body gets her from the chair to the table is a bit of a miracle. She can walk; she just hasn't walked terribly far for a while. Today she wears a pair of loose, wide cotton pants and a quietly flowered blouse that is a little like a jacket. Ruth always teases her that she's a fashion plate, hardly true; but she's very clean and neat, always was. Tomorrow she will put on a dress for when that reporter comes to visit.

Ruth asks, "Iced tea?'

"Yes."

"You're excited. You wish it was tomorrow, don't you?"

"I never wish myself into the future. I don't want to shorten anything that's left to me."

Ruth shakes her head, smiling. "I didn't mean . . ."

"I know. You're not rushing me off."

People are amazed and puzzled that Ellen sends Ruth home at night and doesn't get anyone else in. She still wants that feeling of being able to handle things on her own. She goes to bed at eight, reading for hours, uses the walker for safety when she needs to go to the bathroom, and otherwise doesn't stir things up with visits to the kitchen or the living room. Ruth even keeps water and a tin of cookies and crackers at Ellen's bedside in case she gets hungry during the night. Ellen is an ordinary old thing and also a miracle.

Today she and Ruth were busy. They dug out, dusted, and looked at several photo albums. Sometimes it tired her to explain to Ruth what everything was, but Ruth's utter fascination rewarded her. She showed pictures of places she'd lived when married, widowed—and even the apartment buildings where she lived in the old days in New York. Some of the photos are brown and small.

Ruth is African American, sixty years old. She says Ellen changed her life by giving her the right to ideas and that she will never forget that gift. Ellen pays Ruth, her former student from eons ago, as handsomely as she can. The two of them have become friends, though Ruth can't quite give up the student stance.

Ruth sits across from her now. They eat applesauce, potato salad, and their BLTs. The bacon is a little scratchy going down, but there is plenty of mayo to ease the way. The tomato is surprisingly tasty for the early season. Small pleasures. Don't ever dismiss them, Ellen thinks. Tastes, smells, the feel of things, the sounds of birds, music. And talk. Small conversations with people you like. A good book. That's all she asks for these days.

But it's all starting up again! That's what she gets for living past a hundred years. A guy from the *Pittsburgh Post-Gazette* called her. Once more they've found her.

NINA KNOWS about floods—she comes from this town, so she has to know. Everybody knows. Her own mother who survived the flood of 1936 told Nina when she was a child not to worry, the town was now, as publicity said, "the flood-free city." Ha. Not true. The town made a liar of her mum. Nina saw with her own eyes the aftermath of the flood of 1977 when she rushed back after the disaster to find her mother and father. That's a memory she can't shake. She wants Ben to write about that flood, too, *her flood,* and he has promised he will find a way to angle it in. But because she witnessed that flood and read about the earlier ones—the Great Flood of 1889 and the 1936 flood—she's very aware of the proneness of Johnstown to flooding. Her mother lives in the same little box, the one Nina grew up in, the one that survived waters rushing by in 1977, waters that carried refrigerators, bikes, porch furniture. The destruction that year was so bad it's almost impossible to get her mind around anything worse. And 1889 was definitely worse. It's in all the history books. The town was laid flat. It became an ocean, then a debris-ridden landscape.

Nina, who comes from the not-flood-free-city and whose idea this series is, has been preparing Ben, having told him about the site they are going to see at 1:30, the place in the mountains that used to be a lake—the lake that caused the flood, the big one of 1889, though she's never actually been to see the dam site before.

The infamous lake was man-made of what began as a hole in the earth. A dam was built at one end and voila, the result was a gorgeous body of water on a mountaintop, twenty million tons of water, filled with the best fishing the rich tycoons could buy. The lake was three miles long and one mile wide, sixty-five feet deep. It was surrounded by flora and fauna and felt deeply remote, hidden, and precious. Rich people came to summer there (many from Pittsburgh), but *really* rich people, storybook rich, like Frick and Mellon and Carnegie. The lake was the center of the club they had founded, the South Fork Fishing and Hunting Club. This vacation or summer property was an escape for the privileged, up high, looking down, fourteen miles above the city of Johnstown. A train from Pittsburgh took them right there.

Nina now lives in Pittsburgh. Mostly the migration impulse goes Johnstown to Pittsburgh, small town to big, but one hundred years ago people who could afford it were trying to get out of the burgh to relax at the mountain lake where it was cooler and prettier. Oh, what a story it is. The best and worst of humankind. The wealthy people who vacationed there did not want to think about the dam being faulty. To think about it would be to give up their pleasure for a week, a month, a year while the problem was fixed. And what would they do if it were deemed unfixable? They did not want to know that plants were growing through the huge structure of rocks, creating cracks, they did not want to think about debris pushing at the rocks. It had *always* held, that's what most of them kept telling themselves. There were leaks, yes, but the workmen patched the leaks. That's what workmen were for. The dam would simply have to be shored up as needed. It would hold.

But of course it didn't. After a punishing rain that added another eight inches to the lake on May 30, and then more and more the next day, the dam collapsed. It gave way on the afternoon of May 31, 1889. In a matter of minutes a town was destroyed and 2,209 people died. And the story made international news and stayed in the headlines for weeks in a time long before radios and TV were invented. It was the major news of the day.

She selfishly wishes it were hers to write, but she did the next best (and logical) thing: she gave it to Ben.

"You asleep?" he asks.

"No. Thinking about what we're going to see. Going over facts. Preparing to be Girl Friday."

Nina knows her numbers—eight inches, 2,209 dead, fourteen miles, 4:07 p.m. She wrote all this down for Ben.

Now she gets up and does the toothbrush and comb business, but

Ben doesn't move. "Get your notebook. Come on!"

He looks at his watch. "I'm sorry. I need five more minutes."

"Oh." She has to eat. "I'm going to go see if they can make us milk-shakes downstairs. While you get yourself going." If she runs into some-body her mother knows, what then? Oh, she can't think about it. Her mother is very old-fashioned.

She goes down by the elevator and enters the sunny dining room. It seems very clean, but then everything in Johnstown is clean. It's part of its heritage, she jokes to herself, water washing over everything.

"Do you make milkshakes?"

"Nooo," says the girl at the hostess podium. And before Nina can come up with something else she might order fast, the girl disappears, saying, "But I'll go ask if they can make you one."

Now *that* is Johnstown. Clean. *And* filled with people who wish to please. Right there is the whole spirit of the city.

She sits, poring over the menu. What are they saying in the kitchen? *Oh, gosh we really do need a blender.*

Ben is still not downstairs. What else can she order that's fast and portable?

The girl comes back. She has one of the happiest walks and faces Nina has ever seen. "He says he will make you one!" she announces proudly. "What kind?"

"I need two. One chocolate, one vanilla." She'll give Ben a choice.

"You must be very hungry," the girl teases. She looks too young for the job. Seventeen? She appears to be Hispanic. That's new, recent, in the town's population. Johnstown has always welcomed hard workers, has always been the ultimate melting pot. Clean. A wish to please. Hard-working.

She pays cash for the shakes, which are just ready by the time Ben emerges from an open elevator door and chooses the chocolate.

She points him, once they get to the parking lot and climb into his car, toward the exit they will take. After that, a few seconds in the car, sucking at their thick shakes, she directs him: Market Street to Vine Street to Napoleon, then to Route 56 East. By the time they've finished the shakes except for the last desperate slurps, she reminds him, "You're going to need 219 North."

"Okay, Sacajawea."

He's been studying everything, too. He probably doesn't need her facts. He only brought her along to have time together, like a real weekend date, something they've never had.

"You were gorgeous this afternoon."

"Oh, pooh. I mean, thanks."

Together, a week ago, they sat at her place and looked at pictures of the incredible disaster, a whole town flattened. She told him about her flood, the one she'd seen in 1977—cars wrapped around each other, construction tractors on the tops of telephone poles. Houses downed to nothing but splinters and mud. And about what it was like to fear that she had lost her parents.

For a while now they drive in silence. He puts on the radio trying to find something, maybe a Pirates' game.

She says, "They play tonight."

"Ah. You always know." He puts a hand on her thigh, smoothing it affectionately. "Good. We can watch them while we're rolling around."

"It's a good thing I like baseball. Many women would find that very unromantic."

He gives her a slow, sly smile. She's hopeless when he smiles like that. She could forgive him murder.

He has to turn the radio off because the reception is impossible on the highway.

An idea hits her. "Did you call Amanda when I went for the shakes?"

"I did."

"Did she ask if you were alone?"

He pauses. "No."

"Was she at the house?"

"At her mother's this weekend."

Nina doesn't blame Amanda for anything. And not Ben either. It didn't work out. That's enough for her. "Was it a bad phone call?"

"It wasn't good."

She feels a new uneasiness, but doesn't pursue more.

Finally when she thinks they ought to be close to the dam site, she sees an old man taking slow goosesteps along the road. She asks Ben to pull over for a second. She rolls down her window to wave to the old fellow. "Excuse me, sir. Could you tell us if we're near the old lake?

"Oh, it's right up the road here. No water in it these days. It's not a lake anymore."

"I think that's a good thing."

He nods. "I'd say so. There's a guy works it. Young guy. It's a park now."

She bids him goodbye. Men don't ask for directions, but women like to know where they are and to get various other messages along the way. The old guy was telling her, "You can joke about anything when you get old and can't walk. Perfectly acceptable."

She is going to see her mother tomorrow morning when she will pretend she just got into town—unless somebody tells her mother they saw her about town or at the motel. If that happens, she'll take a deep breath and explain about Ben. Her mother won't like his not being divorced yet, but at least there won't be any lies between them.

"Here we are," Ben says. "Here we go."

A modest sign points them down a road where there is room for about ten cars to park, though there are no other cars parked there at the moment. Up ahead, indeed, is a young fellow working at the lake site as the old man said there would be. She and Ben have gotten out of the car and approach where the fellow sits in a little kiosk, reading. He's red-haired and sports muttonchops, perhaps trying to look as if he comes from the last century. Yes, close inspection shows he's wearing a costume of sorts—nothing official—just a pair of overalls with a battered sports coat over them, but he's achieved a look. He's clearly a theatrical fellow so he must be in need of an audience.

"Where are the crowds?" she asks. "I thought there'd be crowds." Somehow she's formed her question of memorable lyrics. *I thought there'd be clowns.* From *A Little Night Music.*

"Don't know. We'll work it up in a couple of months with publicity for the centennial. We'll get some crowds then. You two want to go in?"

"We do," Ben says. "I called ahead for an appointment."

"Oh, right! Oh, yes, of course. I was just expecting one person. You must be Ben Bragdon."

"Right. My colleague is helping on the story."

"Sure."

"Nina Collins," she says, offering a hand, which the boy takes, flushing. Women don't shake hands in his world.

What constitutes "going in"? There is only land around them. The airs smells fresh, of springtime mud and new growth.

Ben takes out a wallet. "Is there a fee?"

The boy waves Ben's money aside. "Not yet. We're just working up to it." *Working up to* is a phrase he likes.

Then the boy places the book he was reading title down on a shelf, making Nina wonder what it is that keeps him fascinated as he sits up here alone. It looks like a novel. Good. She likes a reader. She used to think she would write novels.

"Here we go, down this path. Follow me."

They follow him and soon they are looking at a canyon, a hole in the ground, huge.

"This was the lake," he says. "Once filled with water and a wonder to all who heard of it until it failed and killed more than 2,000 people."

She knows—a terrible death toll.

There are steps cut into the hillside. They remind her of city steps in Pittsburgh, leading from one hilly neighborhood to a flatter one below it.

"Want to walk down into it?" he asks. "By the way, my name is Silas Andrews. You can ask me anything you want to ask."

"I'm just taking it in right now," Ben says, "trying to see what a stranger sees. I'll have plenty of questions later. I can call you?"

"Certainly."

As they walk down into it, Nina can hardly breathe, the idea of it overwhelming her. She feels like she's drowning under all that imaginary crystalline water she's read about. And also she feels thrilled. She can't explain it. Maybe she feels she's defying death.

"I'll be sending a photographer in a couple of days or a couple of weeks, depending on when they run the story."

"Okay. I'm here. Ten to five. Six days a week."

They all stand in the lowest part of what once was Lake Conemaugh. This expanse of air about them would all have been water. It makes them quiet. Yes. Imagination grows in the quiet. Little sailboats, like beautiful toys, would have dotted the surface seventy-two feet above them.

Seventy-two feet! Ben will need those numbers. He's a little slapdash and romantic in the early stages of a story; he goes for the big picture and looks up facts at the last minute.

"The breast of the dam was there," Silas Andrews says. "See?" Andrews points to a narrow hill. "It gave. And the water flowed right over that way, can you see, down to Johnstown. Well, I'm lying. It wasn't simple. The water took an indirect path at times. Circuitous." She and Ben catch each other's eyes. They understand each other and are amused by Andrews who apparently likes books and words—which they do, too, though Andrews seems more naked in his passion, young.

"This place is amazing," Ben says. He begins scribbling in his small notebook, the one that fits in his pocket. He writes against his hand, then against his thigh.

She wonders what he is putting down. What would she write if it were her story? She would write that they are standing amidst full trees and bushes, next to little park placards, which explain the sanctity of animal life here, that what was once a lake is now back to its original identity—a green valley, a canyon lush with trees, rhododendrons, wildflowers, and ivy, that it defies fact, making it seem impossible the other identity was ever true.

She reads little placards set in the earth. Dandelions of course, she knew those. Yellow trout lily, Mayflower, bloodroot (little delicate white things, wherefore the name?), buttercup—little and delicate again, but this time yellow flowers. And more. Someone has been here to identify them. Lovely.

Sunlight plays on the plants and trees in Lake Conemaugh. Above, there is only clear, cool, spring air, a sky so blue and clouds so white in their popcorn outlines that Nina feels almost dizzy with the pure beauty of it.

"It's a wonder anybody lived," Andrews offers.

"Yeah," Ben says, writing.

There are stories of people who rode trees for miles and miles and were saved—Nina knows a little of those miracle stories, but the best one of all is the one Ben will be tracking—a little girl who rode on a bed, or a mattress rather, and survived and lived another ninety-nine plus years, just a month and a half shy of a hundred. Over two thousand died in a matter of minutes, but some were right *in* the wild waters and managed to survive. Ellen Emerson is the last of them.

Ben is super lucky to be doing this story. Oh, she's grateful she has a job, just impatient with working on the ground floor since she wants badly to be writing stories like this one, that make her heart pound.

Ben, perhaps reading her mind asks Andrews, sounding casual, "Many journalists coming by to look at all this?"

"Nobody much yet. I'm sure we'll have plenty coming up on it, maybe a month from now."

They start to climb back up, the men allowing her the middle between them. At the top of the steps, Silas Andrews leads them to a small building that wasn't visible from the kiosk. "We're going to expand this building," he explains. "There isn't much here now. Just this lobby and the movie theater."

What's there right now is a place for ticket sales and a few maps along the wall. In the center of the room is a little model of the valley, well done and detailed, like a good train set. And, aha, there is even the train from Pittsburgh included. Visitors of any adult size will look down on the valley like gods—seeing, accepting, maybe even complacent.

"Wow! Look at this!" Ben says, coming up to the model Nina has been studying. "Not too shabby."

Andrews, when he feels they've had enough time with the model, says confidentially, "Not that I'll put it this way to other visitors, but you'll want to know, this whole area is a floodplain. The problem is the city was situated badly, just off from where it should be. But if you try to tell people that, it's hopeless, they don't want to hear it, they can't get it in their heads. The city exists. It's there. It's theirs. They won't move. They have their businesses, their jobs, their homes, their families."

Ben says, "I don't blame them. It's a risk, yes. But it's human nature. People in California don't move even though they know they have a danger of earthquakes."

"Right," says Andrews. He frowns. He has a comic face. "It will happen again," he says, wide-eyed, with a shrug. "I guarantee it. I hope not for a while. And I hope I'm up here when it does. Or gone somewhere."

He's right of course. Her mum won't move.

Ben scribbles a few more notes.

Twenty minutes later, with Silas Andrews's help in the way of a hand-drawn map, Nina and Ben are in Ben's rattling Civic, headed to an area known as St. Michael to see what is left of the storied South Fork Fishing and Hunting Club, where the Mellons and Carnegies and Fricks and all their cohorts enjoyed some good snoozes and some splendid meals. After the flood, those club owners went back to Pittsburgh, abandoned the club totally. Ha. They couldn't go back, couldn't face the survivors. They left the structures, never to be inhabited again. But *buildings* tend to stand for a while even when they are not cared for, and the actual clubhouse is reportedly still there. Also, according to her research, three other buildings have managed to stand—houses she or any normal person would think of as mansions but, at the time, were called *cottages.*

"Must be just around the . . . yes, there," she says eagerly.

"Is this it? Is this right?" Ben asks. They have come upon a small crop of buildings. Since they're the only buildings around and his map is accurate, the question is rhetorical. He's just surprised.

The clubhouse is falling apart—of course, she knew that. But it's different from the classic mansions; it's a huge nineteenth-century building, wooden, three stories, with a big rambling porch. "It was once painted red with white trim. I read about it. You know, it must have looked—at one point—kind of like the Sea Mist beach house in Cape May, New Jersey."

"Hm. *That's* what it looks like. A seaside resort . . . a haunted one."

They exit Ben's car. There is nobody around. Once more, she shows off her numbers. "There were forty-seven rooms and a huge banquet hall that could seat 150 dining guests."

"Hmpf." He pulls out his notebook and writes. "You don't have to be my assistant. That's just a pose."

"It happens I'm interested in this too." It's her town, the story of her town after all. She takes in a deep breath. For a moment, they just breathe through their flash of irritation with each other.

"I'm sorry. For a moment it felt like you think I can't do it."

"Of course you can."

"Talk. I'm sorry."

She adds more carefully, "Some of the members had their own cottages, sixteen of them had cottages, but there are only—." Before she can point, he does. "Right. Them."

"Cottages!"

"Rich thinks big, I guess."

There is nobody to stop them. They move forward and soon walk right into the clubhouse. "Ugh," he gasps.

It smells of rot. Things are falling apart and she supposes she and Ben are in some danger of dying at the site (killed by pieces of the old fantastic life falling on their heads), although there are scaffolds holding up some precarious looking roof sections. If she dies here, her mother will wonder where she is tomorrow, and when she is found dead here, her mother will be so puzzled.

The banquet room has a huge fireplace. How wonderful the life here must have been, rich teenagers organizing regattas, attending concerts, engaging in theatricals, lolling about, falling in love. And their parents doing all the same things, no doubt. Those relationships flit through Nina's mind, people living in a Victorian novel.

Ben puts an arm around her. "I'm really sorry for before."

"Lucky bugger." She punches Ben in the arm. "You have a good assignment and me, too."

He doesn't stop hugging her. "What do you think your mother is doing today?"

"Thinking about me. Cooking. Baking."

"Baking what?"

"My guess is a cake. She's a good baker."

"Bring me some."

"I will. Don't let her see your car. Or hear it." His Civic is old and cranky. Her Civic is in better shape than his. She told her mum her car was making a little bit of a muffler noise. Ben, like most men, wants to be the driver, wants to use his own car.

He rests his chin against her forehead for a while. When he moves, it's to kiss her forehead. "Museum next. Show me the way."

"That means we go back downtown again. It's in the place where my mother used to shop for clothes, when I was little. It was my first experience of a big store."

What used to be the Penn Traffic Department Store, a lovely place, now houses the museum collection, but only temporarily, while the building that used to be the town library is being prepared for the permanent collection. Ben takes a last walk around, caught in a coughing fit from the dust and mold, but making a few notes. When he checks his watch, he says, "Yeah. We'd better move it."

As they drive back to the highway, she wishes they had time to follow the flood path. It would take a long time and patience, crawling along tiny rutted roads. But wouldn't he find that interesting?

"The milkshake might be wearing off. We're going to need some dinner. Are we being cautious about going out?"

She thinks about it.

He adds, "I mean, I know you feel awkward because of your mother. We could always get something drive-thru or we could pick up a pizza somewhere."

Suddenly she can't concern herself about being seen. She wants a real life with him. "I'd like to go to a restaurant," she says. "Being out with you. A date. That would be worth it." The town doesn't have a lot of restaurants other than chains out on the highways. But Nina is pretty sure there's a place in town called Johnny's. To sit at a table with him, in public, it will feel wonderful. Maybe whatever it is that has him "off" today, irritable, will disappear.

"CAN I GET YOU ANYTHING?" Ruth asks, pulling up a chair to sit beside her.

"No. But thank you."

"It's like a job—"

"What?"

"You sorting through these pictures. I can't stop looking. The photography's so different. The paper, the poses, everything. I don't blame you for looking and looking."

There is only one sepia of Ellen's mother and father because the photograph was taken at her uncle's church and he got one of the originals. Every photo, everything really, that her parents owned was destroyed, became pulp, including the Bibles, a hundred of them—her father sold Bibles. He was not terribly religious, but he was a decent salesman.

When Ellen and her sister were toddlers, they could listen forever to him reading stories. It didn't matter where the stories came from so far as they were concerned. They asked for stories of any kind, nursery rhymes or otherwise. Some, but not all, were from the Bible. Their father's voice often put Mary to sleep, happily so, thumb in mouth. But for Ellen, well, the stories woke her, excited her.

Now, looking at the faces of her parents, her real parents, she wishes she could have known them longer. She has so little memory of them. Has she made them up? When people get old and they contemplate dying, they usually cope with the end of it all by summoning an image of rushing down some celestial hallway to meet their parents. Ruth is quite literal about it. She expects to meet her folks in the beyond. Ellen jokes with Ruth that she hopes she can manage to recognize her own and doesn't have to end up with the damned aunt and uncle again. She laughed heartily at an image of herself wandering around the pearly gates, irritable. *No. Where are the ones I want? These.* She shows the gatekeeper, Peter or whoever he is, the photo in her hand, the one she holds now, the one that makes her feel kindness washing over her. She thinks she remembers snatches of their voices, but maybe she's inventing everything, influenced by film and TV. Now that she thinks of it, her mother saying, "Would you like a piece of bread?" "Are you hurt?" "Isn't it a beautiful day!" sounds a bit like Glinda the Good Witch—Billie Burke.

Her father, did he have a halting voice? He was a quiet, sturdy type— and she has an image of him walking down the street, pausing, surveying the world, listening to what a neighbor man has to say. In the movie she spins, she's the little girl who stands in the front yard watching him come home, thinking, yes, that one is mine, he is my father. In the photo he looks to be that substantial man of her imagination. Or is it truly memory? Her mother must have loved him because Ellen remembers the inflections of teasing and a slow smile spreading on his face. Well, maybe; she hopes that's who they were. She knows they can't have been perfect. They were people, after all.

She wishes she had things that belonged to them—a shawl, a book, *things,* because objects have power, they just do. Someday scientists will prove it, too, that the coat worn by a man carries the spirit of the man.

"You look a little bit sad," Ruth says.

"Not sad. Just thinking."

"Will soup be all right for dinner? Soup and bread with cheese?"

"That will be fine."

"I think maybe some tea now. And some Girl Scout cookies."

"That sounds about right."

The early spring sun slants through the window. Why, she read an article that college students are lying on the lawns already for suntans. In April! Ellen hopes it's glorious like this tomorrow when the journalist comes to town. Weather makes such a difference in people's spirits. He's only her thirty-eighth or so journalist. She ought to be used to the press by now. So the butterflies she's feeling make little sense.

"I'm just getting the cookies," Ruth calls.

"The chicken tomorrow, did you remember?"

"Yep. I remembered you said chicken for the newspaper man. I shopped on the way here. I have everything—chicken, potatoes for mashing, green beans, and good bread. I wasn't sure my pie would come out as good as I want, so I bought one."

"That sounds perfect. Thank you. And keep some coffee at the ready. I think journalists are big on coffee."

"At least on TV."

"Ha. You got me there. Maybe he'll conform to type. I'll wear the blue dress."

"I brushed a couple, wondered which for sure you would want."

Sometimes Ruth dusts an already very clean apartment, finding ways of being busy enough to keep an eye on Ellen. Now she keeps poking her head into the living room from the kitchen while waiting for the tea water to boil.

Ellen has lived in seven places—no, eight. First the childhood home, gone. Then her uncle's home. School. New York, the rooming house. Finally an apartment of her own in Manhattan. Then a different apartment in New York on the East Side. Her own home in the Moxham area of Johnstown for many, many years. Then this apartment in Southmont.

A few bits of furniture survive from her earliest days. An end table of walnut with the most delicately made drawer and with spindle legs. And a spindle back chair with a carved shoulder piece and a woven rush seat (rewoven twice). Oh, and a very small Persian carpet. Will that man, Bragdon, want to know about any of that, the artifacts of her life? The bed, the dining table, and one of the wingback chairs were things she had in her home with her husband. Everything else in this one bedroom apartment is contemporary in order to brighten things up. White cloth sofa, red leather guest chair. She tends to sit in the wingback, reupholstered once, but she chooses it partly for the support and mostly because it's in front of the window and on good days she can feel the sun coming in on her. Will the journalist want to know about those things? Or just about the day of the flood? One turning point, one day in her long, long life.

She goes back to the photos while waiting for her tea. Oh, this is good: a photo of newspaper journalists in 1889, all of them in bowler hats. Four of her first journalists. There's Ervin Wardman, *New York Tribune*, W. J. Kenney, *New York Times*, Richard A. Farrelly, *New York World*, and Charles Edward Russell, *New York Herald*. They look cocky. Tired and full of testosterone. They'd set up in a shack on the hillside by the Stone Bridge, the site of the terrible fire that followed only hours after the flood. They'd made quite a fuss over her. Well, she was a story. Even her uncle couldn't keep the journalists away from her. She was a good story. The little girl who lived. But even then she knew to invent, to say things a certain way, to hide certain facts, even then.

The teakettle whistles. Ruth bustles around and Ellen keeps working.

WHAT NINA NEEDS to explain to Ben is how fantastic the department store once was because it's . . . oh, a ghost of a building now. The glass windows no longer exist. The architectural insets make the building look like a row of people with their eyelids closed. The big Penn Traffic sign is down. There are no awnings now of course.

He's headed for the front door. "Wait."

He stops.

"I just want to tell you, all this was pretty once, really pretty. There were Christmas displays in the windows. I guess it wasn't that huge a store but it seemed huge to me. I was little. The '77 flood knocked it out of business for good. I read about how it was facing financial hard times before that, but after the flood . . . most of downtown just folded up. It's sad to see things go. It was our department store. And it was lovely. I had some wonderful things from here."

He smiles indulgently and looks from her to the building. "I didn't know what an invested tour guide I was getting."

"Yeah, I know. Sentimental. I always got excited to come shopping here. They had a restaurant, too. We'd make a day of it. Grilled cheese or chicken salad. Nothing with wasabi, believe me. Just plain old-fashioned food. Right. Okay. I rushed you to get here. We'd better go in."

He's been told by phone they don't have much of an exhibit up yet, but they're moving as fast as they can. As if the centennial is taking them a bit by surprise. Lots of stuff is in storage, being rehabbed. His goal, he told Nina, is to get them to let him look at what's in storage.

"If they don't let you see the back rooms, what will you do?"

"I'll have to guess at it. Museums are alike. Letters. Clothing."

Alike, yes, but . . .

Most of the building is blocked off. But they are pointed to a set of stairs and after they climb, they see there are three other visitors today, all looking intently into glass cases and to nearby pages of text that explain what is in those cases.

Handwriting—she loves to look at handwritten passages and so goes to one of the cases. A person's writing conjures the moment in daily life of getting something down—like earlier today, Ben's notebook. She studies one flood-damaged household accounts book. The sign to the side of it explains that a Mrs. Elaine Dougherty kept track of what she needed to buy at market. "Beef bones, flour, cornmeal, potatoes, turnips if they have them, a candy for Todd."

Ben is reading it, too. "Todd—probably her son," he says.

"She was making a potato soup. A broth and carbs."

There are other diaries from before and after the flood. Nina and Ben go from one display case to another, reading the pages that the museum staff has chosen to leave open.

The life of the times is evoked by household implements that survived the flood—a big iron spoon, a skillet, an axe. There are also a set of keys, a trunk, a doctor's kit. And clothing. A woman's dress, a bowler hat, a baby's gown because both genders wore tiny gown-like garments even up to their toddler years. A set of boy's clothing for about age five.

One whole case is filled with photographs. Most of them are of the flood and its aftermath. Some of them are famous—like the one that shows a church in the foreground and another in the background and just about everything in between for city blocks down to rubble. There is a copy of the famous engraving by W. A. Rogers from *Harper's Weekly* of June 15, two weeks after the flood; it shows the rushing waters and turmoil at the bridge where there is the figure of a woman with outstretched arms.

Another whole glass case holds journalistic articles of the time. Ben stays a little longer at that case, reading, and finally joins her at a display of maps and timelines.

"This is all good," Ben says. "But I want the rest." He nods toward a fellow who wears a suit and stands with hands clasped behind his back. "I'm going to try."

Nina watches Ben cross the room and begin to talk, casually, easily, with the guard.

The man Ben is talking to appears to be responding to his affability. At any rate, he guides him to a table and begins to write things down. Good.

She circles the room, looking at everything again, close to tears when she studies the clothing again because now that she reads about it more closely, she learns that the owners of the clothing both died in the flood. How can she *be* a journalist? "Like baseball pitchers," Ben has told her, "journalists need a killer instinct. Got to have it."

She's too soft.

Ben returns to her. "Couldn't crack the guy. He won't let me see the back rooms today. I have to go through channels. So I *will* be back. Who knows how many times, huh? Are you okay?"

"Yeah, fine."

"You look totally gorgeous."

She shakes her head.

"You do. Motel, then dinner, then motel? Or are you too hungry?"

"The milkshake is still holding me. I could use a pause."

And so after another half hour of studying the exhibit pieces, they

drive the few blocks to the Holiday Inn and go up the elevator together. Ben stops at a vending machine on their floor to buy peanut butter
crackers and Coke. He kisses her in the hallway, touching her hair gently
before he reaches into the machines to get his snack. "I'm in love with
you," he says. "Just know that."

Her heart jumps.

When they get to the room, they kiss again and lie down. They begin
to make love, but then they stop. "Let's just lie here," he says.

"Tired?"

"A little."

"Me, too."

His eyes close.

When they go out to eat, they walk with arms around each other to
Johnny's. The day's warmth has disappeared with the sun, making the
evening chillier than she expected. Johnny's is on Main Street, before the
park, she remembers that much. It's one of the few places still functional
after the '77 flood, so she's grateful for it. Ben's hand rubs up and down
her arm to warm her. And then they are inside where the temperature
is just right, the lights not too glaring, the clatter of plates and glasses
enthusiastic without being irritating.

"Let's break the bank," he says. They order Bloody Marys to start,
steaks for their main course. Their hands meet at the center of the table.
She will always remember this. Years from now she will be able to call up
the booth, the lamplight, his face.

He calls for a second Bloody Mary for her, a Scotch for him.

BEN WATCHES NINA walk toward the women's room. She looks back
once to him as if she feels his eyes on her. Women, hopeful sweet ones—
what's the deal with that? The waitress is another, all attentive, like a
good aunt. Nina says it's this town. It's how they are here, bred to be
other-directed. He doesn't know.

Amanda on the other hand . . . today she tried to be nice suddenly, but
it was fake-sounding. Her timing—what was *that* about? She's barked
at him or refused to talk for eight months, but today, a whole different
tune. He feels like a puppet. Before she kicked him out of the house, she
withdrew from him and let him go without love for a year. Then sud-

denly she was filing papers, making him fight to see his kids, making him live down the street at his brother's house—on a sofa bed for God's sake; and then out of the awfulness of the last year, there was Nina. A gift. He planned this weekend away with Nina—so happy about it and suddenly Amanda insisted he call her from Johnstown. As if she knew he'd finally found happiness. Why, he wondered, did he have to call from the road when for eight months she didn't want to hear from him. But he was a worrier, he had kids, and so okay, he called. His feeling was to get it over with, so he could enjoy the weekend. And what did Amanda say? "I think we should work it out."

He could hardly do his job this afternoon, he was so distracted. He listened to that guy Silas, jotted down notes, but all the while he felt split in two. He *is* split in two.

"For the kids," Amanda said.

"For their sake you're saying, and I'm worried about them, I promise you, but what about us? We don't get along. You don't even like me."

"We need to talk of course. It will take work."

She never thought to ask if it was what he wanted. He's totally thrown off course.

NIGHTTIME and Ruth is gone, the cookies beside the bed, the walker at the ready. She keeps thinking about the phone call she got a week ago from the journalist when he proposed this interview. One detail keeps coming back to her. "Let's really dig," he said. "Let's find something new." It was as if he knew she didn't tell everything. And she imagined telling him the things she left out all those other times. Will she? Will she want to tomorrow? Why protect people after all this time? A hundred years— there ought to be a moratorium on polite silence. She wrestles with the problem and eventually sleeps without coming to a solution.

BACK IN THE ROOM Ben pours each of them a Scotch. He pops on the TV. For a while they watch the game, arms around each other.

"Something's wrong," she says.

"With them?" He pretends to look at the TV. "They're winning!"

"With you."

"No."

"Was it . . . the phone call . . . something I should know?"

"No."

"You miss your kids?"

"Of course, yes, but half the time I don't even like them."

"Are you serious?"

"That's only some of the time. Otherwise I love them. Come on. Please. I know that sounded awful. Amanda lets them whine. They have that whiney sound. I hate that. How do kids learn to sound that way?"

"I don't know."

"Let's talk about . . . our teenage years. Our first loves. The cars we drove. The movies we remember."

"How often do you call Amanda?" She's scrunched away from his embrace. "Come on, Ben. I'm in this. I need to know."

He puts down his glass on the bedside table only to refill it. She waits him out. Finally he powers off the TV and says, "We were talking every Monday, Wednesday, and Friday at five o'clock for five minutes about the kids. She always sounded like my calls were a burden she was putting up with. Don't ask me why, but she asked me to call her today. I was surprised. But I called."

"And it was bad?"

"Wasn't good."

"Tell me."

"Let's not ruin this." Though it already is ruined. He feels himself wincing, scowling. He doesn't even enjoy the Scotch. "She doesn't want me to be happy. She must have sensed I was."

"Is it me, specifically? Was she bugging you about me?"

"She doesn't know about you."

"I thought . . . I thought you told her you were seeing me."

"We didn't really talk except about the boys. I was just the guy living down the street at my brother's house, giving her my paycheck, picking up my kids to play catch and take them to a movie and hear them whine. But. Oh. I'm thinking. My brother knew. Maybe Melanie got it out of him."

Now Nina is up, moving restlessly. "What about the divorce? You said it was moving along."

"It was. Very swiftly at first. Then the last two months these cryptic lawyerly messages about working out her demands. I don't know what's in her mind. I honestly don't. If I did, I would tell you."

"Does she want you back?"

He answers her with what it feels like to him, not with what Amanda said this afternoon. "No. She doesn't. She suddenly *thinks* she does."

"Oh."

"Nina. I love you. You've changed my life. You understand?"

"I just want you to be honest. We're living like teenagers. We're sneaking around most of the time. We've never even been to a movie together. Or anything else. This is not how I want to live."

"Me neither. We need time to work it out. It will get better. Amanda will change eventually. She can't really want me back."

"But she said she did."

"She's playing games, but I don't know why."

He is tired, so tired. All that time, a year at least, of begging his wife to sleep with him. Once she said, "You disgust me." "Why, how?" he managed to ask her, his voice raspy and embarrassed. "I can't explain it," she said. His brother tells him contradictory things—that he's nuts for putting up with Amanda, that women just get standoffish sometimes. He doesn't want to live his life without love, that's for sure, not just physical love but all kinds, plain affection, a hand on his shoulder. When someone hates you, when you disgust someone, it . . . messes with your brain.

"Nina, please, come back to bed. Please."

She looks at him steadily. "I don't want you keeping things from me."

"I won't."

She comes to him. He's not sure how to repair the gap. He starts. "I had a Beetle. The running board fell off. I could see the road through the floor. I drove it anyway. Did you drive as soon as you were sixteen?"

She nods.

"And it was . . . blue, green, big, small, yours, your mother's?"

"My father's car. It was a Dodge. I didn't like it. It was bronze."

"Uh huh. Did you ever take boys in the car?"

"Actually once I did."

"Where did you go?"

"His place."

"He was older?"

"No. My age. His family was out of town."

"Uh oh. Naughty girl. Was it fun?"

"Yes. I thought I was in love."

"And he was your first?"

"Yeah. Bobby. A charmer for sure. We only messed around a little."

"In the car too?"

"A bit."

"When you're sixteen, it's just . . . amazing, isn't it."

She laughs ruefully, nods.

"Like now." Between the Scotch and the game of teenager, he manages it. His generally reliable dick flags a little at one point, but he keeps at it. Is she calmed, confident in him, or just quiet? He can't tell. They crash hard into sleep.

Shelter made of scrap wood after Great Flood of 1889. Courtesy of Johnstown Area Heritage. Association

2

Sunday, April 16, 1989

■ "AHA, there you are!" her mother says, throwing open the screen door. "I got up early, I was so excited." Right now it's only eight. Through kisses and hugs her mother asks, "Where's your ride? Where did he go so fast?"

"Left me on the street. He has work."

"And he'll be back for you?"

"Yes. I don't know the exact time, but I gave him your phone number. He'll probably call before he comes by."

"It's such a short visit!"

"Better than no visit, right?"

"Yes, yes, I don't want to be a complainer. I'm ready to make breakfast."

This morning at seven Nina let Ben go out for donuts and coffee and when he came back, she only ate one-half of a donut, rightly expecting her mother to want to cook.

"Eggs and bacon?"

"Sure. I thought you were going to say cake." On the counter is a big, gorgeous cake with chocolate icing. "What kind is it?"

"Triple Hazelnut."

Nina groans. "Can I take a piece with me?"

"You can take several pieces. Give one to that guy who drove you as a thank-you."

"I will. If I can stand to give it up."

The house is as it always was. The kitchen has not been expanded, the appliances have not been updated, the single bathroom has the old pedestal sink and tiles. Her mother insists she is totally comfortable and wants to save money rather than spending it, to be able to give it to her only child.

"I have no need for your money," Nina has told her, which is quite a lie. It sure would be nice to wipe out those school loans to ease her new life with Ben when it happens. But surely her mother will retire one day and will need that little pocket of money, just for bread and milk and lipstick.

The small square kitchen table is already set for breakfast. "Sit," her mum says, "Tell me things."

"Nothing much to tell. I work, I go home, I sleep."

"Work is okay?"

"It's fine. I'm still getting, you know, general assignment stuff. Last week there was a guy with a gun in a house, nobody knew who else was in there, police came, there was a standoff, everybody being careful not to rile the guy, and the standoff took forever. Seven hours. My feet were killing me. Turned out he was kind of nuts. There was nobody in the house with him. I had to make a story out of that."

"Suicidal?"

"Maybe except the gun wasn't loaded."

"It sounds interesting to me."

"Well it was, but I didn't get to write the interesting part—like why he was messed up and what was going through his head, how much of it was showmanship with that unloaded gun and all. I'm supposed to get the facts and make them readable, that's all. And I did."

The bacon begins to crackle. Her mother puts bread in the toaster and opens the carton of eggs. "Will you stick with it?"

"I'm giving it two years. To see if I get moved up to features. If not, I might not stick."

"Two years—anything can happen. Please don't meet someone who wants to take you to live in California." Punctuated by a smooth crack of an egg on the side of the skillet.

"Not likely."

30

"No, if he's a good guy, go to California." Another egg cracks perfectly. "I'll adapt."

"I'd have you flying out there every two weeks."

"Or vice versa."

Soon they are eating breakfast and talking about other things—the good-hearted neighbor who mows her mother's lawn. The toast dipped in egg is delicious. She wishes this breakfast for Ben.

"You were hungry, starting out so early."

"I was," Nina says.

Nina knew to wear a nice dress and flats this morning. Yesterday's clothes are in her overnight case in Ben's car. Soon her mother will mention church.

When they've finished breakfast, her mother says, "I think I'm going to tackle painting a couple of rooms."

"Don't you want to hire someone for that?"

"I think I can do it. See what you think—do we look shabby?"

Nina goes upstairs to her room first. She took away all the posters and decorative items long ago when she went to school. The room is pretty plain: full-sized bed, dresser, and one chair. The next room, her mother's, holds a photo of her father and three photos of Nina in frames on the two dressers. Bedroom slippers under the dresser. Her mother lives a noble and plain life. The job at Memorial in accounts. A few friends. Baking.

Widows' lives are so sad. One day she'll do a story on that subject.

"The walls aren't so bad," she calls out. Her mother says something she can't hear. Nina comes downstairs again.

Her mother's green blazer hangs over the living room chair. "You want to go to church?" she asks brightly.

"If you'd like. I thought we could also put some flowers on the grave."

"Yes, okay."

Another picture of her father, this one larger, stands on the mantle. He was an intense workaholic with his own business in small electrics in Cambria City. It wasn't officially a repair shop but people heard about him and came to him—he could repair *anything*. When the flood wiped out his store, he was especially anxious dealing with the damage and insurance. It seemed nothing calmed him. Before he ever got the store opened again in another location, he had a massive heart attack. At that time her mother was working at the hospital on Franklin Street, but she got transferred to the center downtown. Typing and billing and recording. She started out with a typewriter, but now uses a computer for all that, marveling at all that is new.

"Where do you go lately?"

"Back to Christ the Savior. I like the new priest."

For a long time her mother coped with her grief by going to see *The Deer Hunter*. She talked about it regularly. She saw it at least four times. The church in the film was like theirs. The sounds of the service, just like what they knew. The men were like men she knew growing up. Though Nina's father hadn't been called to Vietnam, he might have been. Many of his friends were and so were people her mother knew growing up—some didn't come back. Worse, some did. The movie came out right after the '77 flood and right after Nina's father's death.

"Off we go," her mother says. They hurry outside and climb into the small Chevy Cavalier her mother bought six years ago.

Nina looks at her mother, neat, trim, well-behaved. She wishes her mother love—companionship at least. Will she ever look for it again? It's sort of old world, isn't it, to mourn forever. She comes at the subject from the side. "You used to complain that if they'd made *The Deer Hunter* here instead of in Ohio, you would have fought to be an extra. Remember? You liked those guys, huh? Those good old ethnic boys."

"No, no, it's just it would have been something exciting for our town. Like when Paul Newman came to do *Slapshot*. It gave us that jolt we needed."

Nina leans over to squeeze her mother's shoulders. Her mother looks surprised.

From time to time, Nina has dropped in on a Catholic church when she couldn't find an Orthodox church handy. One thing about Catholic services is they go fast. They get you in and out. Nina has even dropped in on the Protestants. The Protestants grab you before you've ever sat down. They want your name and address. The Catholics at least don't announce your name from the pulpit and beg you to come back. The Catholics let you be anonymous. But if you want to torture your legs and back by standing for the best part of ninety minutes, if you don't mind being noted, possibly gossiped about, though never hassled, go to an Orthodox church. It's hard to explain why it appeals to her, but it does.

She thinks during the Mass about Ben, hoping that things are going to work out between them, wondering if he's been lying all along about contact with Amanda. She wonders what her mother thinks about, prays for. Her own prayer, even though she chides herself for sending a request heavenward (it's not fair if you haven't been coming to praise, is it, to ask for things?), is that she and Ben see themselves through this time of transition and that his wife stops torturing him and that his stories are good and that she also begins to get good assignments.

The Orthodox service is as long as ever in spite of the fact that the new priest speaks fast. They leave after Communion, even though Mass is not finished, because they have to be home for Nina's ride. The morning clouds have given way to rain. Spring in Johnstown. Rain. Like what caused the flood a hundred years ago. Her mother is prepared with a small umbrella. They run to her car and put on the heater to dry themselves. The running was fun—it loosened them up a little.

Her mother drives, heater going, to the Flower Barn outside Grandview Cemetery.

The woman behind the counter frowns at Nina's request. "Cut flowers?"

"To sprinkle over the grave." She heard that from . . . where did she hear that? From Ben? She's unsure now, but somehow she loves the . . . gentleness of cut flowers, their testament to brevity. The woman gathers tulips, carnations, daisies and somehow makes them look just right bound together by poking in ferns and fillers at just the right intervals. It's such a shame to separate them and toss them. Nina sighs. "How about a second smaller bunch just like that."

"Why?" her mother asks.

"For you. Except," she whispers, "I think I'm going to give you the big bunch."

Grandview is beautiful, if a cemetery is allowed that adjective. It's up high. Nobody lying here is going to be washed away, no floodwaters will rise up this high. The graves are forever.

Her mother wipes away tears. She met Nina's father at the Teen Canteen when they were both seventeen. She says she loved him from the first moment she saw him. They danced all night the first time they met.

"You bum," her mother says to his gravestone. "Leaving me. What was so important about water damage and insurance? Huh?"

BEN TAPS ON THE DOOR of an apartment in the Southmont section of town. He can hardly breathe. He's a little hung over, worried about Nina, too, because she's lost faith, become slightly more cautious with him. He was supposed to call Amanda again this morning but he couldn't find a working payphone when he ran out for donuts. Also, he didn't *want* to call. And when he saw another payphone on the drive to Southmont— and he took his time finding Ellen Emerson's apartment since he didn't know the area—he didn't stop. He didn't need to have his concentration thrown again. Work is what he prides himself on. He hears voices on the other side of the door. "He's here," someone says.

A black woman of indeterminate age opens the door to Ben. He is irritated that his hands are shaking slightly, something that's never happened to him before. There she is, almost in silhouette, his subject, sitting in a light dress in front of an open window, on the sill of which is a potted geranium. He knows it's a geranium because Amanda made him buy her four of them last year. It is still pretty early, ten in the morning—he had to kill two whole hours after he dropped off Nina, but he went over his notes and drove around and pretended to search for a phone. He did go to the park downtown at one point, looking for people to talk to. But nobody was out early on this Sunday morning. He's had this idea that he will do his man on the street routine, find other interviewees that were not part of the plan, because, well, his editor wants "something new" and who can tell in advance where to find that new thing. But there was nobody around in the park except one old guy who wouldn't talk to him.

If this goes fast, he can go back to the park and try again later.

"My name is Ruth. We've been expecting you. Here she is!"

"Hello Mrs. Emerson." He smiles. It's impossible to look away once he is close. He might have guessed ninety, even a bit less. He takes her hand. Now he sees how old it is, slack skin, wrinkled, but her grip is firm.

It amazes him how well put together she is. Her hair, all white, is thin, but shaped like a cloud, puffy with a few dips, waves. Her eyes, nose, mouth, are just slightly pink, fragile looking. And the wrinkles, yes, there are many, but they aren't frightening. He had feared they would be. "You're quite a woman. A survivor. Probably in more ways than one."

"So they tell me."

"Am I your first journalist, this time around?"

"You are." She smiles. "Would you like to sit?"

Ruth pats a smaller chair that sits at a slight angle. He takes it. "Mrs. Emerson. I'm here to talk about the flood. I know you know that and you've talked about it before. My job, my assignment is to talk once more about that terrible day and then your life after. Are you okay with that?"

"Yes. Yes."

"But first I can't help wanting to ask if you have a secret to your longevity. It's an old question, maybe a dumb question, but you're rare, almost a hundred and four . . ."

"Not alone in that . . ."

"Rare enough by my books. And everybody wants to know how—how do you stay healthy and active? Some people credit a glass of wine every day or exercise or prayer or great food . . ." She nods, receptive. "So, what's your formula?"

She appears to think for a moment. "I'm restless," she confesses. "That must be it."

"Hm. Restless."

"I feel restless."

"I might have the same secret as you. I hope it works for me." And doesn't give him a heart attack instead.

"I hope so." She smiles.

Polite. She's polite. Also aware. And amused.

"I want you to talk to me about the flood—easily at first while we get used to each other, anything you remember. Just for now take your time, tell me anything you like."

"Funny. After all these times, I don't know where to start. Do you know much about the flood?"

"Everything I could read. But that's a far cry from living through it."

"My experience or the flood in general?"

"Oh, yours. Start with two o'clock that day. We can backpedal after that."

She pauses, then begins. "There were a lot of families on the street that day. At two o'clock. We were busy packing carts, wheelbarrows. All of us were preparing to move to higher ground. Toys, photographs, were put in the attic, left behind."

He's come armed with a tape recorder as well as a large legal pad and pen. Once she's started, once he has her engine going, so to speak, he sets them up as unobtrusively as possible while she describes water and mud up to people's ankles, then water climbing even higher. He listens, sliding the tape recorder to one side even though it keeps running. He wants her to concentrate on his note taking, which provides feedback as to what he finds important.

She tells of the differences of opinion on the street about how serious this rainstorm and initial flooding was. He's read that. There were big disagreements about whether the dam would really *ever* break, some saying it was imminent, others saying the first group was once again crying wolf. Fortunately his paper and pen activity interests her, for she watches his squiggles instead of watching the tape running—most people are nervous around a tape recorder—and talks easily. Unfortunately the activity of writing keeps him from looking at her, which he wants to do. When he can take her in, he finds himself thinking about how frightened he was when he tapped on the door not long before this and how she's won him over. She's very nice to look at, though frail, and he finds himself fascinated. He's reminded oddly of when he studied his newborn sons, noticing patches of red on their scalps, saliva gathering, and thinking this is what a body is, this is the fragile life of our species.

SIXTY-FIVE MILES away, a young man in blue scrubs taps on a door at a nursing home in Pittsburgh and then enters. "Come on," says the young man. "We don't want you staying in your room." He looks at her name card on the inside of the door. "Mrs. Hoffman? Ready to go out? We have a group session today. It's going to be fun."

"I got tired. I'm sorry."

"You're allowed to be tired. But I think this will perk you up. You are the champion."

"Of what?"

"Longevity. They told me you're a hundred and three. Right?"

"Not yet. Almost. In a couple of weeks."

"Can you walk a little bit?"

"Not too well. Balance issues."

"I'll hold you. Enough to get to the wheelchair?"

"Enough for that. I'll certainly try." She knows she's become deconditioned. It's so easy to let purposeful movement go for a week. She knows diseases flourish in the deconditioned. She was a nurse for most of her life, worked at it for sixty years altogether; certainly she could teach most of the people here a thing or two.

The young man in scrubs puts an arm around her waist and lifts her a little as she walks to the wheelchair so that she's not sure if she's moving herself or if he's doing the work. As they say, getting older is not a barrel of laughs. They will applaud her when she gets to the room they all gather in. They applaud everybody. It doesn't mean anything.

The boy wheels her down a hallway. It's a very well kept facility, so far as these places go.

"What is your name?"

"Lamar."

Lamar moves her to the circle of chairs. All of the aides and the other patients applaud her, as she expected.

A woman, not wearing scrubs—right, uniforms are consistent here so she wears a purple vest—is the activities director, Mrs. Camillo, with a new haircut. And—ha, Anna can still remember names—Mrs. Camillo comes to the center of the circle to address them. She has both hands behind her back, but from her position on the circle Anna can see the woman holds a red ball.

"Today, in just a few minutes, ladies and our two gentlemen, we have an expert coming in to do a session with us. You are going to love it. Our expert is going to do a program called 'When You Were a Little Kid.' But first we have something to remind you of those years. *Play.* The years when we played. Remember that? It's a simple toy, the simplest. Guess what it is!" And then she reveals it. "A ball. Probably the best toy ever invented. We're going to have a good old game of catch. It's good to move our arms. It's good to work on our aim." The simple toy is not quite the size of a basketball. At least it looks soft. Anna hopes it is. It's been a long time since she did anything like this and hardly needs a broken nose on top of all the other broken parts.

The game begins with a small toss to a woman of seventy who looks as if she once played football. Smart start. She hauls it in and chooses to hurl it to the man sitting opposite her. He misses it but the aides run for it and hand it to him again. He tosses it gently to the woman sitting next to him.

They're afraid to throw to me, Anna thinks as the throwers choose others, sometimes for the second time. It's all right with her. She's tuned somewhere else. She can just hear snatches of conversation from a few feet behind her where the expert who is about to be introduced talks with two of the administrators. The phrase that recurs is "elderly depression." Well. She can't argue with that, look around and you see it, but the people whispering on the periphery of the room sound as if they have discovered it. She hears phrases from time to time like, "want to be alone" and "not interested in food" and "danger signs." God help her, she knows all this. She could run this place if they would let her. Yes, big surprise, people get depressed when they become immobile, when they lose loved ones, when they don't feel useful. She's no longer useful. She finds herself, oh it's terrible of her, terrible, wishing for another war, a plague, a disaster, something that would call her up. An imaginary person says, like right out of an old film, "We need all hands on deck for this one." And another imaginary person says, "Right. This one is a hundred and three, but damn, she can still work." She would have to exercise her legs into functionality again, but, even unsteady, she could tend to the wounded. And she would do it well.

An old fury rises. Not being in control of her life. The anger, blood rushing to her head, makes her dizzy.

For a moment she forgets where she is. It's as if there has *been* a disaster and she's been wounded and must get out of the danger zone. She reaches for the wheels of her chair—no, that's not the way, this is one of those new ones with a button to push. She intends to move backward to get out of this place, but suddenly finds herself going forward right into the red ball, which hits her in the face.

Well, now she's in for it. They will think she's hopeless. They maneuver her chair aside and stoop to give her a pep talk. "We're here to help. We're always here to help. What is it you need? Just call on us."

Anna's heart is thumping. "Maybe I don't feel so up to it today. I think I don't."

"Ooooh. You look fantastic. Doesn't she?"

The others agree that she does.

"And you have a birthday coming up!"

She nods.

"Stay for the next game."

"Well . . ."

"Please. Do us the honor."

"All right."

"That's it. That's our girl!"

Now a new person comes to address them, a serious looking woman of about forty, weighting about two hundred pounds. Possibly diabetic, probably has cholesterol problems, Anna thinks automatically. Lifetime of being too nice, too polite, because maybe all that sugar processing messed up the body and brain. Mrs. Salinas, she says, is her name. The woman places her hands together and closes her eyes, "Think of a time when you were a child and of a game you played. Think, think hard. Was it something mechanical? Did you have something to wind up? Was it a ball, big or small? What did it feel like? Did you play with toy guns or other weapons? Did you have a baby doll?" She opens her eyes. "You may close your eyes if you like. Try to get that image of yourself at a young age. Try to *be* it for just a moment. That's right. Close your eyes. What are you playing? What toys?"

The first image Anna gets is of rolling on a large metal can, but the image comes and goes and she doesn't feel certain of it. The others answer in turn, like good children, having been prompted with the right answers. "Ball." "Doll." "Nurse's kit."

"Ah, Anna, did you have a nurse's kit?" the director interrupts to ask.

"Not until I was twenty-two."

That makes them laugh.

"What toy, then?" asks the large sad woman. Salinas.

"Oh . . . a doll probably. Stuffed with straw or something like that." Did she? She must have if she said it.

"Aw, and did you love it?"

She shrugs, heartbroken, memories gone and when she summons something, she can't even be sure that it *existed.* "A can," she says. "I think something like a large can with a picture of a girl painted on it."

"To put things in."

"To roll. To roll on."

The woman smiles at her. Anna looks around. The people who don't need wheelchairs sit in wingback chairs. Some of them are smiling broadly. They liked their childhoods.

"Now, food," says the large woman. "What food do you remember just loving? When did you feel really hungry, really want something? What was it?"

"Ice cream," says Mr. Cobbs. A few others chortle.

"That still happens every night, Mark," the director teases. "Tell Mrs. Salinas about your addiction to ice cream. He loves it still."

"It's good," he says simply.

Anna feels strangely out of sync. They won't believe her if she tells them she's not up to this. They feel their whole job is to keep her here.

"Ice cream! Yes, that's always good. What about the rest of you. Hunger . . . ," says the new person, Mrs. Salinas. Right. "Hunger. You wanted something. What did you gobble up?"

"Cookies!"

"Cake!"

"Bread!"

"Those darned carbs! They love us and we love them *but* not always so easy on the system, eh?"

"Wieners."

"Well, there's something different."

"Tamales."

"Tamales! Where did you get those, Mr. Cobbs?"

"Kansas City."

"Ah."

"Who else? Mrs. Hoffman. What did you love? A memory?"

"Pablum," she says quickly.

"What? What is that?"

"Porridge." For a moment she doesn't know where she is. She was sitting, now she's standing, but the ground is slipping away. She's going to fall. She falls, but there are arms, hands, holding her, letting her down gently, lifting her up again. Suddenly she's crying. Seven people crowd around her, dabbing at her eyes or cooing. She feels ridiculous but she can't stop.

"WE LIVED IN CONEMAUGH," Mrs. Emerson tells Ben. "You probably have the facts down, but just to be sure . . . my father was a Bible salesman. My parents were Victor and Mollie Burrell. There were five of us altogether. I had a brother and sister."

"I read in several articles that you lost all of them."

She pauses, then says, "Yes."

"Yes, I can't even imagine it. And you even had a cousin with you who died that day."

She pauses again, looks surprised or puzzled or is it angry, then frowns and says, "Yes."

"Why did you look surprised when I mentioned your cousin?"

"Did I? Oh, I don't know." Now she tilts her head at an angle, studying him.

He wonders, did he get something wrong? He has to follow the line of inquiry. "Who was he, this cousin?"

"My mother's brother's son. He was twenty." Her lips purse. There's a little something there. Perhaps she didn't like the man? "My mother didn't particularly get along with my uncle, her brother, but that day he sent his son to us to help us move the Bibles and a few household items to his place. The son was the one who came for us. I wonder what would have been different if he'd never come."

"Can we know that?"

"No. No. I can wonder."

"As I understand it, that same uncle raised you after. Is that right?"

"I stayed with them, yes."

"The name of that family?"

"Folks. Paul Folks and Hester, my aunt. He was a minister. They were very religious people and I suppose in sending their son to move us they were aiming to rack up some points in heaven."

He suppresses a joke he is sure she has heard. *Not just folks, eh?* "Why did your mother not get along with her brother?"

"Oh, I don't think he understood her. She had such high spirits and such life in her. He was very strict. She was smart, I mean intelligent in the way of books. He thought she was getting beyond herself. You know how some men are, even today. He was angry that women should have ideas like she had. So there were family difficulties. I'm saying things I never quite said before. You told me I should say something new."

He laughs appreciatively. "You took the assignment seriously. I'm grateful. Yes, my editor wants something new."

"Oh. Well, it's just family stuff."

"You're okay with my saying there was conflict?"

She shrugs. "Yes."

He takes up his legal pad. "Okay. What was your cousin's name?"

"Paul also. Paul junior."

"Let's see. I'll get the names straight, then. Martin was your brother?"

"Three years older than I was. The other person with us was my sister, my twin."

"Her name?"

"Mary."

"Your twin?"

"Yes."

"Did you get along?"

She looks surprised at the question. "Amazingly. We were different. I was the talker and doer. She was the reflector. I was an hour older. I was born before midnight July 7 and she was born after midnight on July 8. We fell into older sister, younger sister roles, which was funny for just a few hours difference in age. We were . . . inseparable."

"So it was a big loss."

She nods vaguely. He doesn't know whether to interrupt and doesn't. Then she answers, "A very big loss."

"Were the two of you—you weren't even four yet—actually walking through water?" He knows the answer to this. It's a test though she certainly seems to have all her faculties in order.

"Most of us were. My cousin had brought a cart for my father's Bibles. Trying to save the marketable goods, you know. We didn't own much. We put the Bibles, a few packages of clothing on the cart and then we topped it with a mattress. And a tarpaulin. To keep things as dry as possible."

"Do you remember being frightened?"

"I didn't know how to feel. I think I went back and forth. There was all that disagreement about whether it was serious or not."

"So . . . back to the scene for a moment, you were walking with your sister?"

"No, no, my sister was on the cart. That's important. She was on the cart the whole time. Because *she* was scared. I acted like I could conquer anything."

"I think maybe you were right about conquering," he says quietly. He is so quiet he can hear the tape running and small other sounds of movement. He becomes aware of Ruth standing in the room.

"Ah, Ruth would like to serve us some coffee."

"Excellent. I'm always for coffee."

"We thought so."

He has a pretty good picture of people moving feverishly to get things from first floors to the second or third floors of their stores and houses. He can write that, about how some damage was already done and people panicked. He can picture this cartload of Bibles moving slowly through the mud. It's a good picture. He wants to draw that for his readers.

Nothing new is coming from her except the negative view of members of her family. Can he fan that material into something?

The coffee arrives on a tray. "Oh, beautiful." It's served in the most amazing china cups (Ben can hardly hold his, it's so delicate), cups Amanda would be crazy about. He ends up saying it—"My wife would die for china like this."

"It was the old way. People got china. Not as much these days."

"Your family was poor, would you say?"

"Poor enough. We lived in a neighborhood that had a lot of immigrants. From all over. Everywhere. Slavic countries toward the end, Italy, Ireland of course. My mother's family had been in this country, but my father's family was newer. Northern Ireland. My uncle blamed my father for dragging my mother down and making her live in an immigrant neighborhood. Bad enough that he was from Ireland! But the neighborhood was wonderful. I loved it. The food smells that would come out of those houses near us! My parents liked our neighbors."

Ben's father's family came from England, but his grandpop married an Italian and then his father married a woman who was Irish *and* Italian, so you can hardly even find the English or Irish in his face anymore. He's all for the melting pot in general. "I know about those food smells that come out of ethnic kitchens. Tell me about the people on the street. The carts and wheelbarrows."

43

"People had every such thing. Carts, yes. Some had homemade rafts with things on top and some carried bundles over their heads. Almost nobody from our end had a horse so it was all what you could figure out. We didn't have one. We pulled the cart along. My father . . . joked that he was the horse."

"That cart saved your life."

"It did."

"Do you still have a pretty clear picture of it—what happened?"

"Mr. Bragdon—"

"Ben, please."

"Ben. The picture is so clear it's as if I filmed it even though of course I had no sense of film—I mean movies were just being invented. I can see it still, that day. I can close my eyes and see it. Exactly."

That last word—it had anger in it. He sips his coffee. It's decent coffee. He jots down, *She can see it still as if it's a film.* He breathes in, waits. There is something going on, but he doesn't know what or how to prompt it. "I would like to see your film," he says finally.

"My father carried Martin on his back."

"Not you?"

"I was trying to be brave, remember? My mother pulled at the cart from the front end and my sister was trying not to cry. My father told her she was needed to protect the Bibles. She hadn't wanted to leave our house. And she never did like our cousin."

"Paul junior?"

"Yes."

"Why?"

"Well, he was an unhappy fellow in general. Then that day he was assigned to fetch us and he did it . . . grudgingly. He was like his father in that he thought he was better than our neighbors. He considered them a lower class of people—and us, too, for living among them. There was a family that shouldered pieces of lumber with baskets on top. He thought they were just coarse. They were Italians." She nods at him. He shrugs and laughs. "They kept catching the sliding baskets and shouting directions to each other. Paul was contemptuous."

Paul? A story? He jots.

She continues, "Other people on the street that day were speaking German, Italian, even some Russian, Slovak, Polish. Paul said Johnstown was working on its own Tower of Babel. 'Babble, babble, worse than children.'"

Ben writes furiously.

"They were the mill workers, mostly. They were a very big part of the town. My mother told my cousin he was being stupid."

"I can maybe give this part of the story a little play . . . immigrants, feelings about the classes, so your cousin can be my example of—" The microcosmic class prejudice mirroring the macro?

"Well. Hmm."

"What?"

"Oh, I don't know. I don't know. Would you like more coffee?"

"All right."

Ruth appears at his elbow with the pot.

"What are those wonderful smells coming out of the kitchen?" he asks Ruth.

"Garlic, onions. And chicken. And I'm making biscuits. For lunch."

"For our lunch," Ellen says.

"Oh, I can't stay for lunch. I mean, I didn't—"

"Oh, dear." They both look utterly surprised.

"Did I say I would?"

"We were counting on it."

"Oh, I see." He looks at his watch. It's after eleven. "I know we need to talk a lot more—"

"Yes, of course. And I do want to show you my albums. I have gathered a lot."

Ruth hurries to explain, "She worked all day yesterday getting those albums ready."

Change of plans. Okay. He can't just bolt. "Of course I want to see your albums. There's only a bit of a problem. I might have to go briefly and come back. I drove into town with a colleague. I told her I'd pick her up between noon and twelve thirty."

"You can use our phone. Can you call?"

"She was . . . doing interviews downtown somewhere." His invention came on him so suddenly he can hardly catch up to the reason. Phone calls. He hates to be overheard.

"Interviews about the flood?"

"Yes."

"How interesting. My flood?"

"Not really. I mean you are the only one left! So just memories, ideas of that one. And then the other floods, too. I . . . she's on the street. I was going to pick her up at the park."

"Would she be willing to come here? Lunch won't be ready until twelve thirty at the very earliest and we usually eat at one or one thirty anyway—and we always have plenty."

"Well, all right. I'll go pick her up in a bit. Very . . . very kind of you."

The albums (so-called) are going to be really worth looking at, he can see that much as Ruth brings them forward. They're full of clippings and of photographs, too.

Ellen opens the one on top. With shaking hands she takes out a photo so ancient and delicate he is afraid to breathe near it. "Your parents?" he asks.

"It's the only one. I'd like you to put them in the paper. A remembrance."

"I'd like to. I'll try. The museum is probably going to want this photo. They'd probably have a copy made if you let them. It's . . . lovely. They look, I don't know, like good people."

"I believe they were."

At ten minutes to twelve, he says, "I should start out now. To fetch my colleague. It's very kind of you," he says again, "to invite both of us to lunch."

EVERYTHING this morning has been speeding by, it seems to Nancy. The time at the cemetery was too brief—just a quick dose of flowers and tears and they are back home. What a strange visit, Nancy thinks, looking at her daughter. Just these few morning hours. And her daughter is jumpy, wandering the house, looking out the front window. Oh, surely she won't have to leave right now when the lunch sandwiches are only partly made. Can't the colleague come in? She'd gladly make him lunch, too. "Nina," she calls. "Lunch. Any minute. I'm just cutting the tomato."

"Yum."

"And then cake."

Nancy knows a distracted person when she sees one. Is it this man, this colleague? Is it a crush or something more serious? Why hasn't Nina *said* anything? Is her daughter's longing unrequited? Damn him if it is. Her daughter deserves someone good.

Her daughter comes to the table, sits reluctantly. Nancy finds herself examining Nina's face. "Who is your colleague interviewing?"

"That teacher, Ellen Emerson, because he's doing a thing on the '89 flood."

"She taught in my high school!"

"I know, Mum. I'm the one who told him about her. I said he should grab an interview before anyone else did."

"You didn't take the story for yourself?"

"I'd never get it. Never."

"Why not?"

"I'm too junior. It's going to be a big feature. But Mrs. Emerson is just one part of it. There's supposed to be a whole series."

"On the flood?"

"Yeah, you know, because of the centennial."

"But you're *from* here. What a crime."

"Tell me about it. I wish. But at least he's a good writer."

"Nice guy?"

"Very."

"Well, I wish he could let you visit for longer."

"I know. He said noon-ish. I'm sorry. I'll come back next chance I get. Maybe next weekend."

"Mayonnaise, ham, cheese, lettuce, tomato. Here you go."

Her daughter is only halfway through the sandwich when they hear the toot of a car horn. "Oh, no. Tell him to come in."

"I know he won't. He's on a schedule. I'll take the sandwich with me, Mum. Mum, I'm sorry. Don't hate me. Give me a kiss. I'm so sorry this was brief."

Nancy is grabbing at a plastic supermarket bag as Nina finds her purse, wraps a napkin around her sandwich, and blows an air kiss. "Oh, I don't need a bag," Nina says. "I'm *fine*."

The girl is almost out the door when Nancy manages to fit the whole cake in the bag. "You do need the cake, though," she calls. So. This guy is definitely in the picture and she intends to meet him. She follows Nina to the car.

"Hello," he says, dipping his head a little to look out the passenger window. He has a disarming smile, but isn't he a little old for Nina? He's definitely sexy—dark ruffled hair, beautiful dark eyes. Very . . . physical.

"I'm Nancy. Her mum."

"Ben. Bragdon. Happy to meet you." He nods toward the bundle in her hand. "Do you need help?"

"It's a cake."

"She said there'd be cake!"

Nina, halfway in the passenger seat, rises up, takes the cake and kisses her mother on the forehead before she sinks down into the passenger seat again. She busies herself, putting the cake on her lap, getting her seat belt on.

Nancy can see the old blue overnight case, her daughter's old reliable luggage, on the back seat. Why did they not stay at the house? Why is her daughter hiding this man?

There are no answers today. The rusty car speeds off. The man, Ben, toots a jaunty horn.

ONCE AROUND THE CORNER, Ben beats himself in the head. "I know I had the phone number. But I got myself into a stupid situation and I lied and then I couldn't get out of it."

"Why did you lie?'

"I don't know. Put the sandwich away. You're invited for lunch."

"Where?"

"Mrs. Emerson's."

"I get to meet her!"

"Yes."

"Wow, great. I've heard about her all these years."

"I was trying to hurry her up so I said you were interviewing people downtown and I had to pick you up at the park. Can you pretend that?"

"Sure." After a while, she says, "Lying sure is a lot of trouble, isn't it?"

"Tell me about it."

"Is Mrs. Emerson still, you know, interesting?"

"She's totally amazing. Sharp. Talks like a smart fifty-year-old. It just comes rolling out of her. Well, she was an English teacher. It stuck."

"How does she look?"

"Old. Clean. Kept up."

"A hundred and four, assuming she makes it. I want that. I want to be that old."

"It generally comes with some physical pain. And loss of looks."

"Bring it on. So long as I have my brain."

"She says it's because she's restless. Says that's what kept her alive. Restless either gives you a heart attack or, if you have the right genes, it gives you longevity."

"My father got the heart attack."

NINA THINKS Ellen is beautiful. Maybe she was ordinary looking as a girl, Nina isn't sure, but age has made her so fine. Not scary at all. Just . . . fragile and lovely.

Ellen tells them, while Ruth sets the table for lunch and Nina sits on a footstool next to Ellen, that she dreamt subsequently, many times, that her family was all under water and that her father kept getting to the surface and diving down again for them, but that he couldn't pull them to the surface no matter how hard he tried. In the dream, her mother, speaking underwater, told Ellen to save herself.

"Such a horrible dream," Nina whispers.

"Yes. It was. Anyway, on that day," Ellen says, restarting the interview on her own, looking straight at Ben, "What do I remember? Besides everything. It was cold. We shivered. My mother pulled the cart from the front and my father and my cousin pushed from the back. It was hard work. I was supposed to cheer up my sister. I was doing my best, telling her things to look at. Should I just keep talking?"

Ben nods.

"My brother Martin wanted to help. He jumped into the water. He wanted to be brave like some of the Italian boys next to us. The water must have surprised him because I remember we stopped for a bit. My mother said, 'Oh, Martin, now you'll be cold, too.' But he tried to pull the wagon from the front along with her.

"It was late in the afternoon when the dam broke up there and the water started down into the valley. I know you've read about it. We still don't have enough words for it. It's because it happened so fast, that's part of the reason. And it was total. And at the time we could not imagine what we were seeing and hearing, but that's what a traumatic experience often is, often unreal, and when it came, we didn't see water. You've both read about the black ball coming at us in the mist and that being all we could see?"

"Yes," Ben answers soberly. "Armageddon."

Nina closes her eyes to picture this evil apparition. She starts small: raining, gray. Then the sound, like a train, like thunder. Who could understand in that moment that the black ball took up everything that lay in its path?

When she opens her eyes, Ellen is saying, "For a few precious seconds, we didn't know. A few people kept doing what they were doing. The water was knee high. Then as it got closer there was a louder roaring noise and by then we knew it wasn't thunder or a train."

"Can you separate what you actually heard and saw as a child from what people said afterward?" Ben asks.

"Ha, ha. That is quite a question. I've spent a lifetime trying."

"Just your best."

"Yes." When she speaks, it's almost objective, as if she's breaking the film down into frames. "My father had run to me and lifted me to his back. I could see everything. Buildings shook. It was like an earthquake. Panes of glass flew out to the street. Other windows were caving in. There was dust and every imaginable thing was moving."

Ben says, "You said in an early interview that you saw bits of buildings, roofs, animals, carts, a car from the train coming along in front of the mass of water. Is that what you *saw?*"

"Not then. Later I saw most of those things. At the beginning I saw the black ball and I saw my family dying. We lost each other in seconds. My mother was calling to us, 'Run for that building.' She pointed . . . left. My cousin was pushing the cart to the right. Martin tried to run with my mother. They'd backtracked a few feet to get to a tall warehouse building. I think she saw her mistake. The water was sort of turning toward her. She waved to me to run the other way. The water hit them. The building went down, too."

Nina has gotten up to stretch her legs and now she looks over Ben's shoulder. He writes *Horrible. Child saw her mother and brother die.*

"I never forgot their faces—I never will."

"I'm so sorry," Nina says.

Ben looks irritated that she has spoken. It's his interview after all. She will try to be quiet.

"Are you okay to tell the rest?" he asks Ellen.

Nina goes back to the low stool. She pulls her knees up and wraps her arms around them to contain herself.

"My father dove on the cart. He had turned me around and was carrying me. I can't tell you *how* he did it, maybe the water helped him to it, but he landed face down, and I fell face up—sort of—and right next to my sister. Do you remember, there was a mattress topping the cart?"

"Yes," Ben says.

She smiles. "We had ourselves a place to land. Next thing was that my cousin landed on the cart, too. Four of us. The water lifted up our cart, it carried us and it jammed us between two buildings. Suddenly we were way up, floating, if you can picture it, and there was a building on each side of us, holding us steady. And it felt almost . . . safe."

"Safe . . . ," Ben says quietly.

"A man who spoke later said he saw it happen. So for that I have corroboration. He was off to the side somewhere in a building that collapsed more slowly and he described this. Otherwise I might have doubted the strange sensation of being carried along, up high, like that.

"My father must have understood that sooner or later the buildings would move and dislodge us and that our little cart would dip and sink and turn over. There was a window next to us—I heard later it was a third-floor window. 'Help me get the girls in,' my father yelled to my cousin. But as soon as Paul stood, we lost our balance. We began to rock. We . . . that's . . . my father fell then . . . into the water. And . . . my cousin, too. But my sister and I—"

Nina can't help herself. She reaches over from the footstool she's perched on and takes Mrs. Emerson's hand. "How awful for you," she says.

"I'm sorry," Ellen says. "I still get upset."

Ruth is at her side now. Nina is holding Ellen's hand and Ellen is saying, "Never mind, never mind."

"Maybe we should give her a break," Ruth ventures. "Lunch is ready. We could stop."

"Are you going to be all right?" Nina asks.

Ellen pats her hand. "I'll be fine. Maybe just a little break, yes. I didn't know it was going to hit me so hard again."

Ruth helps Ellen up and they begin to walk toward the table. It's beautifully set. And there is a gorgeously browned chicken in the center. And there are side dishes in serving bowls.

"Good heavens, do you always eat this way?" Nina asks.

"We do. Yesterday was just a sandwich, but mostly Ruth makes my big meal in the middle of the day. And she does a great job."

There are biscuits and mashed potatoes and a small salad.

"I couldn't have guessed we were getting lunch too," Ben says. "You're very kind to think of it."

After a while, Ruth carving, and Nina helping to serve, compliments abounding, Ellen surprises them with an observation. She addresses Ben. "I think you were disappointed with my story."

"Not at all. Not on your life. I knew it, but it's still amazing. And I'm still totally ready to hear the next part about how you and your sister rode the wave for a long, long nightmare of a time."

"Hmmm." Ellen frowns thoughtfully. "I was surprised anyone wanted to bother with me again. You're right. The story is known."

"You were wonderful. So clear. *I'm* not disappointed," Ben insists.

"Who is?"

Ben laughs. "My editor, maybe, with his 'Get me something new.' But let's face it, that's an editor's job, to say that."

Ellen looks excited suddenly. They continue to eat, talking about what a good cook Ruth is and then about how Nina is *from* Johnstown and knew about Ellen from her mother who went to the high school where Ellen taught. "She was always sorry she wasn't in your class. Nancy Pastorek was her name."

"I only had half the students. But I remember seeing her. I do."

Nina is trying to figure out how to offer her mother's cake without getting Ben all twisted up in a lie, but just then Ruth brings out pieces of pie. Of course they have thought of everything. Ruth is beginning to pass the plates of pie around when Ellen, taking hers, murmurs suddenly, "Is a hundred years long enough to keep a secret?"

Everyone stops moving for a second. Nina gets a chill up her back.

"Of course they want something new," the old woman says soberly. "Of course they do."

Ruth seems to be moving in slow motion, bringing her own slice of pie to her place at the table. The sound of her plate touching the table is the only punctuation to the silence.

"My cousin didn't die in the flood. He went on living. He pushed my father out of the way, off the cart. He's almost certainly responsible for my father's death. He never tried to lift either my sister or me. And the truth is, the truth is"—she's angry now—"he stood up and got himself off our cart and into that third-floor window next to us. He never looked back. He never tried to help us. That's the truth."

"Wow!" says Ruth.

Ben is leaning forward. "The records say he died that day."

"He didn't. He was one of those they marked as *body never recovered*. My uncle insisted his son died in the flood. He made speeches about it in church. I tried to tell my uncle what really happened. He told me I was crazy. And for a long time I thought maybe I was. But I kept seeing my cousin's face. I kept seeing the way he looked when he saved himself—fierce, determined. And . . . I thought deep down that I was right. I think my uncle was angry that he had me to raise and had lost his son. He thought he got a bad bargain. Of course he didn't want to believe his son had simply disappeared on all of us. He said I must never repeat that Paul pushed my father or never helped me and Mary. He said that was all in my mind and that I was crazy like my mother."

"Wow," Ruth says again.

"You didn't believe your cousin died afterward in a collapsed building or in the flood itself?" Ben asks. He leaves the table to get his notepad. The tape recorder is off, in the living room.

"He died *long* afterward. I have proof."

"What sort of proof?"

"He wrote to me. Years later. Through my uncle. An apology."

"Do you have the letter?"

"Yes, I do. I planned to keep the secret, my uncle's secret. When my uncle handed me the letter, he asked me to never let anyone know. I said I wouldn't. He made me swear it. He put my hand on his Bible. So you see, I'm betraying him."

Ben has his fist on his forehead—as if he's trying to push his brains back in. "Are you sure your cousin didn't take your sister, then?"

"I'm sure."

"Her body was never found either."

"I'm sure. I rode with her. We were together. I told her we would be all right. You see, the buildings separated. The cart dropped away and we went under for a while but . . . but the mattress came back up and it floated. That's not the right word—*floated*. It raced like a raft. We might have been riding rapids. But I talked to my sister. I tried to tell people afterward."

"What do you think happened to your sister?"

"I think she lived. I've always thought that. Maybe because she's just right there, in my mind, a part of me. I made a lot of ruckus for a long time. I asked questions all the time. I even tried to find out what happened to her when I was in my thirties. I sent an investigator who told me she died out west. I couldn't make myself believe it."

Nina is jumping out of her skin. Ben has quite a story now. This is better than anything they could have hoped for. Ben will want to verify the letter, but if he does, if it all looks good, what a huge story. And then he should really push for the part about a twin losing a twin and never being able to believe she is gone. That's quite a feeling. He can talk to psychologists, experts on twins.

After lunch is totally finished—Nina helps Ruth with the cleaning up, both of them tiptoeing and doing everything in silence so as not to miss anything Mrs. Emerson is saying about the twins' ride through the flood on a mattress. And before they leave, Mrs. Emerson lets Ben have an ancient letter in a plastic bag. "Don't lose it," she says.

AT FOUR O'CLOCK, they are on way back to Pittsburgh. The interview has taken much longer than they expected. "We can share the sandwich and have the cake for dinner," Nina offers.

"Fine. I mean, I'll take a piece of cake with me. I couldn't eat again for a while."

"Is your brother expecting you for dinner?"

"He is."

"Mrs. Emerson is amazing, isn't she? Can you imagine this little kid going around insisting?"

"You got very comfortable there."

"I'm sorry it bothered you. She was easy to be comfortable with. She knew I was a Johnstown girl . . . she'd seen my mother in the halls at school. How can she remember people so well?"

"Maybe it was a lie."

"No. I'm inclined to believe her."

In a corner of Ellen's living room was a bookcase full of yearbooks—to think she'd cared enough to save them. Ellen had called the people in the high school photos her "other kids." It turns out she had one daughter, but she loved her students with another part of her heart, too, she said. Nina had pointed out her mother and Ellen had said, "Oh, yes. I remember her well."

"Ellen asked me to visit her again. You should know that."

"When did she say that?"

"You were in the bathroom."

"Oh. Maybe when I go back then."

"You don't like the fact that she invited me."

"I feel crowded. You want the truth? When she invited you to lunch, I felt crowded."

"I always want the truth. How are we doing, you and me?"

"I don't know."

"Do you have to call Amanda tonight?"

"She asked me to call her this morning and I didn't."

"Will you tonight?"

"Probably when I get to my brother's house."

"Then we're not so good, are we?"

"I don't know. Amanda is trying to knock a hole in us, that's for sure."

A mere week ago, a day ago, Ben was on the cusp of divorce and glad of it. How did they take this turn so quickly?

"I feel a little out of my mind," he says.

She can see that. He needs to be left alone. She could use a little of that too.

She just wants to circle the wagons in her own apartment, stuff herself with cake, and read a novel.

A few hours later, Ruth asks, "Will you read tonight?" Ellen is still sitting in the living room, not ready to go to bed.

"I'd better. I'll never get to sleep otherwise."

"It was an exciting day."

"I can't take too many more of those."

"Hot tea? I could put a little in a thermos."

She hesitates. "Wonderful idea." She almost never wakes at night anymore but if she needs to go to the bathroom, she will have the walker. She's always felt capable. Today she feels . . . different, a little frightened of something.

When Ruth comes back she says, "I'm glad you told the secret. That cousin of yours was bad."

"Well, a hundred years is a long time to protect him." Her heart is beating erratically. She feels frail tonight, almost asks Ruth to stay.

Ruth senses it and sits. "So you were the big sister, the strong one."

"I thought I was. But I was just more active, more questioning, rebellious, talkative. I don't know. She was the stronger one in some ways. I was just the older one."

"By a couple of minutes," Ruth teases.

"I took on the role as if it were five years. I'd be the one learning rhymes first, showing Mary how to do things. But she was the ace at the adult tasks. I mean yes, we played games sometimes, but by the time of the flood, you know we were nearly four years of age, and we were experts at sweeping, dusting, carrying, fetching, all the work a little kid could do."

"I like when you talk about those days. My mother had us working early, too."

"That was how it was then. I could be distracted by rainy weather, robin's eggs, what people were saying in the next room. Mary never got distracted. She could really clean and she was good at it so she kept doing it. I'd sneak off to leaf through some book."

"Are you ready to get up?"

"I guess."

"It's funny to think of another you."

"We didn't look alike. I was a bit taller which also helped me act the older one. But oh, Mary had delicate bone structure and a darker hair and complexion," she explains. "We weren't identical. If my sister did live, I hope she had a good life." Tears come to her eyes. "Everybody says she didn't live. I need to bang that into my old head."

Ruth holds her elbow and frowns. "Maybe she wasn't strong. Not a fighter. Not like you."

"She was strong, the reverse way; she was the type to cave in, to fall with the punches but the trick is, if you know your boxing, that can lessen the blow."

"You could see that from when she was a little girl?"

"In retrospect. I didn't then. But I pressured my aunt. I insisted she tell me things. And eventually I could put it all together." They have arrived at the bathroom and stopped cold at the door. "I used to wonder why Mary wasn't like me. But the years passed and I saw the world and I thought . . . she had her own way."

Ruth wheels her walker to her. Ellen laughs at herself. All this independence! What for?

"Now, now, I can't imagine anyone stronger than you. I really can't."

"She always knew what was right. She was contemplative. Kind. She put others first. She was quiet. You never knew what she was thinking, but when you found out later, it was always . . . something right."

"I always heard it's amazing being a twin. Like having two selves."

"Something like that."

ANNA IS IN BED already. She can't make herself move but she isn't quite under. She is having the kind of sleep that isn't sleep, exactly, something in between, like being on a drug, an IV meant to keep her from pain. "Think about when you were a little, little girl, safe like that, and just rest," the nurse is saying in a singsong voice.

Pablum. Nobody calls it that. Why did she say that today?

The one nurse leans down to talk to her; she is so close that Anna can smell her breath. Coffee. "Are you still awake? I think you need more blankets."

"Here you go. Two blankets," the other nurse says. "She's had a shock today. Did you give her something?"

"I gave her Clonazepam."

"She's against that. She said never. She always told me never."

"But her chart said it was okay. Maybe she doesn't know."

"Actually . . . she does know. She knows medicines up and down."

No wonder she can't move. No wonder. She feels almost dead.

"She's whimpering. She's having a nightmare, I think. The blankets aren't doing it. We need hot tea and a heating pad."

"No, let her be."

"Should we turn the lights off?"

She doesn't want the dark.

IN HER HALF-SLEEP, she dreams little bits, then in a deeper sleep more. First there is water. Darkness. And then mud.

"Look. Is she dead?"

She tries to lift her head, but can't.

"She moved! It's a girl. Her face is muddy."

She reaches out but there is only mud.

"She said something."

"What?"

"It sounded like 'Alum' or something like that. Pick her up."

"Aye, yes. I think she's injured. Yes, blood, too."

"Does anybody see us?"

They are talking, but she can't tell if they are going to help her. She can't see. There is something in her eyes.

"What are you thinking? Are you thinking . . . ?"

"Let's take her in and clean her up."

"I've got her."

"Does anybody see us?"

"I know what you're thinking."

"I prayed . . ."

The man's body is warm. And she is cold.

"Oh, she's shivery. Dirty little thing. We'll see if someone claims her."

The man is not her father. It's someone else—voice and muscle.

Water and water. She screams. Some of the water is warm.

"Put more hot water in. More." And it gets warmer and is not like the other water, dirty, and after a while she can see. They are the wrong people. Everyone is wrong. The bed, the floor, the bureau are wrong, too. A blanket goes around her, so tight that she can't move her arms; they don't want her to move. She squirms and screams.

"She can't go anywhere. You see? I have her wrapped tight."

"Feed her something. Oats and milk."

"I have it. It's been ready." Another person, an old person. Three voices altogether.

No, she won't eat. She wants to know why she can't move her arms.

An old woman pushes a spoon at her mouth, muttering, "She won't take it. It's good mush, too."

"Burn everything. It's no good anyway. Burn the mattress and everything on it."

"We . . . if we . . . we'd have to move."

"I know."

"Leave the lantern in with her. For a bit. She's scared." That's the man's voice.

"I don't like it." The old lady's voice.

"She'll be Anna. That's a name I like. Go to sleep, Anna. That's right. Sleep and sleep. It'll be better in the morning."

SHE COMES AWAKE. That old dream. One of the bad dreams that keeps coming at her. Like a puzzle, almost all voices. When she's cold. It's about getting warm.

She can't sleep. She sleeps.

The Fenn children, 1887. All would die in the flood of 1889. Courtesy of Johnstown Area Heritage Association.

3

Monday, April 17, 1989

■ NINA TAKES HER CAR to the *Post-Gazette* offices most days, though half the time she hates to put more wear on it by taking it on assignment. Anyway, it sounds a lot better than Ben's car does. This morning the other *PG* employee who lives in her building, Michelle, taps on her door wanting a ride, as she does most mornings. Michelle sometimes offers to take her for lunch as payment and they talk about work—or at least Nina steers the conversation that way.

The first-floor apartment belongs to Michelle who has a large window that faces the porch. And Michelle sits, looking out that window a lot of the time or zips up and down the steps like a roommate, offering pizza or a movie. The whole thing makes Ben crazy. The last thing he wants is a long buzz of a rumor through the offices about his messed up personal life.

Usually Nina has a swagger about not exactly caring if Michelle figures it out, but today, this morning, she doesn't know what she feels. She hadn't bargained on what happened over the weekend. Now she wonders if Amanda has been totally out of the picture all this time. And she feels stupid though she knows she's in a very large company of women who've been conned. And when she examines her feelings, there is still a longing toward Ben—love for him, a wish for him to be okay no matter what Amanda throws at him.

61

Michelle slides into the passenger seat. It's raining a little, not hard. "I looked for you this weekend."

"I went to see my mum."

"Oh. Good. Anyway, I wanted to see *Lean on Me*. If you were interested."

"Did you go?"

"No. We could go tonight. Not crowded on Mondays."

"Let me think. I'm not sure. I might be coming down with something. I feel super tired."

"Okay. Let me know."

Not in the mood for people, Nina wishes she were on the bus, swaying, holding onto the bar on top, reading signs. AT&T FOR THE BEST SERVICE. LA ROCHE COLLEGE HAS WHAT YOU WANT. CONSOLIDATE YOUR DEBT!

"I visited my mum this weekend, too." Michelle says. "Just for lunch on Saturday though. She wasn't so good. Not in good health."

"I'm sorry. What is it?"

"She's overweight, short of breath, not taking care of herself. I wonder sometimes if I should give it up, move back home, make her life better. Like the old days, ha. The unmarried daughter stays at home. You know."

"And the good-hearted unmarried daughter doesn't ever meet anybody . . . and gets depressed? Not a good idea."

"I don't meet anybody anyway."

"Yeah. I hear you. Why do we care? Stupid romantic ideas."

"I guess." Michelle doesn't fancy herself up at all, but she has long shiny dark hair and a narrow but symmetrical face. She's plenty attractive, but down, depressed.

"You should go to movies alone, do things alone if I'm not around. Seriously. You never know what will happen."

"I hate to do things alone. I feel like I have three legs and five hands."

"I know the feeling."

"That's what amazes me. You don't look like you know that feeling. You always seem to have it all together."

"Ha!"

There is a long silence. She almost tells Michelle about her debacle weekend with Ben. Traffic slows. She switches on the car radio. Loneliness is shitty and so many people feel it, have it. And they live with it. Her mum. Mourning for ten years now. Eleven. "Our problems are small. Tiny. People go through awful things."

Finally Michelle says, "I'm going to do more things alone. I am."

The slightly open car window brings in cool wet air. It's not nearly so warm today as it was over the weekend. But that's spring for you. That's what spring is. Unpredictable. It had all seemed so lovely Saturday, in that valley, wildflowers at their feet.

She parks at the Mon Wharf, aware again that if she had the night shift (the better shift though she doesn't want it) she would be doing all kinds of tricks to park closer to the office. The Wharf, where she can afford to park, is dangerous anytime, but at night . . . one of the reporters was killed there at night a few years ago and nobody ever got arrested for it. She walks briskly past the homeless when she is alone, even in daytime, even when she drops coins in their Styrofoam cups. Now she and Michelle go into a silence as they march together out of the lot. Today nobody bothers them.

Ben is nowhere around when she comes up the elevator and into the news offices. Her cubicle is a mess, but no, no note from him. Her ACE—assistant city editor—is Barry, a rotund smoker with an amazing shock of hair as if something he is doing feeds the wild plant that comes out of his head. He comes up behind her, says harshly, "You. Collins. I need you to go to Dormont. There's a house fire. Real bad one, apparently. Call me with anything that looks like space. Take a Jeep."

"I'm gone," she says. So, good, not her car this time. When she gets to the pegboard, she sees that indeed a Jeep is available. She grabs the keys and runs down to the lot and climbs in, breathless.

"You Irish girls," her chief said once. "So tough. Can drive anything, do anything."

"I'm not Irish," she said, only to see how disappointed he looked.

"Collins?"

"You know. Ellis Island." She didn't explain further—that Kolinsky was going to be Kollins, her great-grandparents on her father's side had thought, but the name got changed to Collins by immigration officials who explained to those great-grandparents that they were spelling their name incorrectly. Like so many intimidated immigrants, they didn't pro-test, but traded in the *K* for a *C*. It didn't seem like much. They learned soon enough that some people didn't like the Irish much either and didn't even wait long enough to hear the accent, which definitely wasn't Irish. But Nina's paternal ancestors made their way and melted in the pot along with a lot of others. They admitted later in life that they missed their name. Her father told her so. She never knew his parents. They died young, passing on the gene to him.

The Jeep she's in is as uncomfortable as the rest of the Jeeps are, but this one is especially dirty as well: four McDonald's cups on the floor, and various food wrappers on the seats, not to mention stray pieces of paper. Men! Ben . . . isn't like that. He's more thoughtful, not so completely crass as to leave his garbage around. He's a good guy; she knows it. If he were an actor, which he's not, he would play the best sorts of roles, he-roes. There is something about the way his eyes reflect how carefully he's considering everything. If he were in her mother's favorite movie, *The Deer Hunter,* he would be Robert De Niro. Seeing things, fixing things. Selfish, yes, but also not. Both. Brave.

She has to merge onto the Parkway by taking the ramp around the corner from the *Post-Gazette.* She has to inch over to the left lane, to get through the tunnels. Once she's through the maddening tunnels that make everybody hit the brakes at some point or another, she gets onto Banksville Road and stays left so she can climb up the (exaggerating only slightly) ninety-degree hill that is Potomac. Dormont, Dormont. She doesn't know it terribly well. This modest neighborhood is next door to and poor cousin to Mt. Lebanon where Ben lives (modestly, he would point out, not in one of the half-million-dollar houses). The main reason, he told her when they first met and she was surprised about his subur-ban address, was that it provided the best schools for his kids who are six and eight. He insisted he was not at heart a suburban type.

She's covered several shootings, two suicides, five auto accidents, and two commercial fires. So far all her fires have been relatively mild—no injuries, minimum damage, three paragraphs at most, four if she squeezes various interviews into it. Traffic clogs outside the Dor-Stop, a newish restaurant Ben talks about that does great brunches. She has to idle along the tight street. The restaurant sure looks to be hopping. She'd stop if she weren't on assignment. But around the corner is a fire, and that's work, thank God; honest work will keep her from fretting about what happened last night or didn't; that is, Ben didn't call her.

ONLY TWO MILES away from her, Ben is banging out conjectural paragraphs on an old Corona in his brother's basement. He still needs to go to museum archives or somewhere with the letter purported to be from Paul Folks Jr. He doesn't doubt Ellen Emerson's veracity but it sure would be nice to have proof. The paper is old for sure—with faint lines to guide the writer's pen. It's a confession, all right. Ben keeps it in the plastic bag, sitting next to his typewriter. He intends to build up to Ellen Emerson's story so long as Hal lets him do three or four articles before it. First he'll capture interest with the class warfare angle, then he'll work on the engineering angle. Then, then the human angle, Ellen. He has to breathe carefully, to hope the *Pittsburgh Press* and nobody else scoops him on her, but she promised him the story was his.

He feels a lot of affection for her, as if she's his great-great-aunt rediscovered or something.

He called into the office earlier and said, "I'm working at home this morning. Afternoon at the library. I'll call in." And so he's still in pajama bottoms and his hair is mussed, but there is nobody to see him so he might as well keep working. Which bits go in which article? Does he stay away from the museum details until article four? Not sure. Typing paragraphs helps, even if he's not sure where they will go.

A half hour later, he's aware that he's not thinking clearly. He thought he could compartmentalize, but while he's writing about the flood, the images in his mind are of his wife last night, of the new oddity of being in his house—his own—where he appeared as if on an awkward date and she hosted him for a cup of coffee and a talk, insisting the boys go to bed (which of course they did not want to do since seeing their father in their home was something of an event). He managed to settle them, but how strange it was, climbing the steps, coming back down, catching a glimpse of a perfectly made bed with some sort of new fitted white bedspread in the master bedroom. Everything looked perfect, neat, wrong.

He can't go on living in his brother's basement forever. He needs a home, a base.

Oh, man, last night was horrible.

He climbs up to the first floor of his brother's house where the coffee pot is still on, pours himself a fresh cup, and descends again. The picture in his head is of Amanda sitting in the chair across from the sofa. They each had a cup of coffee then. Amanda said her shrink had told her alcohol was not appropriate if ever they talked seriously. She had dressed artfully in wheat-colored wool pants and a pink sweater, something between her winter and spring wardrobes. Her hair, almost wheat colored, was long and curled slightly. She appeared very nervous.

She began with, "I've tried to understand why you were messing around on me."

He shook his head. It was hopeless. He had already told her repeatedly that he wasn't. And he wasn't. It wasn't until after she kicked him out, not until he'd been firmly ensconced in his brother's basement, living the life of a loner uncle, that he met—well, got to know—Nina.

She continued, "I recently came to think if you needed something that wasn't coming from me, it must be partly my fault. There are plenty of women who don't agree. Believe me, plenty of women have said that men just do that because it's part of their biological makeup. But I've been trying to figure out what I wasn't giving you. And I want to know. I really want to know."

Why now, suddenly, was all he could think. "First off, all that time, I was not seeing anyone." He should have been, but he doesn't say it. "I never thought that way. I just . . . we were just two busy people with kids. You know, busy. But I have to say for whatever record you're keeping and I want to say this clearly, I was not seeing anyone. I'm sorry you thought so."

"You made yesterday's trip alone? You've been alone?"

He paused. "No. That was then. Nobody then. This is now. Things have changed."

"I can't believe that."

Whimpers from upstairs. They couldn't be listening. He had closed the door and put on an audio book, which still hummed in the background, just the slightest little variations on the sound of a voice coming through to him. And there hadn't been the creak of a door opening, though there had been whining when he told them they had to stay in their room. It was that sound he hated—as if his kids were being cartoons of kids.

"They aren't listening," she said. "They're probably breaking each other's fingers."

He laughed uncomfortably and then she did, too. He couldn't figure out how he had once loved her. Ever. It made him feel crazy that he couldn't even remember what it felt like to want her. She was so stiff.

"Tell me about the woman you're seeing."

He took a drink of now-cold coffee. "I don't want to talk about any of that. I just came over to hear what you want to say."

"Oh. So it's all on me."

"You called the meeting."

"All right. I asked to talk to you because . . . I still have feelings for you. They won't go away just like that. I must have been responsible in some way for losing your love. I wonder in what way I sent you to this other woman. And I want to know."

It was almost laughable. She wanted to know what she did? "Well, you accused me of things on an almost daily basis, told a shrink you wanted a divorce, and kicked me out. You persuaded me you meant it. Why wouldn't I believe it? You wouldn't make love to me for a year."

"Were you seeing her before I kicked you out?"

He doesn't know what to do with this obsession of hers. Ninety percent of guys who are accused of messing around are guilty. The joke is that he isn't. But it doesn't matter what the truth is anymore.

He kept his temper. He told her, "I'm so sorry you believe that. I have no way of showing you it isn't true. I wish you'd planted a secret James Bond camera on me that would show you I wasn't in another bed. Or sofa. Or car. Or office chair."

"But now you are."

"That's not up for discussion."

"What if I want another chance?"

"I can't see it."

"Not even for the kids? Not even to try?"

"I can't. You've killed something in me." As soon as he said it, something happened in his body, a shudder for how unsettled he felt, how lost, and he started to cry.

67

"I'm sorry," she said. "I'm sorry I'm upsetting you."

"I should go. We shouldn't be talking without lawyers. We're getting a divorce, and that's messy enough."

"I've asked that the papers not be sent until we give the marriage a chance."

"You don't mean it."

"I do. I want to try."

He was in hell. He left the house, saying he needed time to digest what she was saying. The talk they'd just had felt as disorienting as the first time she told him she was through with him.

He wanted to remember how good he felt with Nina, but Amanda had made it seem wrong to think of Nina at all. He opened the studio bed in his brother's basement last night and lifted the phone. He owed Nina a call at any rate. But what could he say? He couldn't sort his own thoughts. Just then his brother came down to the basement. "Heard you come in."

He put the phone down.

"Anything good?"

"She's changed her mind."

"That's great. Melanie is upstairs wanting to hear. She thought so."

"But it isn't great."

"It isn't?"

"I don't think she really knows what she's feeling or what she wants. She's probably worried about money or she tried being out in the divorced single-mother scene and realized it wasn't going to be easy."

Jake sat down. "I think you'll be okay when you calm down. Just take it easy. Mel said I was supposed to ask if you want a cup of tea."

"Nah. Thanks." He was already full up with the coffee he had drunk out of politeness.

"Take your time. You'll find your way." It sounded like an exit line, but Jake didn't move.

"I've overstayed my welcome here."

"We wanted to help. But this can't be as good as having your house back, we know that."

"I've looked at apartments. I just . . . hate to say it, but I got worried about money."

Jake, heaving his middle-aged spread, sat forward, serious as hell. He looked tired. He looked as if he'd given up, sold out, signed over his identity. "Money is very real. It's got to be part of the equation."

"Right. I will find someplace. I can't go back."

"I can only say, 'Sleep on it.' You know how you get."

He felt the scowl come over his face. "How do I get?"

"Easily offended. Stubborn."

"Okay. I'd better try to sleep. On it or in it or with it. Whatever."

"Is this about that woman you see sometimes?"

Doesn't that have to be "part of the equation?" He almost says it, but he simply turns away from Jake and pretends to straightening the bed covers.

"These things usually turn out to be not so real. Of course you reacted. I'm not blaming you. But reality bites eventually. Your new woman is going to want marriage, kids. You already have kids. Living in two households, mixed families, I've known guys who do it. It's not a picnic."

"I know that."

Finally Jake gets up. "Sure about the tea?"

"Sure."

The moment had been poisoned. He didn't pick up the phone again to call Nina. I'll call later, he told himself. Then he told himself he would call the next morning. He slept badly, hardly at all. He told himself from time to time, "Get up. Work. Work solves life." But he kept trying to sleep instead, to go under, that blessed state.

Now he faces the page again, but his brain isn't directing his hands to type anything.

Amanda stopped working, what, three years ago now. She was a buyer at Saks. And she was, their joke, a *buyer* at Saks. But she is not bringing anything in, if she ever was, and he is her provider. She's stuck—probably afraid to go back to work, even wondering if she can get a job.

He messes around with paragraphs that compare workers and employers with unhappy wives and provider husbands. God, if he had daughters he would make sure they could *do* something, be able to earn a living at something they liked.

He messes with another paragraph about how things don't change when it comes to class warfare. A few years ago when he came to the paper, he covered a story about the fallout of the demise of the steel industry in the city. He wrote about a group that said they were supporting the interests of out-of-work steelworkers. They mainly targeted the Mellons and the banking system. They were very dramatic. They put fish in safety deposit boxes. They chose a church, Shadyside Presbyterian, that had a lot of the moneyed people in their congregation and then they chose a night, the Christmas pageant dinner, and they costumed themselves—gas masks—and they went in with "a weapon." It was ugly. The weapon was a bunch of balloons filled with dye and skunk water. The activists threw the balloons at the diners. The activists lost sympathy from almost everyone after that caper. And they didn't get the steelworkers back to work either.

The anger of the activists reminds him of his wife sort of throwing every bit of shit at him and then wanting her old life back. He scratches the paragraph with a big X. He doesn't have time to mess with a personal journal; he's got an article to write.

THE HOUSE FIRE is much worse than anything Nina has covered before. She manages to get fairly close; she parks almost a block away in a just vacated spot. As she half-runs toward the fire, she can see flames still climbing the roof of the house. Flashes of red, like a strobe, pulse through the black smoke that billows out and up through trees and telephone wires.

The trucks from three, no four, boroughs are working hoses and ladders. She writes down the names of the boroughs. Neighbors line the streets, watching. WTAE, KDKA, and WPXI news trucks are there already. The air is heavy with drifting smoke, and the smell or smells are of what happens when fire meets bedspreads, upholstery, clothing, wood. As soon as Nina gets near the house, she begins coughing, but she presses forward.

She jots down a few more notes to describe the scene, but she stops; something is happening; rising through the crowd's buzzing and murmuring is a keening sound. Several firemen slam a ladder to the second floor where no human being would want to go—and a firefighter in gear carrying his line scrambles up the ladder.

"What is it?" she asks the man from KDKA. He's familiar, a burly older guy named Pete. They've been on the same stories before.

He winces. "It's bad. Woman says her granddaughter is on the second floor. Her husband didn't know they had the kid for the day. He was down the basement and she was somewhere else, somebody said down the street. She thought he got the baby out."

"A baby?"

"I don't know the age. She was screaming at him about a baby. He said he didn't know she had the baby. She tried to go in, but the firefighters stopped her."

Another reporter who'd been canvassing the crowd joined them. He was young, a sometimes stringer for WTAE. She couldn't remember his name. Sean?

"How old? Do you know?" the KDKA man asks the WTAE guy.

"Two. I think they said two."

Nina groans inwardly. She points to the ladder and they all turn. "There's a guy in there—"

"Dormont. Volunteer. He better come out soon or they'll have to go in for him."

She stands at attention with everyone else, waiting. Because of the water pouring into the second floor now, the amount of smoke coming out is greater—who could live through that? How could a baby live through it? All around her are the voices of firemen on their radios but there are more voices that she can't sort out. After several seconds, the red leaping flames appear to be lessened.

All of a sudden, there is a hush. The firefighter is climbing back over the sill. He's carrying a child who is motionless. Nobody speaks or moves. The main sound is of voices far away on the radios and of a screaming ambulance, screeching to a stop. The man climbs down, holding onto the ladder with one hand and only at intervals, gripping the child in the other. The medics take the baby from him as soon as he reaches a low enough rung. All along the street, people are asking, "Is she alive?"

The firefighter is hauled off by his mates. The medics don't answer anyone.

Nina makes her way through the crowd, gagging on the smoke. Her eyes sting, but she sees well enough to see an older woman running after the ambulance while neighbors try to hold her back. At the edge of the crowd is an elderly man on a lawn chair with his head down. Is he the husband? She approaches him. "I'm sorry about your house."

He looks up at her with red eyes. "Is she dead?"

"I don't know. I understand you didn't know she was in there."

"I didn't know my wife was babysitting today. I swear I didn't know. I couldn't have—she says she told me, but she didn't."

His odd phrasing is not lost on her.

"Where were you when the fire broke out?"

"Basement."

"And your wife?"

"Backyard, gardening."

"And where did the fire start?'

"I think it was the toaster oven. It was old. By the time I came up to it, a fire was started and I left the house and went to a neighbor and called 911. My wife didn't know. She was gardening and then she started talking to a neighbor and went down the alley. I didn't want to upset her. I didn't run after her. I didn't know about my granddaughter. And then . . . it wasn't that long—"

The two TV reporters Nina knows have come up behind her and now they have their cameramen training cameras on the grandfather.

"No," he moans. "No, no, no." He puts his face in his hands and won't look up.

The attention of the crowd shifts once more when a car breaks through the tape and comes right to the trucks in front of the house. The mother of the child, surely, from the way she plays out her panic and rage—her car door hanging open and her engine running. "Where's my mother? Where's . . . where's Ashley?"

Neighbors who seem to know her try to lead her back to her car while she flails and insists on answers until she gets them. Seconds later she is in her car and gone, presumably on the way to the hospital before anyone can stop her.

Nobody should have let her go alone. Why didn't a neighbor hop in and drive her?

Nina stands there, trying to decide. Reporters aren't allowed to chase ambulances, but the hospital is where she wants to be. Should she start questioning the firefighters? Stick with the grandpa? Ben told her the best thing is walk aside, close your eyes, breathe. Sometimes all answers are correct. She chose the third option for the moment and once more approached the grandfather. She couldn't help noticing concerned neighbors were keeping the grandmother away from her husband.

"Had you been cooking in the toaster oven?" Nina asks quietly. The man's face doesn't come out of his hands.

"I think I put a piece of bread in but I forgot about it."

"What were you doing in the basement?"

"Taking paint off a table my wife bought."

"I see."

"Sorry, miss, you'll have to move out of the way." A large man flashes a badge. He's from the Allegheny County Squad. "Investigations."

She moves only a few feet away.

"Now, lady. Out of the way."

Lady. She hopes not.

"I'm going to the hospital," says the man from KDKA. "I just got the okay. Ride with me if you want. I'll bring you back to your car."

It's hard enough parking anywhere in the city, let alone at Children's Hospital. She nods quickly and goes with him and his two camera crew, two other men who talk the whole time about whether to go to tomorrow's baseball game if they aren't scheduled to take pictures of a disaster. The one guy handles the cables, the other even now cradles his huge camera over his lap, his gun of sorts, a big blast of a machine gun. Pete drives fast and that's good. They take Banksville Road to the Parkway. Throughout the drive Nina and Pete are mostly quiet. It's a relief that the camera guys keep up a banter. Finally Pete says, "If the kid lives, it's a story. If she doesn't, it's a story. Right?"

"Right."

And finally, they are at Children's Hospital, which sits surrounded by other buildings and offers very little parking. Pete parks on the street at a non-metered spot, risking a ticket. Maybe the TV stations are more generous about reimbursements than the newspaper is. She's glad, anyway, that she's not fighting for parking right now. She has a bad need for a bathroom. There will be one in the ER.

Pete decides to leave one of the camera crew with the car as long as possible, saying the other will wave him in as soon as they get an interview. So she and Pete and the other guy hurry into the building; all the while she's marshalling arguments for her bosses about how serendipitous it all seemed, this offer of a ride from the KDKA team.

As soon as she's in the ER waiting room, she spies the firefighter who carried the baby out of the fire. She wondered what had happened to him. He's still got all the heavy gear on, though his helmet is on his lap. He sits with his elbows on his knees, his head down. Have they checked him out already?

Nina nods toward him, but Pete has seen him too. She and Pete approach, but the man doesn't look up. He's a sturdy, blond fellow with a dirt-streaked face.

Pete barrels in first. "Sir. We saw what you did. I'd like to commend you first of all. Are you all right?"

"Yeah, I'm okay."

"Is there any word yet?"

"No." When he realizes they want more, he looks up and adds, "The medics worked hard on her in the ambulance. I have hope."

"Was she breathing when you held her? Could you tell?"

"At first it didn't seem so. Just as I handed her over, there was something. Black something coughed up."

"I have a camera crew here. Could we get a statement?"

"Not just yet please. Not until I know something." He looks at Nina, apparently curious about her part in this.

"I need to get your name," she says. "*Post-Gazette.* I'm Nina Collins. He's—"

"Pete Marinelli, KDKA. We won't shoot until you say yes." The one tech guy goes to wave his mate in.

The firefighter says, "Doug Wolff. Two *f*s."

"Dormont volunteer?"

"Yes."

"How long?"

"Almost a year."

Pete whistles. "Not so long. Seen much?"

"Nothing like this."

It's clear why children fall in love with firefighters. Heroism is inescapably romantic. And this one adds some decent looks to the mix. It kills her to have to make a break for the bathroom, but better now than later. "I'll give you a moment," she says. "I know this is hard. But I'll need to talk to you. I'll be right back."

In the women's room, she has a jumble of thoughts, a whole salad tossing around. They include the baby, the mother who must be in with her kid, the firefighter, and Ben. Then it's Ben's day, his article, the firefighter's emotions, her need to get a story angle decided. She makes a reminder to herself to call her mother and deal with the disaster of Sunday—was that only yesterday? She thinks about how disorienting this fire is—the possible human cost—and the main thing being the child. Hopefully alive and . . . eventually healthy.

All this, this petit tragedy, reminds her of what Ellen Emerson as a little kid went through.

Her salad of thoughts takes only two minutes but by the time she is back in the waiting room, the camera crew is there. Shit. She's missed it. People are slapping the firefighter . . . Douglas, Doug . . . on the back. Happy slaps. He's crying openly. And then she cries, too.

BEN TAKES a cup of coffee out into his brother's front yard. Pacing the sidewalk from the street to the porch is one of his tricks to get his mind going. Well, to get his mind focused. It's going every which way. Yes, he wants to hold off the Emerson story until he's got those ducks in a row. Can he persuade Hal to wait?

Oh, Ben heard his brother perfectly clearly last night. He should move out. To somewhere. Of course he should. What had started out as the much needed warmth and embrace of family has faltered. He's worn out his welcome and certainly he's never wanted to be a burden. So this is it. He's not going back home. That would be false. That would send a message to Amanda that he is able to consider returning and the truth is he can't even imagine it. The marriage is definitely broken. But now he's faced with practicalities. His neighborhood is too pricey to rent in. Yet if he goes somewhere else it will be harder to see his boys on a regular basis. How easily he let himself fall into this convenience, this basement room down the street from home. Well, the clear solution is he'll just need to allot more time for traveling back and forth. Suddenly he misses the boys, whining and all. Of course they whine. They're kids. They're in despair about his absence. Everything about his life seems cut and pasted, like a Picasso, the shoulder, the head, yes, but not attached in the usual way. He's . . . not himself.

When he paces too furiously, the coffee leaps up over the cup. At least he didn't get it on himself. He checks. No, it's okay. He looks up. Way up the street is Amanda, standing, waving at him.

"HERE, see this restaurant," Doug says. "It's a great little place."

The Dor-Stop. "I passed it on the way to the fire. I've been hearing about it."

"Can you take the time for lunch?"

She's ravenous and she's got to eat one way or another. So she says, "Okay, yes. But I have to be sure I can catch the Arson Investigator. If he's not there, how can I chase him down?"

"I expect he'll be there."

So the fire *was* suspicious.

Back at the hospital, Pete needed to stop to do breaking news for the noon program. When Doug caught her being nervous about getting back to her *PG* jeep he offered her a ride. "Where did you park?" he asked.

"Just about a block away from the fire. The street hadn't been cordoned off yet. How do you have your car?"

"I only live a block away from the fire. I got the call, I drove there. We only have four line officers. The rest of us are volunteers."

"Ah. Okay. How did you park in Oakland?"

"I just did. I didn't get a ticket. Funny. One of those days."

"Luck. To go back a minute—they let you leave?"

"I just did. They didn't stop me. And . . . I'll be reprimanded."

"Listen. Your county man was tough. Impossible to talk to."

"He's usually awful."

Doug parked easily now and started around to open her door for her, but she was already out of the car. He seemed surprised. "So, lunch?"

They went in and sat across from each other. The waitress dropped menus on their table in a no-nonsense way, giving them a reason to be silent for a moment. Nina felt a little awkward, as if this were a date. But the smells, the plates of food emerging from the kitchen, were a plenty good reminder of why she was here.

She wasn't sure what this guy did for a living. Something without regular hours, it seemed. Something that allowed him to jump on a fire truck in the morning. Bartender? Night shift for cable TV? He wasn't wearing a wedding ring, but of course that meant nothing.

She took out her notebook. "I'm going to fill in some things. How long exactly have you been a volunteer?"

"One year minus three weeks."

"How did you decide to become a fireman?"

"My father was a volunteer fireman."

"Nice."

The waitress was back. "Know what you want?'

"The chicken salad," Nina said. "It's quick, right?"

"The special. Very quick. You, sir?"

"Burger. Medium. Everything."

"Fries?"

"Yes."

But people were noticing him. "Were you at that fire?" asked a man at the next table.

"Yes," he said.

"Is everything okay?"

"It is. Quite a lot of damage, but the fire is out."

Nina could see people going back to their lunches reluctantly, wanting to bother him, but managing not to. "They're going to flip when they see you on the news."

He smiled a little. Then he confided in a voice so quiet nobody other than Nina could have heard him, "Already it doesn't seem quite real. I acted. I lived through it. I can relive it in my mind. Sort of as a series of images. But a part of me took a vacation."

"I understand."

They settled into an awkward silence for a moment. Finally she said, "I think the grandfather might have set the fire. I can't write it unless your investigator says so. I wonder what they're finding out."

"The Arson Investigator was on the way in. I'll make sure you get to him. That nasty county man was a *what* guy. The arson man is a *who* guy."

"Tell him to look at the grandfather."

He nodded, not without amusement. "How long have you been a reporter?"

"A year." She laughed a little.

"A rookie like me. Still beating down all the emotions and trying to toughen up. Trying to learn the rules, to be appropriate."

"Toughening up," she smiled. "That's the idea. I never did find out what you do when you're not volunteering to save lives. Did you tell the TV guys?"

"I did. But not on camera."

"They might say in the intro."

He shrugged. "I'm writing my dissertation. They'll say I'm a student."

"Ah. So therefore the ability to jump up at any time."

"And grateful for it."

"What subject?"

"History."

"Sort of a big subject."

"Labor movements. In Pittsburgh."

"Homestead?"

"That's a chapter."

"I thought almost all university people lived in Squirrel Hill."

"My parents moved to Florida. They want me in their house, watching it. I can do that for them. Eventually I'll persuade them to sell. I'll get a degree, well, I hope I will, and then hopefully a job . . . I don't want to jinx anything here by being too positive. And I'll probably move away, so they'll have to sell."

"Are you tired of the burgh?"

"No." He shakes his head sadly. "No. It will break my heart to leave. Maybe I won't teach. Maybe I'll . . . I don't know. Find something. What are historians with doctorates good for? Not much. You?"

"Paying off school loans. I didn't study journalism, I studied fiction, that's what I wanted to do, but I can write articles. I mean so far they haven't fired me. I just have to keep remembering to be objective. Ha."

"You come from?"

"Johnstown."

"The floods."

"The first thing anybody says when I say Johnstown."

"I went there to help after the flood in '77. I was eighteen. It was awful. Were you there?"

"Trying to get there. I was in Pittsburgh that week. On a high school special trip for, well, for some of us who were thought to be . . . promising. I saw the news and panicked. I was only fifteen."

"I could have given you a ride."

ELLEN HAS SPENT a lifetime thinking through things. Family, love, and work are the things that sustain people. Take one away and if the other two are in good shape, a person survives. Take all three away and a person is in despair. When she lost her family, she was too young to have any other kind of relationship. That wouldn't come for many years. But there was work—a version of it—and she discovered labor as her cure. Her work as a child was school. Her work was reading, learning, and she relied on it for survival.

To the rest of the world, as they saw it, she had a new family, her adoptive parents, and she was supposed to be grateful for their generosity in taking her in. But all the while, she knew those parents weren't exactly happy to have her. They were hard people—morally upright, supposedly, and that old cliché about the morality of especially upright people not leading to kindness was true. Ellen was only about eight years old when she came to realize, privately and sadly, that Paul and Hester Folks weren't inclusive, that they weren't forgiving—they allowed others no room for error, no room for messiness—and that they simply weren't . . . Christian, by any decent definition of the term.

She had tried hard to please them, but when any sadness at her losses showed on her face, in her voice, in things she said, those reminders of her inner emotional life angered her new parents. "You must be strong," her aunt said. "Do you see us weeping?" And once when she was a little older, her aunt even said, "This is what God had in mind for you, you coming here to us." Sure. God had picked her out specially and killed two thousand people so that she could have a stricter upbringing? Even as an eight-year-old, Ellen found the math suspicious.

She supposes she was rebellious, a challenge to them, the wrong look on her face when she wasn't monitoring her behavior. They wanted her to learn needlework and they encouraged Bible study. She tried to be good, did those things, actually loved the Bible study because the Bible gave her interesting puzzles to work out. Interpretations. Stories. When she didn't agree with her uncle's interpretations, she learned quickly enough to keep quiet about it. But she read other things, too, whatever she could get her hands on, mostly what teachers gave her. Sometimes her aunt took books away from her with a muttered, "too much of that."

They thought she was already too much like her mother—dangerous, uppity, getting beyond herself. She tried to remember her mother—a happy woman, wasn't she, energetic at any rate, and talkative? But the image was fading.

Ellen's uncle would call her to the rectory office and ask her to stand before him. He would read or write something while she waited. How she hated waiting. He said he was teaching her patience. She looked at the thick adult books in the far end of the room, wondering what they were. Then he would ask finally, "Have you anything to say?"

If she said no, he would stare her down. After a while she began searching for things to say.

Once she asked, "Do you want me to talk about the flood? Is that what you want me to talk about?"

"Think about it, would you? If you brought the subject up, you must have something you want to say. Is there something you want to ask?"

Perhaps he had called her in because he knew something? "Have you heard from Paul?" she tried.

Her uncle's face told her she had badly miscalculated what to ask. He paled; she thought he might be ill. She had told him three times, four times, that he should search for Paul, whose body was never found. In her mind's eye she saw Paul pushing her father into the water, climbing over their bodies to get to the building, as clearly as she saw the boy saving her life while she cried out that someone must save her sister.

"What can you be thinking? I need to understand you. What goes through your muddled head?"

She plunged ahead for the second time that day. "Maybe they died, but not then. That's what goes through my head."

He had dealt with her rebelliousness before. He worked to calm the storm in him. "You have to fight harder against delusions. When people insist on their false beliefs, they end up in asylums, away from the world. Is that where you want to live out your life?"

"No."

"You must learn to accept loss. Loss is a part of God's plan."

Like killing off all those people so she could get a proper upbringing.

"Do you understand?"

"Yes. I have accepted it." She hadn't. She had come to terms with the fact that her mother and brother and father had perished, but not . . . not her uncle and her twin sister. Was it only because workmen had recovered bodies in the first three cases? If that physical evidence was the difference between insanity and sanity, she *was* in trouble. She was like all the wrong-headed people in the Bible, needing to see and touch to believe. Thomas. Wanting evidence.

When she read stories of children on their own, stories not from the Bible, but from whatever books she could get from her teacher at the school, books with children who had run away and, orphaned, survived, often living on their own, she got a thrill, believing for a moment that she could survive, too, if she left her uncle's house.

But, no, she didn't run. Smart enough to know they would haul her back, she stayed. Instead she read; she found books by Charles Dickens in her uncle's library and stole them and read them and put them back. The books kept her rooted and obedient.

Another reason was a bit of kindness coming at her from her cousin, her uncle's and aunt's daughter who no longer lived in the house because she was married. Julia was not like her brother Paul, not mean spirited, but shy, nervous, eager—a recent bride in love with her husband and looking forward to caring for children when they came. Later in her life Julia was unhappy and it turned out that Ellen was needed to help *her*, but at this point, when Ellen was young, Julia was kinder than her parents, softer. She came by often to visit. When she taught Ellen stitching and for one whole month let her help with a quilt, things seemed better, more tolerable. The quilt was a small one, for a baby. Julia was expecting.

Sometimes they whispered as they worked. Ellen confided in her cousin that she might want to keep going to school all her life—at least after she was eighteen—she liked the work of school so much.

"By then you will probably change your mind," her cousin said, laughing. "You'll be on to other things."

Ellen wonders some days, as surely all old people do, if she remembers correctly or if she has made her life up.

Today, Monday, as Ruth fiddles in the kitchen, Ellen sits in her wing-back chair, feeling that the most exciting thing in a long time happened yesterday. She told the truth. She's also sad for the same reason. Even now her uncle's anger edges toward her. Even now, one hundred years later, she can feel his disappointment in her.

So be it.

Ellen has always needed to talk. It's how she became a teacher after all. Yesterday she certainly had her chance to talk and today she is hungry for it again. Mr. Bragdon promised he will come back at least one more time. And with the young woman, Nina, too, who comes from this town.

Talk is necessary. Talk is life. It's her life. It keeps her going.

"Ruth, come sit with me," she calls. "Can you?"

A hundred and four, almost, and she is worried about decline!

The insect tries to live. It's flipped over on its back and keeps moving its legs trying to get a purchase on something solid. Offer it a finger, a tissue, and it scrambles to grab, to keep going. She is that small thing, not ready to give up.

PATRICIA HAYS and Natalie Marshall are both aides at Manor Care Nursing Home, which they generally call The Manor or The Manor House; they always talk while they work, Patricia about things she intends to do, Natalie about her goals for a good life.

"I've got to get over to Marshalls," says Patricia. "I've gotten lax. I can feel my body just wanting to spread. It's from wearing these all day." She gestures at the maroon scrubs they wear. "Some nice clothes would be a motivation. Stomach in and all that, right?" She has short straightened hair and a round face and a big hankering for donuts.

Nat says, "I love, love clothes." She's trimmer, more controlled in her appetites, and hates wearing scrubs.

"I know you do."

"Who's neat is that Mrs. Hoffman next door. She might take forever to get out of her room, but she's a clean one. Decent clothes, too."

"I heard she had a bad day yesterday, a little mini-breakdown. Maybe . . . maybe this is it for her." Patricia pulls the bottom sheet off the bed in the room next to Mrs. Hoffman's room, which is next on their list. "You're right. Her room is always perfect," she says, puffing. "The cleanest."

"I don't know how they keep going on. I don't want to get old." She winces. "I said that too loud. Anyway I want to look good in my coffin."

"You're cracked, girl. When you get that far along, you'll change your mind."

"Not so sure. Anyway, she's a quiet one. She doesn't play checkers when she can get out of it. What does she *do* all day?" Nat checks her hair in the mirror on the wall of the room they are cleaning. She likes her bangs just so—a little over her forehead, but not the whole way. "What does she do?" she repeats.

"Thinks, I guess. And reads those journals. She's still got some smarts." Patricia fits on the new bottom sheet. "Hey, quit looking at yourself." Together she and Nat work and fold the clean top sheet. "I wonder if she's, you know, passing."

"Huh? She doesn't look it."

"It's just she asked me where I grew up and I said 'the Hill' and she said she used to live in the Hill."

"Yeah?"

"She named markets that used to be there."

"So she knows it, but . . ."

"Sure, I know white people used to live there too, more than they do now. But she never has visitors, except once. And it was a black woman."

"Huh. Doesn't prove a lot."

"I know. I know. Just something in the way she asked me about myself. She was interested, making some kind of connection."

They pull up the blanket and tuck it just so.

"Let's go boot her out so we can do her room."

"She doesn't like going to activities."

When they get out to the hallway, they wave down one of the aides that works the activities schedule. She wears street clothes with a purple vest over it—the color code for the aides that take people to chess or films. Maroon is housekeeping. Lots of the residents never figure out who does what. How many times Natalie and Patricia have been asked to get a pill for someone, or a suppository. Hoffman doesn't mix them up, though. She knows a nurse from a nurse's aide.

The serious looking young woman in a purple vest approaches. "Yes?"

"Last we looked, Mrs. Hoffman was in her room and we couldn't do it like we wanted. Isn't she supposed to be out?"

"Ideally. It's not compulsory."

"We just thought it'd be good for her."

"Well, it would. Let me see what I can do. She's down in the dumps lately. I've had a lookout going for things she might want to do."

Natalie and Patricia wait. They hear the aide talking to Mrs. Hoffman. Eventually they hear the creak of a wheelchair and the old lady emerges.

NANCY IS AT WORK, at Memorial, downtown Johnstown, staring at her computer and worrying about her daughter. What worries Nancy the most is that the younger generation won't ever have real romance. All this work to liberate women—and they're still underemployed, underpaid, and they still get into bad situations with men. Why the secrecy about this guy, Ben? Nancy throws a crumpled piece of paper across the room, just a copy of a bill, no longer needed, and wonders at her mood. Of course, yes, she's uptight and she knows it. Old-fashioned. But she wants Nina to have a good life and that includes romance. She shuts down her computer, snatches up her raincoat, and walks down the hallway to where Paula, her only friend at the hospital, works. They are of an age, they grew up at the same time in the same way in the same town, though Paula went to Bishop McCort and Nancy went to Johnstown Central and they didn't know each other before they worked at Con Memorial.

"Have you had lunch?" Nancy asks. Her voice comes out harsh sounding and Paula looks up a little surprised.

"I brought a sandwich."

"I did, too, but we could stash them in the fridge and go out. For a change."

"Well, okay."

There isn't any place good to go, plus Nancy is frugal as well as uptight—though the two things often go together—and so they end up at a McDonald's in yellow plastic chairs, eating unhealthy food, but the French fries are tasty, especially doused in ketchup.

"I went to the cemetery yesterday," Nancy says. "My daughter was in so she went with me. She bought flowers—for me, for the grave." She stops herself from complaining about the cost. With a sigh, she says, "I still miss him."

"Of course you do," Paula says. "You know, it's funny, all my friends who have their husbands still alive and kicking complain about them constantly. I do, too. Men get worse, I think, always underfoot, more sloppy than ever. I guess we all miss them if they go before us. And they generally do."

"I think my daughter's boyfriend is older than she is. I didn't ask. He looks older. A bit. Handsome though."

Paula opens her bun, studies her burger, removes the top half of the bun and takes a dainty bite. "Love. You can't stop it."

"Yours? That son-in-law?"

"Well, the one is okay. He's a provider and he seems okay. The other one is out of work. I don't know. He's out of the house half the time. What does he do? I'm afraid to question my daughter. I think she wants to handle it herself. She's very independent."

Independent. Okay, she'll apply that word to Nina. Working things out. Nancy looks at her watch. "We're okay," she says.

"Relax. I don't care if I am late. I put in plenty of overtime. Always have."

"We're very well behaved. I think we're too good. Don't you think so?"

Paula tips her head. "I took a roll of toilet paper once."

"No! You're kidding."

"I didn't have time to go to the store and we were out. Just the once." Paula laughs. And then Nancy does. As if they are very bad.

They sip at their Cokes for a while.

Paula says, "I think you should maybe start dating. You'd have to really dig deep down to find somebody worth it. But ten years is a long time—"

"Eleven. Going on twelve."

"It's hard to be alone. There's no shame in going out."

"You know, I never met anyone I felt drawn to except for John. We were together from the first second. Did you go to the Teen Canteen? You said you did, right?"

"Absolutely. That was it. That was our social life."

"My mother would drop me off at the War Memorial. She always looked worried. She'd sew me something new to wear. Like a dress, sometimes, a new dress. And I'd go in and stand against the wall, the original wallflower. And when I got home, I would lie and tell her I had a good time."

"I stood against the wall plenty. I had a group of girlfriends. We were all on the wrong side of popular but, man, did we laugh. We'd group together and crack ourselves up."

"One day John came up to me and asked me to dance. I got so nervous, I was shaking." She'd been a good-looking girl, but boys left her alone since her stiffness rang louder bells than her beauty did. "And then we danced all evening." He'd gripped her tight around the waist and clenched her hand in his. How nervous he'd been, too. "And then we went out. And after that we were never separated except for school."

Paula laughed. "Gave your mother some scares, I'll bet."

"Oh, yes. 'He'll never respect you.' But he respected the heck out of me."

"Whoo," Paula laughs. "Drive-ins?"

"Yes. All that!"

Paula crumples her wrapper and then Nancy's before Nancy can grab it. "No. I got it. Well, you were lucky. You really were. Larry and I fight like the devil sometimes. Though I will probably miss him if he pops before I do."

"Of course you will."

"You really should look into going out. I don't mean you have to hang out at bars. I think there are, you know, services that set people up. Dating services."

"I couldn't. Not in a million years."

All day once she's back at work, she remembers specific dresses—the green leaf patterned dress, the bright pink sundress with inset rose petal pieces coming down the right side. She remembers her mother's face. And those walks up the sidewalk to the Teen Canteen. Paying her money, getting her hand stamped, running up the steps to meet John. Then later, when he got a job and a car, he would pick her up. A few times they only pretended to go to the Teen Canteen, had to spend the money in their pockets in case their parents checked. Those were the days, wonderful days.

"I HATE TO THINK I was a difficult child, but I suppose I was," Ellen is saying.

"I can't believe it," Ruth says.

"I was a useful adult, I hope. I helped people." This is a shameless lure. Ruth has already told Ellen that the high school English class she took from Ellen changed her life. She hadn't believed she could read anything of any length, let alone enjoy it. And understand it.

"You helped a lot of people. You were tough. We were all afraid of you. And then we weren't. When you found us and got personal, we weren't scared any more. It's funny to think you weren't encouraged as a child. I always thought you must have been. White family. Books all around. That was what I pictured."

"Some books. Half the time I had to sneak them or fight for them. You know, books give a person ideas."

Ellen is also grateful to her teachers. Two in particular took her seriously as a young child. "I like sciences," she announced when she didn't even know what sciences were. Miss Parks bought her books about birds, rock formations, wildflowers. Since that announcement had worked, she tried, "I like maths." Miss Parks found a somewhat advanced book with problems to solve. Ellen applied herself to the problems every night, but they were too hard for her, dashing her spirits. "I love literature above everything else," she told her next teacher, Mrs. Clarkson. It was true. Mrs. Clarkson supplied her with novels, which she would read for six hours at a stretch if she could get her chores done and then sneak out to the yard. Her aunt looked at her with concern.

Her cousin Julia came over to visit a little less frequently now that she had a baby, Michael. Julia told her mother, "Let her be. Let her read. She has to have something." But that was the young Julia, when she was sweet and before all the trouble.

Ellen made two friends in school, Sarah and Rose. Both were Presbyterian. The three of them took walks together and from time to time compared their churches. The Presbyterians *loved* books, valued learning. Ellen begged and was allowed to go to their church a few times.

Her life progressed as children's lives do, in that half unconsciousness, accented by special events. Before she knew it, years had passed and Julia came to visit with Michael, three, and the new baby, John, one, so Ellen had two children to dote on. She sat with the babies, telling them rhymes, the same ones she used to recite with her sister, well-known ones and others she made up.

I love the sun, I love the moon,
I love the holiday coming soon.
I play in the rain, I don't complain,
I love the lunch we get at noon.

Soon the boys were old enough to fight with each other and they weren't loving much of anything. "I'm never going to be an orphan," John told Ellen one day.

"Why not?"

"Don't want to. Nobody likes an orphan."

"All right then." Little ears had probably overheard something.

She wanted to do something wonderful someday, but what would that wonderful thing be? Go to war as a nurse? Discover something? She couldn't think what. She looked around her and longed for things that weren't hers: children like the ones Julia had, the rough and tumble language of argument she could hear among the immigrant families when she could find them these days (why were Protestants so quiet?), women with jobs outside of the home (right out there, in the world, in the weather . . . why did people refer to them as unfortunate?).

She insisted that the boys stop fighting and she ran through all the nursery rhymes she knew. "Hey diddle, diddle, the cat and the fiddle, the cow jumped over the moon. The little dog laughed to see such sport, and the dish ran away with the spoon." *That* was what she had said to keep her sister from screaming when they rode on the bed, when things slowed for a while and they rode, just before the boy who saved Ellen took her from her sister.

"I wish I'd made the boy save my sister."

"No, Mrs. Emerson. I've heard of this thing called survivor's guilt. I heard about it on TV. You shouldn't have it. Everybody wants to live."

"I know that, but I would have managed. I think I would have."

"I must have given you something bad for lunch. What is this?"

Ellen laughs. "It was the cake."

"I told you I don't trust my baking."

Before her eyes is the flood once more. Now it is just strange, not even frightening, just . . . strange. Crazy, the world upside down and rearranged, dead people bobbing up like clowns. A cow over a moon, a little laughing dog, dishes running off with spoons, it was like that.

"You are strong, I'll give you that," Ruth says. "You made your own way in a time when people didn't. Couldn't have been easy."

One day, some years later, when Julia was over to dinner with her husband and children, Ellen chose her moment to say she wanted to go to lectures at the Presbyterian church.

Her uncle scowled. "Bible lectures?" he asked, in a way that made it clear he wanted to know what was wrong with *his* sermons, his Bible school? Presbyterians, like his sister and his niece, were uppity.

"Not Bible study, no, some new subjects."

Presbyterians, uppity or not, believed in education—reading, writing, and discussing. These were to be lectures on all kinds of things, one every week.

Julia said, "She loves that kind of thing."

The first guest speaker, Ellen explained, was to be a man who'd read law and would talk about the profession to anyone who wanted to know how it worked. The same man would come back later in the year to discuss the court system. The next week was a man who would talk about moral philosophy, and he would explain as well as he could what this idea of "psychology" was all about. The next was a person who wanted to bring new plays into town and thus would discuss the plays being written in Europe.

"I don't know how you can find those things interesting," her aunt said. "They seem very taxing subjects."

"I think I would like them," Ellen said simply.

"She does, she really does like to make herself think," said Julia.

"Perhaps someday. You're still too young," said her uncle.

But she wore them down. A teacher helped out by sending a note home. She got to be sixteen and seventeen years old and during these years, she missed very few lectures. She was learning another truth— that people get used to things. Who would have thought that her aunt and uncle could be persuaded to let her go, let alone give her an early dinner on the nights she needed to be gone. People get used to things.

One Thursday, the speaker was a woman from Pittsburgh, from the

Pennsylvania College for Women. The college had been founded by the Presbyterians and it was thriving. Many young women who did not have decent educations in their own spheres were now attending preparatory classes there to catch up to college level but others went straight for their college degrees. The speaker, Miss Pelletreau, a past president of the college, explained that women who received this kind of education would be leaders in their families and would be better wives to their husbands, yes, but more, too. As the great Dr. James King, physician, a leading man in the practice of medicine in Pittsburgh, had once said in a speech about the potential of women—she wanted to quote it to her audience—"I believe that women have minds of equal force with those of the other sex, that they are susceptible to cultivation, that by proper culture woman may be fitted for any station however exalted."

Ellen raised her hand. "What subjects are taught?"

"Do the rest of you want to hear the curriculum?"

The audience gave a muted yes.

"Four years of college Latin: grammar; then Caesar, Nepos, and prose composition; then Virgil and composition; then Horace and Cicero. In mathematics, we offer algebra, geometry, astronomy. We cover everything. There are four years of Bible study, logic and mental philosophy, four years of history, four years of English, three years each of Greek, French, German. Physics, chemistry, botany. Music and art."

The audience murmured approval.

Miss Pelletreau explained how students lived in the dormitories and how well taken care of they were. "It's hard to be away from home for four years. But imagine. Many people have gone to Europe or New York for long periods to pursue an education. Pittsburgh is not that far."

Ellen's heart jumped. Europe! Why not Europe!

Even then, even in the Presbyterian church's basement, where the audience was preselected for forward thinking, a woman in the audience said, "But these women will never get married."

Miss Pelletreau smiled. "I haven't seen any diminishment in the marriage rate among our young women. The husbands in question, I would say, are of a very high quality."

The talk then turned to Columbia University's having a special college for women, Barnard. And of New York University's taking women. And also the Western University of Pennsylvania in Pittsburgh.

Ellen went up to the speaker afterward. "I want to go to New York University." Imagine, a school plopped right in the city that was the scene of so many novels she'd read.

"Yes, if you want, that is possible. And if you want to stay closer to home," Miss Pelletreau said gently, "our very excellent institution in Pittsburgh may seem quite far enough."

"Yes," Ellen tells Ruth, coming out of her reverie about her teen years, "I had to be insistent, even rebellious, to get what I wanted. So few girls have to do that today."

"Maybe not, but I sure fought for library time. My father sure didn't understand that. I used to tell him, 'My teacher said *I have to.*'"

Right. Ellen had helped others.

As the adopted daughter of a minister, Ellen got a hefty discount at the Pennsylvania College for Women.

When she finally got on a train in 1903, she wore her good wool coat because she didn't have room to pack it. She carried two suitcases of books and clothing. Julia cried, which made Ellen cry and made her feel she was somehow a sad case, never satisfied with an ordinary life as Julia was. Julia carried a squirming little one in her arms. Lucy. Aunt Hester embraced Ellen stiffly, and then, for the first time in her memory, Uncle Paul did too. There was a moment after the embrace in which she almost didn't board the train. They thought she was lost, a lost soul. They wanted to snatch her back.

The train she boarded was the same one that had once brought the wealthy industrialists the other way, from Pittsburgh to Johnstown, for peace. There would always be traffic between the two cities, small Johnstown, bigger Pittsburgh.

"You still want me to sit with you?" Ruth asked, restless.

"I'm sorry. You have something you want to do."

"Could I bring in my book? I got it from the library on the way in here."

"Of course you can."

IN PITTSBURGH, Anna is being summoned again to a group session about memory.

Oh, dear, what is so wonderful about remembering the past, Anna thinks. But they all want her to do it. They believe in it. The activities aide wearing a purple vest has wheeled Anna to the activities room, instead of the large parlor they met in yesterday. Everybody in the activities room, wheelchair or not, is pulled up to a table. Since Anna can't get close enough to the table, she leaves the wheelchair and makes her way a little unsteadily to a regular chair. She must exercise and get her balance back. She knows this.

Soon they are all seated. The activities director, Mrs. Camillo, stands before them, saying, "We very much liked yesterday's session and we asked Mrs. Salinas to continue with her work here. She is sometimes experimental. She is doing very exciting work."

Salinas stands next to Camillo. Both are smiling. Anna wonders if the similar body type makes for a sympathy between the director and the therapist. They look remarkably alike, actually. Through a smattering of applause, Mrs. Salinas says, "Thank you so much."

An aide is slapping down legal pads and pens at each of their places. For a moment there is almost the smell of paint and glue, the smell of primary school. But it's not real, only memory.

"Today," says the therapist, "I would like for you to remember an object from the household. Just a single object. I want you to choose something—it could be a wire coat hanger, simple as that, but make it something you handled, not a toy, something from the household. When you think of it, I would like for you to write it down."

"Would a garden trowel be all right?" Mr. Cobbs asks.

The therapist pauses to think. "Yes. All right."

"How old are we supposed to be—with this thing you want us to remember?"

"Any age before you left home."

"Which home? We moved two times."

"Ah. The home that is most familiar to you before you left for a home of your own."

"I never left," says one woman. They all laugh. "I know. I was a big baby. Lived with mommy and daddy all my life."

The therapist looks both amused and awkward. "Any object then that was in that household. Anything that strikes you."

"Strikes me," the woman grumbles. She says something about a wooden spoon but only the women next to her titter.

"Now for this exercise, close your eyes. Close your eyes tight and just breathe. Nice big breaths, take your time, slowly, in and out." After a while she says, "I want you to see the object, really see it." And then after another long pause in which they worked on visualization, she says, "How heavy is it? How does it feel in your hand? What, if any, smells does it have or conjure?"

"The garden," says Mark Cobbs. "Dirt. That heavy dirt smell."

"Good. Good. Everybody else make sure you find every sensory memory you can about this object. If it had a taste, include that."

Anna opens her eyes. She has chosen a teacup, a pretty thing, real china. Most others have their eyes closed still, so she succumbs. The teacup was light. She used to worry about breaking it. "It's the one thing I have," her mother kept saying, "these few bits of china."

"The shape, the color. The feel. And now, open your eyes and write it down."

They all busy themselves with this task.

Teacup, Anna writes. She examines her handwriting, not so easy to execute and more angular than it used to be.

"I'd like you to next remember a scene in which that object was used. Remember it as well as you can. Bit by bit. Little by little. What was the weather like? How old were you? What might you have been wearing?"

Anna remembers a scene, all right, when she was handling a fragile teacup. It's hard to forget that scene. It was raining. She was seventeen. The long gray skirt, the dark blouse. She has often thought back to this moment. Is that why *teacup* came to her? Was she supposed to remember an important moment or an ordinary one? This was an important one. Crucial. But before she can ask, Salinas speaks.

"And now write down a sort of story that uses that object. It's okay to be creative. You can make something up for this next part. Your feelings are still your feelings. Or you can write it as a memoir, what actually happened to you."

Some of the residents are confused and have many questions. What is a memoir? Why should they make things up? Should they lie? How many things can they say about an object—just describe it?

Anna does not feel confused. She writes: *One day my mother had trouble holding a teacup. I was supposed to go to school, but I knew something was wrong. I understood that she was ill. She thought it was her mind, her memory, declining, but it was her body.*

She looks up. Some of the other residents are writing, some look stumped. Salinas is patrolling the tables. Anna takes up her pen again and writes:

She must have felt a certain urgency to straighten out her life because that was the day she told me she wasn't my real mother. My real mother was a very poor woman who didn't want me. I was devastated and confused when she told me. Was I sad because my mother was ill, dying, or was I sad because now I knew my real mother had not wanted me?

She stops writing. She could go on and on, but her arm is tiring. She hasn't written anything by hand for a while. There's nobody left to write letters to.

But she remembers. She sits like some of the other stunned ones, but thinking, remembering.

"Sometimes I feel I can't . . . think properly," her mother said. Anna stopped abruptly at the sound of her mother's voice. She had been fetching a book she needed for school and getting ready to come to the table for a quick cup of tea, but her mother sounded odd. Anna came to the table only to see that, yes, she was right, something was amiss. When her mother tried to put a cup of tea before her, the cup rattled in the saucer. Anna did not want to embarrass her mother by reaching to help. The tea spilt, almost filling the saucer. "Oh," her mother said.

"My fault," said Anna, "for not taking it out of your hands."

"I'm not myself."

Anna had rushing thoughts: *what does the shaking mean,* and *yes, something is wrong,* and *what should I do.* She felt unsteady herself and dropped into a chair. *I will be orphaned soon,* she thought. This was something she had been preparing for. Her father had lain down five years ago with a heart attack and her mother had not been right since.

"I won't go to school," she said that day. It was raining, it was late in May, the streets were like small streams. She didn't want to go out into the weather even though she liked school. There was no one else here to watch her mother or to run for the doctor.

Had her father died of unhappiness? He often talked longingly of the country where he and her mother used to live. Anna had no clear memory of that time—only sometimes an image of mud and chickens. "Was I happy there?" she asked once.

"Oh, you were just very young," her father told her.

About six years ago her father went back to the farm and stayed for five whole days and came home to them, disturbed and sad. She listened in to things he said to her mother. *I took care of things. I miss it.*

"Why did we leave the place in the country then?" she asked when the time seemed right at breakfast one morning. He told her they had come to the city so he could get work in the mills. "You go where the work is," he said glumly. And then again, sometime later, Anna overheard him talking longingly of the country. She felt awful for him. Would they have been so unbearably poor if they'd stayed on the farm? The fact was, they were still poor. They lived on the South Side of Pittsburgh. She wouldn't have had a good school on the farm, they told her.

On the day of the rattling teacup, she got up and led her mother to their small parlor. Her mother's face was gray. She said, "Go. I'll be fine."

"Lots of people will miss today because of the rain." Anna looked out the window. The rain gave her a sick feeling today; the atmosphere was heavy with it. "Let's sit and read."

"I have my housework to do."

But Anna prevailed. She reversed things. Instead of receiving tea she brought her mother a cup of tea, hands steady, and in a voice measured with enough volume to be heard, not enough to be alarming, she read her mother practically every article on the first two pages of the *Gazette-Times* until her mother fell asleep. She had been correct about other students missing school today. Before midmorning she heard boys' shouts outside their door. She moved over and watched from the window as they splashed through the rain. One of them beckoned for her to come outdoors. She looked back at her mother. She hated getting the bottoms of her skirts or dresses wet, but she had to go fetch the doctor.

She gathered her shawl around her and started for the door. Her mother's voice surprised her. "You remember, oh, a long time ago, when you came home crying because one of those boys told you you didn't belong to us, that you were adopted?"

"I remember."

"And I told you it was a lie." Her mother got up uneasily from the sofa, but began to straighten the newspaper and the antimacassar on the chair Anna had sat in. Her hand was still trembling.

Anna sat down. She knew enough to be expectant.

"But what that boy said was . . . true. You had a family and they were poor, very poor, and could not take care of you. They wanted us to take you and so we took you."

She *knew*, she'd always known there was *some*thing. "When did this happen?"

After a pause, her mother frowned and said, "You were a tiny baby."

"I must have been a very troublesome baby if they didn't want me."

"No. They were poor."

"Who were they?"

"I don't know. They were passing through where we used to live."

"The farm?"

"Yes."

"You never got their names?"

"Oh, I didn't care. I couldn't let them give you to someone who might not care. I'm sorry we were always poor, too. But we fed you. We clothed you."

Anna worried that her mother had chosen today to tell her. It made her want to get out the door to the doctor.

"I have no idea who they were." Her mother began to cry.

"They haven't come by, wanting me back, have they?" Anna teased.

"No! They . . . disappeared. You forgive me?"

The question struck her as wrong but she said, "Yes."

She had been right about the gray clay look of her mother's skin being something serious. She told her mother she was going to the store, but she went instead to fetch Dr. Raymond. He was a short man, stocky and jowly, with pronounced moles. She described all the symptoms she had witnessed in her mother as they walked back to her house: shaking, pallor, fatigue. And she reported in detail behaviors of the last week, like slowed down speech twice for periods of about ten minutes.

"You are very observant. Did you keep a diary?"

"Written down? No. I remembered."

"Impressive."

She didn't see anything impressive about it. A person noticed these things.

A week later, she was an orphan.

The funeral was a small, modest matter. Her mother's body was prepared by women who did that work for the community and the laying out was done at home. A handful of neighbors came and most brought something to eat. Several of them had Eastern European roots and so they brought stuffed cabbage and pierogies. Anna was surprised to see the doctor arrive. He called her aside. "I don't think you should live alone and I don't think you should go to a workhouse. I've had an idea. You could board in our house, go to school if you want, and in your spare hours—evenings, weekends, summer—help me with my medical duties. I think you're a natural."

She didn't know how to respond. In a way she had expected that someone would decide things for her. Several of the women had said they would check on her for a few months and that then she would board somewhere or go to a workhouse. They told her she would need a job.

"You can't live here," the doctor said. "Your parents didn't own it, correct? How would you pay the landlord?"

"Work. A job."

He shook his head. "You'll never get paid enough to afford rent."

She didn't want to be alone. That was part of it. The doctor had a wife and a grown son who still lived at home. It would be like having a family except of course that she would work for her supper. But a family . . . people around . . . she had always wanted that, especially envied neighbors who came from large families, envied the way their voices rose up, the way they called out to each other.

"Think about it. You seem very smart to me. Are you smart in school?"

"Yes."

"I guessed as much. Some girls with money go to college. But poor girls don't and they need to make their way with jobs or marriage. Still, if you have a good mind, there's a way for you to learn a skill, two skills: bookkeeping and a little nursing. I've been planning to hire somebody and there you are. I'd be your teacher."

Mrs. Salinas comes over to her and reads over her shoulder—the small paragraph about the teacup. "Oh," she says. "Oh, I see. You were adopted. And learned it at . . . seventeen. How was that?"

"Odd. Everything seemed so secretive. I went back eventually to trace my roots."

"I think almost everyone who is adopted these days tries to do that. I don't know that it was so common before. People lived with that uncertainty. Did you find your parents?"

"No. I never did." Around them, the others are either working away at paragraphs or falling asleep. Several of the women have decided to bag the project and simply chat with each other. "Why are we doing this?"

"We try to exercise the memory. Just as we exercise bodies. Sometimes it hurts."

That's true enough.

"But we do it anyway," the woman continues. "Adopted isn't always a sad thing. Often it's a blessing."

Blessing doesn't seem the right word. Necessity, maybe. Acceptable reality. "I was an adoptee several times over. I was . . . I can't think of another way to put it . . . always adopted, one way or another."

Salinas frowns. She looks lost for words of wisdom. She smiles and moves on to Cobbs and his garden trowel.

Is remembering really good exercise? Anna hasn't stopped herself from remembering all these years, but she hasn't worked to bring things up. Her visual storeroom is pretty full. The doctor's face as he told her what he could do for her comes easily into focus. The moles, three on the right side near his nose and chin balanced by one large mole on the left side under his eye. She saw plenty of bodies polka-dotted with moles when she worked as a nurse. Old folks. Their bodies popping out moles like teenagers do acne. Yes, the doctor's offer was really her only choice.

That whole night after the doctor made his proposal, she couldn't sleep. Caring for ill people—that seemed right, like what she was supposed to do. In a sense it's what she had been doing for the last several years. The next day she said yes. But she added, "I will need some pay, even if it's small. I will need it one day. I must have something. Otherwise I should take some other job." How had she known to say that?

Dr. Raymond accepted this condition in such a grudging way that

Anna almost withdrew her acceptance. But she was young and without a protector and aware that she needed one. She had all kinds of thoughts about what she would do with the little bit of money she accumulated. If the doctor was amenable, after a time, after he liked and trusted her, she would ask him to drive her to the farm area her father used to talk about. Someone there might know about the people who had abandoned her. If the doctor wouldn't do it, she would use her little bit of money to hire a coach.

That fantasy disappeared quickly. She continued to go to school, but in the doctor's house and in the office in his home, she was working hard with no time for herself. She took temperatures and pulses. She made sure his shelves and his bag were properly stocked. She kept track of billing. And she accompanied him on house calls. He was delighted. She was good at everything.

One thing she learned on those house calls was that there were many different kinds of homes and life habits. Patients were often depressed. She began to understand when alcohol was overused; she fretted over houses that were disorderly. What she saw made her grateful for the clean and orderly house she'd been raised in—and the doctor's house was clean, too, in no small measure because of her—but she struggled to figure out her place in it. She wasn't a guest, not a daughter, more an employee. A bit of a slave.

One Sunday, only two months after she had come to live with the Raymonds, school was finished for the year, the weather was good, and nobody had come running for the doctor, so she went out to the small backyard to read. The doctor's son, who was named Paul, drifted out to the yard and sat beside her, making it impossible for her to concentrate. He was as thin as his father was portly, with intense dark eyes, a prominent nose, and a slightly recessed chin. "Do you like it here?"

"You're all very kind." She looked back to her book.

"I want to talk to you."

"Oh." She put the book down. "I'm sorry." She had a discomfort around him that she couldn't explain to herself but there was no avoiding him now.

"My father says we would make a great match. I mean, I told him I liked you and he said—"

"I'm not here for that."

"Well, not to begin with, but you're here and we like you—"

Of course they liked her. She worked like a demon and asked for nothing. "No, I have to finish school and then I'll figure out what—"

"Lots of people don't finish school. I hated it. I always wanted to jump out of my seat."

She felt herself beginning to diagnose him. She'd been aware he always seemed preoccupied with the next thing he was about to do (which was never very much—seeing about firewood, going to see a friend). He was of a nervous disposition, unsettled. "Things will be better when you have a job," she told him.

"I don't know what I'm suited for. Perhaps you can be my counselor."

"Well, for a while, at the start, take anything."

"Really? Anything?"

Well, no, she was wrong in that. He wouldn't fare well in the mills. Men needed developed torsos and steady hands to work around fire and steel. The work killed enough of them as it was. So did the mines. "Not just anything. But a shop would be a good start. Or sales of any kind. Or, say, government clerking. Something that has a schedule and expectations." She blushed. Something to make him get up in the morning was what she was really thinking. He was lazy.

Her book was on her lap. The most beautiful cardinal had landed, bobbing, on a branch of the yard's only tree, a cherry tree. If only Paul didn't need her right now, she could enjoy this little time without work, this new place she needed to get used to.

"Government?"

"If you like."

"What are you reading?"

"It's a book about anatomy."

"You're studying? On a Sunday?"

She tipped the book up so he could see the title. It was *General Physiology: An Outline of the Science of Life* by Max Vernon.

Then she opened the book again without answering him. Reading a book like this one didn't seem quite like studying. She liked knowing how people were put together. If she could do any work in the world, she would do the job his father did, making sick people well.

Paul got up and paced the yard. "Government, government," he kept saying to himself.

She relented. "It doesn't have to be government. It could be the electric company. I'm sure they need people to keep records."

"You'd like that? If I did that?"

"It doesn't have anything to do with me."

He smiled sheepishly. "Not yet. Someday, perhaps."

She watched his restless, tapping foot. He liked her because she was calm. If only she could scream and raise a fuss, she might frighten him away, but she never did things like that.

For these two months, she had been thinking about insisting on a formal nurse's education. She had met a nurse on one of their cases who got a nursing degree at the Pittsburgh Training School for Nurses. If she could persuade Dr. Raymond of that course for her at the end of next year, she would be able to board away from the house for large periods of time. Nurses *stayed* at the hospital. She would have company—people doing what she was doing—and Paul would forget her.

Paul pestered her anytime he found her alone for the next two years. Even though she got used to him, her romantic feelings were for a boy she knew at school, a boy who liked her, too. Finally she persuaded Dr. Raymond to let her go to the training program she'd heard about in downtown Pittsburgh. "I thought I was teaching you well," he grumbled. "Marry Paul. You have a good effect on him. Marry him and work here."

Learning was important, she insisted, and women were attending four-year colleges. There was another college not far away in the Oakland area and near that was the Pennsylvania College for Women. To ask for a nursing program was modest, she pointed out. What if she'd asked for more?

Dr. Raymond's jowls seemed to sag more when he realized he would lose her labor. She would have to work for him for two years after training if he let her go, he insisted.

She packed her things and went downtown.

Near the hospital on Sixth Avenue was the First Presbyterian Church. It was a gorgeous building, over a century old. On Sundays, instead of going to Dr. Raymond's Catholic church, which was the same one her parents had attended, she tried the church across the street from the hospital. It was strange the way she could predict some of the words as if she knew them. After half a year of wondering at the way her mind worked, it occurred to her that her first parents, the ones who had more or less sold her off, must have gone to a like church. They hadn't sounded much like churchgoing people from what her mother said—didn't she describe them as ragtag, poor, and unkempt, getting rid of a child they didn't want? It made her wonder all over again who they were, what they were like, and why they didn't want her.

"That is it for today," Mrs. Salinas said after several had read aloud their offerings. Anna didn't read hers. She listened to stories of parental embraces and beatings, wondering at the need of old folks to conjure their parents so consistently. Of course, privately, she was doing the same thing. And wasn't a sign of death on the horizon those dreams of reuniting with parents who were long gone? Was Salinas pushing them all toward the gates?

"Gather your pages. We'll keep the legal pads. Until we meet again. We'll see you tomorrow. My loves. I felt like calling you that." She blushes.

We are her children, Anna thought.

NINA, back at her desk at the paper, writing the story about the Dormont fire, reaches for her ringing phone. She sends up a silent prayer that it will be Ben and that all is well. But it isn't Ben. It's Douglas. "Official report. You can say, 'The cause of the fire is under investigation. The investigator has stated he has not ruled out arson.' If you can forgive me for writing copy."

She already has something like this down. "Good phrasing," she tells him.

"But," he says, "I have a tidbit for you. A neighbor told one of the other guys that the grandpa once joked that he wanted to do a kitchen renovation and that a faulty toaster oven might be just the ticket for paying for it. How's that?"

"I can't use it—"

"Oh, I know. I understand."

"—unless the investigator is ready to make a statement about the intention?"

"Not yet."

"Will he give me the neighbor's name, do you think?"

"No. I actually checked. Out of hand rumor, you know."

"Of course. Oh, well."

It happens the owner of the house came up to the burning kitchen with paint-filled rags. In a tabloid, yes; in a city paper, no.

"I thought you might like to know your hunches are probably right. Just for the record."

"Thanks for telling me."

"You're welcome. So. You're still working?"

"Finishing up the story. Now, having saved a few lives today, hopefully you can write that dissertation," she teases. "Put in some good hours."

"Right." He laughs. "You believe in work."

"So I've been told."

"If you need anything else, don't hesitate to call."

"I won't. Thank you so much. For the ride and for caring about my story."

"I'll make sure to read it."

"I'll watch you on the news."

They hang up. Oh, dear. Cute guy, too. Bad timing.

Just then, Ben enters at the far end of the office. She watches him with surprise as he chooses the way past some fifty desks and comes right up to hers, drags over an adjacent chair, and sits. "If I get takeout tonight, can we have dinner at your place?"

But she can't read him. Maybe he only wants to break bad news to her tonight.

"I have food. I could cook. People must be looking at us."

"Never mind. I'll bring something. Meet you there at seven, say?"

"Okay."

Nina, hardly able to contain herself, skims once more—blah, blah, blah—an investigation in progress. The part about the volunteer fireman rescuing the baby is something she was a little freer with—snuck in a bit of feeling. It was thrillingly heroic, and people need to acknowledge him.

AT SEVEN SHARP, Ben carries in a bag of takeout that includes chicken parmesan and a salad and chunks of Italian bread wrapped in foil. He puts the bag of food on the table, which is set with placemats and napkins and silverware, minus the plates, and then unearths a bottle of red wine from his satchel. "It's so good to be here," he says. He hugs her but she squirms out of his arms.

"Talk first," she says. "I can't eat while I'm wondering what's going on."

He takes her hand and leads her to the sofa. The living room of her tiny apartment holds a sofa, a rocking chair, two narrow occasional tables, and a stand with a TV. At the other end of it is a small square table and four chairs near the Pullman kitchen, though four people would surely crash into each other trying to have dinner here. The bedroom is only large enough to hold a bed and a dresser. If the person sleeping near the wall has to go to the bathroom at night, it means either climbing over the other person or exiting the bed at the foot of it.

"Did you have a good day?" he asks.

"How could I have a good day when I'm wondering what is going on with us?"

"You were typing up a storm when I came in."

"I did a story. The fire in Dormont."

"I saw it on the noon news on TV."

She waits.

He says, "It was awful last night. I wanted to call. I couldn't. I couldn't do it."

"You made your call to her and something happened," she supplies.

"She asked me to meet her at the house. That was very weird."

"How?"

"I was in my own house but it didn't feel like mine. I mean, I lived there for almost ten years, but it was almost unfamiliar. My kids were upset, of course. They wanted to hang downstairs with me, but we had to send them to bed." No, that's not what she wants to know. He's blathering. "The long and short of it is Amanda keeps saying she wants to get back together."

She pulls her hand away from him. She's crying before she can stop herself.

"Now listen. I told her last night I don't want that. Okay? I went back to my brother's place. It seems to me his wife . . . has gotten herself involved. Meddled."

"Melanie?"

"Yeah, Melanie has been fanning the get-back-together flames, talk-ing to my wife. When I first went to stay with my brother it was all, 'Stay as long as you want, we love you here,' but now this other message is coming through loud and clear. My brother thinks I should go home because . . . I think it's because Melanie thinks I should and she's been working on Amanda. Please don't cry. Let me finish."

"What are you doing here? Bringing food? Why?"

"I want to be with you. That's what I'm saying. But . . . I'm trying to catch you up on all this. It's very messy. I was working at home today and I went outside just for air and I could see Amanda up the street so I went back inside. Next thing I knew she was at the door. With a speech. She said I was not giving her a chance and not giving the children a chance. She said in spite of the fact that I was 'dating' she knew she still loved me."

"Oh, God."

"It isn't true. She's lying to herself. She just got scared of being on her own. I told her I was serious about you. She said she would come to the offices to confront you if I didn't agree to give the marriage a chance. She wants us to go to a therapist again, a new one, somebody who specializes in reconciliation. She said she would actually sign something (and I had to, too) that if we go for six weeks, six sessions, do the program, and if, after all that, we don't reconcile she'll put her name to the divorce pa-pers. I figure I have to do it. Two months of torture. But what will come out is that she is mainly worried about money and we'll have to figure all that out. At the end of it, let's hope she begins to understand."

"Maybe she is in love with you."

"I don't believe it for a moment."

She sighs, sinks back, and pulls a cushion toward her.

"So long as I stay at my brother's, she's going to think it's in the bag, not to mention I'll be getting pressure from Jake and Melanie. The only good part about being there is it's right down the street and so it's easy seeing my kids."

"I never got to meet your kids. We never got that far."

It's something he needs to solve. He looks around and his heart breaks a little. This place is a solo place, perfect for a young woman find-ing her way in the world. "I could get a room somewhere. Or I could stay here. If I stay here, we'll be cramped. It's really small. But I'd do it if that's what you want. What do you think?"

She studies him for a moment. "Yes."

"It won't be permanent. I'll find us something better. We'll sublet this when we can. Honestly, I'll help. It's going to be rough for a while. I'll go talk to Hal. I'll give him this address for me. We won't try to keep it a secret. From anyone. Okay?"

"Yes."

Finally she lets him hold her and kiss her. "This is big. A major step all around," she whispers. "We're not just playing."

"I know."

"You're okay about work, letting people know."

"I don't care about any of that. Listen. Do you think . . . do you think you by any chance could eat while we work this out?"

"Probably." She almost laughs.

She gets up from the sofa, looking disoriented. She puts plates on the table. "Think it's still warm enough?"

"Sure." He is in a mood to get on with everything, dinner, life, work, everything. "I want to go to Johnstown again sometime soon but not stay overnight. You game?"

"Can we stop at my mum's? Let me introduce you properly?"

"Sure. Yes. Sure." He paces the small space. "I called Ellen late today, just to see how she felt about spilling those beans. She's hanging in there. She asked about you. Some connection I guess she felt."

"Johnstown girls. We understand each other."

"What's a Johnstown girl?"

She shrugs. "Like me."

He watches her pouring the wine. She's lovely. She has pure skin, almost porcelain, and wide eyes that slant slightly. Her honey hair is abundant, wavy or possibly curly, he's not sure what to call it. But her external beauty would have worn thin for him by now if she didn't have the back up of something inside her that he needs in his life. That's the part that brought him here. Tonight. Is there such a thing as a (paradoxical) nervous serenity? He tried to describe her once to Jake but he failed. She's attuned; her tuning fork vibrates, but she operates calmly. Jake thought he was nuts when he described her this way. Jake didn't get it at all. He said, "Anybody can fake sweetness for a while."

They sit and eat. The food isn't as hot as it should be, and the bread has a lot of garlic butter on it. "We're going to smell," she says.

"We'll smell together."

"This is what I wanted," she says. "Being able to sit together and not sneak around. Michelle probably saw you coming in."

"I don't care. I don't care. We're together now."

"I want to go to a ball game with you. And movies."

He laughs. "We ought to be able to manage that."

"But I mean it. Simple normal things. Have people to dinner. I've been wanting that."

"We'll do all of that. Tonight, I'm going to leave. I'm going to be there tomorrow morning when my sons are going to school. I'm going to give it the week to talk to them, to gather my things. I have my first session with Amanda on Friday, late afternoon. I'll come on Saturday to stay— move in. I'll get the boys on Sunday and we'll all do something together."

"You need to ask instead of tell."

It takes him a moment to understand. "I'm an idiot. Tell me what part of that you don't like."

"Just the language."

"If I say I'll work on it—"

"I know you will."

At ten they watch the early news, the story of the fire that Nina covered.

He leaves. I'm changing my life, he thinks, elated.

"The labor troubles at Homestead, Pa.—Attack of the strikers and their sympathizers on the surrendered Pinkerton men," drawn by Miss G. A. Davis, from a sketch by C. Upham, appearing on the cover of *Frank Leslie's Illustrated Weekly* on July 14, 1892. Courtesy of the Library of Congress.

CHAPTER

4

Tuesday, April 18–
Saturday, April 22, 1989

■ AT ELEVEN last night, after Ben left, she watched the news again, KDKA this time featuring the heroic fireman, and went to bed wondering if the fireman would indeed read her article the next day.

On Tuesday morning, a few people in the office mention the article. So it probably passes muster. And she is sent before she can settle down with her cup of coffee—in her car this time—to check out a report of a shooting in Springhill. She spends stray moments imagining herself and Ben tucked into her place, other moments imagining herself being hit by street gunfire. *And a* Post-Gazette *reporter got caught in the gunfire. She is in critical condition at this time.*

When she drove Michelle to work this morning, Michelle said, "I saw Ben last night. Bringing you food, it looked like."

"He did. Nice of him. We had a good talk." How lame she sounded.

Stupid. Having started with Ben on a sneaky note, she didn't know how to explain what was happening now, whatever it was.

"He's a really cute guy," Michelle said.

"Nice, too. Good reporter."

Finally Michelle stopped angling. And Nina thinks now, as she waits patiently for the police to figure out who shot whom, that she must quit worrying and simply take the relationship a day at a time. I don't have to empty half my drawers tonight, she tells herself.

When she finally gets back to the office—someone was shot, but nobody will say who did it or who was bleeding on the sidewalk—she writes her little bit of a piece. Ben comes right up to her desk, once again exhibiting his new, different behavior, and he hands her a can of Diet Coke.

"Oh. Thanks."

"Tonight I'm taking the boys to dinner and spending the evening with them. You okay with that?"

"Of course."

"You get something good today?"

"Boring. You?"

"I'm starting to trace that cousin in Detroit."

"The murderer. That's how I think of him."

"Paul. Yeah. As much corroboration as I can get before I run the thing."

"Sounds good."

"You okay?"

"Yes, really."

When the workday is over on Tuesday night, Nina watches Ben leave the office. She imagines him getting in his car—it's parked on the Wharf, she saw it—driving Banksville Road, coming to his brother's house. What else? The boys coming over. A trip to a McDonald's or an Eat'n Park, right, because he wants to please them and he has little money. Will he take them to a movie? It's a school night. But then he might want to spoil them as warring parents do.

She reads the paper. She looks up what movies are playing. *New York Stories* is still at the Denis. With a zip of excitement going through her, she realizes she can do what she told Michelle to do—she can take herself to a film she wants to see. Go alone. Why not? It would feel good.

Eat something at the Dor-Stop? She starts for her car.

Partway to Dormont, she realizes she's not sure the Dor-Stop is open for dinner, so she pulls into a small place that appears to be an Indian restaurant. If they make palak paneer, she will have it. She is having a good time—an unplanned, spontaneous evening.

It *is* palak paneer for dinner. She fiddles with her copy of the paper, reading just about everything in it as she sits at one of four tables in the small place.

When she leaves she winds up the hill, thinking, ah, yes, she could have had Mexican at Jose and Tony's if she'd been thinking ahead. And she wonders how often she will be on this road with Ben to pick up the boys. Will they like her? And vice versa! Will they stop sometimes to eat at Jose and Tony's?

Luck is on her side. There's street parking on the side street near the Denis. She can't help liking this old, old theater with its rotted carpet and the smell of popcorn bled into the walls and floors, into every surface. She takes her ticket and goes in. She keeps thinking she will run into Ben and the boys in the hallway, but she doesn't. They could be right around the corner, at *Fletch*, and she wouldn't know.

This little triptych of a film has gotten mixed reviews. She has been told that she will like the Scorsese section but maybe not the Coppola section and that she will like and scoff at the ridiculousness of the Woody Allen section. This is, it seems, the typical reaction.

The theater lights are still bright. A few people straggle in.

A man looking for a seat (though there are many) says, "I don't believe it. Is it really you?"

"I think it is," she says.

THE PIECE OF PAPER with Paul Jr.'s letter is so fragile, Ben is afraid to handle it. Ellen—well Ruth—put it in a ziplock bag before giving it to him. The man who wrote the letter was calling himself Paul Fulton instead of Paul Folks. The first thing Ben does with the letter on Wednesday is drive it to Caliban Bookshop where they deal in rare books and manuscripts. "Do you authenticate letters?" he asks the owner, a tufty-haired professorial fellow with a consistently amused look. "Date pieces of paper?"

"I don't do that work myself. I can have it sent to New York. There are a couple of places we use."

He thinks about it. No, it feels wrong. "How about Carnegie Library? Do they have an archivist who—?"

"They use the same guys we do."

"How long is a typical case—if you send a piece of paper to them?"

"Depends on how busy they are. A month. Two?"

Not worth it. No, he believes the letter. He just wants to give his belief in it heft.

He sits in his car, thinking. He goes into Ali Baba and orders a cup of tea. Some sense memory tells him the coffee is not particularly good, some big old machine cranking vats of it out, day after day. While he's there, he goes from time to time to the front window to be sure he isn't getting a ticket. Halfway through his tea he orders a Coke and a plate of lunch known as the Healthy Variety. His little corner of the fridge in Jake's place where he keeps his small packages of deli for lunches was empty this morning, more evidence that this is the transition week. It feels good to order lunch out, like a regular person.

While he's waiting for his Healthy Variety, he goes to the payphone in the front of the restaurant and pulls out his notebook. When Ellen Emerson comes to the phone, he tells her, "My first article goes in next Monday. Now hang on. The first one won't mention you. You are the big story. I want to get all my ducks in a row with the letter from your cousin and all that before I run with it. So don't worry. It's coming."

"*I'm* not worried."

He can imagine her smiling. She has a teasing voice.

"I'm not coming in this Saturday, but next if it's okay."

"Definitely." He can hear her saying to Ruth, "Next Saturday. Ten days from now." Then she warns him, "Plan to eat. Ruth insists."

"I love to eat."

"Bring your girlfriend."

"Yes," he says. "Yes, I will."

Smart cookie, Ellen. He mentioned his wife to her, but she has no trouble calling Nina his girlfriend. Nothing catty, no blame, just . . . fact.

When he's filled with olives, hummus, stuffed grape leaves, an artichoke salad, a tossed salad, and bread, he goes back to the *PG* offices to begin a series of phone calls to the Ford Motor Company archives division. He explains some seven times what he needs. Finally a man who sounds about a hundred years old himself says, "Oh, we weren't so good about keeping all employee records. I dunno. We might have the years you want. What were they again?"

"I don't know the start date. I'd be looking for a termination date in

1911 for a Paul Fulton. Maybe something signed. A signature. That would be gold."

"Gold," the man mumbles thoughtfully. "It might take some time to look."

"I'd need to know in two weeks. Preferably sooner. I'd be very grateful for your help. It's a big article. Can I call you in a few days to check?"

"Oh, sure."

That done, he stands at his desk. Way across the room is Nina, not looking at him. Studying something. Jotting something. Saying something to the reporter at the desk next to hers. Just wonderful to watch— the way she talks, the way she treats people. Yes, she's the one for him.

He goes to Hal's office and knocks.

"Yeah, what?" Hal asks when he comes in.

"Have a minute?"

"Your stories?"

"First one will be ready tomorrow for you. The rest are coming along."

"Anything new?"

"That part is coming. I'm building to it."

Hal grunts. "Hope so. You want to talk about it?"

"Actually I wanted to talk about something personal."

Hal looks at him quizzically.

"The thing is, I've been physically separated from my wife for about eight months. I've been at my brother's house. I gave you the alternate phone number and that worked out. His house is just down the street from mine, so I could be contacted in any pinch at either number. My wife agreed to that at least. But I have to give you a new phone number. I've been seeing Nina Collins lately. I'm going to be staying there. That happened only after I was separated by the way. I know people will assume otherwise, but that's not how it was. The word is, office relationships are frowned upon. I thought you should know that I'm seeing her seriously and that our work won't be compromised in any way."

Hal laughs. "Well, I think I knew that."

"What do you mean?"

"Most of us figured that was going on."

"Really?"

"What kind of reporters would we be if we didn't get nosy?"

Crap. He's an idiot. "Don't take it out on Nina."

"She's okay. Doing her job. Let's see some copy from you."

"Yeah. Coming your way."

Ben wants to be his old self, easy, not nervous. How did he get to be the person he is now? Afraid and falling apart. He tries to breathe deeply. Across the room is Nina, still working, not looking back at him.

BEFORE RUTH LEAVES Ellen—and reluctantly since Ellen is overexcited about Ben's announcement that he's coming back in ten days—she says, "My husband can make such a mess at home. I'm going home now to clean up after him."

"It doesn't seem fair."

"Oh, it isn't. Nothing fair about it."

"My husband was pretty neat," Ellen says thoughtfully. "I don't know where he got it, but I was grateful. He always said it was his Polish parents. They were scrubbers."

"Wish I'd met him. Polish? But named Emerson?"

"Everybody changed their names back then. All trying to get ahead. He was a little sad about it, losing his name."

"What was it? Before?"

"Mizejewski. Today people would likely have kept the name."

Ruth said thoughtfully, "So you could have been our teacher, called Mrs. Mizejewski."

"What would you have thought about that?"

"Foreign. Not as good."

"Right."

"But it wouldn't have been true."

"Um, that's the killer."

"Right."

FRIDAY, LATE AFTERNOON. The marriage therapist, Dr. Caldwell, has made a substantial little presentation and now she asks, "So, will you both agree to no casting of blame, no name calling, in these sessions?"

"Agreed," Amanda says forcefully.

"Agreed." Ben can feel his jaw clenching.

"The marriage faltered, as I understand it, over infidelity issues."

"There was no infidelity," Ben says firmly.

"You're seeing someone now."

"I am. That began almost two months after Amanda kicked me out."

"Explain—both of you—what 'kicked out' meant."

Ben waited.

Amanda said, "I told him to leave. I was distraught."

Ben waited. When she didn't add anything, he said, "Her words were, 'I don't want to see you or talk to you. I'm filing for divorce. I want you to leave the house and not step foot in it again.'"

"Did you say those things?"

"I don't remember exactly what I said."

"Was that close?"

"I don't know. I was angry."

"The anger was because?"

"Other women, like I said."

"The trouble with that," Ben said as evenly as he could, "is that there weren't other women. I honestly wish there had been, now, looking back. I wasn't half alive. All I knew was she was angry all the time, she didn't want me in bed, I was living day to day in a really reduced way. I was extremely unhappy but . . . I was working well. I poured myself into work."

"Why did you assume he was seeing other women?"

"I just did. He is now."

"It took two months on a cot in my brother's basement for me to wake up."

"Back to you, Amanda. Why did you assume he was seeing other women?"

"I can't believe he wasn't. Even now. I was down, I was depressed. I wasn't a barrel of laughs. So I figured—"

"You didn't believe he could love you?"

"No. I didn't." Raspy voice. She's playing it. There's something fake in her performance. Ben's jaw aches.

"I need for you both to just breathe. And calm down. And then, without anything but the bare facts, tell me about when you met. The first moment, then the first moments, then the first week, month, year. A little at a time."

Six weeks of this before she will sign the divorce papers. He doesn't want to go back, not even in memory.

Amanda begins. "It was . . . I hate to admit this . . . it was at a bar. He was with a group of friends. I thought he was appealing. I loved his hair. I could see he was the center of the group. He'd say something and they would all listen and laugh. I wanted to get to know him. My girlfriend said I should buy him a beer and send it over—you know, reverse the cliché—but I couldn't. So she went over to him and told him I wanted to meet him."

"Is that how you remember it?"

Ben says, "I remember I was having fun, feeling good. My friends and I were at the billiards table. We weren't playing very seriously. And when the friend said this woman wanted to meet me, I just thought, well, what a good day I'm having, why not? So then I eventually went over and she was a surprise. I mean I didn't know why she wanted to meet me. I was a working-class type. She was all sort of designer clothes and all that." He keeps his gaze down, trying to concentrate.

"Did you like her at first?"

The pattern of the rug in the therapist's office is made up of leaves that look like human toes, five to a stem. He looks up. "I was flattered. I liked her liking me."

"What came next?"

"I bought her a drink. We sat in a corner. We talked. I walked her out to her car. She was driving a Mercedes—I'll admit it was old; it used to be her grandfather's. I was driving a truck that was missing a lot of metal."

"Amanda, is that how you remember it?"

"Yeah. Yes. I was excited that he seemed so earthy, so sexual, and that he sort of liked me."

"Ah." The therapist is pleased by this. She probably thinks, Get the chemistry going, get the fireworks going, and all is fixed.

"Did you date right away?'

"He called me a week later."

"Do you remember waiting a week to call?"

"I do. I thought we didn't have anything in common but then there was a group going to a ball game and most of the guys were taking their girlfriends and so I asked her. And she went with me."

"I was totally thrilled. I loved every bit of it."

"Where were you living at the time? With your parents?" she asks Amanda.

"No. I was on my own by then. I was twenty-five. I had an apartment with a girlfriend. She was hardly ever there because she had a boyfriend and she would go to his place."

"Whose car did you take to the game?" she asks Ben.

"A friend drove me and we picked her up. Parking was too expensive to take more cars than we needed. It still is," he adds. "It's worse."

"So it was a kind of double date."

The session goes on for another hour. They remember in detail what they were wearing, who ate three hot dogs (he did), how his friends reacted to Amanda (they liked her cautiously, as intimidated as he was). And he sort of fell into the relationship. It never seemed quite right and not even of his choosing, but there it was, a thing that was happening. He doesn't put it in those terms to Dr. Caldwell. He says simply that for a long time he was uncertain but generally cheerful. He was writing publicity for three companies at the time because he was hired by a company that kept finding him gigs. He would do research and write up all kinds of stuff. It was during this time that he got his first bite at the *Post-Gazette* as a general assignment writer, what Nina is doing now. He ate it up. Every bank robbery was his chance to keep his job. That work happiness had kept him from questioning the relationship he was in. He assumed his life was coming together. But—and he doesn't say it quite this way—when Amanda proposed to him, when she said, "Hey, don't you think it's time?," he remembers distinctly thinking he was making a mistake but not wanting to hurt her.

She'd been saying yes to letting him stay at her place, to regular sex, to whatever his friends wanted to do. He was twenty-eight, almost twenty-nine. Several of his friends had gotten married. Amanda was generous with him—let him take her car, things like that. She insisted her parents liked him a lot. He was wowed, he was cowed.

A year later he married her. A couple years after that they had Zachary and then after that Bryson. Those were names in her family, she insisted. Maybe. He guessed maybe. He hasn't met anybody with those names among her relatives. His parents weren't as enchanted by her as hers were by him or as she said they were by him.

Nina. He thinks of her from time to time even in the session with Dr. Caldwell. It's partly because Nina is living on her own in an apartment and he's going to crash there and it feels like the first time, like what he did when he met Amanda, a regression of sorts.

He'd gauge Amanda's talk about her feelings to be only about ten percent honest. He doesn't believe she's in love with him again. She's just depressed. And it's sad. He feels sad for himself and for her.

NINA DECIDES to stay at the office and grit her teeth through the hours that she knows Ben is in therapy with the reconciliation expert. She can't even try to imagine what will happen.

She's finished her article on a guy who was living it up with three stolen credit cards, buying a boatload of stuff before they caught him. Amazing what people think they can get away with.

No assignment, but she hangs around anyway.

Last Tuesday night, when she ran into Douglas at the Denis Theatre, she felt guilty sitting with him, as if she were cheating on Ben. Which in a way she was. Why, of all the movie theaters in Pittsburgh, had she chosen the Denis? Sure it was on the way to Ben's house, another glimpse of his route, his almost-neighborhood. Sure she liked a falling apart old theater better than a sterile multiplex. And yes, she could drive by the scene of the fire again. But she was perfectly aware that Douglas lived somewhere near the Denis. The fact that he wandered into the same movie even now jolts her. Like telepathy or something.

And there was electricity when they sat together. Her fault. She should never have gone there. "You want anything?" he asked.

She'd said no, but he came back with a box of popcorn and some bottled water for each of them and an extra cup. He poured popcorn into the cup for her.

When he asked her at the end of the film if she wanted to go for a drink, she said, "I can't."

They walked out of the theater in silence. Finally he asked, "Are you seeing someone? I mean, with someone?"

"Yes," she said, relieved.

"Is it serious?"

"Yes. Yes, it is."

"Ah. I wish it weren't so. But you know that. We know that. I won't bother you. Should I walk you to your car?"

"Okay."

"It was good meeting you. Alternate lives and all." They both smiled ruefully. "Take care," he said before she drove away.

BEN BRINGS two suitcases and two boxes of things to Nina's place on Saturday, just as he announced he would. With considerable effort, they fit these things into spaces and take the suitcases to the basement. It's a squeeze. Even though he's not a huge guy, when he's in the apartment, his presence is definitely felt.

For a while they just collapse on the sofa, putting on the TV and sitting with their hands linked as they watch afternoon movies.

On Sunday the visit with the boys is brief. He arrives with them. The boys sit awkwardly on Nina's sofa. She gives them each a glass of apple juice. Then they all go out for a walk. Ben shows them around his new neighborhood, pretending to be a tour guide. "And look at these small houses! Workmen used to live here, sometimes ten to a house. Sometimes three to a bed in shifts because of their work schedules. Can you imagine that? A guy gets the bed from seven in the morning till three and that's it. Then he has to bum around for eight hours and finally go to work eleven to seven."

Nina watches the older boy do the math. Zachary. Bryson just finds reasons to run toward street corners and back to his father. The boys are nervous around her, trying not to be, and she doesn't want to push herself on them. They aren't particularly whiny. Ben seems more appealing than ever as he tries to entertain his boys. She wants to touch him, to put her hands in his thick hair, but she doesn't even touch his arms as they walk along.

The day is cool and threatening a spitting rain. "I'm buying the ice cream," she announces. "Right around the corner." That earns her a few points with the boys. They actually look at her for a brief second. Easy, she tells herself. These things take time.

After the ice cream, Ben nudges the boys toward his car. "Article's in tomorrow."

"I know!"

"It looks good."

Men, possibly relief workers, in front of a shack made from debris from the flood of 1889. Courtesy of Johnstown Area Heritage Association.

5

Monday, April 24, 1989

Upstream/Downstream Drama of Wealth and Class Tied to Great Flood
Club near Johnstown Attracted Tycoons 100 Years Ago

Pittsburgh Post-Gazette, THE JOHNSTOWN FLOOD SERIES

BY BEN BRAGDON

When the snow thaws, people begin looking forward to summer and vacations. Not everybody can afford a vacation, of course; some are too poor to go beyond the backyard or the neighborhood park. Immigrant laborers tend not to think in terms of vacations. Work is simply what they do every day. People with middle-class incomes save up and go to the seashore, that great source of renewal. Really wealthy people have a broad choice—private resorts, the Riviera, exclusive hotels. Those wealthy citizens are shielded in many instances from the fact that people who actually live and work in the resort areas they favor are often extremely poor. The Caribbean islands are a case in point.

Not much has changed.

The Johnstown Flood, a disaster of mammoth proportions, which happened nearly one hundred years ago, is inextricably linked to the idea of wonderful vacations for the rich.

A hundred years ago Pittsburgh boasted some of the most entrepreneurial and influential men in the world. They were the ruling class. And when they decided to form a private club that ran a private resort, it's no surprise that someone dubbed their club the Bosses Club. They chose—or were chosen by—a spot in the Allegheny Mountains, an area so beautiful, so full of verdure and natural life, that it could provide another world for these men, away from business, finances, and the daily details of manufacturing. At the risk of putting Machiavellian mustaches on all of the bosses, it can be noted that they wanted a club, private, almost secretive, away from common workers. The one they built was not ostentatious like some clubs for the wealthy, Tuxedo Park for one. Theirs was simpler: beautiful, comfortable, and, best of all, only an hour from Pittsburgh. They bought a piece of land that included the South Fork Dam. It had originally been built as part of the canal system that would link points east to the rivers. But there is waste often in great projects and some of that waste gets accounted for under the name of progress. The progress in this case was the railroad, which could deliver goods much faster than the canal system ever could.

The dam wasn't needed any longer. But there it was, just sitting there. It held in place a natural basin of water that happened to look like and be a spectacularly beautiful lake. The property, including the lake, sat idle for several years. Because it changed hands and purposes several times, maintenance was spotty.

A businessman named Benjamin Ruff took a look at the place and decided it was a perfect vacation spot. There was some secrecy in putting together the charter and selling memberships to the club. The idea was like an early version of time-sharing in that there would be a large clubhouse that could accommodate 100 to 150 people. Any member would be able to stay for two weeks. To stay longer, members had to have their own cottages. The highest rank of the wealthy built sixteen cottages in all. Their club was named the South Fork Fishing and Hunting Club.

They knew they sat atop a mountain and that down below was the city of Johnstown, a thriving small town with mills producing iron products at top speed and efficiency. They knew there were mill workers both in the town and on the hillsides as well as, sprinkled among them, store owners, doctors, lawyers, and teachers; and they knew that some of the workers at the club would come from that population. Horses and boots were the means of transit.

Since what happened on May 31, 1889, was one of the biggest stories ever told internationally, since it was the first and largest domestic disaster in the United States, people have been trying, and are still trying, to explain it.

The men on top of the mountain died a long time ago but they endure with naming rights over towns, libraries, and businesses. They include Andrew Carnegie, Henry Clay Frick, Robert Pitcairn, Andrew Mellon, and Henry Phipps Jr.

Pitcairn was born in Johnstone, Renfrewshire, Scotland, but he immigrated to the United States as a boy. As a young man working for the Eastern Telegraph Company, he became friends with another Scotsman, Andrew Carnegie. They both showed immediate promise and rose to more and more power there as they did when they later worked for the Pennsylvania Railroad. Carnegie left to form a steel company, with Pitcairn eventually becoming superintendent of the Western Division of the railroad at the time of the flood. Pitcairn lived in Pittsburgh, at Ellsworth and Amberson Avenues. He was a religious man who helped found the Shadyside Presbyterian Church. For a time he was choir director. He was married and had three children. He telegraphed the first order to send supplies as well as undertakers to Johnstown after the flood. His telegraph was to the *Pittsburgh Commercial Gazette*, which in turn contacted the mayors of Pittsburgh and Allegheny.

Andrew Carnegie was perhaps the most famous and successful Scottish immigrant to land in Pittsburgh. He immigrated at age thirteen with his parents from Dunfermine, Scotland. He is emblematic of the classic American story of a boy who with brains and effort could rise from a lowly job to become a multimillionaire. His early years were spent as a worker at a bobbin factory, then he worked with Pitcairn in the telegraph company, later took a directorship of the Pennsylvania Railroad, and finally started Carnegie Steel—which with mergers eventually became U.S. Steel. He became known in his later years as an important philanthropist. His money often went to peace initiatives. He was scholarly and, as such, he believed in free libraries and established them not only in the United States but in Scotland and England.

Henry Clay Frick was born in the United States in Westmoreland County. Ambitious and determined to be rich, he formed the Frick Coke Company. The steel mills needed coke. While on his honeymoon, he met Carnegie and eventually became chairman of the Carnegie Steel Corporation. He was responsible for forming the South Fork Fishing and Hunting Club. As a founder and charter member of that club, he was presumably informed on all aspects of the club and its lake from the beginning. After the dam broke and the city of Johnstown was flooded, Frick organized with other wealthy Pittsburghers to send relief. His wealth was spent to a great extent on artwork. One of his legacies is his mansion, which is now a museum housing the Frick art collection. He also bequeathed to the city of Pittsburgh upon his death the property that is now Frick Park.

He did not get along particularly well with Andrew Carnegie. Frick is perhaps remembered most for the steely determination that resulted in the union-busting assault by Pinkerton detectives on striking steelworkers in Homestead. The Homestead Strike, as well as the Johnstown Flood, are blots on his record of philanthropy. Perhaps telling is the fact that when anarchist Alexander Berkman attempted to assassinate him, he took two bullets to the ear and neck and four stab wounds to the thigh while fighting his attacker and he returned to work a week later. The flood that killed over two thousand people destroyed Johnstown, which was home of the Cambria Steel Works, his greatest competitor. While nobody saw the flood as purposeful, it confirmed a public perception of his having a persistent streak of villain's luck. His best friend was Andrew Mellon.

Andrew Mellon was also American born, the son of the

Pittsburgh banker and judge Thomas Mellon and Sarah Jane Negley. He, like Frick, became an art lover and collector. He showed an early aptitude for finance, turning a profit in a lumber and coal business and moving on to captain banking and industry, notably coke and aluminum. He became extremely wealthy, reportedly only a step behind John D. Rockefeller and Henry Ford. Under Harding, he served as secretary of the treasury, attempting to tackle the national debt that sprang from World War I. He counseled reducing taxes on the wealthy. By the Depression, he showed his hard-line attitude by advising President Hoover to "liquidate labor, liquidate stocks, liquidate farmers, liquidate real estate . . . it will purge the rottenness out of the system. High costs of living and high living will come down. People will work harder, live a more moral life. Values will be adjusted, and enterprising people will pick up from less competent people." He was not popular with workers. This advice came forty years after the disaster in Johnstown that destroyed the lives of so many laborers.

Pitcairn, Carnegie, Frick, and Mellon were only a few of the members of the South Fork Fishing and Hunting Club. Some others whose names strike Pittsburghers as familiar are Scaife, Knox, Bidwell, Lippincott. These and others of slightly lesser wealth vacationed with each other.

Most residents of Johnstown had not actually seen the club on top of the mountain. It was highly restricted as well as high up on a hill. But the word came down through Italian workers and a few adventuresome investigators that it was a paradise on top of the mountain. The scenery was beautiful. There were deer gamboling, rabbits jumping, fish leaping up in a silvery sunshine. Most Johnstown residents never got to see it but they must have filled in the details as their individual imaginations allowed. Perhaps they'd seen painted drops at the Opera House. Almost everyone had seen Garden of Eden illustrations in their Bibles. The intellectuals, and there were a number of well-educated residents, might have relied upon their Greek and Latin to see what was up there as a new-age Mount Olympus—Zeus with a gun and Artemis sauntering through glades with a parasol and a bow and arrow. One way or another, rumors made the club an ideal playland. Doves flew, sailboats skimmed the lake, the food was good, the clothing fashionable, the music mellifluous, the theatricals entertaining.

On the day of the flood, it was raining, so residents of the club were not hunting or sailing. They might, however, have been relaxing in front of the big fireplace in the clubhouse.

In the town were merchants carrying dry goods to higher floors, scholars and educators and businessmen frantically picking up papers, finding which ones were important and moving them, too, to higher floors or higher ground. There were laborers' wives who had been thrifty in preserving foods and now were lugging dried fruits and vegetables along with them wherever they were going—walking, carrying things through the floodwaters on homemade carriers of all sorts.

They had heard that the dam might fail. Should they believe it? There had been threats before. The dam had broken in 1862, though the damage had been minimal and the dam managed to hold. But there was definitely significant flooding and so they had to preserve what they could.

Two of the people on the street were Elmer and Victor Laslo, brothers, who worked in the mill. They were both large, muscled men. They were found dead a week later three feet from each other with a part of a roof they had clung to.

Another group of people, a family named Peterson, consisted of Alvin, his wife, Mary, two teenage boys, and three young girls ranging in age from ten down to two. They decided to stay in their house. He worked as a clerk in the bank. They must have moved up to the second floor, then the attic, then hung on the rafters until they could poke through the roof. Other flood victims reported they saw the father on the roof, pulling out the children. The whole family of seven was found dead the next day.

Rose May Hubert was the mother of seven children. Her husband was a mill worker. They were seen by other flood victims hanging on to pieces of flotsam. Rose May got her hands around a tree that rode wildly and slammed into the shore. She lived, but the rest of her family died.

It's true that, against the odds, many people lived through the flood. There were however significant medical problems—dismemberments, wounds that left scars, mental trauma. Clara

Barton arrived in the town to organize efforts to tend to the ill and wounded. The potential for rapidly spreading disease was high, but because the valley was doused with donated disinfectants, doctors, remarking how surprisingly little disease there was, had to contend almost solely with typhoid.

Altogether it is believed 2,209 people died while the lake raced down to the city. The flood wave reached the city in one hour, and devastated it in a mere ten minutes. The aftermath was more protracted. The water moved crazily over landscape and buildings, finding outlets until it finally calmed some three hours later. At that point, late afternoon and early evening of May 31, some survivors still floated on bits of lumber. Debris piled up at the Stone Bridge and caught fire. Many who had survived the water perished in the fire. The town then looked like a lake, a huge one, much bigger than the gorgeous one that had been on the top of the mountain. The national and international presses covered the disaster almost unceasingly for a month.

The members of the club maintained secrecy about the workings of the club and about their whereabouts on May 31. They sent relief to the victims in various ways. Carnegie built a library in the town. The club members, however, never submitted to interviews about the flood or the condition of the dam. They did not suffer any lawsuits. They did not return to the South Fork Fishing and Hunting Club. The club, a place of great beauty, disintegrated slowly, unused.

Next week read the story of the dam—how and why it failed.

Nina read Ben's article on Monday at work, wondering if it was a good idea to put off the story of Ellen Emerson, which was such a coup. She pictured Ellen in her apartment reading the first article. How strange it must be to have a whole complex life that keeps being defined by a few minutes of trauma. Like everyone else, surely Ellen had small ordinary days and sad ones and joyful ones. Human beings find ways to get over all kinds of things, though losing family is surely the worst.

Nina picked up the phone to call her mother. She'd let it go for too long.

Basketball team at the Pennsylvania College for Women, 1906–1907. Courtesy of Chatham University Archives, Pittsburgh.

6

Ellen and Anna
Autumn 1907

■ MELBA VAN HUSEN owned the Brownstone in New York that had been broken up into rooms for rent for which she sought working women and NYU students of a certain character. She charged them eight dollars a week and for that they got breakfast and dinner daily, peppered, in each case, by the word *respectable*, amazingly fit into sentences and paragraphs that would seem to have no particular use for it. Sometimes there were respectable eggs or a respectably cooked beef roast with potatoes.

Ellen took a room there. Her room was tiny and fitted out with a gas fireplace that required coins to operate. The university buildings were around the corner. Although Ellen walked to Washington Square, most of her classmates—in this case both men and women—commuted. The program Ellen had entered was the graduate program in education.

"Why don't you take a teaching job now?" her Aunt Hester had wanted to know, for she was already more than qualified with four years of college when some teachers had only two.

Ellen said, "This will make me the best teacher."

"You don't have to be best, do you?"

But Ellen managed to nod disarmingly. Her uncle and aunt finally took her to the train station and watched as she boarded for the long ride to New York.

So she'd made it there finally. She often stood at the window of her room, lonely and wondering if she should give up all this nonsense and go back home. But she loved meeting the people in her classes and she especially liked those who were themselves immigrants or the children of immigrants. A small social group formed naturally of Irish, Poles, Italians, Greeks, people from all over the world who had fought hard to make it to a university. When they weren't in their small group, many of them tried to fake it, to pass as long-term American residents. But they had somehow found each other—the strivers. The things they carried for lunch often looked more appealing to her than the steady diet of ham and bread she was allowed to keep in the house kitchen for her lunches. The small traces of accents in their speech fascinated her. The lack of politeness in some of them, the sense of rush and tumble as they fell into classes and rushed out, did not appall her. Some walked long distances, others took the Broadway coach that was public transportation, others came over from Brooklyn, and everybody talked about the subway system that was going to open soon and bring some of them to school on underground trains.

Things changed in amazing ways. If you thought ahead, you realized that someday the men who scooped up horse dung probably would not be needed anymore. The world was changing—movement was changing—and one sign of it was the increasing number of horseless carriages on the street.

All this started a few years before. She had been a regular Sunday guest in the home of her best friend at the Pennsylvania College for Women. Progress was all the talk at those Sunday dinners. The conversations with Susan Gresham's father came back to her. He had wanted an automobile, was eager for the day he would own one.

Susan. Her friend. Ellen was here partly because Susan had died close to the end of her senior year and she, Ellen, was the substitute. What the parents could not do for their daughter, they did for Ellen. They supplied the tuition money and the travel money to get her to New York.

At the window one day she watched three street sweepers, two lamplighters, and several couples walking by, aware of feeling bereft. She was very lonely, but if she left, she would be a great disappointment to the Greshams. And Susan would have encouraged her to stay, to find her way.

Finally she turned from the window. Three Dickens novels sat on her desk. She'd read them before, more than once actually, but the assignment she faced now was to trace his development as a writer over time. *Did* he develop over time or was he simply superb from the start, adapting to whatever came his way? Most assignments begged a question, but she was fairly adept now at simultaneously rebelling against that question and playing the game. Her papers at the Pennsylvania College for Women were "unusual but not uninteresting," as one professor had put it. Dawdling at first, she studied the drawings in her copy of *Oliver Twist.* Nancy. Yes, she remembered Nancy, for whom she had cried buckets of tears. Then Ellen turned back to page one, thanking Charles, as she called him in her inner monologues, for being so prolific and for being able to fill up so much of her own life. Oh, what might this canny writer have made of the flood and *her* odd childhood?

Macabre snapshots, moments in her experience of the flood, visit her as she sits to work, wondering what she would look like in a Dickens illustration. The horse passes by her. She screams. The man she thinks will help bumps up against the mattress. She sees he is dead. Working backward, reversing time, the raft gets caught between two buildings.

Should she have done something then? Grabbed her sister and gone into the window after her cousin? But all the while she was calling for her father, wanting to believe he would surface and find them again.

After two months at NYU, she definitely had her favorite person, the person who made a day good just by being there. Bill Mizejewski was his real name once upon a time, he explained to the other students, but now he was plain old Bill Emerson. His parents had wanted to give him and his brother a chance in America and that meant an English-sounding name.

"How did they come up with Emerson?" Ellen asked.

"I don't think it was Ralph Waldo. They just chose it. Saw it on a stationery shop once and then later on a jewelry store sign and figured Emersons were enterprising people."

"They must be thrilled you're going to a university."

He grinned. "They are."

There was something four-square about Bill. Brown hair, slightly elevated cheekbones, not very large brown eyes, height and weight about medium. He was so outgoing, he became the leader of the group she talked to most. Ellen had already fallen a little in love with him for his good spirits when one day in the study lounge she heard him mention to the group of like friends that tended to gather around him that he had married at nineteen. She was so surprised, she dropped her book, and grabbed it up, embarrassed. It turned out several of the other students were married, she learned over the next weeks, two women and seven of the men. Ellen felt foolish having fallen for Bill when he was so socially and personally *advanced* and even more foolish for having mistaken his friendliness for interest.

After that blow to her fantasy, she tried to be quiet and unnoticed, but somebody, often Bill, pulled her into conversations. Would she teach in New York, did she think, or take some other sort of job there?

She didn't know. She wanted to see Europe; she wanted to go back home. "I have contrary impulses," she said. "To expand my horizons, to shrink them."

There were times—it was only something of a private insanity—she would pass someone on the street who had the right color hair and eyes, the right age, and she would think, "My sister. That could be my sister." Crazy. To lose her *mind* seemed the worst thing of all.

Bill Emerson said, "Something is making you sad."

She put her sandwich down. "Maybe." She was just plain lonely. A person didn't say that.

"I wish I could help."

If Bill Emerson could have a job and go to school and be married, too, then she could at least fit a job into her life, she decided.

She was careful about choosing. She read the *Herald* every day, studying ads. When she saw a position for night copy editor on the paper, she wrote for an interview, signing her name, E. Burrell. But when she got there, the editor shook his head and told her he would not hire a woman at night no matter what her qualifications. He didn't particularly want one around in the daytime either, he muttered. "We get kind of rough in here."

"I need a job," she said forcefully. This was not literally true. She had enough money for basics. The man looked at her as if she'd given him a headache. If only women would let themselves be taken care of, his sigh seemed to say, so that predators couldn't get at them.

"Sometimes publishing houses hire," he said. "Some copy work is given out to be done at home. You might get some of that. Are you qualified?"

"More than qualified. Where? Who might be hiring?"

"I'm not going to help you to that. *I* don't know. Conditions change by the week."

She got up to leave.

"Try Greaves or Greenleaf. Try Greaves. I really don't know anything about it."

She caught her breath and walked straight to the Greaves offices. She'd studied ad after ad for seamstress, nanny, clerk—hardly anything for positions other than those. And of course, they'd want to hear she couldn't help it, that she had no other means of support.

When the editor at Greaves agreed to see her, she was unprepared for what would pass as an interview. The man who ushered her into his office was abrupt, burly, dark-haired, and olive skinned, nearly forty years old, she guessed. "What is it?" he asked.

"I need to work here."

He almost laughed, but instead ran his forefinger rapidly under his nose, as if irritated. "Why is that?"

"I have a college degree, I'm getting another, and I think there must be more to the world than what I've seen so far. I want to be out in it, working."

"You don't wish to be paid?"

"Of course I wish to be paid." She saw a version of herself standing up, walking away from this man who sounded arrogant to her. But she sat there and waited.

"You think you'd be a good proofreader?"

"Unquestionably."

"That's strong language." He laughed comfortably.

She laughed, not meaning to.

He drew a packet of pages to him and plopped them in front of her. "Let me get you a sheet with the symbols on—do you know the symbols already?"

"No." Symbols?

For about three minutes he fumbled among papers and finally produced an instruction sheet. She had time to inventory him: quickly moving eyes, chipmunk cheeks, a bit of girth, something almost embarrassed about him. Gruff, but also . . . busy, shy? "See what you can do."

"Where do I work?" She looked about.

"Take it home." Her spirits sank. "Bring it back in a week. You'd better write down where you live." He fetched her more paper and pencil. "You lose that and . . . I don't know what to threaten you with. You lose that and more than one life is ruined, mine included." He watched the orderliness with which she wrote down name and address. "Ellen," he said, "and from upside down, it looks like Burrell. Where do you go to school? Barnard?"

"NYU."

"Right." He took the piece of paper and read her address. "And you live around the corner from the university. So one way or another I can find you if I need to. I'll pay you six dollars for this job if you merely try. Ten if it's done right. You'll return in a week. Three o'clock next Monday. Don't let me down."

"I won't."

He reached out to shake her hand. "Arthur Greaves is my name. In case you want it."

She didn't want to work at home. One week. And it was only part time, but the little money she made would be wonderful and she would use this work experience to look for something else. Walking home, past school, she ran into Bill Emerson running for the coach that would take him to his job clerking at a men's clothing store. He stopped to greet her, panting. She told him her news. "Good going, Burrell," he said. "Very impressive!"

She didn't want to work at home, but that's what she was handed. She wanted to explain that to Bill, but he had to charge off for his ride. He was lucky. He said he didn't want to work in his parents' butcher shop anymore and he had managed to find himself something new.

At ten that night, having for hours reviewed everything she needed to do (and shadow edited without writing a thing down), she finally put pencil to paper and worked for two hours. Employment suited her. Absolutely. Bulkhead against undermining loneliness.

Ellen's light hair had darkened over the years to a chestnut brown. It had a slight wave to it that was going to serve her well in years when it became acceptable to cut it. Wound back in the style of the time, it was not the worst hair. Nor were any of her features out of line or outsized. She was acceptable-looking without being a beauty. There were actresses who had no more looks than she did, but they liked the limelight and that light, falling on some paint, heightened plain looks to momentary beauty. Late at night, when she was too tired to proofread any more, but too wired up to go to sleep, Ellen looked at herself in the thin glow of the lamp at night, thinking, What will become of me?

Outside an occasional carriage went by over the cobblestones. Lovers, she always thought when a carriage passed by at night. The landlady had occasional visits from her lawyer. Millie, the other student in the house, went out three nights a week and came home rumpled. But even on the street, she could see love was everywhere, everywhere.

She set out the clothes she would wear the next day. Thanks to Aunt Hester's needlework and more to the Greshams' generosity, she had several skirts and blouses of good quality. Aunt Hester had taught her to recognize decent stitch work and solid materials. Her aunt had also taught her to mend anything that could be saved. Now, looking through the choices—gray or brown, black or burgundy? And which blouse?—she saved the nicest, the burgundy, for when she would take the pages back to Greaves Publishing. Not in a week. She knew she would be finished early and that it seemed wasteful to let the work sit around in her room when someone could be putting it through the next stage.

If Greaves liked it, she would agree to do a little more, but she would make it clear to him that she was looking for something else, work that would be less isolated.

She stared into the night for a long time, knowing, before she knew, that she was about to hurt herself with love. Later she came to believe that love was decided in the first moment between people, nothing to be done about it except run and did you ever really get away?

Four days later, Greaves growled, "A week is what I said. What is this? A problem?"

Perhaps it was foolishness to bring the work in on a Friday, after all. She should have come Thursday when she was actually finished.

Greaves watched her. "You want another assignment?"

"You haven't checked to see if that one is right."

"True. Sit." He turned page after page until she was sorry she'd asked him to look. "Tell me about yourself," he said finally.

"I went to the Pennsylvania College for Women. I could begin teaching now, but I . . . liked studying and I wanted to see more of the country. And so I'm here."

He nodded. "But where do you come from? What family is outraged by your wanting to live in a big city you were not born in? You weren't, were you?" She shook her head. "I didn't think so."

"I was born in Johnstown. I was raised by an aunt and uncle. He's a Methodist minister, but I ended up at the Pennsylvania College for Women by making friends with some Presbyterians."

He laughed. "Grooming the wives of ministers."

"Exactly. It's almost a system."

"Why were you raised by an aunt and uncle?" he asked easily. When she hesitated for only a second, he added, "I'm not shock-able. If it's illegitimacy, I don't care. There is always some story that explains it . . . Ah. The flood?"

"Yes."

"I'm sorry. That town! Vale of sorrows. There was flooding again this year, I read. Wasn't there?"

"Nothing disastrous."

"But who needed a reminder, eh?" He appeared to slow himself down to ask, "Your adopted family is still alive?

"Oh, yes. I'm not abandoned. Or destitute."

"Restless," he pronounced. "I certainly, certainly understand that. In my deepest soul, I understand. So we must get to know each other. Do you want more work?"

"Yes."

"A double load?"

"Yes. I think I can get it done in, say, ten days. You didn't comment on my first."

"I'm sure you know it's perfect and you're just wheedling to hear it spoken." He began going through the pile on the desk, putting down a thin manuscript and choosing a heavier.

"I never know."

"But since you're always perfect, it's a pretty good guess. Make a few mistakes every once in a while just to have the experience. It can be thrilling."

"I don't know about that."

"Of course you do."

In the outer office, three people bent over their desks and made small marks on paper even though each desk also held a typewriter. At one of the three desks was an elderly woman. So Arthur Greaves was willing to put a woman in the offices. Good.

Ellen had no sense of how long she would live and what changes she would see. Already it seemed amazing that more and more people had automobiles and that the lightbulb and the typewriter had made their way into most office buildings. Edison and others had made pictures *move*. Invention was all around her. A sense of the *unusual* and of *possibility* filled her that day as it had the day she rode a gigantic wave of dirty water through crashing debris, and somehow lived, defying all odds. Things she had not conceived of—radios, televisions—would become something to shrug at. Wars in Europe, Korea, Vietnam, all were in the early gestures of becoming. It was impossible for her to guess these things—or that she would one day live contentedly in the town she had once fled, believing it too small for her spirit.

She continued to do work for Greaves.

At Christmastime, she made a trip back home and spent time with her cousin Julia and her children, especially having fun with Julia's third child, Lucy, a sweet thing of five.

THE PROBLEM Anna had was being good at everything. Dr. Raymond wanted her back in his office as his assistant. But the head nurse called her in and told her, "We have two possible positions for you. There is Pittsburgh Home Nursing, where you would be placed in homes as the cases come in. There is also . . . ," the woman frowned. "Perhaps you've heard. Miss Carter is leaving us. We will have need of a head nurse here to teach the new classes."

Anna's heart told her this was the job she wanted—training the young women correctly, making sure they knew what they were doing. Still, she couldn't accept it. "I made an agreement to continue working for the doctor who boarded me and paid my expenses when my mother died."

"Really? You mean years ago?"

"Unfortunately. Yes." Raymond was a good doctor but a cheapskate.

The student nurses *were* the nurses at the hospital. They paid their way with work, being put on revolving shifts. They learned bandaging and wound care and fever care. They assisted the doctors in surgery. They learned to give injections and to place intravenous needles. They did everything except make big decisions and perform the surgeries. There were times Anna felt she could actually do the surgeries, but she never dared say so.

"I made a promise," she said. "I gave my word. But if it's possible, I would like to come back in a head nurse position in two years."

"Impossible. We'll have a whole new class to choose from."

"Perhaps if I came in on my days and hours off—there aren't many of those but I would come in if it helped. Perhaps then you could keep me in mind."

The superintendent was shaking her head no, but then she stopped and nodded.

Anna had excelled at the study of the body, the way muscles worked, the factory of organs doing their jobs, the bones with hinges that allowed movement. She never knew why this came to her naturally. Her father and mother had shown no such interest.

"You will be exhausted."

"Yes."

"Where will you live?"

"In the doctor's home."

"I see."

Dr. Raymond was thrilled to have her back. So was Paul. Every time she looked up, he was studying her. "I don't want to get married," she told him. "Ever." That wasn't true, but she was worried it was her fate.

"You're just shy."

Shy. She hated the word. She was just quiet, but she knew her mind.

She exhausted herself with work, it was true, but she also kept learning. Head lice. Wounds that did not heal. Broken bones needing to be set. Mothers who had babies and rejected them, not feeding them. She found wet nurses, soothed distraught mothers, comforted abandoned babies. She had found something she could do well. She didn't expect to have a life beyond this.

In this early period nursing was often evidence of a woman without a family or a place to live. Many of the nurses grouped together in graduate nurse homes. The nurses got rented out—as the superintendent had offered to do for Anna. They never had any money. Well, fifteen dollars a week when they had work, but when they didn't. . . . Sometimes the working nurses would help to support the ones who hadn't been called. It was strange to hope for a long lingering illness in a comfortable home, but that was the safest bet. Anna kept contact with some of the women who had graduated with her. When she visited their graduate nursing home, they told her tales of their assignments. They showed her a printed advisory that had been distributed to all the group homes. They were already laughing as they handed it over.

When night comes, the patient, glowing with fever, says frequently: "Miss S., do not sit on that hard chair during the night. Look—this bed is a double one, with room enough for two. Come share it with me, for you need rest. Do please me; it will be a comfort to have you near me."

Now here comes the temptation to a nurse to please her patient, but stop a moment, think of your patient's and your own welfare.

A patient must have undisturbed rest. Can she have it if the nurse turns or even moves? Does it not annoy a sick person? Is it right for a nurse to allow herself to try to rest with a patient who is restless, coughs, or has fever? Certainly not.

How the nurses laughed. "They're afraid to say 'he,'" one said.

Anna added, "The reasons they give us! They think we're too stupid to understand."

"What if he's young and the bed is nice and the fever is low?" said the most comical of them with a raise of her eyebrows.

Anna laughed the whole way home. One thing she knew about bodies: they wanted to be touched. She wanted that sort of love, but could not make herself fall in love with the doctor's son. During her training she had fallen in love three times, once with a doctor and twice with patients who were warm, calm. She had not climbed into their beds, though she had wanted to.

BY JANUARY, Ellen had proven herself so quick at everything Arthur Greaves gave her to do that she was invited to take a desk in the office on Friday afternoons, Saturdays, and full time in the summer. The offer answered everything she had hoped for.

She was moving on, moving. She got letters from Julia about her children and the joys of raising them. Julia's life was orderly and normal and lucky, the way things were supposed to be. Ellen understood the message.

By the end of the first year, Ellen recognized that she was in love with Arthur Greaves. Around him, she felt alive, full of wit.

"What do you think?" he asked of a manuscript she had just read for him and that he was deciding whether to acquire.

"I found it earnest until page seventy-eight, and appealing, but maudlin after that."

"Exactly, but can it be fixed?"

"Yes, if he is willing to take a new direction."

"I think so, too. But how will we specify that direction? I mean who is to provide the example?" He raised his eyebrows.

"Me?"

"I think you're an expert at checking the maudlin."

All day she glowed to think he had noticed her, thought about her. Saturdays were her favorite, being at the office alone with him. He ordered lunch up and they ate together. She knew he liked her and that was enough for her. The color of his skin, his burly shape, were part of her dreaming life, day and night. Nothing could induce her to quit her job and move on to some other chapter in her life. His company was worth everything to her.

Her life? She suspected she'd found herself a Rochester, but there would be no transforming fire to make him hers. On weekdays, she overheard him talking about his wife and children. She knew he was out of reach.

One Saturday in spring, she was working on a particularly difficult novel when the door opened. She jumped in surprise. "Hello?" she said.

"Hello." The woman who stood there was well dressed in a cream-colored linen two-piece dress, much fancier than anything anybody wore to the offices, with white lace at her neck and a hat that matched the color of her suit. "Is Arthur here?"

Before Ellen could stir to bring him out of his office, his door opened. There was no doubting the fact that he looked surprised. He still held a letter he'd been reading. "Lydia! I didn't know you were coming in!"

"I made up my mind suddenly. I thought we could have lunch."

He nodded. "Lunch. All right. Lydia, this is Ellen Burrell whom I've been telling you about."

"The talented editor."

Talented.

"Ellen, this is my wife, Lydia."

"Enchanteé," Lydia said. "I'm practicing for France. I didn't guess you would be lovely, too. I thought all editors looked like Arthur."

"Happy to meet you," Ellen replied.

Arthur said again, "This is such a surprise. You want to come in?" He indicated his office.

"Oh, no, I'm perfectly comfortable out here. I understand you're working. But I don't mind sitting out here."

He waved the letter. "Let me just put this back and we'll think about lunch."

Lydia settled in the chair nearest Ellen and smiled at her.

"You're going to France?" Ellen began.

Lydia raised her voice just a little to include the next room. "This summer. He's promised, haven't you Arthur? But only for three weeks. We haven't been for five years and I miss it."

"I miss it and I've never been there except in my imagination. Books, you know."

"You must then. If you already know it's for you. France is beautiful."

"Will you go to Paris or somewhere else?"

"Paris and the countryside both, with a little help from the trains. At least that's what I hope." She looked inquisitively at her husband who had returned. "Am I planning too much?"

"No, no." He looked out the window. "I'm trying to figure out whether we should all have lunch here—it's being delivered and I think there will be plenty, but I could go out and ask them to add another sandwich—or whether we should all go out. It's clouding over."

"Are you especially busy?"

"Very."

"Well, then let's picnic indoors."

"Would you like *me* to go down and order another sandwich?" Ellen asked. But as soon as she made this offer, she saw it put a barrier between her and Lydia. She was on a program to do things (like going into restaurants) most women didn't do alone. She explained, "I know where the shop is. I always notice it on the way."

"I'll go," Arthur said. "Why don't you come with me, Lyd? Experience the routine you keep asking me about?"

"I always ask him about his life," Lydia said softly. "I'm a little tired. If I could just sit, I would like that better. Would that be all right?"

"Of course." And he was gone.

"I won't bother you."

"It's all right. I forget to take breaks. This can be hard on the eyes."

"I imagine. I couldn't do it, I know that. You like it?"

"I do."

"People like different things. I like home life and children. Although this morning, I didn't like them very much. They were fighting, nobody could calm them, and I didn't want to be in their presence. So I dressed and came out. Do you not like children?"

"I love children. I always have."

"Did you think of, did you ever think of becoming a teacher of children, then, or a governess?"

"I did. For a long time I thought that's what I would be. I decided I would be a teacher at a very good school and so for that, I went to college, but then I decided to get another degree. I'm still in school. Did your husband tell you?"

"He did. I don't know how you do it all. Do you have time for music and dinners and relaxing?"

Ellen searched for the right answer. "My life doesn't seem to be going in that direction."

"Or travel? You wanted to travel."

"Some day I will."

Ellen thought the phrase, "When I find someone who wants to go, too," and Lydia might have been thinking, "This woman needs to be taken care of by someone so her life falls into place." She must have bumped into the thought, "You must think of coming with us," because she spoke it out loud. Her words clearly surprised her. She'd made a crazy chess move and now had to make other moves to make sense of the first. "I know you're not a nanny and I do understand that's beneath what you can do, but if you would want to give the children a few lessons while we're away, just every once in a while give me and Arthur time to ourselves, that might be just right for everyone."

Ellen understood what Lydia was saying. Inside her, the balloon that kept her spirits up deflated. "That's a very kind offer, but I'm sure there will be work that needs to be done here."

"Oh, I expect so," Lydia said, not completely disappointed. "My husband told me you come from Johnstown. And you were in the flood."

The conversation always went there, and after Ellen had answered the inevitable yes and acknowledged once more that she had lost everyone, she felt so badly for Lydia that she changed the subject to France, which she suspected would lighten the mood. "Did you see the Eiffel Tower when you were there five years ago?"

"Yes. Twice. Once with the children and once without. I could have gone three more times, but of course there is so much to do. My sister went with us, and a nanny. The children were smaller."

"Four children, I think Mr. Greaves said?"

"Yes. They were three, five, seven, and nine then. Now add five to each one."

"Now they'll need to be occupied cleverly."

"Precisely. Do you have recommendations? Anything is a help."

Ellen thought and then said, "A language class. Time in the gardens to run wild. Spending money to learn how to get around. Games for the train. Plenty of reading material. I'm trying to think what reading would be good at their ages . . . Let's make a list."

She took a clean sheet of paper and began a list of books—*The Jungle Book*, *Pudd'nhead Wilson*, all of Dickens. She stopped to ask which the children had already read. This activity kept them occupied for several minutes. While making the list, she tried not to be too clever because her recommendations, coming out of her so facilely, had cut Lydia down, she'd seen that. When Arthur returned, they were all relieved.

"Here we are," he said. "I'm the delivery man."

"It's fun, isn't it, to make a picnic indoors." Lydia cast about for some-place to eat.

Ellen knew Arthur's desk was hopeless, so she began moving things off her desk. While Lydia wandered into Arthur's office, Ellen ran to fetch a few plates from the washroom down the hall. Feeling foolish, she said, "Lunch is ready. I mean it's set out."

Arthur looked at her kindly. None of them could help it. The idea had taken root and it was too late to pretend it hadn't. Over lunch they decided that if she took four manuscripts with her and spent a little time with the children she would more than earn a trip to Europe.

And be part of the family. And remember her place.

THE SHIP'S PASSAGE was rough. One morning when she was reel-ing with seasickness, Ellen left her cabin and went up on deck. She was surprised to see Arthur up there, looking out to sea, his hands in his pockets, head inclined forward. Watching him made her feel intrusive and so, without making a sound, she turned back to leave him alone, but the glimpse she had had was of a troubled man. When Ellen made her way to her cabin, she thought she did so quietly, but before she reached it, she heard Arthur's voice behind her in the passageway. "Ellen? Are you all right?"

"I just needed some fresh air."

"You want to go back up?"

So he knew she had left after seeing him. He was clever in all things. "Thank you but I feel better now." She excused herself and went back to her cabin, thinking she was getting very good at self-control.

The rough passage took a week. At the end of it, they were in Cher-bourg. Disembarking from the ship, Ellen felt the disorientation of an-other country, another language, was the exact outside model for her inner feelings. She could not at first understand the rapid voices and inflections, nor could she summon whole sentences when she wanted them. Prepared she was not. The onslaught of sounds and sensations overwhelmed her. The Greaves children ran ahead, led by Jenny, the explorer, followed by Arthur Jr. who took the position of sensible leader. While Lydia closed her eyes and breathed it all in as if she had come home, Arthur busied himself with porters, luggage, money changing. When he had a pocketful of francs, he nodded and they moved on to a coach and then a hotel where they would stay for one night until they could board the train for Paris.

Ellen thought she would never remember any of it because it was happening too fast. The farmerish look of the coach driver, the new smells—what were they? hay and honey and butter combined was the smell so far as she could tell—the guttural and nasal sounds of French voices, the tight quarters, hard beds and harder pillows, the second breakfast of the morning, just because the children wanted to go out to have more bread and coffee.

"Coffee?" Ellen asked Mary, who was only ten, and a charmer. "Are you sure?"

"Mother said when in Rome . . . I don't like it but I'm going to learn to. Do you?"

"I love it."

"I love the bread and butter."

"I love that too."

Mary smiled at her. "Did you wait a long time for this? Europe?"

"It seems like a long time. I would read about it in all kinds of books. Let me think. I was about your age when I first decided I had to travel."

"That is a long time." Mary buttered her bread, soberly considering such a delay.

Arthur beckoned the waiter to bring them more of everything. He smiled and said something humorous to the man. How strange people were. He had seemed so abrupt and frightening when she met him and now she saw children hanging off him and that he had a kind of acceptance of—respect for—everything around him.

When they boarded the train to Paris, she managed to sit far from him. At the hotel, she stayed with Jenny and Mary, with whom she would share a room. This skill at physically positioning herself gave her a little confidence. Lydia wanted her company on walks, to talk about the look of Parisian women and what they wore. Ellen struggled to catch up to everything they talked about, everything she saw. One day Arthur walked with her, asking how she was faring. Sometimes, no matter how hard she worked, she ended up face to face with him. And even at the Eiffel Tower, after she took care to climb the stairs a whole staircase below where he was, the children ran up and back because Mary worried that she was slow because she was tired. So in the end, she climbed one whole section at Arthur's side.

Mary was her favorite. Partly, she just liked her name.

During this trip, Ellen further defined her role in life—defined it right out of the fiction she had read from childhood on. She was the outsider, the governess, the trusted companion, the relative taken in. She would have no Balzacian bitterness. Only self-effacing English goodness. If her feelings leaked out, she would remove herself from the job at Greaves, from the city, if necessary.

The Greaves children loved Ellen. They took to touching her, then hanging on her, an arm around her waist or shoulder. They were real and sweet, complex and intelligent.

When the trip was over, she went back to her little room in New York, and alone, for the first time in a long time, she cried for the loss of a whole family she would have to give up. How to quit, how to tell Arthur . . . ? He had done so much for her. She must never seem ungrateful. A rustle in the hallway caught her attention. Soon after, a letter scraped its way in underneath the door. Aunt Hester, she thought, a death announced. Her heart pounded right up into her head.

Bill Emerson. In a few moments her head stopped throbbing. Bill Emerson wrote: *You are the envy of our whole class. How was the trip? Would you consider telling us about it at a fall picnic in the park near our house in two weeks? We will provide the food. You are the entertainment.*

Work resumed. It was better to feel sharp pain in the heart than to feel nothing. She chose it.

School resumed. She told of her travels to a group of students who managed to get to Brooklyn one Sunday for the picnic near Bill Emerson's house. But her European trip was not the only thing they were interested in.

Bill Emerson had an announcement. He would be graduating mid-year and had just been offered a job with Westinghouse in Pittsburgh. "I think I should take it." His wife nodded. She was thin and serious looking. "I will write plenty of letters," he promised. "Only, if they guess I am really Mizejewski," he said, "I might be out of luck."

Love resumed its held in check position. For a whole year.

"You must work here full time now," Arthur said.

"I don't know. I wasn't thinking when I took this—"

But somehow movement happened instead of speech. She moved. He moved. They were squeezing hands, then embracing. "You can't help it. I can't. I've examined it every which way. It's nobody's fault. We were meant to be with each other, to know each other."

He smelled wonderful—of what, she didn't know—coffee, the starch of his shirt. Clean and human at the same time. She thought she might never be able to move away from him.

His voice caught. "I don't know what I'm proposing. Some vast change, I know that. I don't want to hurt you. Above all things, I don't want that."

To imagine him away from his family was not possible—or not something she wanted to be responsible for. She wanted to run away, but she stood there and let him hold her. She had never thought she could be this sort of person, but here she was.

At first they made love in the office. When Saturday seemed too far away, they came in early or stayed late on a weekday. Did the others guess? They thought perhaps yes. When they realized they couldn't do without each other, try as they both did even after the first confessions, Arthur rented a small apartment in a building two blocks away on 24th Street. He told the owner that he and his wife came into town on business several days a week and needed a place to rest. If Ellen had to greet the owner on her way into the apartment, she allowed herself to be called Mrs. Greaves. She took to carrying an assortment of packages so that it would seem she had been shopping.

Her thoughts gave way to each other, inner argument, until she became used to all the feelings. Things weren't always the way Uncle Paul preached they ought to be and they never had been from the beginning of time. Arthur loved her back. That was the miracle.

She loved him. Sometimes she thought she would die of it, but she didn't. Yet she felt an uncomfortable detachment from herself. She supposed that was a permanent feeling, detachment. A kind of floating.

"I'll leave them. Divorce."

She shook her head. "I can wait."

"For what?"

"Until the children are grown. Established. It will be easier. Don't leave them now."

"But your life meanwhile. . . ."

"I am all right."

"I don't want to cause you harm."

"We'll know what to do when we know." She supposed her Methodist childhood had taught forbearance. For whatever reason, she got used to the present arrangement—as people do to all sorts of things.

Arthur was a gentle lover. They talked for hours about everything—religion, her adopted family, what she could remember of her real family. He talked freely about his children, about the business, his parents, his childhood friends. After two years she told him about her cousin Paul causing her father's death. He was so sad for her! Sadder than she could have imagined.

Her history was there with them all the time. But they had eager minds. They talked, joked, compared notes on things they read. They catalogued the changes of the world around them. George Bernard Shaw. The *Titanic*. The trouble in Europe. They ate up information, distracted themselves with it, fell into routines, and got older. They even argued sometimes. They were, in a word, married.

She moved to her own apartment on 27th Street, though they kept the tiny one on 24th. She spent most Christmases, New Years, Easters, Fourth of Julys alone. She remained thin. She was always polite and neatly dressed. People trusted her.

Aunt Hester died, but Uncle Paul went on living and preaching, although he was ailing by then.

One day in 1913, she went home to visit him. It was clear from the start that he was very agitated. He greeted her strangely.

Julia came to visit and whispered, "He's been very strange. I don't know. Maybe a parishioner in trouble?"

Finally after Julia left, Uncle Paul called Ellen into his office where she'd stood on the carpet so many times. This time he asked her to sit down. What could it be? Then her uncle showed her a letter he had received that he was about to hand over. He showed her that inside one envelope was another.

Her uncle said, "The first letter is from a woman who sent on the second letter. The woman knew . . . a man, a man who didn't die in the flood, but lived until six months ago, leaving instruction that his letter would be sent on only after he died. He addressed the letter to you. It's a terrible thing that he did. We mourned him once, and now we mourn him twice more, for . . . his life, for . . . the terrible disappointment he was and for his real death, too. I'm sorry."

She read the first letter.

I have been instructed to mail this letter to you upon his death. He hoped it would get to you. We were married for ten years. He had many struggles and a tough life, but he managed to keep a job and we were thankful for that.

And then:

Dear Ellen,

If you are alive and I think you are, I hope my father gives you this letter. I did not know where else to write to you. What I did was terrible and it is to you that I owe the biggest apology. I possibly could have saved you or your sister—I doubt both—but I took care of myself. I found out later that you lived and I was relieved about that. I have no clue as to my cowardice except that I probably was always a coward. I pushed your father aside, I ignored your pleas, and I saved myself. For what, I cannot say. Regret certainly. And a feeling of never being able to return again or to be myself. I changed my name. I went by Paul Fulton. I got work in a Ford automobile factory. I had trouble with alcohol for some years. My later years were better. I found church again. That helped. I did wrong and I know it.

In hopes of God's forgiveness and yours, your cousin,

Paul

Ellen had two feelings, one of shock (she was shaking, every part of her was electrified) and the other was of calm (she had *known*, seen, that he left her and her sister; she had not been imagining things after all). The letter told her that he had felt guilt, but not enough of it to change his mind when he hurried to save his own life, not enough of it to come find her, or to come to see his father. After she read the letters, she said, "I'm sorry."

"For what?"

"For you. What you've been through."

Standing, she leaned over and kissed him on the cheek. "Thank you for showing me the letter."

"It's yours," he said. "It was addressed to you. I hope you'll burn it." His hands loosened and tightened with the many things he couldn't keep in his grasp. "Let's talk again tomorrow."

Back in her old room, she cried for her father for a whole night. He might have lived if only Paul Folks hadn't wanted so desperately to be free of all of them. She stayed in her old room and cried until she was exhausted with the untidiness of her grief.

TIME CONTRACTED, expanded, evaporated.

One day in late May, five years later, in 1918, she opened her door to two visitors. She had known Julia was coming with her daughter, Lucy, and she had wondered why the letter didn't sound happier. As soon as she saw them at the door, her mind raced ahead to figure out the trouble. She guessed it before it was announced.

ANNA WAS MARRIED. It was 1918. She was Anna Raymond now for she had given in to Paul some ten years ago because she wanted to get on with her life, make a family, have children. But things didn't go her way; she was barren, apparently, or so the doctor she consulted concluded.

Anna was married, trying to keep the marriage afloat, and the world was at war. It was a terrible time in Europe, the news worse every day. One early March Sunday she sat at breakfast with Paul, reading the papers. He made anxious designs in the butter with his knife. "Are you still hungry?" she asked.

"No."

Her love was not what she had imagined when she was a girl. It was not romantic but instead was closer to the love of a nurse for a longtime patient. She was Paul's comforter, his caretaker. She spent time away from him trying to think what he needed, time with him hoping not to agitate him. "Should we go for a walk later?" she asked. It was something she could enjoy. There were few days when she was not working. She continued to work because . . . because she liked it and because there were no children, but also because Paul's employment had been spotty. He'd lost his temper at work more than once, frightening employers at the bank and at the Water Department and now she knew things were iffy again. She suspected he'd been fired again.

"I've been wanting to enlist."

A jagged fear went through her. Decisions he made when he was agitated tended not to be good ones. Take your time, she told herself. Don't jump to say anything yet.

"They need men. That's all I know. They need men."

She nodded slowly. Speeches went through her head about his age, about married men, about his general nervousness, but she kept quiet and folded the paper.

"I want to make you proud."

"I am." So, he had been fired.

"No. Don't try to coddle me. They say the army makes a man of a fellow."

"That's an old saying. It also does other things."

"Kills?"

"Don't say it."

A part of her thought it would be a relief to have time to herself. He could go to Fort Dix or one of the training camps. He would probably not make it through. On the other hand, there was a good chance the army would reject him for one of several reasons. "Come. Let's walk and think."

"It's freezing out."

"Not that bad. Bracing." Exercise was good for him. It diluted the tension.

"Bracing." He smiled. The tenderness she felt for him as he found his scarf and coat was what came over her sometimes when they both gave up trying to change things. They walked for ninety minutes. They came home and she immediately stoked the fire and began to boil water for tea.

He took her in his arms. "Don't give up on me."

"I won't."

"You'll write to me. When I'm gone."

"If you go, I'll write."

"No tea." He turned off the burner. The small house his father had bought them was cozy; the bed covers were piled high and warm. "There's more than one way to get warm."

That night, late, he told her the rest of the truth, that he had looked into enlisting but there'd been doubts about his age plus his work record.

As she'd suspected. "You should just stay and keep your job."

"The job doesn't matter."

"Well . . ." She waited for him to say he'd been fired again.

"I've been investigating ways to manage getting into the war. I've already booked a passage. I'm going to France."

"I don't understand." But she did. She'd heard of men doing just that, joining the American Field Service, driving ambulances. It was extremely dangerous work.

"I'm leaving in a week. I have to do this. I know I have to do this."

"Are you going to try to join the Field Service?"

"Maybe. But I've made a connection with a guy who tells me how to go about joining the French Army."

A BOUQUET OF FLOWERS stood on Ellen's table because she had thought of this as a happy visit. And she had been influenced by the French—let in the light and fresh air and decorate with flowers and fresh fruit. Her apartment with its few well-placed paintings made the place look like something Monet might have done, worldly and full of pleasure and beauty. Julia and Lucy noticed nothing of this. Lucy cried nonstop.

"I understand," Ellen said. "Don't cry."

Julia said, "We allowed her to give lessons to children in a family in our neighborhood. They seemed highly respectable."

"They are!"

"No, Lucy. Let me tell this. Their young uncle lived in the house, too.

He's twenty. I think I would kill him if I could ever find him."

"Where is he now?"

"Gone to Europe."

"I see."

"He'll come back. He was frightened. He'll come back," Lucy insisted.

"Please, Ellen, help her to be sensible." Julia turned to her daughter. "He is not going to come back to marry a sixteen-year-old who is having a child. He is simply not." And back to Ellen she continued, "You see, as his sister puts it, everyone would know. And it would harm both of them, his sister says. That's hardly true of him, but it will certainly harm Lucy no matter what."

Lucy continued to cry. Ellen took her hand. "We'll figure it out."

"We . . . we want to tell people she has come to live with you, to study at a school here. If you could help us name a likely place . . . if she's away for the whole next school year—"

"Does her father agree?"

Julia nodded, but it was clear there was a breach between them. Julia who had had a perfect life until now looked old and worn. Her husband, she admitted, blamed her for what had happened.

"Does your father know?"

"No. I'll tell him eventually. I think I will. It all has to do with how . . . things turn out."

Ellen's head spun. Everything she had woven carefully to give her the life she wanted was coming undone in an afternoon. She was thirty-two. Women were about to lift their skirts and bob their hair.

"It's a horrible thing to ask, but we can't think what else to do. We'd give you money of course to take care of her. And I'll come to see her . . ."

"I don't want money. I have a salary."

"But will you—"

Ellen nodded that she would accept. She stood and looked about, thinking where to put an extra bed, and knowing her cousin probably was shocked by the small size of living quarters in New York. "I'll figure it out," Ellen insisted. Lucy was crying a little less now.

Ellen came back to the table, motioning to Julia that she wanted to make Lucy talk. Julia frowned when Ellen asked, "What is his name?"

"John."

"What did you like about him?"

At first Lucy shook her head unable to talk, afraid of her mother, who clearly didn't like this question.

"There must have been something. He had a good strong name. John. Is he handsome?"

A nod. "But that wasn't it. He made everything seem humorous. Things you would never think to laugh at. I never laughed so much in my life. I know he'll come back for me. We could live in Europe."

"He'll never come." Julia looked out the window, to the blue sky outside her daughter's prison. She turned back to Ellen. "Don't encourage her. He has a reputation already as a cad. He got out of town in twelve hours after she told him and out of the country twenty-four hours later. I think I haven't slept for weeks. I ask myself a million questions, but they always come down to: How could this happen? How could it?"

Ellen rapped her fingers on her thigh. She studied a plume of curling smoke starting up from several buildings away and said to Julia, "We ought to go out to dinner. We must do pleasant things, the theater, a concert while you're here."

"It's not a vacation."

"Of course not. When you go home, you'll want something to talk about." Next she turned to Lucy. "When I get quiet, don't worry . . . I just have a lot to figure out. I had the thought we might actually get you to a school while you're up here." She saw Lucy's surprise. "We can make the lie true."

"No," Julia said, "no, not out of the apartment. She must not be seen."

"But it would be unhealthy to—"

"Just imagine if someone from home comes up here—and sees her—my life will be ruined and so will hers."

Lucy looked as if she might protest, but she didn't.

Ellen busied herself making them a late lunch, all the while thinking about that small apartment she and Arthur kept for themselves. All this hiding!

Julia said, "I couldn't put this in a letter. I know we've sprung it on you, but letters . . . someone somewhere might see the letter. Things go wrong. I want to take every precaution."

Anyone looking at Lucy would know from her distraught expression that something was terribly wrong. They'd guess—as Ellen had the moment they walked in. But Julia, so broken down, needed a plan she could believe in. And so they arranged that Julia could return to New York in three weeks with a few more supplies for her daughter. Fictions were needed and Ellen spun them easily.

ON THE DAY BEFORE Paul would leave—that was back in March 1918—Anna told him she had hired a car to take him to the train station. From the way he held her, she understood that the idea of being a soldier had already significantly changed him. His grip was firmer, for one thing. "You seem different," she said.

"I am. I'm an army man at heart. I know that, even though the Americans don't."

"Your parents are coming over later. For dinner. It's only right."

"He tried to change my mind."

"Both your parents are worried about you. Your father is . . . slower lately. Have you noticed? As if he's always distracted."

"I never thought it could happen to him."

It's not senility. It's illness. She can tell. But she can't get the doctor to confide in her. "I'm making a beef roast for all of us. You have to see them before you go."

"Thank you. I'm sure I'll remember the meal for the rest of my life. How did you do this—get off work to be at home?"

That was different, too, that he'd asked her about herself. He was simply nicer. "I just insisted."

They took the afternoon to hold each other, to say sweet things, to make love. Finally it was time to get up and host his parents.

Conversation was spotty as they ate, tense. At the end of the meal, his mother finally cried out, "What possessed you? I don't understand. They'll send you back surely."

And his father said, "Hush. Not now."

But Paul answered, "Verdun. Anna would read about it and worry. That much bravery, that much blood. And I ended up wishing I was French, out there and brave. I mean I am French in my blood and so—"

"You see," his mother told his father. "He doesn't understand. This conflict has nothing to do with us." She turned to her son. "You must change you mind."

"Maybe for once I know what I need to do," he said, with a trace of humor. "Maybe for once I'm being smart."

Anna served a yellow cake with jam on top along with coffee though there was a pot of tea for Mrs. Raymond. To the best of their ability they had accepted her as a daughter-in-law. Nobody else had been able to handle Paul. But Anna never felt she had fully lost her identity as their employee, a servant of the family.

The strangest thing was Paul—so eager to get away from her, to be on his own, and at the same time so much nicer to her, and, it seemed, more solid as a person.

ELLEN CONSIDERED calling Arthur to tell him she would take a few days off work, but rather than risk Lucy's story to the telephone, she went in to the office on Monday to explain. It was a beautiful late May day. The air coming through the window of his office was warm and damp. Outside the trolleys clanked and automobiles made their duck sounds. Ellen wore a much lighter dress than the one she had first come to the office in, sixteen years ago. Like everyone else, she had been shedding bulky cloth, going from corseted thick dresses, to tubular dresses, to loose blouses and skirts, the latter of which fell six inches above the ankle. Today her dress bared part of her lower arm and those same six inches of leg. Her hair had not been cut short yet, but curled into a soft coil at the nape of her neck.

Arthur's face immediately registered his worry. It was not just that Ellen would spend time away from the office. She now had a new focus in her life, a person to take care of. He was displaced in the way men are when their wives have children.

Ellen said, "I'll be back and forth, honestly. I can do the Jones manuscript at home and still keep my niece's spirits up. I can't bring her here. I mean, I would, but her mother doesn't want her to go out anywhere. I can't imagine being a prisoner for six and a half months."

"*You* will be. In a way."

"I know. I know. And . . . I have to find her a doctor."

"She hasn't seen a doctor?"

"She has, someone out of town. I don't know how Julia found him, but she found someone and got the confirmation. I'm afraid Julia is losing her mind over this. She feels it's her fault, that she didn't protect Lucy."

"I can give you the name of a doctor who is good with women in her condition. He's . . . I'm sure he's of the world. No judgmentalism."

"Sweetheart," she said. But the word sounded a little odd, metallic. In the outer office she gathered her things, trying to slow herself down. It was all right to be gone from home for an hour or two. And yet she felt a pressure to get out into the warm damp morning air and back to her charge. She stopped at a bakery on the street level to buy Lucy an apple strudel. There were several customers before her. While she waited, she looked out the large window to the street. People were walking. People were outdoors. No matter what Julia said, it seemed wrong *not* to go walking today. Yes, she thought with conviction. It was bad enough the child would be penned indoors in the last months of the pregnancy. Now was the time to show her there was still life to be lived, to give her an image of . . . *life.*

Out on the street, Ellen looked up at Arthur's window and saw him looking down at her.

The bakery had slowed her down and yet she found herself shifting her packages to browse through a bookstore and come up with a book of poems she thought Lucy might like. And then, breathless with hurry, she stopped at the Washington Square Extension of New York University for a catalogue of classes that a non-graduate student could take. Just in case Lucy could be comforted by the work of learning.

When she got home, she found her red-eyed cousin sweeping the apartment. "What are you doing?"

"I have to do something for you."

"It's very nice of you but not . . . expected. Listen. We're going to have a secret from your mother. For a while, anyway, you must go out every day. There is too much to see to stay cooped up in here."

"What if I run into somebody from home?"

"It won't happen," Ellen said. "Today we'll eat lunch out. And we'll walk around the neighborhood. I'll show you the park—we can get a newspaper. I need to find out what's at the theater."

Lucy nodded skeptically. "My mother says I must sit and think."

Ellen put packages away. "If we eat a late lunch, we could each have a small piece of strudel now."

"It looks wonderful."

"I've had it before. It is."

Ellen took the broom and put it away in the sliver of a closet that held such things. Her cousin sat heavily. "When you sit and think, what do you think about?"

"John, of course."

"Did you love him?"

"Oh, I did. Very much. I do."

Ellen chose two of her nicest dessert plates. She was quite a scandal herself, living alone, having her own things. She handed Lucy a plate, napkin, and fork. "Tell me about him. How long had you known him?"

"A year altogether."

"You liked him right away?"

"Oh, yes. I'm supposed to hate him now. So my mother says."

"I think she wants you to see he hurt you, that he was careless with you. Don't you think?"

"No . . . yes. He was very impulsive. I didn't want to—but I couldn't stop thinking about him, you see. And it seemed natural—I can't talk about this." Ellen realized Lucy thought of her as an aging unmarried woman who had experienced nothing. Ha.

Her own answers to the questions she'd posed to Lucy:

Yes, very much.

Ten years.

No.

Yes.

The strudel was deliciously flaky. Food. Always a part of renewal. Tragedy reduced by the taste of a sugary strudel. They went out to walk. They did not talk about John any more that day, although they would talk of him often enough in future. They didn't discuss what would eventually happen to the baby, but it was surely in both their minds as they walked. Julia had intimated she would make "contacts" on her next trip into the city. The three of them would totally erase a year from the young girl's life.

Later that day, when they pored over the catalogue from NYU, just before supper—the sounds of traffic thickening outside the window—Ellen said, "You could think about getting a teaching certificate one day. When you taught the children, your job, did you like it? Were you happy doing it?"

Lucy shrugged. "Well, I suppose. To tell you the truth, I'd rather be a seamstress." Her eyes clouded over.

"What are you thinking?"

"What a long life I have ahead if I live through this—a life with nothing much in it. I'm trying to get used to the idea."

"It's only one possible idea to have. You could try others."

Lucy nodded. "Like that I will live."

"That's a start."

The current fashions were kind to Lucy. Loose blouses allowed her two and a half more months of summer before she felt she had to hide. After the first two weeks she cried hardly at all. "It doesn't seem right to feel I'm on vacation." But she couldn't deny being pleased with strolls in the park. The doctor she'd seen at the end of the first week there (Lydia's doctor, Arthur's wife's doctor) told her soberly that she was healthy and said that he could arrange for adoptive parents as soon as she told him to go ahead. Lucy's mother came and went, relieved that the doctor had the correct contacts to make an adoption possible. She called Ellen a savior, a miracle worker. She had even given in to the idea of Lucy's going out in those first few weeks before her pregnancy showed.

After Julia left for home, Lucy said, "I don't think I can stop going out."

"I know."

They went to the theater (six times), concerts (four!), bookstores (many times), hurrying to experience as much as possible.

Three months later, Ellen dug in her jewelry box for the false ring that she wore when she went to the little apartment to meet Arthur. She could do without it; she didn't care. "You can make something up."

Lucy told a woman in the park that her husband was studying in Italy.

"Studying what?"

"Architecture."

Lying was so very simple, she told Ellen, it frightened her.

During the summer, Ellen had seen Arthur at their apartment only five times. She still loved him, but she could sense a fresh uncertainty in him. He knew she would leave him before she knew it herself. He said, "I've done you harm after all. You need to be with a family. I can see that. I'm angry at my selfishness."

"We have time to think about things now. Nothing could stop us then. You said so yourself. You can blame me as much as I can blame you."

"Tell me what you want. Anything. I'll do anything."

"I don't know. You can't keep me on staff if I only do half the work."

"I can if I wish."

"I need to be useful. Suddenly, I feel anybody could edit—"

"Not true."

"I know that. But I also feel nobody can keep my cousin in spirits better than I can. Of course, I may be giving myself too much credit."

"Tell me what you want."

She did not say, "Marry me."

Lucy told Ellen in September as they sat at dinner, "You have the most *motherly* personality, much more than my own mother does."

"Your mother is just reacting to circumstance," Ellen said. Later she added slyly, "As I've looked around, most girls find their own mothers flawed. It's some law of nature. I probably would have found my own mother flawed if she'd lived long enough."

Lucy persisted. "Think about it. If you're thirty-two and I'm sixteen, you see, you could have been my mother. You would have had me at sixteen. Just like me. I wish you *had* been. My father rejects me now and my mother is so sad, all she can think to do is hide me. But you're different. You're nice, even though you've had a very different sort of life."

"After this year, you will be fine."

"My mother said I have to keep secrets for the rest of my life. Never ever tell anyone, not . . . another man, even if I love him. Do you think my mother is right?"

"Absolutely not."

"Really?"

"There are all kinds of men. Some are capable of understanding." Lucy appeared to think about this. "You don't want one who doesn't want to know the truth about things, do you?"

"I don't know." Lucy put her hand on her belly, which was now large enough to show. "I still think about John. What if he tries to find me in Johnstown? What if my mother keeps him away?"

"If he wants to find you, he will. Even your mother can't stand in the way of it."

There was no word from John, though, and Lucy got bigger and bigger.

"I don't hate him. I can't. I wonder if the baby will look like him. I wish I could know. I wish I could be an angel in heaven and watch the baby grow up. Does that shock you?"

"No."

"Nothing shocks you! Why is that?"

Ellen made a face and laughed. "I always read a lot. All kinds of things. I think you need to read more." Ellen tapped a favorite stack of novels on the end table.

That September, Ellen had brought her cousin a different sort of book, too, the ones she would be reading if she took two courses in the extension program at NYU's program in the School of Pedagogy. Ellen chose English 3, Rhetoric and Composition, described as "a study of the art of composition. Themes, written exercises, individual criticism. Readings," and English 12, History of English Literature, described as a "review of the growth and development of the literature." Ellen felt she could handily *teach* the courses that were described and that thought began to niggle at her.

"This isn't so bad," Lucy said at the time. She was not in the mood for more Latin and Greek. But she only dabbled in the new textbooks for minutes at a time, losing interest.

During October, Lucy stayed in, and tried harder to do her studies while Ellen went to work more often. At work, a new formality came over her and Arthur. How is everything? he would ask. She would tell him things were fine. The two men now working at Greaves looked at her curiously. Why was she working away from the office so much of the time? What was the deal? One day Ellen got an invitation to Arthur's eldest daughter's wedding. The same invitation appeared on the other desks. December 15. The invitation was a polished piece of printing.

"It will be lavish," the copy editor said to the designer.

"No doubt," said the designer. "I certainly will not miss it."

"None of us will," said the copy editor.

How could Ellen be away from Lucy in December? She told Arthur privately what the problem was and he said to reply in the affirmative and to make an excuse at the last minute if she needed to. She measured the lilt and tempo of his voice, the temperature of his smile as he answered. The idea that they were veering away from each other gave her so much pain, she felt sick. And yet she was one of the two turning away. How had it happened? She could not imagine being without him. She had not sketched out her future.

One day, reading the newspaper, she happened upon an ad for a secondary school teacher. She tried to put the paper aside, but went back to the ad, just to read it. Again, she put the paper away from her. When she cleared her desk, the ad leapt out at her again. No. Perhaps she could move to a different publishing house.

During November Lucy stayed indoors nearly the whole time. She was supposed to write letters to her mother, fictions about her life, so that if anyone were to see the letters, there would be details of this young girl's experience taking classes in New York. "Let's do them as compositions," Ellen suggested. "Let's describe the school halls, the building. I can tell you the bare facts, but you'll make it interesting. Then I'll . . . show you what to edit." There she was, being a teacher; she had tricked herself.

Another trick: just as suddenly she became a mother.

When Lucy gave birth to a slight little girl on December 10—after Ellen had run for the midwife, then the doctor, and after Lucy had fallen asleep, exhausted—Ellen could not give permission to the doctor to take the baby away. She was losing her mind. The decision came up in her strong, as if she had made it a long time ago. But it was madness. She had no baby clothes, no diapers, no wrappings, nothing. The doctor was angry; the midwife looked at her curiously. But still she didn't back down. "This is not what we arranged," the doctor said sternly and the midwife, in a tone of offering peace, asked, "Will you want me to bring you a few things while you . . . decide."

"Decide?" the doctor asked. "To strap this child with a child?" But he knew what Ellen intended.

"I can move. I can easily say she's mine."

"You won't escape censure either."

"No, I won't."

The doctor looked as if he wanted to pace, but could not find the room to do it. "How upsetting this will be to your cousin. You've considered that? She thought she could begin to forget. Now she never can."

"I hope in the long run she'll be glad."

The midwife put a hand on the doctor's arm. "I've seen it before," she said. "She'll know for sure in two days. I'll bring some things."

"The baby's mother is going to have to feed her then. That creates a bond."

Lucy was half asleep when the midwife put the baby to her breast. It took a moment for the connection to work, but when it did, the doctor and midwife left. Lucy nursed her child without looking at her.

After a while Ellen lifted the baby and rocked her gently. She would say it was hers, send Lucy home in a few months, move to a different apartment, answer people's questions with whatever tragic story came to her. Husbands went to war in Europe now that the draft had been extended. Many of them never came home. Ellen's fictional husband would be one of these. Ellen held the baby close to her and it felt right. When the child cried, she crooned and comforted her. She thought about Arthur. He had said he, too, loved the name Mary and had chosen it for his own daughter—whom, Ellen knew, continued to be generous and loving to everyone. She remembered how kind Arthur's daughter had been to her on the trip abroad. She thought if Lucy would agree, she would like to call the baby Mary. Then Ellen got frightened about naming the baby for her lost sister. She added a Rose to the beginning. Rosemary.

She woke Lucy and persuaded her to feed the baby again. Lucy held the child uneasily while her cousin, her smart cousin who lived in New York, went out to buy things: blankets, crib, tiny nightgowns, and diapers.

Ellen didn't go to Jenny's wedding because she couldn't bear to leave the baby for that long. And also, she was carefully monitoring Lucy's acceptance of the new arrangement. With care, with attention to every detail, she could make it work.

ANNA HAD SUFFERED two early miscarriages in the past and the doctor (not Dr. Raymond) had told her she was simply not meant to carry a child. Her body couldn't sustain one, he said. He implied she wasn't living correctly: she worked outside the comforts of home and had chosen a life of stress near illness, he told her crossly. The result was her barrenness.

But she was pregnant again and this time, this time, she had a feeling it might work. She had wanted to write to Paul as soon as she knew, but she was afraid to get his hopes up and disappoint him. He was in the most dangerous kind of position—he had gotten himself in the French Army quickly, with little training, and this was the army that saw so many casualties. He wrote letters to her when he could—and he sounded good. France was his natural home, he said. The bread, cheese, wine, trees, flowers, everything that wasn't war, was exactly right, perfect.

Finally one day in late July she sat down and wrote him a letter about her pregnancy and said that she had high hopes. She imagined how happy he would be when he read the news. It was pouring outside but she was eager to mail the letter.

She was about to fetch her umbrella when there was a knock at the door of her house. As soon as she opened it, she knew.

The man who delivered the rain soaked telegram said, "I'm sorry, Ma'am" and reached out to touch her shoulder. When he walked away, she shut the door and didn't open the telegram at first, only held it, letting the letter she was about to mail fall to the floor. She made her way to a chair and sat still for a long time, maybe an hour. Finally she opened the telegram.

Each word that had been carved into the buff wetted paper seemed a rebuke for the amount of time it had taken Anna and Paul to find their ways in the marriage. The telegram was from the Red Cross.

It is with deep regret that we must inform you of the death of your husband Paul Raymond. He was killed in action while fighting with the French Army near Château-Thierry, Department of the Aisne, on 15 July 1918. He is buried with his gallant comrades near where he fell. As further information becomes available, it will be forwarded to you.

She slowed down and read each word several times. He was gone.

He had wanted to be brave and perhaps he was, but he was gone.

France. He had wanted that, too, and now he would be there forever. His family name, he'd explained, had once been Raimond. His great-grandfather and grandmother on his father's side had been French. He loved the language. He loved the beauty of the countryside when he found areas untouched by the war. He had had less than four full months to experience France before he died there. She found herself hanging onto the fact that he had had some joy in the landscape and the language. She sat for two hours until she was nearly due for work at the hospital. She would have to see Paul's parents first and tell them. She would have to let the doctor help her find someone to send to the hospital superintendent with the news. Three days bereavement leave, that's all she would be allowed.

It had not been an ideal or romantic marriage, but she mourned it anyway.

She put on a coat and found an umbrella. Outside the rain continued to come down steadily. How she hated the rain, always had, always.

At first she had thought to join one of the nursing units being sent to France with the somewhat illogical idea that if she were nearby, her husband would be safer. But two factors got in the way. She had an excellent position as head nurse and instructor at the hospital in Shadyside and Paul was adamant that she should stay at home to be near his parents. He had written to her that ships carrying nurses were under constant threat of attack by German U-boats. Didn't she know they often sailed under complete blackouts? Didn't she understand how much anxiety she would give him if she joined the war?

She did know that. She had two friends from her nursing class who had become volunteer nurses and one of them wrote her letters in which she did her best to find humor in the situations—the exercises and drills they did on board a ship, the things they said to each other, the fat doctors. But there were sober portions of the letters, too, one of them about how religion was a great help when they knew how much sorrow and horrible injury they were going to have to bear up under.

Through the streets Anna walked that day, five and a half blocks to Dr. Raymond's house. Her work uniform of a dark dress and white apron was soaked. She didn't care; she was trying to figure out how she would break the news.

"Terrible weather," a man passing her said cheerfully.

"Yes." But her voice was so depleted, he probably didn't hear her.

Finally she was at the door of the Raymonds' house. It was a Friday. The doctor would likely be in his home office. Shaking, she removed the telegram from her small purse and knocked. Then harder and harder.

Mrs. Raymond came to the door. Once more there was no need to explain. Faces said "death" quicker than any telegram could.

Mrs. Raymond screamed "No, no, no." She pushed Anna and the telegram aside.

The doctor came running. He understood. Anna handed him the telegram. He opened it and read it slowly with one arm around his sobbing wife. For the last several years he had been looking old and weak, now he seemed very ill. He pulled Anna to him and hugged her. The embrace felt wonderful, needed, but his wife cried, "He would never have gone if she had loved him!"

Was that true?

The doctor ordered his wife to make tea. When she arrived with it, he poured a good dollop of whiskey in each cup. "This will help."

Anna drank hers. And it helped.

"I'm pregnant again," she said quietly. "Four months now." They needed something to keep them going, even though she was afraid even as she made the announcement that she might lose the baby.

"Thank you for telling us," the doctor said. An odd thing to say.

"Is it Paul's child?" his wife asked.

Anna almost laughed. That it should come to this, her need to say, "Of course."

She kept working, knowing she would have to take a substantial leave when the others noticed her condition. She and the baby hung onto each other through that fourth month and after. Other letters came finally, one from a comrade of Paul's, another American, explaining that he had been killed near Reims and that he had served bravely. If it's a boy, she thought . . . but Paul seemed like a bad luck name. She wanted a good, steady name. She remembered her first love in high school, the boy Michael—what had happened to him, she wondered. He was possibly in the war now. But so long as she didn't know anything bad, she kept thinking Michael would be an excellent name. And a girl? Elizabeth, Elinor. She liked all of those names.

When she was nearly six months pregnant, she couldn't hide it any longer and was asked to leave her post at the hospital indefinitely and to "behave accordingly," as a woman having a child.

And when she was seven months pregnant, and by then living in the doctor's house again, having lost her independent source of income, she finally did what she had promised herself she would do for many years. Putting aside the feeling of foolishness (she could hear the doctor's wife again, calling her foolish and a spendthrift), she hired a car for a day.

The weather was fine—crisp, even cold, but sunny. She wore an extra shawl and warmed herself with a lap blanket. There were bits of colored leaves left on the trees, not many, but enough to keep the season from seeming bleak. The car was a Standard, quite a beautiful thing. The driver seemed surprised at the assignment. He was an elderly man with thick glasses. "Farmlands?" he asked. "Indiana, the little town in our state you mean?"

"Not the town. Into the county. Can you do it?"

"Yes, I can get there in a couple of hours. But tell me where you want to end up, a destination."

"I won't know until I get there."

"Uh huh." He cast his eyes over her whole form, trying to figure what was going on, but thought better of asking directly.

And then they were off. The ride was rough, much of it on bumpy dirt roads. But she was happy that she was doing this finally. She was living in the doctor's house because he had owned the one she and Paul lived in. And then he'd sold it after Paul died, explaining to her that it was wasteful for her to live there. She didn't have enough money to buy it from him.

The rolling farmlands in Indiana County were brown with the season. She asked the driver to find her a church. He asked the first passerby he could find and was directed to a Methodist church a quarter mile away and also to a general store near it. It was ten thirty in the morning. "I like to drink milk," he said.

"I've packed sandwiches, enough for you."

"Ah. I have my own. Salami. I hope the smell doesn't bother you."

"It won't."

Anna ate a part of a sandwich when they stopped so that her driver could have his break. She looked down the road to the Methodist church, eager, and her driver noticed and started the car again, drifting toward it. "Well, it's what you wanted," he said doubtfully. "No services on a Saturday, you know."

The church doors were locked but she had luck in the rectory next to it. The minister's wife answered. She was a cheerful woman, rosy and outgoing. "He's making a house visit, but I could show you the rectory books. It would be all right, I'm sure."

"Thank you. For the year 1886. Someone else would have been the minister."

"Oh, yes, my husband's father. But he did keep records."

"Good, good."

When the woman dug out a book, she asked, "What are you looking for? I'll help."

"Just all the births, baptisms."

"All right. It's kind of scratchy, but here you go. What name?"

"I'm not sure. Girl children in born in 1886 with a birth date of May 8."

There were none. One boy. They looked back two months and forward several months and did not see much. An Elizabeth Baker in September. Nobody named Anna. There was a Collette Angier in October. Had Anna, too, had French parents, poor ones in her case, who didn't want her? With the dusty old book before her, her spirits sank. She looked back a year and forward a year seeing how impossible it was to guess now what had happened. She didn't know who she was *before* she was Anna Burkhardt and then Anna Raymond. "Is there a Catholic church around here?"

"Two. One near and one far."

"The people who raised me were Catholic, but . . . I wanted to be thorough. I thought I might have started out a Protestant."

"Humph. I like a puzzle."

"Could you point my driver to the Catholic churches?"

The next part was easy. The first Catholic church was three-quarters of a mile away and the priest was a young man, eager to help her. She was thinking now that perhaps she was baptized when she was adopted.

The young priest said, "Burkhardt? We've had a couple of Burkhardts in the books as I recall."

Together they searched. They did not find a baptism anywhere for an Anna Burkhardt. But there was a marriage recorded for Francis and Emma. Her parents. There it was! An address for her parents! Their early days when they lived on the farm. This was just what she wanted. She copied the address down though it was only a road—Curtis Creek Road—and she hurried to the car. The priest followed her and gave the driver directions to Curtis Creek Road.

When they got to the farm, she saw the brown shreds of corn plants that had been harvested and she thought, "My father liked this place, wanted to stay here."

"Not a very big farm," said the driver. "You want to go up to the house?"

"Yes."

The driver wound around a road that might previously have seen only carts and horses and up to the house. A woman came to the door immediately from the sound of the car engine. She wore a faded dress with a sweater over it. She had been scrubbing something; her hands were red and raw. Her first reaction was to be terrified. She looked out to the fields, hand over her heart, to where a man working alone hammered at stones and then she looked back to Anna who was getting out of the car.

"Please don't be frightened. I only wanted to know about the farm. I think my parents used to live here. Perhaps you bought it from them."

"My husband bought it from a Mr. Hoslip. Is that who you mean?"

Disappointment settled over her. What a foolish trip this was. Hoslip. She tried to remember if she had heard the name.

"Do you . . . need water or tea. I have tea."

The driver was out of the car and wandering around, looking. It didn't take long to figure out he was looking for the outhouse.

"Out back," said the woman.

"I will need it, too," Anna admitted. "We've driven from Pittsburgh."

"Of course. But we're the Youngs. We bought from Hoslip if that's who you want. I don't know where they moved to. My husband might know."

"Before the Hoslips?"

"My husband would know. Please. Come in."

"Thank you. I am Anna Raymond. My maiden name was Burkhardt."

"Burkhardt. That's it! I heard him say Burkhardt. Please sit."

So this was it, where her father used to live and wanted to live again. Why did she not remember any of it? Nothing. Not a thing.

"Would you like to look around?"

"May I?"

"Yes. I have a baby in the bedroom. She's just getting up from a nap. She might start screaming. I'll make tea. Then I'll fetch her."

"Mrs. Young? I could bring her to you. I know how to hold a child. I'm a nurse."

"Oh, yes. Well, yes. But you're dressed nicely."

"I don't care."

Anna wandered the rooms. Nothing looked familiar, nothing at all. Out one of the back windows she saw her driver pacing.

The baby was an irritable red-faced child in a small crib with rocker-chair bottoms, perhaps something homemade. Anna lifted the child, who screamed at first but softened in Anna's arms, curious, examining her. "That's better," she said and carried her out to her mother. "It's very kind of you to make tea."

"We could share our lunch. It's just soup."

"Thank you. We've eaten. But I'll go out back for a minute if you don't mind. Does your husband come in for lunch?"

"Yes, any time now. And he's seen the car, so he'll be here."

"He might know something about the Burkhardts' friends."

"I don't know. He doesn't talk to folks much. He just does his work."

Anna knew from having treated many pregnant women that she was going to have insistent needs for chamber pots and outhouses today and for the next two months. She could picture it all anatomically—the baby taking up more space, pushing at her bladder. In her mind was a picture of her child, sensing things, hopefully gathering strength.

By the time she had finished outside, her tea was well-steeped and poured into a cup and Mr. Young had come in to see what the fuss was about. He was small, wiry, taciturn—if not outright suspicious. He had thin light-brown hair that stuck up when he took off his cap.

Anna asked her question.

"Friends? I wouldn't know. You'd have to go door to door to see who your folks talked to. They didn't tell you or mention any names?"

"No. They left here when I was a baby. They didn't much talk about it."

"And you are looking for . . . what?"

"I don't know."

"That's a long trip for not knowing."

"It is."

"You like riding in the car?"

"I liked it. It was exciting."

"You knew your grandmother?"

"No. Never knew her."

"Well, it's not my business, but she had her own place five miles down the road. In Ninevah."

"Where am I now? This place?"

"East Wheatfield Township."

"But my father's mother was in Ninevah?"

"I don't know how I know that—yes, I heard from someone who bought the place when she died. That was a while ago. You didn't know her?"

In her mind, she revised her statement. Yes, she remembered now, the woman had come to visit Pittsburgh for a day or so when Anna was a little girl. A frightening woman who examined her, studied her. She was told her grandmother died soon after that. And the property was rented out for a time.

"What is your baby's name?"

"Ivy."

"Beautiful name." Red-faced little squealer. Who would Ivy be when she grew up? "Would you be able to point my driver to the old Mrs. Burkhardt's place?"

"You're having a long day in that car," the farmer said. His wife shot him a look that suggested his tone was not very friendly.

"A once in a lifetime kind of day, yes. Thank you for your hospitality. I'll let the driver know we're ready to start and let you get to your lunch and your work."

People like this lived a hard life, not that her father's factory life was much easier. But this was . . . isolated; that terse sound of voice had traveled with her father to Pittsburgh.

"Another place?" the driver asked querulously.

She almost said no. "But we've come this far. I'd hate to make a second trip."

"We are kicking up a lot of mud."

"I expect so."

And then they found it, a farmhouse along the river. Modest plantings in the back. A feeling stirred in Anna: she'd seen this before. Riverbank, barn, chicken coop, frame house. She'd visited here. They didn't tell her they visited here, but . . . odd that she didn't remember the other place. This one . . . she had a feeling about this one.

There was no one to answer the door, but the door was open. She slipped inside. Nothing was instantly recognizable and yet she felt she'd been here.

"Nobody here," said her driver when she returned to the car.

"Out working perhaps. The crumbs on the counter are fresh."

"I see. Does that mean waiting?"

"No. Let's look for three neighbors. I'll stop after three. There. See that house?"

Her driver nodded. She climbed back in the car and he drove down the road.

"We just moved here," said the first neighbor, only a small distance away. "We heard about the old lady Burkhardt, though. People say she drove a tough bargain."

"She lived long alone?"

"I don't know. I only heard about her. I think she was widowed young, so probably."

The second neighbor was a man, very talkative. "Oh, yes. Her husband used to work for my father. A long time ago, this was. Then he died and her son worked for my father for a while, but he inherited a place with his wife so they worked that."

"Burkhardt? On Curtis Creek Road?"

"That was it, yes."

"But the mother lived here? Alone?'

"They visited, wanted to get her to sell and move over with them. She was a tough old bird and she said no to that. They checked on her from time to time."

"Did you know them when they adopted a child?"

"No, I never knew about that."

"Before they moved away."

The man shook his head and thought. "They had a niece visiting once. I think they maybe adopted her. I don't know."

"A niece? Not a stranger? I've come to find out about a baby—"

"No, this wasn't a baby. This was a regular little girl."

"Oh. Did you know of a poor couple around here who gave up a baby?"

He appeared to give this a lot of thought. "I don't know that I ever did hear of that. Any baby is a hand on the farm. Even a girl."

"Maybe they were passing through—the people who gave up a baby."

Embarrassment crossed the man's face. People didn't talk about things like this. They kept their family secrets tight. "I don't know of anything like that. I always thought it was the niece they took on. They moved to Pittsburgh right after. Put their farm up for sale and the Hoslips bought it. I don't know any more about it. I'm sorry."

"But the mother's place was rented out for a while?"

"For a pretty long time."

"Funny. I feel like I've been here."

"Well, the niece . . . if that's you . . . was here. I saw her here. Feeding chickens. In her night clothes."

"Yes." She wanted to cry. She was exhausted. "Yes."

The third neighbor knew nothing.

"Best to leave some things be," said the driver who'd begun listening in. "Best to get back home."

So they gave her up when she was older. How awful must she have been?

She let the driver lead her to the car and wrap her up. The roads were bumpy and she worried the jostling would bring on labor, but she fell asleep in spite of the rough road and slept much of the way home.

Two months later she gave birth to her son. Some people, those who knew her, understood that she had lost a husband. Others looked skeptical and assumed the husband was a fiction for a woman who had gone astray.

Two weeks after she gave birth, she worked for the doctor again, it couldn't be helped, but as soon as she could persuade him, she took her job at the hospital again and allowed her mother-in-law to take care of the baby. It was very hard, giving up her son for those many hours and to a woman who didn't much like her.

She'd had trouble coming up with a name that appealed to her. The Raymonds had talked her out of several, including Michael, urging her before the baby was born to name him Paul, but she held firm and finally settled on Edward. Edward, Ned for short, just a good name with no associations.

ELLEN HAD TO MOVE now that she had a baby. Arthur helped her to pack up things from both apartments and he hired movers to get those things into one she'd found on Orchard Street. She no longer worked at Greaves but had taken the position she read about at a nearby public school. These days she wore the wedding ring Arthur had bought her, but that was all of Arthur in her life. Ellen told anyone who asked that her husband had been killed in the war and it seemed they believed her.

People liked her. People liked her in the way they would later like the actress Katharine Hepburn. She was practical and clear-eyed, good with her students, capable in the world, and she seemed to approach things with logic and humor. People also assumed she was the very conventional person she seemed to be—perhaps not the first to cut her hair or to shorten her skirts, but when she took her turn at these things, they were done with taste. At times she would look in the mirror and see herself as others saw her: clean, hard-working, intelligent, upbeat. Stoical in loss, a truthful person.

Privately, the lies she had needed to tell, first to be able to spend time with Arthur, then to take care of the baby, confused her. The truth was, she felt lost. Searching for comfort outside herself, she began to go to church again. The hymns still moved her, and the idea of a community of people singing together, bad and good voices alike, seemed a wonderful metaphor for the world as it should be. Tell everything, a voice in her said. But to whom should she tell it? A minister? She considered it. And what good would it do Arthur or his family or Lucy or Julia or Rosemary? It was wrong to unburden herself at the expense of others.

She loved to take walks with Rosemary, first in a buggy, then holding her hand when Rosemary was a toddler. Other mothers chased after their children on the street, making Ellen perfectly aware she was not the youngest of mothers. On weekdays, because of the teaching job, she had to leave Rosemary with a woman who lived two buildings over and had three of her own.

One day, it was autumn, a Saturday, a knock came on her door— nearly four years after she had taken charge of the child. Ellen opened the door without calling out, "Who's there?" She had no idea who would come by, but she didn't feel frightened. The knock had a friendly rhythm.

Nearly every answer she needed stood before her when she opened the door. In a person. Bill Emerson. It was as if she'd been adrift for a long time and in an instant the world righted itself.

Here was the person to whom she could tell everything. Anything. Oh, his face. Warm, compassionate, even though it showed a new emotion or a mixture of them, fear and eagerness at the same time.

Almost a year later, when Rosemary was not yet five, they married and moved to Johnstown. That was 1923. Bill who now had a law degree from the University of Pittsburgh decided to leave Westinghouse, though they still wanted him, and to take a position representing Memorial Hospital. Ellen got a job teaching English at Joseph Johns High School. Life became regular, ordinary, and strangely refreshing. Ellen, Bill, and Rosemary lived in Moxham in a house they bought. The twenties roared in the big cities, but in Johnstown, just to hear a little music, to go to a play, was exotic. Sometimes they travelled to Pittsburgh to hear an especially good band.

Bill knew everything about Ellen's life that there was to know. He was solid. Earthy and straightforward. Able to take a secret, unfold it, refold it, and put it back in his pocket. His wife had died two years before he contacted Ellen.

They sat on their front porch one summer, watching Rosemary play in the yard. Ellen closed her eyes. She wished Rosemary could be a more joyful child, a playful girl, but the little girl carried Lucy's sadness and there was nothing Ellen could do to budge it. Perhaps she was at fault, too old to be a mother. Bill put an arm around her. "What is it?"

"Us! How we got here! Where I never thought I would end up."

"Do you miss New York?"

"I don't think so. Oh, maybe a little."

"Were you thinking about Arthur?"

She hadn't been. Arthur had been replaced by Bill in some tricky cutting of a silent film just as once Bill (very much married and not the sort of man who would act on desire no matter how strongly it hit him) had been replaced by Arthur who was more cynical and far more willing to take what he wanted. Now she understood that her early feelings for Bill had been returned all along, from the start. He'd fallen in love with her, too, the out-of-town girl in a rooming house, trying to figure out how to take what New York offered.

Once Bill said he blamed himself for not *being* Arthur, a man who took what he wanted and lived with the guilt.

But that wasn't Bill.

Sitting on the porch, Bill's arm around her, both of them watching Rosemary, she felt safe. "This is my life now, this is how it has turned out," she thought. What she meant was, she had stopped moving in unpredictable ways; her raft had brought her to a place that was safe and there she would stay; there would be a good thirty more years in the Moxham house, she figured, followed by their tidy, ordinary deaths. She was wrong. She lost Bill after thirty years, that part was right, but she just kept living.

Sometimes he's right there, still with her. Every once in a while she dreams of him and he's so real, making toast or grumbling about some problem at work.

Hours, minutes, years contract, expand, and evaporate in mystifying ways.

WHEN EDWARD was four, Anna fell in love. She knew William Hoff-man was a wonderful man, she knew that; she also knew her life would be hard if she acted on her feeling, but there was nothing she could do. He was, the more she knew him, the person she wanted to be with. When Edward was nearly five, they married, but she'd already turned their lives upside down, way upside down. William was a Negro and the Raymonds, once they found out about him, told Anna she was no longer welcome in their home.

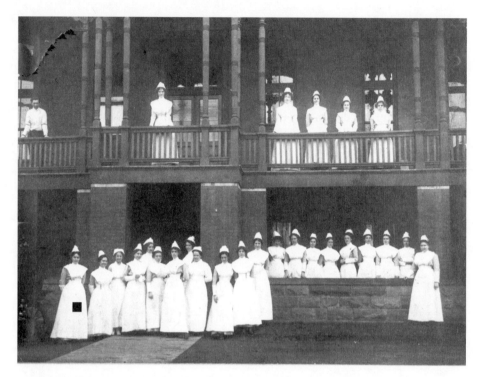

Conemaugh Valley Memorial Hospital's School of Nursing class of 1917. Courtesy of Johnstown Area Heritage Association.

CHAPTER

7

Saturday, April 29–
Sunday, April 30, 1989

■ TOMORROW is Orthodox Easter Sunday and today Nina is taking Ben to Johnstown to meet her mother properly. There's another visit to Ellen happening, too, that's how the weekend plan started, but it's also time to bring her mother on board about Ben. They're taking two cars because Ben is coming back on Sunday to finish up his article and she's staying over on Monday, a little holiday with her mum.

"Two cars," he mutters. "It's crazy."

"I know. Don't be nervous. She'll like you. And vice versa. I mean, she's . . . you know, from J-town. Totally likeable."

"How did you define that J-town thing again?" he asks as he helps her into her car.

"Oh, you know, nervous, high strung, alert, but also very patient. Describes every woman I ever knew there. It must be in the water."

"There must be exceptions."

"Not too many."

"'Love is patient, love is kind . . . '"

"Don't take that tone with my mum, okay? Don't be sarcastic. She won't like that. She wants you to be the man she always dreamed of for me."

"Oh, well." He makes a funny face. "No pressure."

"No pressure."

She watches in her side mirror as he goes to his car. The old Ben. And not. Everything is changed, changing.

Their first stop—before the important reintroduction of Ben to her mother—is to be lunch with Ellen Emerson. To prepare for the likely size of that Emerson lunch, they hardly ate breakfast, just a half piece of toast each, all the time marveling over the fact that Ellen was slender. "That comes with extreme age," Nina explained.

"You should eat lots more," Ben teased. "It's Ellen's secret, you know. She stored up. You could live to a hundred and ten years old. You could have two more husbands after me."

She heard him, the assumption that they would marry, but she had her mind on other things this morning over the toast and strawberry jam. "I think you should add as much about Ellen's life after the flood as you can. People will be interested. I mean, in how a life was lived. That's what I want to read about."

"I'll include it if I can. Hal disposes."

She balked again at the limits of daily news journalism. "I mean she went from carts and horses to cars, for God's sake. She went from gas lamps to electricity. Talkies must have seemed like the end result, like, what more could anyone want, and now of course there's TV. And cable. I wonder if she could get interested in a computer? And now, if things are going faster . . . we'll go from airplanes to what? You could end with the question of what we'll see developed. Like James Bond devices and cars that fly and watches that talk."

"Teleporting, you mean?"

"Little personal wings to travel up over roads."

"Drop down for a donut, power back up to the rooftops. My kids will like that, all right."

Yeah, well, clearly the half piece of toast wasn't doing it for him. He was thinking of donuts.

Anyway, on the slight breakfast, they start out.

The day is cloudy and cool. Every once in a while a sprinkle of raindrops hits the windshield. Spring—you never know what you're going to get other than hope. Orthodox Lent is a matter of waiting for the spring to spring. It's a routine of being very hard on yourself. Nina doesn't observe it but her mother makes a pass at it every year. It means very strict dieting. Almost nothing is allowed. Her mother tends to fall off the wagon several times during any Lent when faced with extreme hunger or temptation. Tomorrow the fast gets broken with a traditional ham and fixings for Easter dinner.

Nina has explained about Ben in a phone call. *The man you saw in the car . . . Ben . . . yes, I'm seeing him. He's separated from his wife. He's seeking a divorce. He's living with me in my little place until we can find a bigger one.*

Her mother had made it through each revelation without protesting or wailing. She said, "He seemed . . . very charming."

"He is. He is that."

"I'm glad you're happy."

She is, she is. Happy but worried. After all he has to put in many more therapy sessions. And when she asked him yesterday evening how the latest had gone, he said, "It was awful." Then he didn't say anything else about it all last night, just sort of drank beer and seemed private, closed.

For a while she drives along, fiddling with the radio, watching Ben in her rearview mirror tooling along in his car, and she wishes she could be with him, so she could ask him, "Awful in what way yesterday?"

He appears to be drumming his fingers on his steering wheel. She gets a flash of thought about Douglas—a dumb thought about wouldn't it have been nice to go to a film with him again while Ben was busy. Wow. No controlling the mind.

When they are a little over halfway there, she begins to toot her horn and points to the right and puts on her turn signal.

He toots back. He's nodding. He's seen the sign for food.

A minute later she pulls into the lot of Dean's Diner.

"Great idea," he says when they've exited their cars. "I was considering eating my thumb." Ben smiles his sweet smile and things feel right again.

"Let's not get too much. We're only two hours from a big lunch."

The diner is busy with people who probably come from miles around to have a Saturday breakfast out. The air smells of pancakes and waffles and bacon. They are lucky to get a booth just as it's being vacated by a man and woman in flannel shirts and jeans and still sporting their bed hair. Nina loves diners, loves the way people feel so at home there. "Diners could cure America," she says. "We need more of them."

"You should write that up."

"I should."

"I mean it."

If she had a column, that would be one of her entries. Or several. She takes a minute to consider. She could drive around visiting diners, describing them.

They sit before their table is cleaned off and scrunch back to avoid any flying bits of waffle the waitress dislodges as she wipes, simultaneously handing them menus high up in the air.

"I'll bring water. You going to want coffee?'

They say they do. And then they give the menus a quick once over.

"Portions look big," Ben observes. "Want to order one big special and share it?"

"Good idea." They put the menus aside. "How are you?" she asks.

He shrugs.

"Is it my mum?"

"No."

"Last night? You told me it was hard."

"Yeah it was, kind of. Sad."

"Can you . . . tell me? We're in this together."

"Well. Caldwell pressured Amanda. She was tough on her."

The waitress is back. Clunk, clunk go the water glasses. Then the cups, then the carafe of coffee. "You guys know what you want?"

Ben orders, explaining they will share.

Nina waits for a minute. "Pressured her in what way? Fairly did you think?"

"She pressured her to give up the fantasy that I'd been fucking around all along. So it was messy, but the fact is Caldwell believes me, so at least I don't have to fight the therapist. The only thing is, Amanda, when she finally said she had no proof, just her feelings, she started crying and she couldn't stop. I should say sobbing. It was strange and I had no choice but to comfort her. I didn't want to put an arm around her, but it was clear Caldwell wanted me to, so that's how Caldwell messes up my head.

Anyway I did it and I felt awful. Like touching her was a betrayal of you. But whatever was going on with Amanda was scary and deep."

"Oh." He didn't want to comfort Amanda but he did. Nina didn't want to feel tenderness toward Amanda and worry for her but she did. Amanda was way ahead here. And Nina didn't want to think about Douglas every time things got dicey, but she did. "I'm sorry you had all that."

After they share the special (scrambled eggs and sausage and hash browns and toast, plenty for two) they indulge in a coconut cream pie with a meringue of four inches because the place is famous for pies, it's clear. Almost everyone is ordering pie—to eat there or to take home. And the meringue is downright insane, giddy with height.

Then they are on the road again.

ELLEN IS WEARING a flowered dress of lilac and cream. She feels wonderful, twenty years younger. Having young people visit is the ticket. She must do it more often. Call people. Make them come. Have parties!

"You must have slept well last night!" Ruth says. For Ellen is standing at the dining table, surveying the settings, not sitting and reading as she usually does. "Your walk looks strong today."

"Well, 'strong' might be too strong a word for it. I like moving. I used to really move. I could fly down the street. I feel I could almost do that now."

"You want to show off for the reporters."

"I guess I do."

"Don't get too reckless on me."

Ellen pulls out a dining chair and sits, chastised. If she breaks a bone, her life is over. If she so much as bruises herself, she becomes a burden to Ruth. So she breathes for a while and then gets up and crosses the room to her big chair. Then with irritability, she picks up the book she was reading—*Anna Karenina*. She knows it almost by heart. Well, there are worse ways to spend a day than rereading the big ones. How marvelous it would have been to have turned out to be a writer. All the pain in life is worth it if you can be a Tolstoy or Austen and use it for others. She thought for a while that she would or could do it, but then she didn't, perhaps lacking the constitution or the right brainwaves for it. She was a crack editor. Well, that was her function, all right, all her life. A person can't be just *anything* they wish. All those kids on TV have that wrong. You have a maybe and then there are circumstances. There was Arthur Greaves at that crucial point in her life to turn her into an editor.

Karenin is telling Anna she must quit paying so much attention to Vronsky in public. Poor Anna. Poor all of them. A paragraph later in *Karenina,* Ellen puts it aside (their trouble will keep and keep forever) and picks up a photo album, wondering, Anything here for the reporters who are coming in an hour or so? She wants to give them something new again, addicted already to pleasing them.

No, she thinks, how can she interest them in all this; it's mostly family. She studies a page with Julia, who became so completely destroyed by her daughter's folly that she never recovered. The picture is of the two of them, Julia and Lucy, when the daughter must have been about twenty-five—yes, about the time Lucy was about to get married, for she did marry, at twenty-five, and it should have been a happier thing. But Lucy was simply making herself acceptable in the world, marrying a hard-working, sober, and always quiet accountant, nothing wrong with him, but she didn't love him. He was her Karenin. She had had her Vronsky briefly, never got over it, never found her romantic self again (though Ellen is glad Lucy didn't need to throw herself under a train). But oh, these photos, no sweetness in Julia anymore or Lucy for that matter. To think what sadness can do.

Rosemary, too, only the flicker of a smile, a sad child, her daughter—or does she actually sometimes think the phrase, *Lucy's daughter*?

She could cry even now that Rosemary had drifted away from her and Bill when she knew they weren't her real parents.

The next photo is of Rosemary's husband, the Reverend Driscoll (trying to look like he could enjoy a game of golf—couldn't enjoy anything much, not even a good birthday cake, that man). But yes, Rosemary had a punishing sort of religion in her blood; Lucy and Julia and Hester all had it. It felt right to them. Rosemary managed to find a man who was too much like her great-grandfather, a man who judged, who thought God was about judging.

Judging is some people's pill against weeping, she supposes. And so Stephen Driscoll was where her Rosemary had ended up. Ellen loved Rosemary steadfastly through the three years when Rosemary stopped speaking to her, through the tearful reconciliation. They even had some good times later when Stephen Driscoll claimed work demanded his presence, allowing Ellen and her daughter to take a trip to the Delaware beach together.

She leafs back to the early years, studying Rosemary's face, her posture. Even Bill, so in love with life, could not budge the little kid who was born sad.

And then there is a knock at the door! Aha, the young people are here to dispel the gloom. Today there will be joy. Ruth's roast beef smells delicious. The door opens. Ben and Nina shake off a dusting of mist from their coats. And Nina hugs Ellen, unafraid, a good hug, the way young people do these days. "You smell lovely," Nina says.

"Soap. It must be the soap."

NINA FEELS SUCH a connection with Ellen that it makes her insane to be here as a fifth wheel, not being the one asking the questions. As Ben sets up his tape recorder, she whispers to the old woman in her pretty lilac dress, "What were you looking at before we got here?" nodding toward the photo album. "Something for us?"

"No. Just looking. My daughter."

"Can I see?"

Ellen hands the book over and Nina studies it.

"It's not a typical story."

"Oh. I want to know about your life."

"If I explain, will you two keep it out of the paper? Am I nuts to ask that of journalists?"

"You have to ask him." Nina points a thumb to Ben who has finished his set up. "I have no killer instinct."

"I would honor your wish—*of course*," Ben teased, twirling an imaginary mustache. "Tell me it's not germane to the article."

"I don't think it is."

"Okay. What's the scoop?"

"My daughter Rosemary was actually the daughter of my young cousin who got pregnant. She was just a girl, Lucy. And Rosemary's grandmother was my first cousin, Julia. My husband and I raised Rosemary."

"Mr. Emerson?" Ben asks.

"Bill Emerson. The stoutest heart you could ever meet. I was lucky. I was a lucky woman."

Nina can't help blurting, "Stout heart. I like that."

"I like it too," Ben says, flirting, and taking the stage back. "Tell me, when did you meet Emerson?"

"In university in New York. He commuted. I lived near campus. We knew each other in my first days in New York. We married some fifteen years later."

Wow, there's a story there, Nina thinks. Was it a long and tortured courtship? A first marriage? She wants the dope.

Ellen looks at her to explain, "He was married at the time we met. He was a mature, married student with a home. I was a Johnstown girl in a boarding house getting to know the city. Then, a number of years later his wife died. She'd *been* delicate. I didn't know that at the time but I did know she was very thin and pale. I learned later she'd had several bouts of pneumonia in her history. And then she didn't make it out of her thirties . . . and Bill and I met up again."

"Do you have a photo of yourself in college? When you first knew Bill and you were in the rooming house and all that?" Nina asks.

Ellen flips back to find it.

Nina and Ben exclaim over one photo of Ellen, huddled in a coat, standing with several fellow students, mostly men, on a cold day outside a building, "Is he here? One of these guys?"

"No, not in that picture. Maybe a later one." Ellen flips forward looking, and pauses briefly at one.

"Oh. Who is that fellow?"

"The man I worked for when I worked in publishing. Greaves Publishing House. That's Arthur Greaves."

Nina senses in the tiny silence something of Ellen's history. Not everybody has a portrait of a boss among family photos. "Imposing fellow. May I look?"

Ellen hands over the album and Nina studies the man, trying not to make too much of it. The man looks like a boss, power coming off him. An interesting face. Men dressed so formally in what Nina's fellow students had often referred to (to the consternation of teachers) as olden times—as if there was only now and forever ago. A whole movie plays in her head. The New York streets, with some combination of cars and horses. The young woman shut up in the boarding house. The letters to home. Counting money. Taking meals. Reliance on work as the social outlet. Is she right? Is her movie right?

She leafs back to take the pressure off that one photo and she finds what she has been imagining as the stills in the film about the brave girl from Johnstown who went to New York. There is one photo of four women, each with a book in hand. Students.

"Oh, beautiful. Sweet! I love this." The long skirts, the coiled hair. And such a hopeful look on each of their faces.

"Schoolgirls," Ellen laughs. "With a bit of clothing to manage."

"I'll say." Nina can feel Ben rustling behind her. "I guess you want a piece of this action," she teases him.

"Well, yeah. I don't want us to tire her. I have just a few simple questions. I don't know how much of this I can use—the filling out of your life. I'd like to. But to start, I want to move back a bit in your biography: Did you like being in college in Pittsburgh? Was it frightening, and did it feel far from home?"

"Pittsburgh. Yes. I loved every bit of it. Of course I was nervous at first, but several of us had a rescuer, another student named Susan. She was one of those bright, generous spirits. She saw who needed a friend and she gathered three of us right away, the first day. Her parents were local—they had a home, a magnificent home, on Amberson Avenue. At first I thought, why does she want to bother with us, but she was, as I've said, perfect. A great soul. For one thing, she was physically beautiful and the thing is, she was not caught up with herself over it."

Nina leafs back in the photo album.

"You won't find a picture of her. I just never got one."

"You remained friends after college?" Ben asks.

"Oh. No. That's the thing. She died in our senior year. She was twenty-one when she died."

"Of what?"

"A horseback riding accident. She lingered for two days. The doctors couldn't care for her at home; they took her to the hospital. It was not a pleasant place—lots of very hard cases. But she was so bad . . . she was paralyzed. And then, she was gone."

"I'm sorry. This is still sad for you."

"Oh, yes. You see, for a while I had a fancy that she was my sister, that she was adopted into her new family, but then I saw two photographs of her as a baby and I knew it wasn't so. I know that was more than a little crazy of me. It was just that we all felt close to her. She was *like* a sister. A sister substitute. And I loved her. We all did."

Nina sighs, nudges Ben with her foot, thinking, "Use it, mention it, how she suffered yet another loss, use it."

Ben asks, clearly thrown by the episode of another sadness, "School during this time, was it difficult? Did it prepare you for employment or was that not on your mind?"

"We were very sad during our senior year and for the first time school seemed . . . yes, difficult. But employment, being out in the world, it was very much on my mind. I'd wanted that from the beginning. I wanted to see things. Europe. And New York. I didn't target any other city in the U.S., but I definitely wanted New York. I still had that in my heart."

"Were you training to work in publishing?"

"Oh, no. I'd never thought of it. I was being primed to take a teaching job at some private school or become a governess. And truly, all I knew at that point was that I wanted to *go. See.* When I heard about graduate work in New York and that a few women had gone, I thought that was for me."

"You got used to being unusual."

"I guess I did. I didn't try to be set apart, but it kept happening. Once Susan's family learned I was the girl who'd survived the flood, well, they kept treating me as special. And when she died, they insisted on paying my way through school in New York. I tried to refuse, but it was . . . very tempting and when I saw that they needed me . . . as a daughter substitute in this case, I let them. I sent them gifts over the years. As I could. And I always wrote to them."

"Was school in Pittsburgh not very challenging then?"

"Oh, no, I got a good workout there. I just thought of it as . . . not onerous. And such a beautiful place. It was—you know this, I suppose—

the school is called Chatham now, the same school, the same location, different name."

"Ouch. I don't know what it was called," Ben admits.

"Pennsylvania College for Women. Then sometime in the fifties they changed the name. Easier to say, for sure."

"I drove through there once. It's gorgeous up there."

"Oh, yes. It was like a retreat every day. It was our own South Fork Fishing and Hunting Club. I'd say that. Maybe we didn't have a lake but we had sports and music and theatricals, all that. It was very privileged. Lots of Presbyterians! And classes were hard enough, really. Latin and Greek and history. I loved it."

"And New York?"

She stops, thinks. "Lonely at first. Also spectacular—all that mind power at work, all those immigrants, the life of possibility. It still is that to many people. I haven't been there for a long time. Except in movies."

"Would you like to go back?"

"Yes. Yes, I would, to see it."

Nina is trying to think how they might manage such a trip when Ruth walks into the room. There has been some clatter of dishes, but not enough to make it hard to talk. The aromas, however, are encroaching seriously by now. "About another half hour," Ruth announces.

Ben says enthusiastically, "You've done it again! You have us salivating!"

"I love to cook."

"I'm going to want to ask you a few questions for a quote later on. Okay?" he asks Ruth.

"Me?"

"About being a high school student with Mrs. Emerson as your teacher."

Ruth, surprised, nods and goes back to the kitchen.

"New York," Ben prompts.

"Well I lived in a rooming house. And then I wanted employment right away. And so I went out and got myself a job. It was in publishing. With the firm called Greaves. They did very good work. Very good. I was happy there for a long time."

"You worked there when you adopted a child to raise?"

"I quit about that time and turned to teaching. I was a single mother. Very common these days. In those days not. I wore a ring. I faked it. You could always say your husband died in the war. Plenty said that. Nobody knew beans."

"How brave," Nina bursts.

"I didn't feel brave. Only confused. And determined." She looked at Ben. "My relatives have died. My daughter Rosemary had a son and he died, but his son is still alive, I believe. Somewhere in Vietnam. He doesn't know of my existence. They found that pregnancy of Lucy's so shocking . . . she was just a girl then . . . it affected everything. I don't think you should print that part."

Ben nods. "I can fudge it. I'll simply say that you and your husband adopted a daughter and raised her." He frowns. "It won't make any difference in the flood story."

"Thank you."

"In all this time, did you talk a lot about the flood?"

"Well, people always asked, yes. My boss at Greaves. Others. As soon as I said where I was from."

"And when you said you didn't believe your sister had died . . . did this idea persist into your twenties and thirties—beyond the idea about Susan?"

"Yes. Yes, it did."

Nina approves of this line of questioning. She gives Ben a nod, whether he wants it or not.

"And that investigator that was sent. That person who told you she had died out west—was this during the years you were in New York?"

"Yes, the same time."

"How did you find a detective?"

"Oh, my friend, my boss at Greaves, found him for me."

Ha, thinks Nina. Oh, yeah.

"The investigation was thorough?"

"I believed it was. I told myself it was. Private, confidential investigations the firm advertised. They were considered good."

"What did they find?"

"They followed a family named Wilson that lived in Ferndale. The

Wilsons seem to have adopted a daughter about that time and she was called Mary. Then they left the area and moved to Idaho. When Mary was twenty-seven, the article said, all three of them died in a fire. Mary would have been only twenty-five. But the detective said they often got ages wrong. The girl had had some sort of injury before the fire and she was not quite right, he said. He believed this was my sister, Mary. Mary Wilson."

"You didn't believe it?'

"I didn't know what to think. I tried to teach myself to believe it. I tried."

"Did thinking about . . . the flood recede then? Eventually? As a memory?"

"Well, I suppose so. I mean it was always there with me, like a shadow. But in my waking life I thought about it less as time went on. I'd get occasional dreams. Once I got my husband to take me on the path of the flood, the path of the water. A very sobering day out, let me tell you. And once after that, after he died, I drove myself up the mountain and I did the same trip again."

"What was that like?"

"Sad, of course. I wasn't out of control with emotion, but it sat heavily on me. I saw images not only of my own family perishing down below in the town itself but also of so many families on the steep hills being just . . . swept away. It made me thoughtful. You know, wanting to assign blame, realizing that blame is complicated. Lots of thoughts. I see you studying your notes . . ."

"Oh, sorry."

"Go ahead. You can ask anything."

"When did you lose your daughter?"

"Almost thirty years ago now. She died of cancer. It was terrible. It's always terrible. It was."

"You cared for her?"

"Yes, I did. Of course I loved her. And I stayed by her side. We had gotten past the time when she thought of me as a sinful and loose woman who had raised her with wild ideas. By that time, Lucy was dead, that was part of it, and maybe I was all she had, but she did warm to me again. I was there whenever her husband wasn't. She thought he should be there at the end to close her eyes when the time came and . . . get her into heaven. These things are funny. People. Ideas. My daughter and I weren't exactly a match. I don't like people who flog you with God. Do you need to explain that part of my life?"

"No. I think I can fudge it."

"Fudge again. You must be hungry."

Nina is thinking with delight of Ellen as a sinful and loose woman. How wonderful. But she is also thinking, Ben, Ben, ask more. What if the sister lived? Right? Just . . . what if?

"What was the detective's name?" she asks.

"Sklar. Henry Sklar. New York office. Oh, in case you are wondering, I tried to contact him later and he had gone out of business, and by the time I traced him, he was dead. I wanted to go over the paperwork myself."

"Of course," Nina says.

"How pretty you are," Ellen tells her. "Your mother was a beauty, too. No wonder."

Ruth comes into the room then and announces, "We're ready."

They go to the table where the roast beef looks to be everything the aromas promised.

"Please don't be upset," Ben warns, "if all this amounts to a paragraph or less. My articles tend to be cut heavily in the editorial process. I just want you to know that in advance. Oh, and it won't be in until next Monday. I'm writing about the mechanics of the dam this week. I'm actually still finishing it. I have my computer in my car. I'll be at it tonight."

"Those are long hours."

Work would keep Ben awake tonight, typing, proofing, while Nina went with her mother to midnight Mass.

It confuses Nina that, sitting at the table, marveling over Ellen, she pictures herself telling Douglas about the events of this day. How does that firefighter keep climbing into her daydreams?

Now Ben sits in the little living room in Johnstown, hoping Nancy likes him as much as he likes her. He figures she must have been a great mother. Nina has all the virtues. He's imagining Nina growing up in this simple house, this modest neighborhood, carrying her books to school, making friends, fretting over this or that—for he is sure she fretted. She bears the burden of being an only child, feeling she should be everything to her parents.

There are no pretensions in this house—matching couch and chair, all in a camel color. A rose-colored carpet that has seen some traffic, but stands proudly bearing its vacuum cleaner stripes. Family pictures only, no art, mostly Nina at different ages. He likes the toothy one when she was eleven or so. She sees him looking at it and says, "Yes, I had braces."

"Who didn't?"

"You?" Nancy asks.

"No, but everyone I know had them."

"Do you have brothers and sisters?"

"A brother. He lives in Pittsburgh. So I see him a good deal. I stayed with him for a while."

"I can't believe you brought your computer."

"Well, it's a way to get my article ready. I need to submit it tomorrow at the latest. So I'll work a little tonight. I understand your Easter Mass is long."

"Very long. We'll start at 10:30 and we probably won't get back here until 1:30 or 2:00 in the morning."

"Wow."

Nina adds, with a whimsical smile, "And we have to stand most of the time. It's one of the tougher religions."

Ben is glad there is no move to urge him to accompany them. He'd go crazy, mind zipping here and there with hours to reflect on all his worries, Amanda being the biggest one of them, living arrangements being second biggest, so it's a good thing he has sentences to marshal into shape.

"Would I be able to read what you're working on?" Nancy asks.

"If you want. It's about drainage pipes. The fact that they were needed and if they'd been there, there might not have been that flood. Pretty amazing to think about it that way. Tomorrow, if we can, we want to go up to the site where they have a new film running. Then—we got this idea from Mrs. Emerson—we want to drive the path of the flood."

"I was going to put the ham in about nine in the morning. Is that okay?"

"Oh, sure. I mean, say we start out at ten in the morning-ish. I think the ride would take about two hours. We would still have time for your big meal before I have to leave."

"Good, good."

"Would you like to come?"

"Oh, thank you but I'll be basting the ham and cutting potatoes for the potato salad. And don't worry about me. I like doing that."

"Well, we'd like to take you out to dinner tonight."

Nina groans and pretends to collapse on the sofa. But Nancy is smiling.

He hastens to say, "I know you have Mass tonight, but before that, if you'd consider it, we'd like to take you. Just some place you've been wanting to go. Name it."

Nancy laughs easily. "Well, there's a place up near Richland that does pasta. I was thinking of taking you two."

Nina sits up surprised at her mother's easy corruption, and then plays at collapsing again.

"No, no, my treat," Ben insists. "Come on, Nina. We'll want to eat again by tonight."

"She was always very dramatic," her mother confides.

"I thought you were fasting, Mum."

"Well, I've broken it so many times by now . . . and here you are, visiting."

They let him set up and work at the dining room table from five to seven and then they go out, Nina driving.

"What will the article be called?" Nancy Collins turns from the front seat where they insist she sit to the back seat.

"Oh, I don't know. My working title is "What Went Wrong." The headliners will change it to what fits and what they want. This one is about the architecture of the dam and the way the water behaved. It was hard to research. And I feel like a fraud. I'm not an architect. But I at least know how to get it to layman's terms—terms I can understand."

Nancy smiles, pleased with him.

WHILE THEY WAIT for a table at Rizzo's, which is packed, they study the photos on the wall of the founders of the place: the Rillos (one of

194

whom eventually married a Rizzo so there wasn't too much trauma in terms of name change). The photos then show the generations of Rizzos running the place. "When they say family-owned in Johnstown, they are serious," Ben quips.

Nina gives him an encouraging look. They find the stack of menus and snatch one to study in advance.

Ben says, "These prices are amazing."

Her mother chose an inexpensive place since he's paying.

"Small town," Nancy shrugs.

They are getting along! It's going to be okay, Nina thinks, putting an arm through his. "Ben? Remember I told you my mother was in the '77 flood and my grandmother was in the '36 flood? You can maybe ask my mum some questions."

Nancy, studying the menu, looks up. "Really?"

"No promise that he can use it—"

"I do want to hear. I'm getting the veal piccata."

Nina releases Ben and puts an arm around her mother and squeezes. "Do you see something you like?"

"Fettuccini Alfredo. At least no meat. So I can minimize the guilt about going to Mass."

"I'll do fettuccini Maria."

"Aha. You're getting your fresh vegetables," Ben comments.

When they are seated, Nina prompts her mother to begin. "Tell him about Grandmum."

"Sure," Ben says.

"Well. My mother was only sixteen in the '36 flood. She lived in Cambria City and she was home alone. Her mother and her two sisters cleaned houses for a living and her father was at work in the mill. Anyway, my mother sewed all the time and she was in the middle of making a dress. But some soldiers came to the door and said she had to leave. She wouldn't. She was making pea soup and she was sewing. One soldier turned off the stove and carried her out—that's what she always told us. She grabbed her sewing. They put her in the back of a truck; she was terrified."

Nina adds, "There was a lot of transport. Lots of people being taken up the hill. They took her to Brownstown. But here's the thing—"

She pauses. A waitress has plopped down menus again though they know what they want. Before they can say anything the waitress is gone.

Nancy looks relieved that Nina has taken over. "Here's the thing that always got to me. Waiting to find out if her family was alive. She told us it was awful being an orphan for fifteen hours, not sleeping at all."

"Tell the funny part," Nancy says, "about the dress she was making."

"It is funny. She was shivering and used it like a shawl. Pretty soon people admired it, and, well, she ended up in business afterward. It was sort of like advertising her skills on the spot to a captive audience."

"And did she find everyone?" Ben asks Nancy. He's not taking notes. Well, Nina knows all this, so it doesn't matter.

"Some trucks brought the rest of them up to Brownstown the next morning. She always told us how relieved she was and she cried every time she told it."

An apologetic waitress comes back to take their orders, which include Ben's request for a bottle of wine. They watch her run off, thinking perhaps she hasn't heard everything. But she's quick, no nonsense, bam-bam-bam, she's got it down. She practically runs from table to table, to the bar, to the kitchen, doing her thing, and pops back with a bottle of wine.

"Your grandma died when?" This is to Nina.

"Three years ago. Heart. Mum, tell the part about after the flood."

"Well. Her sewing machine was washed up onto a high cabinet and it was a heavy old thing so the cabinet was splitting, but the sewing machine was saved in the long run. She got it oiled and she used it again. And the soup—it was in a big pot with a handle—it ended up hanging on a curtain rod."

"And my great-grandfather who hated waste ate the soup!"

Ben laughs but still doesn't makes any notes. "A happy ending," he says. "Everybody survived."

They all lift their glasses of wine and toast.

Nina says, "Our flood, '77, my mother's and mine, was bigger, worse in most ways. More deaths and this time I was the frightened one." But she's told him all this before. The first time she was away from home. Two days of terrifying news on TV. No phone lines, no power. Her boyfriend Bobby, sixteen, on the same high school trip to Pitt with her, Bobby, always different, who'd taken a car to Pittsburgh when the other kids hadn't. How, against all National Guard warnings, he took matters into his own hands and drove the two of them back into town.

"I was alive for that flood," Ben reminds them. "I saw it on the news. It was really something. Crazy."

"Oh, it was," Nancy exclaims. "Cars being lifted up and moving on their own. Things rushing down the street in the water. Lawn chairs, even a little organ. When things calmed down my husband and I went out and started walking. Mud everywhere. And looters down in Coopersdale—I guess you heard about them. Army trucks along the road. We were officially a national disaster."

Ben is listening, passing the basket of bread that has arrived.

"The town was supposedly flood-proof," Nina reminds him. "I learned it in school. So did my mother."

"The Flood-Free City. The Friendly City. And the City of Beautiful Women," Nancy recites.

"It's still friendly," Nina says.

"And the women are beautiful," Ben says on cue.

Nina jabs him. "Of course you have to say that."

Nancy laughs, explaining, "It was a guy on WJAC radio who started it. It spread like wildfire. All the women kept quoting it."

Nina is pretty sure Ben isn't going to write this after all. It's just her life. Ah, well. Everyone thinks their own trauma is the most potent. Still the images are strong: Bobby, sixteen and precocious, with his little VW Bug that could hardly get up over the debris. And how kind he was, really, and how the soldiers took pity on them and let them in.

"Bobby is in Boston now," Nina's mother says. "Did you know? Starting a residency."

"Medical?" Nina asks, surprised.

"Yes."

"He did med school?"

"Yes. I talked to his mother one day at the Giant Eagle."

"Whoa, that's a turn."

"Engaged. Settling down, I guess."

"Good for him." One of those pinging, tiny losses. First love gone. Bobby, a great guy.

Ben pours more wine for all of them and lifts his glass. "To survival. You got back to town and your parents were all right."

All right in a sense. Her father had been looted, too. The register money was gone and anything else the looters could carry out. Stereo, two TVs, and, funny, like some reverse karma, somebody's sewing machine.

When Bobby got her to the house and her parents weren't there, he stayed with her, drove her to the hospital where she found her mother outdoors, pouring jugs of water from an army truck to take into the hospital. *Still alive.*

"The army truck," her mother says.

Their shorthand. Her mother hugs her again here at Rizzo's.

IN THE CAR on the way to church, Nancy says, "I like him. A lot. Are you . . . worried about the age difference?"

"No. We get along."

"And you like his children?"

"I don't really know them yet." She had pictured the children before she met them as little miniature Bens. But they look more like their mother. Hey, you can't order up children.

The Mass is interminable. Nina tries to achieve a holy state, but whether it's the beef for lunch and the pasta for dinner that corrupted her or her own faulty self, her mind wanders terribly imagining various future and past lives for herself. At one point it's Douglas who drives her into town during the '77 flood. He tells her he's going to volunteer at the firehouse one day, like his father does. Douglas, yes, somehow shape shifting in her mind with Bobby. She shakes her head and focuses. "Have mercy on us, oh, God, according to Thy great goodness, we pray Thee, hearken and have mercy," says the priest. Interesting, insisting that God hearken.

There are Easter eggs at the end of the service at 1:40 in the morning. They play the game of who cracks whose and her mother wins.

When they get home, Ben is up working still. Then comes the odd part, where she goes to her childhood bedroom with Ben. They are both very quiet and very tired. They just hold each other and sleep. It's as if they've lived a whole life and moved into old age together.

ON SUNDAY MORNING Nina and Ben zip up to the Park Service to watch the new film about the flood. It's very unsettling and meant to be so, like the buildup in a thriller. Water swelling. Water boiling. Cascading. It's awful, watching doom as entertainment.

Then she and Ben begin the drive from the top of the mountain in South Fork down through the little towns. Ben drives his old buggy while she dictates the directions given to him by the director of the flood museum. *Cataclysmic*, she thinks. That word keeps being the only right one. She and Ben imagine how John Hess ran his train a few yards ahead of the oncoming water with the whistle blowing to warn as many people as he could warn. One of the heroes. Risking his life. "Amazing that there are people like that," she says. "Like the boy who saved Ellen."

The drive takes them almost three hours. The water took only one, stopping at two or more points along the way and pushing a mountain of wreckage ahead of it.

The ham is spectacular. Ben eats well and then packs his computer and his care packages of ham and potato salad and he's off.

Nina and her mother sit on the sofa and watch TV for the rest of the day, Easter Sunday, April 25, 1989.

Sightseers on rooftops after flood of 1889. Courtesy of Johnstown Area Heritage Association.

8

Monday, May 1, 1989

Structural Faults Led to Great Flood
What Went Wrong

Pittsburgh Post-Gazette, THE JOHNSTOWN FLOOD SERIES

BY BEN BRAGDON

On May 31, 1889, a forty-foot wall of water and debris sped down the mountain from South Fork into the valley that is Johnstown. It hit the city just before 4:10 p.m. More than 2,200 people died and the town was almost completely unrecognizable.

George Swank, an editor of a local newspaper, wrote: "We think we know what struck us, and it was not the hand of Providence. Our misery is the work of man."

One problem was that the townspeople had heard warnings for several years that the dam was unreliable and might break. They became so used to those warnings that even on the day of the flood, those in the telegraph office measured the danger by the level of water in their own offices—only a few inches. If warnings had been heeded, some of the disaster might have been averted. But ordinary citizens fretting about water on their first floors were not the culprits Swank referred to. There were sixty-one members of the South Fork Fishing and Hunting Club to blame, sixteen of them wealthy industrialists with big names. Many were politically connected. Attorney Philander Knox would become attorney general to presidents McKinley and Roosevelt and also would be secretary of state to Taft. John Leishman would serve as a U.S. ambassador. Andrew Mellon would become secretary of the treasury under no less than three presidents: Harding, Coolidge, and Hoover.

The lake that was the centerpiece of the South Fork Fishing and Hunting Club had once been a canal feeder for the water-way systems of transport. When trains took over the same work of transporting goods and passengers, the canal feeder stood idle. Benjamin Ruff purchased the canal from a congressman who had purchased it from the state. Ruff saw the potential of the idle body of water and its dam. It looked to him like a perfect setting. He began to spin the idea of a resort lake and a club for exclusive members. He approached fifteen wealthy Pittsburghers and sold them shares.

The lake was only viable as a lake because the space that held the water had been dammed up. Work had begun in 1838 on this body of water, a canal feeder, more than forty years before the flood. The earthen dam was 850 feet in length and it was planned in such a way as to have adequate spillways. Engineers specified that it should be 62 feet high. It would take, they thought, a year to build. They were wrong. Because of delays having to do with both finances and illnesses, the whole project was not completed for fourteen years. The dam followed current practice for such structures and was deemed competently done. Specifications were made so that spillways were secure and that no water ever came over the top.

As a civic project the canal feeder was doomed. Progress got in the way. Railroads, the new means of industrial transport, took over and the canal basin stood idle.

The dam broke once before 1889. In 1862 heavy thunderstorms caused spillage and the cause was found to be a portion of faulty foundation. The blame went to local citizens who were believed to be stealing lead from the pipe joints. That early break in the dam caused little actual damage and perhaps inured inspectors for years afterward.

For years the lake, the former canal, had only a low level of water and in some places the lake bed was actually bared. When Congressman Reilly sold the lake to Benjamin Ruff, he took a loss on his own purchase price. Perhaps he aimed to recoup some of his loss by removing the old cast-iron discharge pipes and selling them. He is believed to have done so.

Ruff repaired the dam by blocking the stone culvert and using whatever he could find to make a wall: rocks, plants, boughs of trees, waste of all kinds, including manure. Heavy rains ruined these repairs twice—in 1879 and in 1881. However Ruff and his engineers persisted in their course of shoring up rather than dismantling. Only months later, there was enough water in the lake to make it possible to stock it with fish. A railway tank car brought a thousand black bass from Lake Erie.

It has been easy in retrospect to vilify these men, partly because of their great wealth and privilege. But they certainly didn't see themselves that way. As David McCullough writes in his exhaustive history of the flood, "They were men who put on few airs. They believed in the sanctity of private property and the protective tariff. They voted the straight Republican ticket and had only recently, in the fall of 1888, contributed heavily to reinstate a Republican, the aloof little Harrison, in the White House. They trooped off with their large families regularly Sunday mornings to one of the more fashionable of Pittsburgh's many Presbyterian churches. They saw themselves as God-fearing, steady, solid people, and, for all their new fortunes, most of them were."

From 1881 to 1889, rumors of a dam break spread through the city every time there were heavy rains. But local engineer John Fulton, sent up to examine the dam, pronounced it safe. And the townspeople got used to flooding. Altogether there were seven floods in that decade before the flood of 1889.

Perhaps the most prestigious person in Johnstown during these years was Daniel Morrell. An area of town is named for him. Morrell was head of the Cambria Iron Company, several banks, and the water and gas companies. He lived in the finest house in town on Main Street. His Cambria Iron Company was the top producer of iron in the nation. Morrell was enough of a visionary to see that the new process (Bessemer) of converting

iron to steel was the industry of the future. He financed explo-
ration of this technique and soon became the greatest steel producer in the country.

Morrell eventually became a member of the South Fork Fishing and Hunting Club, partly because he had been concerned
about the dam and wanted to keep an eye on things from the
inside. He'd sent his engineer, John Fulton, to inspect the dam,
and even though the members, particularly Ruff, took umbrage,
Morrell persisted. He even offered to contribute some money
toward repairs. Fulton's conclusion was that the dam needed
overhauling; it definitely needed to have the discharge pipes
that had been removed replaced. There were other engineering
problems only discovered later. One was that the dam sagged
in the center where it needed to be highest. But Ruff and the
club members decided not to pursue an overhaul, even with the
generous offer of money from Morrell.

Most warnings for years included the dangers of heavy rain-
storms on the topography of the area, known to be susceptible
to flooding. The rainstorm that hit the town on May 30 and May
31 of 1889 was extreme. Morrell was no longer around to chas-
tise the club members. He had died in 1885 after having slipped
into dementia. Ruff had also died two years before. Their disagreement was not carried on by current members.

It rained so hard that businesses were shut down and the
town was waist-high in water. A telegram arrived midday to
various telegraph offices warning that the dam was liable to
break. When the message arrived in Johnstown, the freight
agent Frank Deckert didn't read it. Others in his office treated
it as a humorous repetition of what they had been hearing for
years.

Up at the lake, water was rising and the dam was groaning.
Club member Elias J. Unger went out to inspect the dam and he
concluded things looked dire. He ordered workers to cut more
spillways and to try to clear the spillway that had been netted
to keep fish in. The screens that had been installed were meant
to keep the fish in the lake for club members (so those special
fish would not escape to streams that would take them to local

fishermen); those screens were clogged with debris. Unger's men, working in heavy rain, were not able to change much.

Unger then sent John Parke on horseback to make warnings to the people of South Fork that water was beginning to top the dam. Parke asked the telegraph girl in South Fork to use the telegraph to alert Johnstown. After that, for hours, some two dozen people traded messages back and forth, in person, on telegraph lines—all warnings that something might very well happen this time. There was no system in place. Communications were chaotic, with many of the telegraph lines downed by the heavy storm. It didn't help that some skeptics still thought the fuss was not worth it.

Clubmen up at the lake saw the water cut a channel and then begin to flow faster. They were helpless to do anything at that point. Suddenly the whole dam gave way and the lake became a monstrous body of water moving down the mountain. The break happened at 3:10 p.m. Then the water of the lake made its whole disastrous journey into the valley.

Most of the town was destroyed. Houses and businesses, once there, were gone. Over 2,200 lives were lost, including whole families. There were many orphaned children. And there were many single survivors of large families. The club members, most of whom were not in residence, never came back, though several were involved in the relief efforts and about half gave money.

It should be noted that two men, ordinary men, risked their lives during the disaster to warn others. One was the engineer John Parke who rode a horse over dangerously muddy terrain to the town of South Fork to warn residents earlier in the day. The other was John Hess, a railroad engineer who rode just ahead of the wall of water with his train whistle blowing for as long as he could manage—and that was only a few minutes—before he had to jump off the train. His train lasted only a few seconds longer before it too was swept up but its whistle was the crucial warning for the people of East Conemaugh. At the lowest point in the valley, the people of Johnstown had no miracle. The clogged screens, the lack of drainage pipes, the refusal to overhaul the dam, finally took its huge toll. And the Johnstown Flood was world news for months to come.

This article is the second in a series about the flood and the upcoming centennial. The next installment is about the survivors.

FROM HER MOTHER'S house on Monday morning at eleven, Nina dials the Bureau of Vital Statistics in Idaho. "My name is Nina Collins. I'm a staff reporter for the *Pittsburgh Post-Gazette.* I'm looking for information on a family named Wilson. During the years—"

The woman who answers sounds overworked and overwhelmed though it's only the start of her workday. "Whoever you are—"

Nina has already said who she is. And she hasn't had a chance to say much else.

"—there are a lot of Wilsons in Idaho."

"I understand that. What I wanted to ask is—"

"I need first names, birth dates, and addresses. Also there's an eighteen-month wait on searches."

"Get back to you later," Nina says. Dumb. She is. What does she think she can accomplish? But she can't seem to stop so she calls the Carnegie Library in Pittsburgh to ask what newspapers she can look at for in and around Boise, Idaho, in 1910. That Pittsburgh librarian refers her to the University of Idaho where another librarian, the fifth one she talks to by that point, says there weren't any big papers beyond the *Idaho Statesman,* but there were a few miscellaneous publications before 1912, before the Caldwell papers took over. Nina's mother pours her a cup of coffee and listens to Nina's end of the phone calls. She has an insanely proud motherly look on her face as Nina explains to the Idaho librarian that she is looking for a corroboration of a house fire that killed a family of three, name of Wilson—a long shot, she knows, that she can find anything to offer Ellen.

"Fires got reported," the librarian says. "Fires were news and there were plenty of them. But I don't have the time to go through it all, I don't see how I can manage it. I'll call you back if I get a chance to check the *Statesman* for you."

Idaho. Why did the only clue that might possibly bring closure to Ellen Emerson have to be so far away?

"I'm jealous," her mother said, sliding into a chair across from her.

"Of what?"

"Mrs. Emerson. She has a hold on you."

"Oh, Mum. It's just work. Come on, you know I adore you. But now you have me worried. I was going to suggest we visit Ellen today. I don't want to upset you. She's asked to see you and she's nice, really."

"Oh, I know she's nice. I guess I'm just needy. Forget I ever used the word *jealous*. I ought to be ashamed of myself."

"No shame, no blame." Nina did her best to just sit and drink coffee and marvel at the day off they both had. Finally when her mother went to the bathroom, she dialed Ellen Emerson who said, "Of course, of course, please do come over."

"But not for a meal! We can't come until after lunch. And my mother insists we bring a care package of ham and potato salad and a few slices of her latest cake. It's a chocolate cake. But she wants it to be for you, not to feed us."

"We'll have an old-fashioned tea then. I have cookies."

"Well, if you insist."

Before they go to visit Ellen, Nina and her mother walk up to Koch's drugstore where they hope they will find a copy of the *Post-Gazette* and will be able to read Ben's story. They find yesterday's *Press* is still there, but the *Post-Gazette* isn't stocked any more. The drugstore is small, the last of its kind; most of its goods are dusty. The place won't last much longer, not with the chains moving in.

When they get back to the house, Nina sees the blinking light on the answer machine. The message is, to her astonishment, a call from the woman in Idaho, saying she has tracked down the story. Nina hurries to return the call.

"I found it. Believe it or not. Mother and father and daughter were killed in a house fire. Wilson."

"On a farm?"

"*Statesman* doesn't say exactly. Almost everybody was farming something or other."

"No details about the people?"

"No."

"Photographs?"

"No photographs. The house was totally razed, maybe that's why."

"Ages?"

"No, nothing, not in the article I found. I could keep after some of the single sheet papers. But probably not till next month."

"Right. Let me think. Could you show someone where to look then if I can . . . if I can find someone out there to help me?" She might be able to locate a journalism student to be her surrogate investigator. It will probably take a hundred phone calls.

"Sure. Oh, hell, let me try first. I'm probably going to get in some sort of trouble, but I'm getting used to that. I'm supposed to be culling books we're getting rid of."

"I thank you. You can't believe how appreciative I am."

Nina planned to leave her mother's place later today, but now they have the afternoon visit to Ellen and also, seeing her mother's face, seeing how happy she is, Nina decides to leave at six in the morning tomorrow instead. Barring a storm or an accident on Route 22, that will get her to Pittsburgh in plenty of time to change clothes and get herself downtown to work.

Ah, finally, Ben's article. Nina reads it at Ellen's place while Ellen fusses over her mother, showing her the yearbooks she still has. "I would see you walking 'the halls with your boyfriend back then," Ellen says. "You were one of the happy people. Nancy Pastorek. I remember you well. In high school some kids are clearly miserable. But you . . . you were in love."

"I was."

"And it lasted?"

"Yes. We got married. We stayed together. But he died young."

"I know. I remember reading it."

"You keep track of people."

"Not on purpose. It sort of comes naturally. One of my skills. If you can call it that."

Nina puts down the newspaper.

"He did a good job, didn't he, your Ben?" Ellen says.

"Yes."

Nancy says, apologetically, "We tried to get the paper this morning but our store didn't have it."

"Ruth went downtown for it. Ben said he would send it, but I hate to wait."

Ruth comes into the room. "I'm not good at waiting either. I'll be standing at the door to the Rite Aid waiting next week when the piece about Mrs. E. is in. I'll want more than one copy of that one. He might quote me."

"Oh-oh," Ellen teases. "What did you say?"

"I said you were a lot of trouble, very demanding and difficult."

"Oh, dear."

"No. I said you were a great teacher. You got me reading. And you showed me a life outside my own. And now we're friends. Stuff like that. And I said you noticed people. Paid attention."

"Well, you could have told them what a pain I am sometimes," Ellen says. She smiled conspiratorially. "The photo I gave Ben was from fifteen years ago, so I'll look younger than I am! He called this morning to say they had okayed the photo but would send a photographer for a new photo if I wanted. I told him I didn't think I'd need to bother them with that."

The tea Ruth serves makes Nina think of those good old "olden times" when there was afternoon leisure. Conversation, kindness, a pot of tea, and a plate of English-style biscuits with chocolate icing—what else could a leisured woman wish for? Ah, yes, the answer: employment, purpose.

"It's been a good visit? Your weekend visit together?" Ellen asks the Collins women as they sip at tea.

"Wonderful," Nancy answers. "Very full."

Nina adds quietly, "We did the ride along the flood path yesterday, just Ben and I, the one you talked about, and it was long, and it was sobering, just as you said. Before that—I don't know if you'd want to see this—before we took the drive, we watched a film up at the site. It's hard to watch, actually, to feel trouble coming like that and nobody knowing what to do."

"I think, mostly, nobody wanted to be foolish," Ellen says quietly.

After a pause, Nina tries, "I've been wondering, who did Henry Sklar actually talk to when he found the witness who said the Wilsons moved to Idaho? Neighbors, pastors?"

"He didn't say. I wanted to follow up years later when . . . when I ended up back in town, but many phone calls later I had to accept the fact that Sklar was gone and there were no records to be had."

"Why no records?"

"When he retired, he destroyed them, so I'm told."

"Did Arthur Greaves have a report?"

"More like a letter. After he died, I hated to bother his widow for it. I went to Ferndale once, to look at where the Wilsons must have lived, to imagine a life there. I tried to imagine Mary there. The letter said something about Mary Wilson being slightly retarded. I know that's not a word they use anymore, but it certainly didn't describe my sister. She was quiet, but she was sharp."

An injury in the flood?

A shrug, a sigh, the end of the tea, embraces all around, Ellen's embrace much stronger than Nina would have expected. And then they leave.

TO NINA'S SURPRISE, the librarian, an overachiever after her own heart, calls back late in the afternoon. "Yes, Ms. Collins, I found one other story on the fire. The man was a former railroad engineer. He'd moved from Kansas City where he worked for the railroad there and then he worked for the railroad in Boise."

Not a farmer after all. "Kansas City? When?"

"Says 1901. Before that he came from Pennsylvania."

"Where in Pennsylvania?"

"Doesn't say in the articles."

"The wife, the daughter?"

"Nothing on them."

"Nothing at all?"

"Nothing."

"Thank you."

It is just before five. She thinks for a moment and calls the flood kiosk at the flood site and asks for the fellow with red muttonchops. "What was the furthest point the flood waters went? I mean . . . where did the flood end up?"

"Oh, near southern Indiana County. The town of Ninevah, in Westmoreland County. Now it's called Seward."

Not Ferndale.

So perhaps *not* the Wilsons. It's possible that mysterious adoptions happened more than once. "What was Ninevah like?"

"Just a small town. Farms around it, of course."

"Farms. Hmm. So does that mean space between neighbors?"

"Like let me look . . . I'm looking at some records we have here. Let's see, some debris washed up in Seward—*Ninevah*. Yes. I got that right. Great name, isn't it? And around there was East Wheatfield Township. Indiana County. If I have my facts right. *Wheat field.* I doubt they grew wheat there but it was a farming area. Did I answer your question?"

"Yes, thank you."

ELLEN CAN TELL that Nancy Pastorek is worried about her daughter. Daughters marry whom they marry and mothers don't get a vote. Ellen couldn't do anything to stop her own daughter—who was by then defining herself as *Lucy's daughter* when she met her minister-husband. It all happened in a rush. Before Ellen knew it, Rosemary had married Stephen Driscoll, a man who had the blazing eyes and the high forehead of those whose mission it is to spread the word of salvation. Oh, Stephen was a well-meaning, if high-foreheaded, man, but he was bound and gagged with scripture. From the beginning, he made Ellen uncomfortable. The relationship started after one weekend when Lucy came to visit and decided it was time to tell Rosemary the truth about her parentage. First Lucy and Rosemary had taken a long walk and both had come home weeping. Rosemary was twenty-five at the time, the world was at war, and Rosemary had not attended college as Ellen had hoped she would. She simply wasn't interested. She was only working outside the house at a secretarial job because Ellen and Bill valued work so much.

"You should have told me," Rosemary charged when they came back from their walk.

Ellen looked to Lucy who said nothing to help her out. "I was abiding by Lucy's wishes."

"All this time. You let me go on, not knowing."

"We were all doing our best."

"And it makes so much sense."

"What does?"

"That I'm more like my real mother than I am like you."

Oh, that hurt. It was true, though. The old Lucy was gone, no longer spirited at all. That had happened to Julia, too, both of them after a brief bout of youthful exuberance ending up like Hester, militarized with goodness, duty, rules.

Lucy sat down in Ellen's living room, her whole manner slowed down and careful. She appeared older than Ellen at this point and she was, as they had often noted, sixteen years younger. "Rosemary wants to come stay with me for a while."

Ellen felt the words stab. It turned out Lucy didn't intend to tell people the truth or anything so drastic. But Rosemary would be "visiting" Lucy—lengthy cross-town visits being much more the thing in those days than later when transportation was so much easier. At the end of that weekend of truth telling, Rosemary packed a suitcase and accompanied the woman she now privately called her mother out of the house. Before they went to Lucy's, they made a stop at an unfamiliar church, a Methodist church downtown, where they met the new minister. Driscoll. Of the blazing eyes. Rosemary talked to him after the service. It was love at first fiery glance for both of them. A week later, Rosemary came back to live with Ellen and Bill, the parents who had raised her, but there was a clear shift in her relationship with them. Ellen and Bill digested all the downward glances, the vocal hesitations, pursed lips, flinches when touched, and they felt horrible.

At dinner, Rosemary said, "I told only one person about my situation. I told Stephen. I didn't want any sort of secret in our marriage."

"Marriage! Already?"

Rosemary said yes, she wanted to be married very soon. The next day Driscoll came to visit. He frowned and looked at his bony knees as if deep in thought. He ate supper with them, concentrating on cutting his chicken precisely. Then he went home.

"Why is he so uncomfortable with us?"

"He's working things out in his mind."

Thank God for Bill who was smiling, trying not to laugh.

"Don't worry. He's hard on my real mother, too. He thinks people have to pay for things. 'No free lunch' is his favorite saying."

Ellen said, "Don't take Driscoll so to heart." She added, "Many people would understand. Your mother did nothing wrong."

"She thinks she did."

"She should forgive herself."

The biggest problem with Driscoll was that he was not intelligent; as a thinker he could not include contradictions. He was a stuck man, depending on something outside himself always to get him through any situation. He looked like a man, acted like a man, but he was emotionally a child.

Ellen waited to hear Rosemary say, "But I love you of course. You have been a wonderful mother." Rosemary couldn't say it, not then anyway, because all along she had thought her adopted mother too . . . *modern*, too accepting of error, in need of some straight and narrow. Six months later Rosemary was married and out of the house.

And then for some reason—not from lack of punctuality or pilfering from the cash box or anything like that—Stephen was transferred to a different church, this one in Loretto. Soon Rosemary and Stephen had a son who was one year old and Stephen Driscoll—who could count marriage, the ministry, bad bony knees, and a child—did not have to go to war when so many in the country did.

Ellen watched the rosters of boys' names in the paper, boys she had taught in school. She mourned them, sometimes getting images of them that caught her off guard for weeks. She continued to care for Rosemary, taking her food, gifts for the child, doing what favors she could, being a grandmother. But if you had asked her—and only Bill did—Rosemary was not the daughter she would have chosen. She and Rosemary were one of those parent-child mismatches, the mother in this case being the wilder spirit.

She got only three more years with Bill. She watched him age, watched his heart weaken.

"I'm sorry I can't seem to do the long haul with you," he said.

"Don't talk that way."

"I can feel it. It runs in my family. Early exits. I've far outlasted all of them. I hope you'll meet someone good. You'll hear my cheer if you meet someone good."

"I don't want that."

After Bill died—this was in 1948—and after a suitable time had gone by, people kept trying to match Ellen to available men. But nobody appealed to her.

And retirement didn't appeal, either. She was sixty-three when she was widowed and she didn't want to give up work. She became sixty-five and then seventy. Oddly, the school officials didn't boot her out. She realized only later that she was listed incorrectly by her graduation date instead of her birth date and even though she'd been written up as a flood survivor, bureaucracy being what it is, nobody did the math; so she kept teaching. It was amazing and lucky for her that sometimes red tape got so tangled.

Thank heaven for students.

And thank heaven for books. At the library they ordered books specially for her. They let her say what she wanted to read and she galloped through some nine books in between the ones her reading club read each month. She knew all of Steinbeck and Hemingway and Faulkner and Welty as well as the new books—*The Diary of a Young Girl*, *Under the Volcano*, and *A Streetcar Named Desire*, a play. Eventually she would know *Peyton Place* and other popular books as they arrived and caused sensations.

She welcomed the school year always, when it was possible to drown in work, to be selfless with regard to others, to be around young people with all their promise. To this day she loves the smell of September— apples, the chill on the breeze. If she closes her eyes and concentrates she can smell those old school smells of disinfectant and chalk dust. That remembered smell, even after all these years, gives her butterflies.

Rosemary, long gone, and her blazing-eyed husband, also long gone, and their son, gone. Having survived every trap and disease over in Vietnam, her grandson came home to drugs and so the enemy got him anyway. Enemy. Strange thought.

"Who are these people?" Nina had asked on Saturday as they sat looking at Ellen's books. Nina of the beautiful mother, the mother with a love match, and Nina who wants to be a writer and is afraid to keep trying.

"My grandson."

"Not alive?"

"No. Drugs."

"How sad. How sad for you."

Nina is her spiritual great-granddaughter. "Come back with your mother some day," Ellen had said.

"Really? She would be so excited!"

"Yes. We'll look at her class yearbook and she can catch me up on everyone."

And they came. Nina brought her. Lovely. It was lovely.

"GOD, I MISSED YOU," Ben says.

She and Ben are hurriedly brushing their teeth, she's got a fresh outfit on the bed, waiting. She says through toothpaste foam that she read yesterday's paper and liked what he did.

He says through toothpaste foam that he's getting the Ellen article ready for next week. Detroit has confirmed Paul Fulton. The article's theme will be survivors. All sorts.

"Did you ask about doing the other floods, too?"

"Didn't. I think that's pushing it."

"Oh. Well. My mother's fifteen minutes of fame, I thought." She sighs and begins changing clothes. "What did you do last night?"

"Went to see the boys."

"Good. Where did you go?"

"Nowhere. I sat with them at the house. For a while."

When she has her clothes on, she says, "Ben? Is there any coffee?"

"Yeah. I made a pot."

"Let's sit."

"We don't have time."

"I know. Let's sit anyway."

"What was it like, at the house last night? You and Amanda?"

"No, no, no, don't try to make—"

"I'm not trying to make anything. I need to know. Was she friendly? Did you feel any warmth toward her? I deserve to know."

"Yes and yes, a little. I can't believe we're doing this now. We need to—"

"We can talk more tonight."

"That would be better."

"I'm just acknowledging what's happening. We're not moving forward as we were—"

"I live here. I went to meet your mother."

Nina sat there and let his phrasing settle over her. "We're too crowded here."

"I know that. I'll go look at a place tonight. May 1 is the big turnover date for apartments. I can find us something—"

"Ben. Ben? I'm not ready to move. I need time. I wouldn't mind at all if you moved and had a place. But . . . if you want to know the truth, I think you maybe ought to try the sofa in your house. You'd be seeing your sons, Amanda would have a fair chance, you'd know what you felt. Well, sort of. Feelings are tricky buggers."

"Are you kicking me out?"

"No. I'm saying we don't know. We want to feel secure and know we're okay for sure, but we don't know. Ben? We've practically stopped making love. That means something."

"We make love."

"Not for a while."

"We'll get back to it."

She laughs in spite of herself. She feels so sad, so sad, why has she begun all this now?

"Is this about that firefighter friend you made?"

She pauses, breathes in a big lungful of air, drinks coffee. "I honestly don't know. I only know we're not quite comfortable with each other any more, you and me."

"Did your mother say something against me?"

"Are you kidding? She knows a charmer when she meets one. She liked you."

"Nina, don't do this."

What is she doing? She isn't sure. Is she sending him back to his wife, like she's in some 1920s movie, paying for the sin of desire? Or is she just figuring things out?

As if both of them are obeying a train whistle or a class bell, they put their cups in the sink and start for her car. Nina taps on Michelle's door, but Michelle is already gone.

She's driving today. They take turns now, share a car and the parking cost. He touches her shoulder. "You must be tired. You started so early."

"A little. You're working on the Ellen piece today?"

"Mostly."

"Sure you can't add the other floods?"

He's shaking his head. "It doesn't come naturally. I don't want to get typed."

"As what?"

"Feature only. That's more your bailiwick. I want the political investigations eventually. That's what I want."

"Oh, for another Watergate."

"There's always a Watergate something."

"I thought you *wanted* the flood assignments."

"Don't get me wrong. It's been fun. I love Ellen. She makes a great story."

Nina shrugs. Little pieces of her life are breaking off. How strange today is, a gorgeous spring day, no rain, people walking with a bounce, and she started a mess this morning. What kind of a nut is she?

Penn Traffic Company delivery cart, circa 1910. Courtesy of Johnstown Area Heritage Association.

Ellen
August 26, 1950

■ THE BUICK had stalled once, then caught. She thought, "Well, what else to do on a Saturday?" Before she had gone far, she pulled over at a bakery first for a raisin cookie, one of her favorite things, a little like a Fig Newton but full of raisins instead and a good fifteen times the size. On the street strangers greeted her with a hello. Inside the bakery, the clerk knew her by name because she'd gone to the high school. This was the thing, the small town thing, that she had come to value. Friendliness caught on and spread like a cold. The legacy of worker poverty was probably partly responsible. Parents and grandparents of immigrants had once packed many people into tiny homes with tiny bedrooms where they must have felt every breath, every heartbeat of the others. And the closeness stuck. That was her theory.

Ellen had determined to teach a segment on the floods in her classroom this coming year. It didn't immediately fit into a high school English class, but these kids needed to know about it. She would make them write something or other, an imagined tale of a survivor. Hopefully she would get them interested enough to ask why the dam failed and she'd tell them objectively that there had been warnings. Because wasn't there a lesson in the idea of ignoring warning? Believing all would be well simply because you wanted it to be?

Next, brushing off those cookie crumbs, she drove downtown and managed to park at the end of Main Street. There she looked at the foot of the hill that rose up to be the Westmont section. This is where the water had hit and begun the backlash, the back-flood. This is where the mattress her sister rode must have changed direction. Was it here? And then . . . where did it go? Everyone's answer was the stone bridge where acres of debris piled up and burned for days. Because nothing was found, ever. She should have made the boy save her sister first. Bill told her it was normal to let herself be rescued, but she was the stronger one physically. She would have held on.

Bill had studied the maps when she asked to see the old dam site, the place it all started. And then they made their way down into the valley, the fourteen miles it took for the wall of water to get to town. The water met various points of resistance, but it kept descending, getting larger all the while. Bill made a rolling motion with his hands. "The bottom water was digging at the river beds or the surrounding earth, getting friction from the mud, the top water cascaded over the bottom water until it rolled. It was like a waterfall circling back on itself and becoming a big ball, then bigger and bigger." Yes, that made sense; even in drawings there was a rolling motion to the water.

A woman passing with her little daughter called out to Ellen as they walked past her. "Beautiful day to be out." The woman turned back and smiled, then continued to walk briskly, holding her daughter's hand, both carrying bags from various stores, perhaps school clothes, yes, that smell was in the air. It made people want to buy new shoes, new dresses and shirts and pants.

Ellen was normally a dry-eyed, logical person, but something happened, she got dizzy and couldn't do the trip that Saturday. Soon she was taking herself home instead. Tomorrow, tomorrow, she would drive up the hill to where the flood started and once more wind her way down from Lake Road.

And she did. The next day she made it to the top where a coal town had sprung up after the flood. Now there were smaller, unostentatious houses for working people in the vicinity—the houses wouldn't have been here then.

She started her drive down the hill, formulating what she wanted to tell her students. She passed Mineral Point where the telegraph operator had relayed frantic messages. Mineral Point had been interesting—like something out of George Bernard Shaw, a perfect community for workers—where Morrell who owned the Cambria Iron Company set up a furniture making enterprise to turn out furniture to be sold in the company store to fill the homes of the workers. Talk about thinking of everything, talk about playing God, wanting to make the world just right. Morrell was a Quaker, and highly moral, known for his benevolent treatment of the working man. He'd set up a first hospital, that kind of thing. Practical, too, he must have been. For him, economy *was* morality. No. Reverse that. *Shaw* was like something out of *Morrell*.

No car was behind her, which was to the good, because she hit the brakes several times to look at the point where the North Fork met the South Fork to become the Conemaugh; and then she sped up. She was the water, relentless.

Could she get a school bus to bring the high schoolers along this route? Would they know how to look past the ordinary contemporary houses and the barren patches of land to imagine what once was? (It turned out the school wouldn't approve the money for the bus.)

She passed through East Conemaugh. Nothing wrong with this place now, it seemed. It had been reborn. A handful of businesses could tell anyone who was looking that Eastern Europe had settled some of its best here. There was a residence hotel, then Slovenian Savings and Loan. The Franklin Works to the right. A couple of teenage girls walked down the street, talking, gesticulating broadly. Do they know what happened right here? Ellen thought. But, of course, they were on to more interesting things: fashion, boys.

She kept going. The bridge. Woodvale. Poor Woodvale had been the Cambria Iron Company's model town—another perfection engineered by Morrell. There were 255 frame houses, a beautiful Maple Avenue, with trees; that area suffered the highest per capita loss of the flood's *many* targets. Woodvale Heights survived, but Woodvale itself—and Franklin—had been virtually wiped out. We never know what's going to come to us. Get used to surprise. That's what life is. Plan to be surprised and you'll be surprised anyway.

The German area of town still boasted the St. Joseph German Catholic Church. One end had been pushed in, but the place was rebuilt now, so the German pocket was thriving.

She's already told her students, "This valley *is* the melting pot. This is America, right here."

She began to come down into the city eventually to the large expanse of space where the flood had split into three large raging rivers and where she had been rescued. Somewhere in the chaos of that moment she lost her sister. People said there was a pile of junk on the mattress and that she was simply a crazed child. But where exactly did the mattress *go?* she'd asked at least a thousand times right after the flood. Where is it? One person on the street told her maybe Franklin Street. But everyone else's opinion was that it turned in the current and went to the Stone Bridge and the conflagration. Sklar said the answer was Ferndale and a Mary Wilson who had died out west. Ellen had marshaled all her will to believe it.

In town, Ellen went to the end of Main Street where the house still stood that had become Clara Barton's headquarters. She turned a corner and got herself to the main part of Main Street, past Glosser Brothers and the park and across from the park the Alma House where 264 lucky souls had crowded together on a top floor to spend the night of the flood—and lived. Luck. Then she moved up Washington Street, past Gautier Works, past Penn Traffic Department Store where she bought all her clothing and cosmetics, and to the Point where the Stone Bridge with its multiple arches stood and where the huge conflagration had been. Everything was calm now. A few leaves on the trees had begun to turn early. The sun shone mildly on the place where young and old had perished terribly in the middle of the night. She heard her child's voice calling, "Somebody, please get my sister." She'd cried it for hours. "No one there," she was told. "Just debris."

Finally Ellen went home.

Her daughter, Rosemary, was sitting in a car outside her house.

"I didn't know you were coming by today," Ellen said.

"Things were rough at home."

"Rough? How? Get out of the car. Come in."

"Oh, not physically. We had an argument though."

Ellen unlocked her door and waited for more.

"It's about money, sort of. Stephen is talking about quitting the ministry, getting a job in something else—he's really not suited to anything else." It was true, he wasn't. "I told him no. We're going to have some medical bills. That's the problem. I got bad news. I have a breast lump and it's bad. I don't know how long I have. I want to see David get to college and through college. That's what I want."

The news was all backward. The money was nothing. The disease was everything.

Surprise. There you had it again. You never could know. You couldn't guess what was coming. Ellen dropped everything to hug Rosemary close to her. "We'll fight it. Tell me what to do."

"I went to a doctor in Pittsburgh. He wants to send me to someone he knows in New York, a doctor who is trying something new. I don't want to go, but Stephen wants me to go, and I guess if I want to see David grow u— . . . I guess I should. I'd rather have the money for him."

"I'll take care of his bills."

"I'm sorry. I'm sorry for the things I said. I got mixed up about . . . whatever life you led before you adopted me."

Ellen simply shook her head.

"My real mother, you know, compared you to Ingrid Bergman."

Ha! She doubted she had the passion or guts of Bergman, but she did manage to have sex without marriage, that was about the size of the comparison. "Of course I'll take care of you, whatever you need."

"Thank you."

"You should go to New York. I'll pay for it. I'll go with you."

So a sort of rapprochement was the result of the cancer diagnosis. To be honest, Rosemary was weakened in every way. She didn't have much fight in her and that included whatever energy she used to be judgmental and bitter. Two years later Rosemary was gone.

They kept dying. Her sister gone, Susan the replacement sister gone, daughter gone, cousin before that. And Ellen kept living. She got used to it, living.

Cigar factory girl. Courtesy of Johnstown Area Heritage Association

CHAPTER

10

Tuesday, May 2–
Friday, May 5, 1989

■ "Who was your visitor?" Patricia Hays asks. She's folding up the walker to put beside Anna's bed. "You did really well today!" Yes, Hays is the one who is so curious about where Anna lived.

"A woman I knew for a long time. She was the child of one of my son's friends. I knew her when she was a little girl."

"Glad to see you had a visitor. Your son comes around?"

"He was killed in the war."

"Which war?"

These young people! "It was World War Two."

"Oh. That's a long time ago."

"Yes. I didn't have him for long, but I can see him still. He was a very wonderful young man."

"And you lived in the Hill with him?"

Anna puts the poor girl out of her misery. "Yes, we did. My first husband died in World War One—that was 1918. Then I raised my son for a while. Then I met my second husband and he was—" she still has to revise mentally, from Negro to black to African American. "He was African American."

"So then you moved to the Hill?"

"That's right. There were people who didn't much like the idea of us

225

in other parts of the city. We made them nervous. I had a good home in the Hill. I was happy there."

"Cool. And you must have made good friends because you had a visitor."

"I did have good friends there. My son's good friend had a mother who was my good friend. The woman who came to see me was her grandchild."

"And does that mean your friend is gone now?"

"A long time ago. Everybody is."

"Hmmm. That would be real hard. Do you want yesterday's newspaper? You never even opened it."

"Put it aside. Not much in the mood for it."

"What would you like to do?"

"Nap. I guess it's the big preparation. You know."

"Oh, heck, don't talk like that."

Anna is settled in bed, so the girl leaves. Even here, even now, she is sure her life would get some censure from certain of the residents. Yes, things are much better for African Americans today, but they are not yet okay. And mixed marriages—some people still don't like them. Miscegenation. What a word.

Naps are usually easy for Anna—fifteen minutes, an hour sometimes, and she wakes refreshed. But this time she doesn't go under. Perhaps there's too much sun sneaking under the blind, too much noise in the hallway.

Once more she wishes for a disaster—the nursing home washed away or bombed and her needed to tend to the wounded. Finally, she'd be at work again, making decisions! Then they would see what she's worth. Then they would know that her body might tire more easily, but that she is a miracle in an emergency, knowing just how to care for people, how to provide comfort.

Raising herself up, she puts on her bedside lamp, and takes up yesterday's newspaper. On the front page is a story of a black boy killed in gang crossfire. In the Hill. Oh, it wasn't like this early on. Except for the riots in the '60s and '70s, there were plenty of calm times, good times. She even had a social life then, friends, jazz clubs, the most wonderful music ever, right there. Will was so hurt by these things in the news.

"Stupid, crazy boys. How will we ever turn things around," he would say. "Do everything right and still . . ." But he didn't live long enough to see the gangs, the worst of it. Will Hoffman gave her her third name and the best part of her life. Anna Burkhardt had become Anna Raymond, then Anna Hoffman. The third part was definitely the best. Well, there was a fourth part, supposedly not so nice, at the beginning, but she doesn't know who she was then, Anna something or other.

She turns the pages, takes up a new section. Sports. She got interested because Will loved a good game. They used to listen on the radio, oh, long ago. The baseball season is in swing. Sometimes she watches. How he would have cried when Clemente died! She did.

She picks up another section. There's an article on the front page about the flood that once was, down the highway in Johnstown. A terrible, terrible thing. She can't bear to read about it. Anger fills her when she tries to read about the people who let it happen. Her heart begins pounding and she has to put the paper aside.

ON TUESDAY EVENING, Ben said, "I have to go to an evening session with Amanda on Friday. I'm sorry. This is where it gets dicey, but you shouldn't think I'm leaving you. They really make you spend time together. Believe me, I don't want it."

"It's okay. You should go. You should know."

"It's not okay."

"Is it an overnight?"

"No. It's like a mini-retreat. We have to go to the lodge in some country club—South Hills. There are other couples. It's like I think from seven to eleven. I expect I'll get back at midnight."

"It's okay; do it."

"Are you breaking up with me?"

"No, but I want you to live somewhere else. This place, right, we're driving each other crazy? And also you won't really know about Amanda unless you spend time with her. Dinner, that kind of thing, not just therapy."

"I can't believe what I'm hearing."

"I think we both need to know what we're doing. Not rush."

"I'm going out for a walk," he muttered angrily.

By the time Ben gets back, it's late. Nina is awake. She hears him undress and bed down on the sofa. She could go get him but instead she lies there and cries it out, tears in her ears, the whole business.

On Wednesday they drive in together, mostly silent. Her heart hurts, everything does, it's like having the flu.

She watches him across the room as he settles in. Sometimes she looks up and he's watching her.

After a while, she taps on Hal's door.

"What?"

"People like the flood series."

"Right. Oh, yes, thanks for pushing it. Points for you there."

"What if I did a sort of sidepiece, about the '36 flood and the '77 flood?"

"Why?"

"Well, it's interesting. Tough little town. Survivors. All that. My family experienced those floods."

"Oh, a personal piece—maybe a little essay, a column? When you have something, we can run it by Stu, see if he wants it."

So. Hal didn't say an outright no. All the while waiting for an assignment—another shooting, another fire—she messes around with a few paragraphs and stops. It's not coming. She's too nervous. She's trying so hard for *size* (not a "poor me, poor us" sort of article) that she's paralyzing herself. It's that pot of soup on the curtain rod that interests her. It's her mother hauling water into the hospital.

She leans over her desk to eat a quick lunch when noon comes around. And damn if somewhere in her care-package ham sandwich there isn't the seed of another idea—a phone call she's been wanting to make. She looks about. Ben seems to be seriously occupied, which is good because she doesn't want him to hear her on the phone. Last week he started coming up to her desk now that they're a known item. Only they might not be an item much longer. She calls a number, another, and another until she get a quick moment with a researcher at Pitt who is rushing off to a luncheon but promises to call her back after four. Well, she's started something. Hopefully she can be here at four.

After lunch she gets an assignment. But it's easy, about fundraising at the various colleges and she is able to get the information she needs by phone. She writes paragraphs as the information comes in. Finally it's four, then a minute after. And wouldn't you know it, Ben comes up to her, puts a hand on her shoulder, as if they haven't been at odds, as if everything is all right.

"Are you sprung early today?" he asks.

"Not really."

"What's up?"

"Some drudgery. I'm sorry to hold you up." She makes a gesture as if sending a small boy out of the room.

"You're telling me to entertain myself?"

"Uh huh."

Boys—they aren't too good at being hurt. His face kills her. He walks away.

What if the professor at Pitt never calls back?

She is typing suppositions, all she knows to do at this point. *In 1889 most adoptions were not legal matters and often there were no records.* Is this true? She needs to do the research. Like a tabloid writer, she pushes forward, in spite of not having facts (she heard such a writer interviewed once and the woman said, "Oh, I just make up studies and quotes.") *People with high social standings and financial means were more able, if not more likely, to employ attorneys in order to make adoption formal. Many fictional accounts show us childless women who adopt the children of servants. Children born out of wedlock did not always end up in orphanages. Even then, there were adoptions of convenience. In many cases, perhaps, the adopted child never knew the truth. An easy foray into imagination gives us scenarios like the devoted servant who seemed more like a mother than the mother.*

The phone rings. Finally.

"Hi. It's . . . Doug."

She recognized his voice on "Hi." Her face flushes.

"I said I would leave you alone. I don't want to be a shit. But I'm finding myself thinking about you and wondering if things are the same with you."

"Yes, sort of. Well, not completely."

He hesitates.

"I mean yes, but complicated."

"Well, then. Would you ever consider just getting together as friends? A movie? A burger? Some talk?"

"No kissing?" She laughs awkwardly. What a complete idiot she is.

"Right. No kissing. If those are the rules."

So it's up to her. "A movie, hmmm. When?"

"Would Friday be possible?"

"It's funny but that's sort of just about the best time for me to do it."

"Atria's for the burger? Say, seven?"

"Okay. Meet you there. Could you give me your phone number again, just in case I need to—"

He gives her his phone number, which she jots on a scrap of paper that she stuffs into her purse, her face feeling even more flushed. She's not the true blue gal she always thought she was. She says, "Count on me unless you hear from me."

"Great! Great."

No mistaking that enthusiasm. Her hand lingers on the phone when she hangs up, so that it vibrates a second later when the phone rings again."

"Rebecca Silverstein."

"Oh. Oh, yes."

"I tried you a minute ago but you were busy."

"On the phone. Sorry."

"I'm glad I gave it another try. I have to go soon though; I have kids."

"Thank you for calling back. I'll try to be brief. I understand you've done some work on memory in children."

"Yes, that's my bag."

"Could I come talk to you, get some reading? I won't take too much of your time. I just need to be sent in the right directions."

"It's a new field of study—the things we're working on now."

"And also, I'd like to know if anyone is doing research on twins. And memory."

"Identical?'

"Just twins. Fraternal. But possible differences in mind and memory."

"I could graze the subject a little. I do know someone in Ohio who has a paper people respect a lot. I could put you in touch with her."

"That would be fantastic."

"Well, I also teach tomorrow afternoon. I could meet you at four at my office. Not for long but we could make a start."

"I'll be there. Thanks."

BEN CAN'T SUMMON a smile today. He can feel the pull of muscles downward, his face sagging. How he wishes he'd never met Amanda those ten years ago. It's Nina he wants. He's lately had some of the coarser guys at the office congratulate him—as men do in that smirking sort of way—about snagging Nina. And they don't even know her.

Across the room, she shuts down her computer and gathers up various pieces of paper. It's his turn to provide dinner tonight. So he will either make his famous pasta with garlic, butter, and cheese or he must think up a good takeout.

"Chinese?" he asks when she comes up to him. He's grateful for that small move, that she came to him.

She pauses. "Can't ever seem to get in the mood for Chinese. Well, we have the ham and potato salad my mother sent—"

"I think maybe we need a ham break if that's okay with you. Pasta or pizza?"

She hesitates. "Pizza. I'll make a salad."

"Good." Soon they will tuck into her little place, and have their difficult conversation. "I'll order it once we get there."

They walk to her car.

His boys asked, almost in unison, last night as he sat with them in their room. "Who's that lady we had ice cream with?"

"A colleague."

"What's that?" Bryson asked.

Zachary said, "It's about working together. Right?"

"Right."

"But you sleep at her place?"

"For now." At the time it was a lie and now the lie seems to be coming true.

"Where do you sleep?"

"On the couch," he lied. And again, that became true last night. Words are funny things. What was the chapter in his college class textbook: "Saying it makes it so."

"The arrangement is temporary," he told his boys. "She's nice, isn't she? She's a very good friend."

The boys shrugged in physical unison. "She likes ice cream," Bryson offered.

The air in the car is vibrating with tension. "I'm going to have dinner with my kids on Friday—before the thing I have to go to."

"Oh, that's fine."

"I'd ask you to come too, but—"

"No, no, no. It's okay. Where will you take them?"

"Someplace simple. They like burgers. Chicken fingers. They do like my pasta, though, just so you know."

She smiles. "I like it. It's fine, once a week."

The plan was for him to do Tuesday, Thursday, and Saturday meals but last weekend with visits to Nina's mother and Ellen Emerson, they are off schedule.

"I know sex isn't what it was," he says carefully. "I'm not a young stud, but this is temporary, I'm sure."

"Well, you're in the sessions with Amanda; that would get in the way. I understand how if you concentrate on her, you can't think of me. Either way, you're caught in some kind of betrayal."

Right. He's in limbo. Two weeks ago, he couldn't even remember wanting to touch Amanda. Now he has a sense memory of the way it was between them, no fireworks, but something and it's alarming to him that he feels that something again for her when she's quiet, nice to him. There was maybe three minutes in the last session when he was able to feel attraction to her, maybe seven minutes at her house on Sunday.

"And since we're on the subject, and I'm not great at talking about this, but when we make love, I'd rather we kissed and touched for a while and that you didn't go down on me right away."

He's taken off guard. "Really? Most women would be giving me awards."

"I'm not most women. Plus many of them would feel the way I do. You can be a bit unilateral—'I want it so she must want it.'"

"Look. I'm going to call Amanda and tell her I won't do Friday. What do I need to go to some fancy clubhouse to—"

"No. Go. I made another plan. Doug—you call him *my firefighter—*

called me today. We're going to have dinner on Friday. It's just as a friend. No secrets. You were busy and so I said okay. Just don't take the kids to Atria's. We're going to Atria's. In your neck of the woods."

"I thought you weren't the sort to play games."

"It's not a game. It just happened. I like him. And if we don't make it, you and me, I'm going to give it a chance. I didn't engineer it. It just happened."

He feels himself trying to stitch himself together all through the evening. Then she says, "You don't have to find your own place right away. If you put it off for a month, you could rent starting in June. What I'm saying is you could live with Amanda and Zach and Bryson for a month, give it a real serious look, then you'd know. You'd know and I'd know. No regrets."

Where is this coming from? Who is she?

Rebecca Silverstein, about forty-five, with no-nonsense hair, salt and pepper, a nice bob, has pictures of a man and three children all over her desk. She smiles but she also looks at the clock before they begin. "So, I don't know what your focus is, but yes, there are people doing important studies about childhood and memory. It's a hot topic. I've done some research on it, but I have to say there are studies way ahead of mine. Some scholars have been examining large populations over twenty years to measure how much is retained by children and when it starts and what factors play into that. May I ask why you're interested?"

"A case I'm possibly writing about for the newspaper. Trying to make sense of something."

"I'm curious. It must be something fascinating."

"It is. Well . . ." she can't mention Ellen Emerson. "It's a case of a traumatic experience. One twin survives and the other one is lost. The first believes her sister is alive but the sister is not found. Everyone assumes the sister died because if she didn't, why did she not ask for and find her family? That's the main point. That's the most important question. I would like to know if there's a chance the second child might have lived and not . . . *said* anything. I'm not explaining this well."

"No, you're doing okay. What age?"

"Four. Almost four."

"The crucial age. Absolutely. It's when memory kicks in for most. So your subjects are absolutely right there at the nexus between forgetting and knowing."

"Wow."

"And you've somewhat begged the question—if one child could remember and one not remember after a trauma. I'd say yes, it's possible. And the reasons I would give as the potential causes are: differences in the mental capacities of the victims of the trauma *or* differences in circumstances after—if one felt protected and one didn't."

"Ah. That's a possible factor in this case."

"Then there's the role of language in conceptualizing and categorizing trauma. I can't emphasize this enough. This is my main interest in the subject. The power of words. If a child is allowed to use words, that child is more likely to remember. If others use words around the child to give memory a base, yes, even *more* likely to remember. If you think back, how many times is a memory really what someone else told you? A parent says, 'You were so insistent that we buy you a new book every two days.' You might think you remember it, but you conjure the image by being told that you did it."

"I understand."

"So, you're not going to tell me specifics?" She waits, raised eyebrows. "Okay, all right, say it's a car accident. If adults are asking, 'What did you see, what did you hear?' the memory is more fixed. Or if adults tell what they saw and offer perceptions. 'You held onto me, but then there was a big crash, but I kept holding you.' Or if the adults feed back repeatedly what the child said. 'You heard the other horn blasting and you said you put your hands over your ears.' That last image is remembered. It's been recycled through the adults, but it's remembered, called up. In some form. But if nobody talks about the accident, it's less likely to be remembered as such. And what if there's a lie? 'You had a bad dream. You never liked loud noises. You dreamed of a car horn, really loud, and a crash. In the dream you had to put your hands over your ears because of the sound.' It's actually possible that the child will remember it as a dream."

"I understand. I do. I feel it."

"I believe you. So these twins . . . if there were differences in the ways they were talked to, it's possible one would remember and one wouldn't.

Also of course, a very simple additional reason is physical harm. A concussion can wipe out a lot, a whole lot. If memory is wiped out at the crucial stage, well, it might be gone for good. Is this at all helpful?"

"This is very helpful."

"Good. Good. I've copied three articles for you. They're respectable work—sound scholarly articles. They pretty much explain what I'm saying. How about if you read them and get back to me with any questions? You've made me *very* curious."

"Sure. I'm really grateful for your time. It's almost suppertime. And you have kids."

"Thankfully my husband is good with food."

Nina leaves with a sheaf of papers, hoping she will understand what scholars have to say. But she already has corroboration of what she told herself all along—different circumstances producing different relationships to memory. Ellen, the talker, made her memories stick.

"WHAT'S THE MOVIE?" she asks.

"There's not a lot. Do you like whacky?"

"Not much."

"Well, otherwise—we've already seen *New York Stories*—there's an Australian thriller, there's a comedy called *Skin Deep*, there's a baseball movie with some good people."

"Baseball. Love it."

"That's at the Galleria and the Denis. We can make one or the other."

"It's okay if we don't."

He puts his menu aside. "Very okay with me. I'd be happy with face to face."

She wonders if he has any friends that he seems so . . . available. "Did you get a lot of fuss made over you? After the fire?" She is having that experience of his looking unfamiliar, then familiar, then unfamiliar again.

"Plenty. Also a reprimand and a speech about not putting expectations on myself."

"And you didn't set the fire?"

He laughs. "Oh, no. You've been reading the accounts of insane criminal firefighters."

She has. People who need the work or the heroism so badly that they set the fires in order to be called to them. In some cases, they just plain love fire. "Very scary people."

"They are."

She looks around the restaurant—they've been seated upstairs at Atria's and of course she warned Ben not to come, but she finds herself checking the room anyway.

She orders fish with lots of vegetable sides. He orders a burger and fries.

"How is the dissertation going?"

"It's going. I had a pretty good week."

"Which chapter?"

"Oh, early. Revising. The one on women in the workplace."

"I guess if I think it's an uphill battle for women now, I can't even imagine what they went through decades ago."

"Yes, true, in a way. I don't know—it seems there were determined women in all sorts of areas all through history, not in the numbers there are now, but they existed. The individuals interest me—I mean people who didn't work in groups, in factories. Women in telegraph offices. That kind of thing. I can't do much with them in this . . . I want to call it a book, presumptuous of me . . . but maybe some day. I have to stick with organizations, even loose ones, and attempts to get better treatment. Nurses, for instance, horrible conditions, got paid almost nothing, had to buy their own uniforms out of their miniscule pay. Teachers. It took a long, long time to persuade teachers that unions were okay."

"Why?"

"Associations with labor versus the genteel cleanness of teaching, I guess. But it had to happen. Women who taught needed the pay and the recognition. Around 1916, it became formal. The AFT. You're interested . . . in this?"

"I know a teacher. I'm trying to guess at her life."

"Well, she wouldn't go back this far. By the '40s, things were more established."

Nina held her tongue. Ellen went back very far. "And if . . . say somebody ended up poor, destitute, what would that person do? For work. And I'm not talking prostitution."

Doug looked curious. "Pittsburgh?" he asked.

"For example."

"Well, determined women did have jobs. I'm doing some paragraphs on the Amalgamated Clothing Workers, the Amalgamated Textile Workers, and the telephone operators' branch of the Electrical Workers. You really want to know this?"

"Yes."

"Okay. I suspect a reason. A story?"

"Maybe. Hopefully. I don't know yet."

"Okay, there were other factory jobs that attracted numbers—lots of bookbinders, boot and shoe workers, cigar makers, garment workers of all sorts—and, if this helps you in what you are thinking about, you can't help noticing the physical work in these factories was hard and there were probably fumes, too."

"I'd never have made it. Fumes kill me. Headaches, digestion, the works. I require good air."

He smiles. "There were exceptions. A few. How would your violin have been? Musicians. They had a successful union early on."

"My violin would give you and everyone else a headache. Other work?"

"Hotel employees. They had a union. Post office clerks—up and coming job. More women working in the wars of course, including the First World War. Then the numbers went down when the wars were over. But in general they went *up* over the years—the result being more and more women working outside the home. On the other hand . . . well, about half were in domestic service or clerical jobs. For a long time. And that might not have been highly satisfying to a lot of them."

Ellen's twin—one scenario: forced into domestic service. If she lived.

"Have I helped you?"

"I've been trying to construct a picture of the last century—in case I write this thing I have in mind."

"Good."

Gradually his face comes into focus and doesn't contradict itself. Their food arrives. She hasn't found anything to dislike about Douglas, wishes she had, for it would close this chapter and simplify her life. He asks her all kinds of questions about her home life, about being an only child, the Orthodox faith, her parents, her first prom. What does he want to know, what answer is he searching for? They dawdle over coffee and dessert. Then they wander to the bar to watch the game.

"Spanky," she says when he comes to bat. "Mike LaValliere."

Doug smiles. "You know these guys."

"Like they're playing in my backyard."

The time for the movie comes and goes.

"They're going to have to kick us out. I could show you my house or is that off limits?"

"It's not that. I should go. I'm going to visit my mother tomorrow, early."

Douglas squeezes her hand before they part. The touch zigzags through her.

"I'LL BETCHA THINGS were a little bit different when you were a nurse, huh?" says the chubby jolly nurse as she releases the blood pressure cuff.

This is one of those days Anna thinks what she wants to say, but it doesn't come out right away. She has a frustrating delay in whatever sends the signal from brain to tongue. "You betcha," she answers finally.

"Ha. You're funny. Like how? No penicillin, right?" The nurse's hair is blonde and curly. She is like an outsized version of the fictional nurse in *South Pacific.* No, no, Anna never went to the South Pacific and she manages to hold her tongue because just the reference to that funny song will confuse this well-meaning nurse who is eager for a connection—what is her name?—Ms. Kelly.

"When I started out, we never thought about penicillin. It wasn't in our imaginations." The truth is, they weren't supposed to have imaginations; they were a form of domestic servant, doing cleaning for a living—cleaning of all sorts, day and night. That's how student nurses in hospitals were used. To this day, Anna is known for her cleanliness. Her drawers are perfect. If she gets a spot of tea on something she begins scrubbing it herself.

"We nurses, we'd like for you to talk to us about it sometime. We'd like to know how it was—your work in the early days."

"Hm. If you want a start on it, I don't know if you can find it, but there's a book."

Ms. Kelly's face falls. "I don't know if I can find time for research. We just wanted to hear from you."

It's an old novel, she's thinking of, and it might not be around. What she manages to tell Kelly is, "It was called . . . *The White Linen Nurse.*" Was that it? She thinks that's it. "Unfortunately the picture it gives is not too rosy. That was the worst of it, when it got like that. We were the robots, the machines."

"Oh."

The doctors, even now, weren't completely different. "Don't worry. I chose it. I wanted the better parts of the job."

"I'll bet you were good."

Good? She was fantastic. "You betcha."

Nurse Kelly thrusts a thermometer into her mouth, the sort that beeps when she hits a steady temperature. "You are so funny. I'll bet the others don't know what a sense of humor you have. You hide it. Sly little thing."

Sly, hmmm. Nothing beeps. Maybe she's running a fever. Oh, how she ran toward it, the work, the toil of being one of the nightingales, the *garde-malade.* How she ran to it. She wanted to help. An arm was lopped off in a factory, a woman with children coughed up blood, she wanted to know about that, not hide from it, *do* something. Was that stupid? Always searching for some answer, some how-to-live, how to stay alive.

And she did help people. Most of the time.

One day she was aware of the cross look she got from her supervisor in the elevator at the hospital. Anna was asking the man who operated the elevator what was wrong because something was wrong, he was red-eyed and she thought perhaps he'd lost a relative, a brother, in an accident. The war was over at that point, but there were factory accidents every day.

"How are you, Mr. Hoffman?" she asked as she always did. The way he smiled at her each day as she approached—it lifted her. "Oh! Are you all right? Your eye—"

"Got something in it. It hurts a bit."

"You're weeping from it."

"That can't be helped. My eye just keeps coming up with tears."

"Come with me, let me look at it."

He hesitated but he came with her, after locking the elevator door open. Anna was aware that the supervisor followed them and when

Anna looked back at her she saw the woman's face filled with fury. Anna continued what she intended to do, briskly examined the man's eye with a light and a magnifier, saw a foreign object but wasn't sure what it was. With care and patience she got it out. "Keep washing it," she instructed. "Do you have an eye cup?"

"No."

"A whiskey glass?"

"I could borrow one. Don't worry. This was very kind of you." He was already on his way to the elevator he'd locked open. Maybe three and a half minutes had gone by. She worried that small delay would get him into trouble.

"Don't you ever do that again," said the nursing supervisor.

"What? Help a patient?"

"Use our things on a Negro employee."

"He works here. He certainly ought not to be miserable."

"He's going to lose his job once I report what he did."

"If you need someone to blame, blame me. You heard me ask him what was wrong. I insisted he come to the station so I could look. Make sure you tell them that."

"I will."

"How did you expect him to do his job? He could barely see, his eye was weeping so much."

"Well, then, have it your way; you're the one in trouble."

Anna waited for something to happen, a letter dismissing her. But mainly it was the nervous waiting that constituted her punishment. Each day she saw the cross face of her supervisor reminding her she was being watched. Now when she caught the elevator, when she and Will Hoffman greeted each other, there was conspiracy in their murmured comments about the weather or the news. He understood she had fought for him.

One day he asked, "How is your son doing?"

She said, "I miss him when I come to work, but he's fine—healthy and growing."

"What does he like to do?"

"He's only four. He seems to be eager to try just about everything. Last night he told me he'd like to go fishing. I'm not sure where he heard about fishing, but I have to figure out a way to take him."

He nodded, looked as if he would say something, then he didn't.

One Sunday Anna had to go into work especially early because there was a trolley strike, which affected several other employees. The student nurses were still in residence, but they required supervision. As a head nurse who'd been married and had a child, she'd established living off campus, as it were. She was walking briskly along Fifth Avenue—it wasn't even seven in the morning and she had been walking for blocks when something alerted her to a figure ahead of her, working in a garden on one of the Fifth Avenue estates. That man looks like Mr. Hoffman, she thought, but then she thought it was just the problem of her thinking of him, thinking she saw him. Oh, the mind! She was already winded from the long walk. When she got up close, he turned, with the most amazing timing, as if he felt her coming. But his surprise was almost as great as hers. "How—?" he began. "I mean, today, I thought—"

She was usually off on Sunday but the strike, she explained, made everything different.

He put down the shears he was using. "I'll walk with you."

"You work at this house, too?"

"Here and a couple of other places."

"But won't they mind?"

"I'll explain."

Explain what and to whom, she was about to ask, but they were busy walking together at a fairly brisk rate. "How many jobs do you have?" she asked instead.

"The elevator . . . gardening . . . I do light carpentry work on people's houses around where I live. That's mostly about it."

A car on the road veered crazily as the driver craned to look at them. "We make quite a picture," he said.

She nodded. They were just friends, she told herself, sympathetic to each other; they would always be friends, and some people would not understand.

They walked several blocks, not in silence exactly, but with a halting conversation about the strike and about their work in the hospital. "I'm sorry about my supervisor, the way she treated you."

His jaw tightened. Finally he said, "I put my mind to how you treated me. That seemed the important thing to remember."

"Did you always live in Pittsburgh?"

"Born here. My mother's parents came up from Alabama, but my father's parents were working here. You?"

"There are some things I'm not quite sure of. I was probably born in Indiana County. I grew up on the South Side and I still live there. Unfortunately."

"You don't like it?"

"The house and its owner are . . . difficult. The owner is my mother-in-law. But she cares for my son while I work and that seems to be the arrangement that's best for all of us right now. My in-laws sold the house I was living in. I need to work. I want to work. She's just as happy to have me away and to have her grandchild to herself. But I worry about him. I shouldn't, but she's not the kindest soul—to him, yes, she is, but to the world, no, she's bitter."

"I wondered."

"About what?'

"Many things. Everything about you."

She heard it beginning. Her breath caught.

He said, "I think about you all the time."

They were on Aiken Avenue. Her heart pounded and her knees threatened to buckle. She remembers very distinctly that she stopped and held onto a decorative iron gate around one of the properties. "I know nothing about you," was all she could think to say.

He paused for a long time. "Should I tell you things? Do you want to know?"

"Yes." She let go of the gate and began walking again. "Three jobs, I know that. Three at least."

"I had a wife. She left me seven years ago. She left with another man. We were together seven years before that. I guess maybe sevens are my turnaround time. Anyway, I had to track her down to get a divorce, but I always had in mind that I wanted to love someone again. I don't have children. She has two girls with her new man. I'm thirty-nine." He paused, then continued. "I have a house. People laugh because they think I should use my money for fun and live in a room instead of a house. But I have a house and it has a small yard and I bought it and it's where I want to be."

Something about the way he said "yard," made her know without asking that the small outdoor space meant everything to him. He was comfortable in earth, friendly with the physical world. She pictured a yard providing him with vegetables.

"I've counted six people who have stared hard at us. If you'd like for me to stop walking with you, I will." His face furrowed again, his jaw tightened and she recognized his reaction to anger, insult.

"No."

And then his face relaxed. They walked a few more yards in silence.

"Would you ever come to my home? It's in the Hill district. Would you consider that?"

"I've never been to the Hill. It's up over Centre, isn't it?"

"I would find a car. *Hire* a car. If you would come."

"No. I can walk. You walk home from work, don't you?"

"You would need a car to get back to the South Side. With the trolleys down. At night."

"Yes, that's true."

"Will you come tonight?"

"No. I can't possibly." Then she thought about it. "Well . . ."

In a way it would be easiest tonight. If she were released at five, which she might be—her mother-in-law would not know anything about the hospital workings in a time of strike and might expect her as late as ten.

She thought of his route to work. He must come down off the Hill, walking down Centre to the hospital most days, and on other days, walking the rest of the way to Fifth Avenue to the houses where he tended gardens.

"If you say yes, I will come for you and walk with you, and then get a car for later. I'm not a bad cook. I could make something for dinner."

She wanted to say no, to stop all the trouble she could predict before it happened, but there was no way she could look at his face and say no. She was already in love with him, and just now admitting it to herself. His face, manner, voice were already part of her comfort, part of what made her feel seen. She didn't have the common white person's perspective that Negroes were different or not handsome. She found him handsome, a pleasure to look at. "Ah, well . . . I don't even know what to call you. Mr. Hoffman seems all wrong."

"William," he said.

"I know."

"Will. Some people call me Will. And your name is Anna. I saw it written at work. I try not to say it in the elevator."

They were almost at the hospital.

"I might be able to come tonight. If I get released at five—schedules are uncertain, I might be needed—if I'm released at five, I will come. I'll need directions—"

"I'll be at the door on Centre. In case. I'll wait until . . . six, seven. Try to send a message if you can't come."

She was drifting off to sleep when Nurse Kelly came back into the room. "Sorry. Checking. Are you okay?"

"Hmmm," she said. "Mmmm."

At six thirty Ben herded his boys out of the Eat'n Park, and though he hadn't planned to go to Atria's because he simply hadn't planned what he would do with them, it ended up seeming so much the better choice. But Nina had claimed it as her territory tonight. My God, he wondered, how is Nina going to resist falling in love with the firefighter and does she want to resist it? Ben had seen the clips on the news and he practically fell in love with the guy himself. So now, this of all things, is the house of cards Amanda started.

"Why are you hurrying, Dad?"

"I have to get you to Aunt Melanie's house. Right? Your mum and I need to be someplace at seven. So haul it."

"Haul ass."

"No. Haul *it*. That's what I said."

"What's 'it'?"

"Never mind."

They cackle in the back seat.

He drives shouting, "Sit back!" and dealing with his colliding feelings. Nina is exploring her options. It's only fair. He is. No, it's more that he's excavating, digging for hope that he doesn't want. And of course the guy is falling in love with Nina. Of course.

"This car is old," Zach observes.

"I know it, buddy."

"I know about your meeting. Mommy's happy about it."

"That's good."

"Are you happy about it?"

"Happy enough." He runs his hand along the torn upholstery of the driver seat. New apartment or new car, what will it be?

Amanda is standing outside with her sister-in-law, ready to hop in. The boys take too much time going toward their aunt so that their mother has to bug them to hurry up. They turn back, curious to see what happens when she gets into the car. Ben knows they would like to see a classic lean and kiss hello but he cannot give them that. Instead he waves and tosses a kiss like a football their way. They accept it, sort of.

She looks nice, Amanda. Soft pants, these dark, soft sweaters she wears, dark gray—winterish again, she's always cold. She wears shoes with a small heel.

"I wonder who these other people are," he says. He feels itchy. He hates a group confessional.

"Other people in trouble. Marriages like ours."

How funny to think of it as an epidemic. Like something out of a Greek tragedy (or comedy). A plague has hit Mt. Lebanon: anger, no sex, mismatched expectations. And he is a fraud if he is supposed to be trying to find his way back to her.

And yet, when she smiles and murmurs her worry that others will hog up all the time and they won't get to work on their stuff, he says, "We'll do our best." His hand finds the worn upholstery again and he adds, "This car is going to embarrass you. Probably some valet will ask to park it and it will make its belching-farting noises the whole way to the lot."

"I'll survive the car."

That response surprises him and squeezes a little at his heart.

THE BOOK she's trying to read is too heavy to prop up, so Anna starts leafing through the newspapers again. She's become a character—she heard the aides talking about her earlier. "Oh, she wants *all* her papers. Until she tells you to throw them away, you have to save them for her. She's very neat but she'll pile them up. She's paid for them and she *wants* them. Like people who smoke the last tobacco leaf off a cigarette. If she hasn't read the whole damn thing, she isn't done. It's like a job to her. She doesn't have anything else to do."

The embarrassing thing is the aide is right. It *is* how she thinks—finish everything. She always had a schedule, always worked every corner of a thing, a bed she was making or a book she was reading. She is hospital corners all over, in every inch of her being.

So she takes the Friday paper and begins the leafing through, checking off what she's already read, making a note of what she wants to read. When she comes to the entertainment section, she lets out a moan. "Oh. Oh, how did they do this—" she says aloud. And then she shakes her head and makes herself read, only her eyes blur and she can't. She's going mad. This is it, this is the madness she has kept at bay with all her routines, come to get her at last.

One of the aides comes into the room. "Did you need something?"

She shakes her head weakly.

"Are you all right?"

"This picture. I . . . I can't get over it. Who do they say it is? This man."

"Some actor."

"An actor." Yes, it's in the movie section.

The aide takes the paper. "He's in some movie. *Lean on Me.* I heard of that. I think it's supposed to be good. He plays, let me see, yeah, a school principal, name of Joe Clark. That's what it says. We should get you people out to the movies more."

"I want to go. I want to see it."

"Way to go, Girl! You got excited, huh?"

She almost tells the aide, "He looks just like my husband, this actor. You wouldn't believe how much he looks like him." But she hesitates.

"Should I take the paper?"

"No."

"Oh, you want it."

"I want to cut this out. I keep a box of photographs. It's in my bottom drawer."

"Okay. You want me to cut it out for you?"

"Be careful."

"The whole article or just the dude?"

"The whole thing."

She almost laughs. She is mad, yes, but this aide thinks she is way off her rocker. Way off. It's because she was thinking about Will so much today, but the actor does look just like him, and if she sees the film, if they take her out or bring the movie here, it will be, maybe, like having him alive just a bit for a while. She'll cry and cry. She watches the aide clip the newspaper and at least the girl does it cleanly.

"You want me to put it in the drawer?"

"No, let me read it."

"Okay. I'll get the drawer open for you. That way you don't have to get down and tug, you could just drop it in, get one of us to come and close it for you. Whoa, you got your stuff in here. An award, I see that. A nursing award."

"Don't leave it open. I can't stand an open drawer."

"Okay, Mrs. Hoffman. Your call."

A life in a drawer. The aide is not likely to understand how she's winnowed her life down to that size. Let the girl live another eighty years to understand that.

"What about these other newspapers? You ready to trash them?"

"No. I'm not quite finished. Never mind, take Monday. The one with the flood article."

"You finished that one!"

"No. It gives me the creeps. I always said I'd choose fire before drowning."

"Ew."

"Well, we're all different, I guess. To me it's as bad as being buried alive."

The aide takes the Monday paper and leaves, finally.

When Anna reads about the movie, her mind does leaps of all sorts. If Will had been an actor—and he was nothing like—he might have played this character. No, no, what she means is, if he'd been formally educated and been a teacher, then a high school principal, he might have *been* this character. Can fiction come so close to type? But she keeps reading and sees that the character was based on a real man. She feels, for the moment, for this evening, as if Will is just around the corner, out in the hallway—he's close tonight.

At the hospital door that first time, the day of the strike, he waited for her as he'd promised he would. It was autumn and beginning to darken after five. Leaves blew around at his feet. He wore a suit and carried in his hand a fedora softened by age. His face was . . . happy and full of hope.

They began walking.

"How was it today?"

"Difficult. We had two emergency surgeries. But mainly the superintendent was her horrible self."

"It should be you in that job."

"I find myself thinking that." It was always exhausting work, always rigorous, always a worry watching the students take on more than they were capable of, but, yes, she thought she could run the whole thing if they asked her.

"I hope to make the rest of the day good."

It was strange. People didn't do things for her. She'd always been the one who served, even with her parents, but especially since her mother died. The fact that William wanted to treat her gave her a thrill. "Thank you, William."

"Will. Will, if you would." He put on his hat. "It's gotten chilly," he said. "Are you warm enough?"

"I'm all right for now, while we're walking."

"I have a heating stove. I'll get that going."

He wanted to know everything—how she got started in nursing. She told him about Dr. Raymond, her apprenticeship, the marriage proposals from the doctor's son, her insistence on going to training at the school. "It was a fight. The doctor told me I was learning perfectly well from him. I told him that one day he would die and I would lack a sponsor. Meanwhile I was sure I wasn't ready for marriage so I kept saying no to his son. Well, that refusal so insulted Paul's mother that she *wanted* me to leave. Under normal circumstances I wouldn't have been able to get into the school until I was twenty-two at least, but the doctor vouched for me and they could see at the school that I already knew a lot about nursing and so they let me in. The others were older. I was like the upstart little sister."

"I can see it." He smiled. "Just this turn here and we start to climb uphill."

The houses were beautiful. "I always heard it was beautiful here."

"Well, here, yes. Not so fancy I'm afraid when we get up to my neighborhood. Just small houses, some not so good. Are you all right?"

She had worked downtown at first, and then the hospital and its training school moved to the Shadyside area. She liked the second place better even though it was farther from home. Home. "I married the doctor's son eventually. It was . . . difficult much of the time. I knew I was a calming factor in his life. Sometimes it seems like he went to fight in the war because he wanted to die. It scares me to think it, but I do."

A man parks an automobile ahead of them in front of one of the fancy houses. He gets out and stands by the car until they reach him. "Is this man bothering you?"

"No, he's not. We're friends."

"Well, then."

After a while, Will said, "What we're starting. It's going to be like that."

"I know."

"Not everywhere. I know some decent people."

The Hill, at that point, housed lots of Eastern European and Jewish immigrants, so it was easier once they passed the boot factory and the cigar factory and got there. Anna had read that H. L. Mencken described Pittsburgh, as "the heart of industrial America," which made everybody at work sort of proud, but then there was argument because there was also Mencken's insult about Pittsburgh's being ugly and dirty and smoke-filled.

"Is the factory work good?"

"It's pretty lousy, but you have to be white to get a union card to do it. I'd rather keep to what I'm doing."

Eventually Will led her to a small house that fronted on the street and was not imposing in any way. She saw that his hand was shaking as he opened the door. Inside it was clean and neat, ten times poor, and yet more appealing to her than her mother-in-law's house. He'd set the table with unmatched china plates. "I made everything in advance."

"Oh, what if I hadn't been able to come?"

"I would have had two meals with the same food." He'd made fried chicken, collard greens, and baked potatoes.

She touched his arm. "Why don't you have another wife?"

"I wanted you."

That's what he said. Oh, he's right around the corner today, very close. She supposes that means this is it, that she's going to die, that he's come to get her. How strange that she still isn't ready to go. She puts the newspaper clipping inside the Bible in her bedside drawer so that nobody makes a mistake and tosses it out. Tomorrow she will compare the photo to the three of Will in her drawer.

The second time she went to his house was when she lied and told her mother-in-law that she was called to work on her day off. He arranged his yard work to other hours—one house he did at ten at night the night before. They spent the whole day together. They loved each other—had loved each other from the start. Sometimes it just happens that way.

Ma Raymond was scandalized when Anna told her she wanted to marry again. When she learned who it was, she tried to keep her grandson for herself, but Anna insisted her son be with her. Little Edward helped. He kicked and wailed, a good little solider, until Ma Raymond didn't want him anymore. They went up to live in the Hill where they made a life. They suffered their enemies and mostly were happy.

CHAPTER 11

Saturday, May 6–
Sunday, May 7, 1989

■ NINA IS IN HER CAR, enjoying the sweet slap of the windshield wipers and the rain—just a sprinkle. She's not fully awake. Last night, late, she sat with Ben when he came in. She'd been listening to the Pirates on the radio, the end of the game and the talk show after. They'd won, that was great. And then she sat with Ben and told him about her evening with Douglas and he told her about his session with Amanda. She had a sip of scotch with him. She'd had wine at dinner. Mostly she listened. She told him she'd talked to Hal and had written a small piece on the other floods.

Ben said the session was not as awful as he had been sure it would be. He said Caldwell suggested that he alternate, that he spend a week at his home with Amanda and another with Nina or on his own, that he needed experiences of both to make a decision.

Nina said, "I agree with that. I think I said so."

"My decision, though, is already made."

Tonight Ben will pack up a few things and move to Amanda's place for a week.

She turns on the radio, sings along, shuts it off. She'd forced herself to knock on Hal's door. She'd said, "How is it? My article?"

"We'll do a small sidebar. Cut it a bit. We'll run it alongside Ben's on Monday."

Ellis Island immigrants on dock. Courtesy of the National Park Service, Statue of Liberty
N. M. and Ellis Island.

"Right, well, is there room for more?"

"More what?"

"More feature material about the lives—"

"Funny you didn't lobby for the whole series, you're so keen."

"Are you kidding?"

He squinted hard. "Partly. Mostly."

Well, damn, her mother was right. She needs more killer instinct. "Well, what if I write some additional related stuff? On my time. Will you look at it?"

He appeared to consider it. "We can't overdo it. Yeah. I'll look."

"Good."

"Meanwhile, find what's his face. He wants you to cover the guy threatening to jump off a roof in East Liberty. I think they have him down now, but we need the sequence, how they talked him down, where they carted him off to."

In her satchel are the pages she got from Silverstein. She'll go over them again at her mum's place tonight. But she's read enough to get the idea that it's *words* that make the difference. If you have words for things, you are likely to be able to remember those things. If you are four years old and highly verbal, you will remember specific incidents better than a four-year-old who is more visual. How strange, how strange, ears win over the eyes. What about smells, touch?

Today she'll go to see Ellen again. She didn't tell Ben she called seven, then eight, nursing homes around Johnstown from her desk asking how many residents were a hundred and four. She learned there was only one, a hundred and two. An African American born in North Carolina.

She didn't tell him when she broadened the area and called more places.

Nobody wants to be foolish.

What is the sense of calling twenty-five nursing homes in western Pennsylvania? If Mary Burrell had lived, she could be anywhere—Idaho, Connecticut, Frankfurt, Germany. Anywhere. She could have died at eighty-two or ninety-nine and if she had an altered name, nobody would be the wiser as to who she was. But Nina has started and she can't stop. She understands Ellen, head bangers for sure, both of them.

"CAN YOU BELIEVE IT?" Ellen laughs. "These nineteenth-century Russians put us to shame. Just one little meal for two people—" She begins to list what they ate: "They order three dozen oysters. Then soup with vegetables. Then turbot with sauce because of course they are influenced by the French so they want their sauces, then roast beef, then capons, then sweets. And of course wine with everything. And cheese. Amazing isn't it?"

Nina groans, "I'd want to stop after the oysters and maybe soup with vegetables. What vegetable? What can you grow in Russia?"

"Good question. Potatoes, turnips, beets . . ."

"You must want me to make that meal for you," Ruth teases.

"Even I probably couldn't manage it," Ellen sighs. "Not any more."

Nina is frustrated that she doesn't know much about Russia. Her heritage. Her great-great-grandparents would have been on that farm, growing beets, maybe cucumbers, Russians being big on cucumbers. She wishes she knew more. "I should read Tolstoy again. And Dostoyevsky. Oh, and a whole lot of other things."

"Well, they're fun. Tolstoy was half Jane Austen—always reporting who looked down, whose eyes sparkled, who sighed and trembled, and always with that romantic focus on who was the best match, who would marry whom. He knew romance was everything. He was very interested in behavior and flirtation and love."

"Anna Karenina didn't come out too well."

"No, no she didn't. Do you ever put yourself back a century and imagine yourself there?"

"Sometimes." Nina looks about the room with its few pieces from a century ago right along with contemporary pieces, like the sofa. She tries to concentrate on Ellen's question. What she really wants to do is *ask* questions. "Well, if I look at my great-grandmother, I'd have to guess that I'd be a peasant. I'd be on a farm, growing whatever they grew or taking care of the lambs."

"Aha. But you have heroine's blood in your veins. You might have wanted to get off the farm—unless of course, you loved it."

"I would have loved it . . . unless I read books. If I read, I would have still loved the farm but wanted to live what I read—in the cities, at balls, at great dinners. A conflicted soul."

"We've got it then. You would have been the beautiful, intelligent shepherdess who moves out of her station. If I were in Russia—which of course I wasn't, I was here—and if I examine my probable life of a hundred and ten or twenty years ago, in Russia, say, I would have ended up a governess. Not too far from how I did end up, eh?"

"It's lovely that you think about things like this."

"Is it? Stories intrigue me."

"Speaking of, I read a draft of Ben's story on you. It's good. I wish it were four times longer and had all of your life in it, but he's supposed to stick to the flood."

"Ah."

"I'll have a little piece in too, a sidebar, about the '36 flood and the '77 flood."

"I was here for both. The house in Moxham in '36, this apartment in '77."

"Was it frightening?"

"I didn't know where my daughter was. This was '36 of course. Bill found her at a friend's house. The streets were filled with water. People had to abandon their cars. He brought Rosemary and that whole other family to our house. I remember we ate on the second floor, in candlelight. No power. Some journalists came to find me and others who had survived the '89 flood as well. Now . . . I'll be famous again. For fifteen minutes."

"You know that expression?"

"Yes. The blond boy. Yes, he's quite a character."

Yes, still sharp, still sharp.

Nina didn't know how to start with her own interview. Finally she just did. "Suppose one day I want to write something different—"

"What?"

"I don't know. Something. Say a big long article about you."

"Oh, I'm not material for much more."

"You are. But if . . . could I ask you a few questions? Things that couldn't fit into the article about the flood."

"Hm. Like?"

"Your husband, Bill Emerson. What was he like?"

"Well, it's easy to talk about him. Some people are blessed—simply born happy and he was one of them. His family had emigrated from Poland and changed their name—I think I told you. He had one brother. His father was a butcher; his mother made pierogies and haluski, which they sold at the shop. They were precisely who my uncle and my cousin would have avoided. Well! What's to do with the fact that Bill and his brother were lightyears smarter than my old uncle? But Bill never pushed himself in people's faces. He just did what he did well and people responded. Even Julia and Lucy were crazy about him. Well, he was about five-eleven. He had thick brown hair, a little curly, brown eyes. He got stocky as he got older. He always noticed people who needed to be taken care of—he could always tell. The way he got married the first time was a little of that—a frail woman who was devoted to him (people were). And he felt responsible for her. He says he loved her after a fashion but it was almost like loving a sibling. It wasn't magical; it was about comforting and support. She was never healthy. When she died, several women tried to get Bill's attention. He always told me he kept thinking of me during this time. He moved away from New York, took a job in Pittsburgh, Westinghouse."

"What did he do?"

"Oh! He started out in business at Westinghouse but he ended up in the legal department and then he went and got a law degree. At one point he made some inquiries and when he heard I was on my own, in New York, teaching school, he just arrived at my door one day. I was never so happy to see anyone in my life."

"He sounds wonderful."

"I adored him. Like everybody else did. He was one of the first people I met in New York and I thought he was the most wonderful person I had ever met. I was devastated to find out he was married. I felt like a fool. I must say he never treated me that way, though. He was genuinely happy to see me."

Ruth has come in and taken a seat. Ellen appears to make a decision and speak to both women.

Nina asks, "After his wife died, why didn't he come for you right away. Since he felt that way?"

"He thought I was with someone. He had picked up hints. And. Sometimes rumors fly even when you think nobody knows your business."

"Was this . . . Greaves?"

"Yes. Arthur."

"It seems very romantic. I think you're the Tolstoy heroine."

"So lucky I didn't have to hit the subway tracks."

"Were you also in love with Arthur?"

"Yes. My, you have a way of asking questions. It was very complicated."

"I can imagine."

"Can you? And maybe, yes, maybe that cliché that I did need a good father for a while to make up for the bad father, Reverend Folks, in my life. Well, if that's what it was, I gave my youth for it—that need. But Arthur was a good man. He didn't want to hurt me, I didn't want to hurt him. It went on and on until I realized I wanted to keep Lucy's child, I wanted to devote myself to the next generation. Once I took on Rosemary, Arthur and I were able to part. I thought I was meant to be alone and then Bill appeared at my door."

Ruth is smiling slightly, shaking her head. "Whew," she says. "Mrs. E, you are some hot number." But when she notices Ellen's eyes are moist, she says, "I'm so glad you had Bill."

"I was very lucky. Amazingly lucky."

"I love hearing about you," Ruth assures her.

"Oh, well."

"Thanks for telling us," Nina says. Just then the teakettle sounds. Ruth is up and moving and in seconds a plate of white cakes appears on the dining table. "Tea is on the way," she says.

Nina wonders, How much can I push? The subject she wants to broach is painful as well. And suddenly, under the delicate clatter of cups in the kitchen, she just asks, "Can you remember what it was like being a twin? Can you remember very much about that?"

"Yes. I think so. I remember a feeling. A good feeling."

"Did you look alike?"

"No. Not very much. She was the prettier one, so people said. Well, I learned that later from my aunt. There were no pictures, but when I got my aunt or Julia to talk I got a clear memory of her: dark brown hair, blue eyes, a very delicate face. My hair was a more mousy color. I guess I made up for it by being the noisy one when we were little. I asked questions, I made protests, I'm afraid I bossed Mary around some. I was that kind of kid."

This time Ruth puts the teapot and cups on the table as well. "Mrs. E. likes to move," she explains to Nina. "She says the more she moves, the more she can."

"Excellent."

"Are you one of those exercisers?" Ellen asks Nina.

"I should be. Haven't been. Slacking off. I'm making a vow right now to get back to it." She watches Ellen get up, hovers a little behind in case she is needed as a human crutch, but Ellen makes it smoothly, and proudly, to the table in a few good steps.

Nina says, "Tell me about your sister. I never had a sibling. I didn't much like being an only child."

"No, it's hard. I was essentially that in my second life, with my uncle. I was the only child in the house. I could still remember my sister. Because we'd talked constantly. Or I should say I talked at her. She was the best listener! And then she would say something that let me know she was fully there. Like when she told me our cousin was not a good man. She had the courage of her convictions. I thought I was the leader, but she was. She was leading me in some way."

"What did she like? Dancing, singing, painting?"

"We were just little things. I don't know that we did much dancing and singing. She liked stories, of course, everybody does. I entertained her with this and that. I was the entertainer. She liked pleasing people. Order. We were given chores. She was a demon cleaner-upper."

"Does it bother you to talk about her?"

She appears to consider. "No. I feel I'm struggling though to explain. She just was. Like a part of me. Like my other self."

"Your quieter self."

"Nicer self."

Ruth makes an exasperated sound. "There is nothing not nice about you."

"Thanks, but I know my own selfish nature. If Mary had been a young woman in New York, she would have tolerated her loneliness. Withstood it. I tried to cure it."

Nina ate her white cake, surprised she could like something so much that had no chocolate or nuts in it. She couldn't admit that she had been calling nursing homes—such a useless endeavor, one after another, broadening the circle. How long would it take to cover the country? And what if Mary had lived and was just as independent as Ellen—in an apartment somewhere in, oh, Idaho, again. Far-flung Idaho. Nina feels defined by irrationality. "My life is so small."

"Well, almost all lives are. Small."

"Yours doesn't seem so."

"A disaster is a big thing. But the lives . . . if they go on, they still get measured in the small strokes."

"I'm thinking about that."

"Where is Ben today?"

"In Pittsburgh. With his kids."

Ellen studies her, makes a slight nod. The woman misses nothing.

NANCY STILL USES the old 1920s vanity her mother had when she sits to comb her hair and put on makeup—three shallow drawers on each side, very practical if not exactly pretty. Bobby pins and scrunchies in one drawer, powders and rouges in another; Nancy doesn't much like changing things that don't need to be changed. A brush of her hair, a touch of lipstick, and she will be ready to go. She's taking Nina to Conzatti's this time; it's like the beginning of a routine, even though it's only twice—dinner out on Saturday nights.

Oh, she can't be this mother who guilt trips and leans on her daughter for company. Her daughter needs that phase of life in which she forgets to think about her mother. Almost everybody has that span of time when parents are taken for granted. They're alive, they're there, they're in your blood, you don't need to keep seeing them.

They will go at about seven. She can hear Nina in the living room downstairs, clicking on the lamp, then a minute later walking to the kitchen. Water running—that would be the teakettle. If she goes down, she will be in her daughter's way, so she lies on the bed, trying not to muss her hair. One time, she and her friends talked about movie stars and musicians who peak too early and never can come up to the standard that made them famous. Her conclusion is that love can be like that. If you fall hard and get it right early, nothing else ever looks good.

What do movie stars do when they crash? Some disappear and drink. Others write memoirs or take small roles or work at being producers.

You have to reduce expectations, get rid of pride, find joy in the non-exciting, the ordinary. Be alive. She wants to be alive. But how foolish is she? Who will look at her now, spreading hips, eye and cheek lines, all the usual damage that clothes and makeup cannot hide.

Ellen Emerson said Nancy was a beauty in high school. Maybe. That seems too strong a word. She was lucky to have decent looks just when she needed them—that mating time of life.

Something is wrong between Nina and Ben. Is he going to marry her or not? And then Nina told her she met a guy who wants to see her and he's nice. A sort of backup plan. And that thought of two appealing men gives Nancy a twinge of jealousy that shames her. She wants the best for her daughter.

Self-pity. Oh, she just gets lonely. Admitting it makes her cry, and now she has to start all over again at the vanity.

NINA IS AWARE that things got quiet upstairs. Perhaps her mother is napping and that's to the good, it will give her time with the articles she brought with her, things she's kept in her bag, not wanting Ben to see, not wanting to have to answer questions about her foolishness. When she imagines telling him that she called (now) some thirty nursing homes, she can also imagine his rational argument for why that doesn't make sense. *But if her name changed in 1889, if it did*—and he shrugs and says, *It really is impossible.*

And what will she do with all this information she's gathering? She has a tiny idea that if she writes it right, she can try it on Hal—a piece about grieving, a twin's grieving. And so with her teacup rattling in its saucer, she comes back to the living room and studies like a schoolgirl cramming for a test. What kinds of things can she use in the article? Why did Mary, if she lived, not remember who she was?

Answers: Someone lied and told her everyone was dead. And took her away. Okay, that's kidnapping. But who would the child complain to if she thought her whole family had died?

Or she suffered a trauma and was confused for a time. Not a talker to begin with, other voices took over her voice. She was silenced. Their interpretations became her memories.

Or she died.

Or she was worn down with promises—*we'll take you back when the flood is over, this is just temporary, etcetera.*

All right, why would someone want her?

She might have appealed as a farmhand, a domestic worker in training—and damn, she was already good at it at the age of four. So perhaps poor people who wanted help took her on. Or dumb people who simply didn't hear the news and didn't know what to do with her—almost impossible. Or the oldest story in the world, Biblical in fact, of the childless woman who wanted someone else's pretty child.

She takes up her pages. *Endel Tulving on multiple memory systems,* Dr. Silverstein has scrawled on top of the copy's pages. Okay, 1972, this chapter from a book seems to be about episodic and semantic memory—distinctions made. We possess more than one type of memory, says this scholar. We can remember incidents. We can remember ideas, sweeps. Nina puts the article aside to look at the next.

Wow. Aristotle. That guy had a hand in everything. Way back when, he said a person can remember something generally (say unhappiness) without a specific incident or could remember an incident that is time specific. No beating him for categorizing.

Even Henri Bergson gets in on the act, asking, How do we think, how do we remember?

Well, all right, if Mary lived and if she remembered specifics, she would have acted on them at some future point when she was old enough to do so. Unless she hated her family, which doesn't seem likely. Unless she fully believed they were all dead. But no, if she remembered, she could have gone back to visit her uncle at some point to find out what she could.

Nina comes back to the power of words. If all memories are reconstructions—if we use the present knowledge to put together a story of the past—what happens if there weren't words, then what?

Something unlike Ellen's experience—Ellen who used and heard *words.*

Her head aches. She feels like she is back in school again. Aristotle, Bergson, Pierre Janet. She marvels that apparently she would not know how to put her car key into the ignition without memory, that getting through life is a matter of knowing how to do things. Who can afford to learn everything all over again? Amnesia! The worst nightmare.

Ben smiling at her over a cup of coffee in the break room at work. Douglas going into the house on fire and coming out with a baby. Are those first glimpses of someone so strong that they define everything that comes after, so that we are not only experiencing the new but also working on a memory system at the same time?

On a single sheet of paper at the bottom of the pile is the name of a woman who teaches at Ohio University. And a scrawled note: *Research on twins.*

She can't call tonight. Normal people take their weekends seriously. So Monday. She must wait.

"I have this feeling," she tells her mother as she drives them to Conzatti's. "I feel like I could find out something, give her an image (it might be horrible and sad, but it would be closure). I feel like I could find something out, but I don't know where to start."

"It's a feeling?"

"That's all it is."

"But if you're calling nursing homes—"

"Caught! All right. More than a feeling. A wish. At the worst I could write a feature on children and memory and try to get Hal to take it. That won't help Ellen much."

"No. But it will show what you can do."

"I guess. I'm so hyped up."

"Too much tea? Ben? Has he called?"

So it always comes back to Ben. "I told him to go home, to give himself to the home situation and not do it half-heartedly. I don't want to marry him if he doesn't know what would happen if he gave his marriage a try."

"You're braver than I ever would have been."

"I don't feel very brave. Can we not talk about it?"

"Of course. Um. What will you have for dinner?"

"I think ravioli. And lots of bread and butter. You?"

HOW STRANGE, how strange to appear at his home, the one he pays for, and like a traveler, an old cousin, carrying a small overnight bag.

The boys are all over him; he's the tree trunk and they are the squirrels, climbing.

"If you want a shower," Amanda says, coming into the living room from the kitchen, "I put out fresh towels." She is wearing a light blue dress and a sweater of medium blue and flat shoes. Her hair looks nice in that way it does when she's just had something done, like highlights.

"A shower would feel good."

"No!" cry the boys. Bryson insists, "Watch *Big* with us. It's about a guy who gets grown up right away."

"I remember. I saw it."

"We saw it too. Let's watch again." They watch everything at least five times. They learn the lines, like alphabets, like prayer.

"I'll watch a little. I really want a shower."

"Why?"

"I don't know. Just do."

Amanda follows them into the family room and sits. "Are you watching, too?" Zach asks, surprised. Bryson looks at her, wide-eyed. "I thought you didn't like this movie."

"I like it. I'll watch for a little bit. I'm getting things ready. Baked potatoes. Steak. Green beans. Salad."

"I thought chicken fingers." The whiney voice again. Zach is too old to sound that way.

"Tomorrow's lunch. Try to eat the steak."

Zach shrugs. Somehow he ended up not a big meat eater. And Bryson does whatever Zach does. Ben still likes his meats and so does Amanda, there, something in common. She sits with one leg crossed over the other, jiggling her foot.

She's trying so hard. It makes Ben sad, but he doesn't hate her.

The one thing he allows himself to like about being home is the space. He could almost jog around the house. The family room has a bar, only slightly tacky, a locked cabinet that the kids will figure out how to break into when they are in their teens, or before. He'll have to get rid of it. "Is there anything in there?" He points.

"I think so. I haven't used anything."

He fetches the key from its hiding place in the kitchen between two stacked ramekins and while he's in there, he fetches two glasses with ice.

On the counter is a bottle of red, open for their dinner. When he comes back to open the bar, he asks, "Something for you?"

"No. Thank you."

"Sure?"

"Maybe in an hour or so I'll start on a bit of red."

She used to ask for Bloody Marys when he opened the bar. The mix is still there, little cans of it. His Scotch looks to be the same level it was when he left. In some things, time stood still. Maybe.

The jiggling foot in its pretty little flat shoe—pompom over the toe— is the giveaway. Amanda is never very calm and she is trying to just sit, but her foot wants to move somewhere, do something. "Are those new shoes?" His voice betrays the worry about cost. He hasn't bought himself anything for a long time, but then he doesn't much care about fashion.

"My mother bought them for me."

Another maybe. He doesn't know where truth is.

The boys laugh when Tom Hanks sees himself in the mirror, all big. "They want to grow up fast," he whispers to Amanda.

Amanda says, "All boys do. Girls, too."

He watches for a while, for as long as his Scotch lasts, and he can't help remembering the bottle he left at Nina's, the one they took to Johnstown. She usually refuses, too, just like Amanda. Well, he doesn't choose souses for his spouses.

Finally, the boys are so engaged they don't even much notice or care when he goes upstairs for his shower. The towels are white (with kids in the house?) and he is pretty sure they're new. Does Amanda have a job on the sneak? But, oh, once he is in the shower stall, huge and with a center ceiling nozzle, all very state of the art, a tile ledge to sit on if you're a woman and want to shave your legs or if you're an old fart and just want to sit down—he likes it, the space.

He scrubs well, not sure of what the evening holds. Will they touch? He doesn't want to think ahead to what it will mean to sleep in the same bed. Does Caldwell know what she is doing? Is she some equivalent of a Catholic priest, refusing to acknowledge that some sacraments were not meant to be upheld?

Wrapped in a new white towel—man, what are these things made of?—he steps out of the bathroom and into his bedroom. He's so uncertain of everything. He'd wanted Nina to be his ballast and she's sent him off, floating, uncertain. To make room for the fireman? He lies down on the bed, still feeling sad and worried. He is almost asleep when he hears, "Oh, I'm sorry, I didn't know—"

He's covered, well covered in the huge wonderful towel. "Where did we get these?"

"My mother."

"Why is she buying you things?"

"She felt bad for me. That was part of it. I think also she wanted me to be able to snag a you-know—"

"Someone not like me."

"I guess." They both laugh a little. "I'll put off dinner until you're ready. I can make them the damned chicken fingers if they can't wait."

"No, I'm ready. Just let me get dressed."

"Is work good?"

"Okay. I have a big piece in on Monday."

"What about?"

"The flood. Another flood piece."

He sees in her hesitation and the cast of her eyes aside that she has not been reading the paper. Well, that's one big mark against her, more evidence for the negative. When she leaves, he dawdles for a while before finally dressing and going downstairs.

Dinner is good. Very good. The wine is more than decent. Maybe Mom bought that too. Eventually the boys are persuaded to go to bed. Amanda has another movie, *Rain Man*, for them to watch. He's seen it over at Jake's house, but he doesn't say.

"Would it be okay if I sit on the couch with you?" she asks.

"Yes." He moves over an inch or two unnecessarily.

At one point in the film she takes his hand. At first it seems an assault, then it's not bad at all. Late in the film, she starts to cry. "Sorry," she says. For a moment it's as if he's with Nina, a similar emotional reaction, but she is not like Nina who is much earthier. Still her tears are heartfelt and he comforts her with an arm around her.

Eventually he kisses her. Is this what he's supposed to investigate? Ah, well, sometimes the body gives cues and you either fight them or you don't. They go up to the bedroom and find mostly old patterns. He holds her from behind, he urges her clothes off, he undresses hurriedly, she lies on the right side of the bed, he takes the left side and supports himself partway over her for the prelims. It's all very familiar even though it's been a long time.

"Thank you," she whispers, "thank you."

Oh, Nina, he thinks, where are you?

T HE NEXT NIGHT , Sunday night, Nina is alone in her apartment. With her small life. The apartment—she wanted it to herself again—now it seems haunted, Ben's voice, his body, there and not there.

When Michelle taps at her door, she feels both irritation and relief. "Hey. Come in."

"You have a minute?"

"Sure, what's up?"

"Nothing. I just needed to hear a voice."

"Me, too."

"Where's Ben?'

"He's with his family this week. We're alternating." There. No pussy-footing around. Just say it.

"That's very advanced."

"Or backward. Depends on how you want to interpret."

"I don't think I could be that advanced."

She didn't think so of herself either. But here she is. What she's supposed to do by most people's count is call Douglas and explore a connection with him as Ben explores one with Amanda. She's such a nerd. She can't make herself do it. "Let's eat some cookies my mother packed."

"Okay." Michelle seems relieved she is being asked to sit down.

"Coffee?"

"That goes great with cookies."

"Agreed."

"Are you seeing the firefighter you told me about?"

"No."

"What happened there?"

"Nothing happened. I just can't."

"Why?"

"I'm too Johnstown."

"What does that mean?"

It means ridiculous. She putters in the kitchen, starting the coffee. "It's hard to explain," she says finally.

"Try."

"Um. Oh, addicted to the high road." Michelle looks confused. "Okay, holier-than-thou."

"You should be tough."

"Yeah. Hey, I have a piece in tomorrow. Not assigned. A little feature. Working my way up. Toughly. It's a tiny step."

Johnstown

VOL. XXXVI., NO. 1853.　　　　　JOHNSTOWN, PA., FR

OUR CALAMITY

Johnstown Sitting on its Ruins and Mourning its Dead.

Mills, Buildings, and Homes Gone, and 5,000 People.

NO WORKSHOPS NOR BUSINESS HOUSES, AND ONLY HERE AND THERE A HEARTHSTONE.

Whole Families Swept Away, and All that Remain in Deep Bereavement.

The Heaps of Wreckage Still Filled with Victims, and Hearts Still Bleeding.

TENS OF MILLIONS OF FINANCIAL LOSS, AND ONLY THE FUTURE TO RESTORE IT.

Misery, Poverty, and Death Our Portion, but Friends Are Helpful.

The Ruined City Now Under State Control, with a Ray of Hope Ahead.

sumed before your eyes, and the same fate your own a moment after!

But the flood had not yet done all its work. Cambria City remained to be destroyed, and the railroad towns below if it could reach them. Cambria went, like a child wipes out a pictured village on its slate, and then on the waters flew. But soon they were out of the mountain and away from home, and then, as if repenting the last blow struck, the cruel current weakened and spread and all was over.

All? To many it was but the beginning. The fierce rush was over, but the back-water remained, and thousands of people. Their refuge was the wreckage left behind and the few buildings that, sheltered in some way, survived the shock. But all around were buildings falling. Crash succeeded crash, wild shrieks for help were heard on every side, and "our turn next" was the thought in every mind.

And then there was the darkness coming on, and the rain had again set in. Wife, husband, children—whole families separated—no way to get news of one another, and the long hours of the night ahead. Nothing to do but sit and wait in dread, cheering others if you could, and being cheered by other souls in turn—helping and being helped the whole night through.

Darkness soon came, and then the fires, and the added horror that sight of a conflagration always brings. Down at the bridge—what a glow it made! People were told the wreck had been fired to clear the way—to break the jam. Well that they believed the story! St. John's Church, with a corpse in it, fired no one knows how, and then the houses on both sides of it. How like guards the people watched the flame, and questioned one another! It's going down; it's blazing up again; it's coming this way! Calls from roof to roof, "What's burning now?" and answers that in the awful stillness succeeding the first wild hours had an awful sound.

"Who are you?" "Who's with you?" and so, in the way that rumors fly, from mouth to mouth a good part of the whole day's story went, and hearts that had hoped sunk in despair, while hearts that had feared and quailed for loved ones thanked God that they were saved.

All through the night house upon house that had partly held together after the first great crash and had stood the awful journey down and up and down again, went to pieces with its occupants, and then came heroic deeds of daring by which many were saved, and the most frightful experiences until other roofs were reached, only to be gone

It was not long, however, before he came. It came first in the form of a big corps of reporters from Pittsburgh, and at sight of them we knew that we were again in touch with the great world outside. They had to surmount many obstacles; not merely houses in the streets and wastes of water everywhere, and, in a general way, take chances with us, but there were many dreary miles between them and the nearest telegraph station. But they performed their duty nobly and we owe them much. Then in came the farmers with their Saturday marketing, many of them in ignorance of our plight until they struck the hills overlooking the track of the flood. There were few to sell to, but, bless their souls, they didn't want to sell. All they had was the suffering people's, and they were only sorry they didn't have more; and to prove their sorrow they went home and got more, and have stood by us ever since. Many of them came to town with teams and wagons and set to work as only a farmer can to clear the ground. Right there they were at home, and every stroke counted.

Saturday was a terrible day nevertheless. Not a living man, woman, or child but was bereft of relative or dear friend. Bodies were recovered rapidly. Here a banker or merchant, by his side a laborer or perhaps a despised Hun. Here in the filth, all that was left of a sweet, refined woman; there and all about her the bodies of strangers dead. Here and there, wherever the wreckage landed, a fond mother with her dead babe tight clasped in the arms of death. The leveler's work was thorough.

So the day wore through and night came again. Headquarters for relief had been established, a general morgue opened, and at the most accessible points up and down the valley dead-houses were located. There were also hospitals, to which many sick and wounded were removed, and every moment saw stretchers moving along.

With night came total darkness. The electric-light house was wrecked and the gas house demolished. Only on the hill houses was there even oil, and only here and there on the hill would a faucet run water. These houses were open to all comers, friends and strangers alike, and all were crowded. But they could accommodate only a fraction of the sufferers, and many spent the night on the mountain or straggled out to peaceful and hospitable country homes where every comfort was afforded them.

Then came the Sabbath, but it was a day of rest in Johnstown. The work was taken up where it was left off the night before. Hundreds of bodies had been

CHAPTER

12

Monday, May 8, 1989

Oldest Flood Survivor Visits Memories, Reveals Truths

Pittsburgh Post-Gazette, THE JOHNSTOWN FLOOD SERIES

BY BEN BRAGDON

The Johnstown Flood of 1889 was a capricious god. In the maelstrom that was the tumbling water of the South Fork Dam, there was a group of people huddled on a roof that floated, and though it was a strange ride, they thought they were safe and that they would live. There was a boy riding a tree trunk that careened crazily through the water, making him and everyone who saw him certain that he faced imminent death. The boy lived. The group on the roof died when the roof went under.

By June 1, 1889, there were many such stories of deaths and survivals. The flood's oldest known survivor, Ellen Emerson of Johnstown, for years has told a story as strange as any other. She now lives in an apartment in the Southmont area of Johnstown. The building is well maintained; she has daily help, but she has insisted on her goal of remaining independent.

Mrs. Emerson's personal history is unusual for a child born in 1885. She got an undergraduate education at what is now

Chatham College in Pittsburgh and a graduate degree at New York University. For many years she worked in publishing as an editor at the Greaves publishing house. She married William Emerson in 1918. They adopted a child and took that child, Rosemary, to Johnstown to raise her. Rosemary, who died in 1952, had married Rev. Stephen Driscoll of Johnstown.

Mrs. Emerson has often spoken of the day of the flood. In 1889 she was one of the most colorful survivors. Journalists from around the world wanted her story. And she, a child of four, told it well. But she asserts now that she told it only partially, understanding even as a four-year-old that some of the truth made an unseemly picture of the relatives who would take her and raise her.

Mrs. Emerson's parents were Victor and Molly Burrell. She had an older brother, Martin, and a twin sister, Mary. She remembers her family rushing to put what goods they could save in a cart. They didn't have a horse to do the pulling so her mother and father and a cousin, Paul Folks, drew the cart themselves. Around them on the street were neighbors also packing up goods and moving to higher ground. The first layer on the cart, Mrs. Emerson explains, was made up of stacks of Bibles, since selling Bibles was her father's business. "We couldn't tolerate the loss of his inventory," she says. "But of course, in the end, just about everything that everybody owned was lost.

"On top of the Bibles were a few items of clothing and some blankets. And on top of that a mattress and over it an oil cloth. We were going to my uncle's house and we knew we would want one more bed. But also the mattress just fit the cart and it acted as a cover, a cap, to protect the Bibles."

At one point as they moved along slowly, they and their neighbors heard the famous sound that some thought at first was a locomotive. But soon enough, Ellen Emerson says, the panic began to hit. "Only it was too late. By the time people turned and could see the wall of water coming at us, there was no time to go anywhere."

The flood itself, a huge disaster that claimed 2,209 lives in a matter of minutes, is difficult to comprehend because of its speed. "Everything happened suddenly. I saw my mother call to us to run to a building. I saw her and my brother start toward it. And I saw them swallowed by water."

What happened next was as strange as any story of the flood. Mrs. Emerson's father grabbed her to put her on the cart. Her sister was already there, terrified from the start by the warnings of disaster and the ceaseless rain. The movement of the water tipped both Ellen Burrell and Victor Burrell up to the cart and for a while the cart moved through the rapids like a huge raft. Paul Folks, the Burrells' cousin, had managed to hang on. At one crucial moment, Mrs. Emerson says, things changed. Her cousin pushed her father from the cart into the swirling water as he climbed on. "This is something I never told before, except to my uncle. He was adamant that I never say it again. He told me I was mistaken. He told me I was made crazy by the trauma."

Everything about that day was traumatic—with strange rescues and survivals and more often swift deaths.

"The cart jammed between two buildings. For a moment we were still. My cousin climbed into the window of one building. He didn't take us. That was perhaps a sin of selfishness. What he did to my father was worse. It was a crime." Mrs. Emerson says that she and her sister lost the cart beneath them when it was dislodged from the buildings but that they rode on the mattress for a significant amount of time that she estimates to be about four minutes. She reports that she repeatedly comforted her sister. They saw horrible things. They saw death all around them. "There'd be a man bobbing up, a horse bobbing up, dead, all dead. Sometimes there'd be a shout from people hanging on to planks of wood or a roof."

One such instance of other survivors was a roof with a family huddled on it. "The son was a boy of nineteen. His parents screamed at him when he grabbed a set of roofing tiles and used them to swim toward us. They were terrified for him. But at just that point, we were close. Our mattress veered toward their roof and I tried to stand. He grabbed me and tossed me to the roof. When I saw him start to swim back to the roof, I screamed that he needed to get my sister. He was surprised. He hadn't seen her. He tried to swim back but just then the water changed course and the mattress sped away. I think I screamed for hours."

The roof that the boy who saved Ellen rode on survived and it hit ground hours later. The boy's name was Martin Venders. "Martin. Like my brother. If you like coincidences," she says with a smile. Venders lived to the age of seventy-five. He became a banker in Cleveland.

Ellen Burrell's uncle and aunt, the Reverend Paul Folks and his wife, Hester, said they would adopt her. They were alarmed by the story she told about her cousin Paul Jr. They knew she had lost everyone, so they assumed she was crazed with grief. Still, she insisted on seeing the bodies of recovered victims. When her sister could not be found among them, she insisted that her sister was alive. Mary Burrell was never found and is listed among the unrecovered dead. "I tried to find her years later. I had a private detective searching records. He said she died in Idaho. I still believe he had the wrong person."

For all of the times Mrs. Emerson as a child was told that she had remembered the events of the day incorrectly, she held on privately to her convictions. One day years later a posthumous letter arrived from her cousin Paul. He had given instruction to his wife to mail it after his death. It was a letter of apology for what he had done to save himself at the expense of others' lives.

When Mrs. Emerson is asked the usual questions about her recipe for survival, she says, "I'm restless. Always have been."

The people of Johnstown have been called strong. They began to make coffins and to line up the dead on church pews as soon as the floodwaters allowed them to move. Clara Barton set up headquarters. Men went back to work in the mills eight days later. "The most terrible thing had happened, but the living kept living," she says. "And I just kept on with it."

Family Survives Multiple Floods in Vulnerable Johnstown

BY NINA COLLINS

The city of Johnstown is situated in a valley and especially vulnerable to flooding. Residents know this well. They have heard stories from parents and grandparents and great-grandparents.

Early immigrants from Europe experienced the Great Flood of 1889. While subsequent floods, two of them major ones, did not cost the numbers of lives that the first flood did, they wreaked significant havoc on an already nervous population.

The Flood of 1936 happened in early spring and was caused by three consecutive days of heavy rain and a substantial runoff from melting snow. At one point the water level was fourteen feet high. Two dozen people died and many buildings were destroyed. In fact property damage was so substantial that President Franklin Roosevelt agreed to tour the damage.

To be fair, Pittsburgh residents of 1936 suffered an even worse version of this flood. On the same dates, March 17 and 18, snow melted, rivers rose, and water reached over forty feet. Altogether 100,000 buildings were damaged; the death toll was sixty-nine people.

In Johnstown, with the knowledge of what had happened in 1889, people were understandably frightened. Here is one story of many: A family of hard-working Russian immigrants was away from home at their jobs, the women cleaning houses, the men in the mills. Only sixteen-year-old Maria was at home. She was sewing. Dress and shirt making was the women's secondary employment. The women were never idle at home, but always sewing. When soldiers came to the door to tell Maria she had to leave, that they were there to take her to higher ground, she refused. When they insisted, she tried to get them to carry the sewing machine. They hurried her to a truck outside. They were saving lives, they explained, not machines. She was distraught. She had left a large pot of soup on the stove. It would be destroyed. Her sewing machine would be destroyed or stolen.

To be spirited away by strangers, when she understood she would lose everything, was hard for her, but even worse was not knowing where her family was and if anyone was taking them to higher ground.

It turns out it took a whole day for Maria to find them in Brownstown, up on a hill where all the houses were crowded with strangers. Years later, Maria, married by then, taught her own daughter Nancy that things were safe. Roosevelt had dedicated money to reroute the rivers and Johnstown would never be flooded again. Nancy grew up learning that Johnstown was

"The Flood Free City." It was also "The Friendly City" and "The City of Beautiful Women"—this last according to a WJAC disc jockey.

Nancy married and had a daughter. On July 20, 1977, there were thunderstorms trapped over the Johnstown area. The rain had been heavy for days. Creeks swelled, the new channels Roosevelt had had built overflowed, small streams swelled until their water cascaded wildly, creating new unplanned channels.

Nancy's daughter was only fifteen at the time and she was in Pittsburgh on a special university visit. Nancy and her husband survived the water rushing down the street and filling their basement. As soon as the water receded, they went to work, him to clean up a small shop he owned, her to Memorial Hospital. There was no water, electricity, or phone service anywhere. The town was cut off. Nancy's daughter could not find out if her mother and father were alive. She got a ride back into town with a friend who ignored barriers and warnings and drove over fallen trees and debris. They found houses down everywhere, trucks and cars wrapped around each other, trees down, and mud and wreckage everywhere. Finally she found her parents alive and working. They were not among the eighty-five dead.

I, the writer of this article, am Nancy's daughter. My mother, born Nancy Pastorek, went to the high school where Ellen Emerson taught. Her mother, my grandmother Maria, returned to her home in Cambria City in 1936 to find her sewing machine on top of a wooden cabinet and the pot of soup attached to a curtain rod. We've all learned to fear the power of water. We've also learned how lucky people are when they suffer a traumatic disaster but do not lose the people they love.

"GROUP SESSION," the aide says. "We're supposed to get the butts moving."

"I don't have much of a butt."

"That's true. You want the wheelchair?"

"Let me see if I can walk." What a glorious day it is outside her window. "Oh! We should meet outdoors," she says, getting out of the bed with some difficulty. Her mind tells her body to move but her body balks. The aide helps her up. "Can we change the meeting place?" she asks.

"Well, no, it's in the gathering space. Easier to hear each other. Most people have hearing aids."

Bless her ears. That's one part of her that's working overtime. When she stands, she totters, and the aide has to catch her. The legs are not working overtime. "I feel so . . . very tired today."

"Did you have breakfast?"

"Um, yes." This is a lie. She skipped it.

"Excitement, then."

"Maybe that's it. I'll . . . I'll need the chair after all, damn."

"I'll say damn, too. I'm going to put a pillow on the chair to cushion your bony butt. Were you always thin?"

For a long time she was. Then she had a period of contentment and she spread a bit in the hips before she knew it was happening. But at one point she lost the weight without trying. Age. "Whew. I'm winded. Very tired."

"Too much exertion. You're sure you ate?"

"Um hum." Not last night either. For some reason she couldn't make herself want anything. And the result is she doesn't feel all that well today. She knows she must make herself eat lunch. "Maybe I should skip the socializing."

"Really? But that's the cure for everything, they say. People. Friends."

"Well, all right."

She's in the chair minutes later and the aide is trundling her down the hall. She wants to lie down; she wants nothing more than she wants sleep. She closes her eyes.

Her very good ears tell her something is up. A hush and a giggle. Ah, yes, here she has tried to forget this marker, but they won't let her. There is a large sheet cake in the center of the room and real cups next to a carafe of coffee as well as paper cups near a jug of cider. A hand drawn sign with gold glitter inside the numbers says, "A big 103."

"Happy birthday!" everyone cries out.

Oh, how she wants to sleep.

"And now," Mrs. Salinas says, "we want to sing to you." When they warble at her with their wavering off-key voices, she begins to cry. Maybe because they sound so bad or maybe because she's thinking, All this for me and no oomph to give anything back.

"We're going to have our regular session," says Salinas. "In a bit. But first we want to hear from our birthday girl. How did you do it? How did you get to a hundred and three?"

They quiet down for her answer. She is thinking how people die near their birthdays and she has the feeling that today might be the day. She feels the big black void filling her and it's bigger than she is. Everything in her wants to give up. And why not? Why not, so long as it doesn't hurt?

She has to say something. "I went into medicine. I was a nurse. I had access to the magic pills."

There is a smattering of laughter. Perhaps her joke is not so funny to some.

"What did you eat?" Salinas's favorite question.

"Everything. Absolutely everything. And a little wine and beer."

The group likes this answer and so they applaud her. She's fighting so hard to remember their names. Ada, Marion, Velma, Vicky, two *V*s, that's right, Mark, Richard, the only two men. The other names won't come to her. She knew them yesterday. She pulls herself together to say, "This is very nice of you."

"But we want to know about you. Your life. You were a nurse where? For how long?"

She just doesn't have the strength it would take to explain that she started at sixteen and worked private duty after she was sixty-five. Altogether she worked sixty years. And she was proud of it. She answers simply, "Mostly Shadyside Hospital."

"What is your worst memory?"

"Being cursed by a man whose life I saved. He wanted to die. He was angry with me for bringing him back."

"Oh. Maybe he was grateful afterward."

Anna doesn't think he was. She thinks he wanted to die. Period.

"And your best memory?"

"Too many." She saved a baby once who couldn't breathe. She met her husband when he was working the elevators at the hospital. Along the way there were a couple of awards and when she left the hospital (though she didn't stop working as a nurse) she got honored for her years of service.

As a nurse she witnessed the deaths of people she had come to care for. That was hard. The idea that she was supposed to stay removed, professional—it never quite took with her.

"Too many!" Salinas smiles. "We'd love to see pictures. Did you wear long uniforms in the early days?"

"Down to my ankles."

"Anything you'd like to tell us?"

"I'm so tired. I'm sorry."

"That's all right. It's the excitement. Let's have a little break."

"You want the paper?" Ada Tully asks her.

"No, thank you. You keep it." It's the copy the institution subscribes to.

"She gets her own copy in her room," the aide explains.

"La di da," says Vicky, whose comments are almost always negative, couched as teasing.

"There's a good article about the Johnstown Flood," Ada comments.

Anna tries to smile agreeably. That is one article she won't read, but she doesn't say so.

"I read one last week," one of the men says.

"This one is about the girl who rode on a mattress and lived. A mattress. Can you imagine?"

A darkness closes in and around Anna. She is sure she needs to sleep. She struggles to stay smiling, to be the right sort of recipient for all this kindness. "I am so very sorry, but I need to lie down."

"We're cutting the cake. Take a piece with you."

"All right."

They put it on a piece of heavy foil and she rides with it in her lap.

When the aide gets her back to her room, she ventures, "Didn't much like all that excitement, did you?"

"I tried."

"Sure you did. Let's get you to bed. A nap is a good thing."

Even the movement to the bed winds her. Her eyes are closed before she knows it. She doesn't care, she doesn't care, she doesn't care.

"Would you like some water?"

"No."

A small voice in her says, "You should. A sip."

"You want the newspaper?"

"No."

It will be like drowning. She didn't want it to be drowning. But there's that time when the swimmer stops fighting and feels ecstasy. So it's only awful for a while.

JIM PAGERINA squeezes her shoulder. "Liked your little piece."

"Thanks."

"I guess you want my job."

"Yes."

"Heeeyy."

And there's Ben, standing at her desk. "Can we have lunch at least?"

"If I'm here."

"I'll go out for two sandwiches in case. Hoping."

She'd almost rather go out. What if Ben makes her cry for all to see? But the assignments editor gives her what amounts to an office assignment, so she's going to be here. "Follow up on the CMU hiring freeze. Admins, chairmen of a couple departments, faculty. Okay?"

"Okay. Can do." She makes phone calls for an hour. In between, looking about to be sure nobody is paying attention to her, she calls the professor in Ohio who has done research on twins.

It's a surprise when the professor herself answers the phone and Nina has to shelve the speech she has ready for a voice mail system. The professor is fairly peremptory until Nina mentions her talk with Silverstein. That slows Professor Krakowski down some.

"Okay. Oh, how is Rebecca?"

"She seemed to be thriving."

"Good. So, what do you want to know?"

"I'm interested in memory in fraternal twins, different patterns with regard to memory?"

"Memory. That's a huge subject. I mainly study twins, not necessarily memory."

"I know. Are there studies of twins who get separated . . ."

"Sure. Oh, sure. That's a popular one. If you want some light reading—"

"No, I'd want more the real scoop. And if there is anything about memory or mental capacity in—"

"All right. I deal with that some. Tell you what. I could send you my bibliography. Do you have a fax?"

"Yes, we do, the office fax." She gives the fax number. "When will you send? I don't want it to get lost."

"I'll send in about five minutes."

Watching the clock, she types distractedly and then gets up and moves quickly through the office to where she can hover at the fax machine.

It's in. Two pages. She folds them and tucks them in her bag. Then she slips into the ladies' room where, in a stall, she looks over the bibliography. She's got to get to a library. That means heading to Oakland after work where she can start with Carnegie Library and then move on to the Pitt libraries—and, hey, yes, all right, it's a little something to do while Ben goes to Amanda and the boys.

When he arrives at her desk, sandwiches in hand, he has such an eager look. "God, I miss you," he says.

"Me, too."

"You miss you, too?" The old tease. And it's true. She lost some of her self along the way. "Say," he adds more seriously, opening today's paper on her desk, "here we are, together, in print. Nice, isn't it? You had that up your sleeve."

"Feels good."

"I know you'll get to do this kind of thing in future."

"I hope so."

"I got you a Reuben. I remember you liked them—when was that? I hope you still do."

"I like a Reuben."

"I got two so you don't get a choice. I had a sort of monomania going there."

Jim Pagerina taps her on the head when he goes by.

"What's that about?" Ben asks. "Is he flirting?"

"He's afraid I want his job. I do."

"This little article stirred something up."

"Yep. Killer instinct."

"I called Ellen this morning. She said you went by there on Saturday. That was just a visit?"

"Maybe. Are you checking up on me?"

"Curious."

Her sandwich is still hot. It drips with butter. She does not want to hear about his time with Amanda, but the fact that he doesn't want to talk about it is saying something anyway. While she's bantering with him, an angry headache creeps up her neck to the back of her head.

He should be saying, "It's awful. It's torture. I slept on the couch. I couldn't bring myself to touch her."

She should have kicked and screamed and said, "Don't go."

She's relieved to be interrupted and told to go see about a grade school with a gas leak and a couple of children falling down, overcome.

She eats the Reuben hungrily in the car, then manages to get herself to East Liberty, where she spots the TV crews—the people she knows from KDKA and WTAE.

"Anything happening?" she asks, going up to them. Pete is there again.

"The kids are happy," he says. "They got out of school."

"Can you say how serious is the leak? Who's talking?"

"Don't know yet. Some inspectors are in there. Some parents have taken their kids to be checked out."

"Say, whatever happened to that little girl from the fire?" one fellow asks the others.

"She's going to be okay," Nina tells them. "I got the word." Doug checked several times.

MELISSA KELLY SIGHS and studies Mrs. Hoffman. "Don't you want to wake up? Don't you want to have dinner?"

It sounds like "No." She's not sure.

A piece of birthday cake is sitting on the nightstand, untouched. "Oh, Mrs. Hoffman, this is no way to spend your birthday." She presses a hand to Anna's head. Uh-oh. Slight elevation. As she gets a thermometer from the cart, she pokes a head into the hallway and asks one of the aides, "Did you see Mrs. Hoffman up today?"

"Her birthday party."

"Oh, and she went to meals?"

"I don't know about that."

"Ask. Please ask."

Yes, the breathing is not so good. "Here you go sweetie, let me get your temp."

"Argo." Or something like that. Unintelligible. Over a hundred, no, over a hundred and one. Oh, damn. On her birthday. Of all things. Damn. She tries to dial the main office from the hall phone. Busy. Damn again. She runs down the hall, almost running into the aide she sent for information.

"They said she wasn't hungry."

Right. Oh, crap.

The director is not in the main office. She'll be back, but in the meantime . . .

Melissa Kelly picks up the phone and dials 911. "We need an ambulance. Patient is showing signs of pneumonia. I'll start an IV drip and some oxygen. Probably she is going to need antibiotics, but her doctor is—never mind. I'll call. Yes. Full code."

Another nurse drifts toward her and Kelly calls out:. "Would you bring me an IV and oxygen? To Mrs. Hoffman."

"Sure." The other nurse hesitates. "Mrs. Hoffman?"

"Yep."

Kelly goes back to the room and looks at the chart again. Yes, full code. This one is supposed to want to die. That's what the other nurse's hesitation meant. But this woman chose to live, at least when she signed in, and there was nothing naïve about her, she was a nurse after all. Kelly can hear at least seven people who tomorrow will be reprimanding, even if they don't say the words aloud. *At this cost? And she's a hundred and three? Can't we just forget to notice what she wrote down ten years ago? Can't we just . . . slip? Goof up?*

Kelly can't think that way. Oaths were written for her. She hates to see a person who can still think, who can make a joke, give it up.

Anna does not look like her usual self. Her hair is awry and her eyes are distant. "I'm pretty sure they're going to give you antibiotics in a little bit. I'm waiting to hear from your doctor. But for now, some water. Right? Will you try? You want to try, don't you?"

A very muffled line sounds like, "I can't talk." Anna looks at the cup, but can only manage the tiniest sip.

"Good. And one more."

The IV equipment arrives with the second nurse. "You want help?"

"You do the oxygen. I'll do the IV."

She hears Anna groan as the cannulas go into her nose. Her hand waves as if to pull them out, but instead she adjusts one.

"This is going to pinch," Kelly says.

Anna nods slightly. Her eyes close.

A few people gather in the hallways. The litany out there is of people saying, *We never had her birthday party. She was so tired. Did something happen? She's way up there in years. You can't expect—she was a quiet one. I never knew what she was thinking. Maybe she was quiet but she wasn't mean.*

A clatter that can only be the EMTs dragging a stretcher down the hallway quiets the speakers.

"Name?"

"Anna Hoffman," Nurse Kelly answers.

"Age."

"A hundred and three."

"She doesn't have a DNR?"

"Nope."

"Wow. Interesting. Give us some space. We're going to move her."

"I'm glad to see you're moving fast. We had a team in here last week that couldn't be bothered."

"Just doing my job. How are you, sweetheart?" the one young guy asks Anna.

"Urngh."

"A little pokey today, huh?"

"Today is her birthday."

"We can't have that. I see the cake. Obviously not touched."

"She's out of fuel. She skipped meals."

He nods, grunts as he and his mate cradle her and slide her onto the stretcher, then begin to bundle her up. After a moment, the one in charge leaves the strapping to his partner while he takes a call. When the call ends, he removes a vial of antibiotic from a case and injects it into the IV.

"She's—" says the second guy. "I give it one percent."

Soon Anna Hoffman is gone, down the hallway, to an ambulance, to St. Clair Hospital.

Two newish aides come in. "Should we do something to her room? Pack things up?"

Nurse Kelly reminds them that orders of that kind come from central office. Otherwise they have to leave things where they are. Nurse Kelly has plenty more rounds to finish. There is a little tug, something sad in her. Well, you can't help these things, attachments. This one reminds her of someone, she's not even sure who.

When the others are out of sight, she sits on the edge of the bed and pulls the cake to her. There was no plastic wrap on it so the outer layer is crusty and dry. She eats it. She doesn't need the sugar, but on the other hand, she needs the sugar.

HE'S LOSING NINA. Her face, the way she won't look at him. He's not sure he can explain to her that he doesn't love Amanda but that his body appears to be responding to the routine of the trip to Mt. Lebanon, the boys hugging him, the shower, the bed, Amanda's body. It comes to him as a remembered series of physical sensations as if he got into a car he used to own and after a second his hands knew exactly where all the buttons and controls were. But his heart is something else. It's with Nina.

He's driving fast, but why, he doesn't know. He pulls in at a gas station on Banksville. What's the hurry to get home? There he said it, home. Oh, he's out of his mind. Just work, work, work, that's the only solution. Next article is on the reconstruction of Johnstown with sidebars to give the schedule of festivities (funny word to apply to a flood) for the centennial. Why celebrate? He'll ask the question and then he'll answer it. Celebrate the human spirit, the survival, the determined animal nature of living. Animals learn to run on two and a half legs when the other one and a half get chewed off. Snakes grow another couple of sections. People build houses where a house went down, find new husbands, wives, families—*restless*, Ellen Emerson's word. He's losing Nina. He's losing pure joy.

He needs to spend time with some male friends, certainly could use a long bout of testosterone-fueled joking in a bar. That's what guys do when they don't feel in control of their lives.

He's just sitting at the gas station in one of the spots for people using the convenience store. He gets out of his car and checks the payphone. It appears to be in working order. He looks at his watch. Give her a little time. He wanders inside. Coke? Candy bar? He settles on an ice cream sandwich. Great way to layer the stomach for supper. Without the friends, there is still the possibility of a bar, a way to spend more on a shot of Scotch than he would if he had a tumbler full at home.

Oh, it's glorious today, real spring weather, not that early humidity and high temperatures that plague spring weddings. He finishes the ice cream and then goes to the payphone where he drops in coins and calls Nina's apartment. No answer. Machine. I love you, he wants to say. But when her voice asks him to leave a message, he says, "Thinking about you. I miss you. Can't wait to see you at work tomorrow." And then he can't think of what to say next so he hangs up on an unresolved musical note, a tone that cries out for an ending.

Fuck it. Fuck women altogether. She's probably off with her firefighter and here he is pining for her. He slams into his car only to drive a mere eighth of a mile or so and to pull into Atria's lot. Sure, he says to the valet who approaches him. Right, he forgot that here someone else must park the car. He goes inside where he orders his pre-dinner drink and watches local news on TV. Mostly they talk about baseball and he thinks how Nina loves it, always knows more than he does.

What is he doing indoors? It's beautiful outside! But an outside umbrella table will not put him in company with other despairing men, so he stays at the bar. Then he finds the hall payphone and calls Nina again. When her machine comes on a second time, he hangs up. Not home. He thinks of all the places Nina might be.

Two days from now he will take his boys to a Pirates' game without Amanda. She doesn't like baseball. Or Nina, who does, but it's too early to do that to the boys again. Four days from now, if he says yes tonight when he goes home, he will go on a weekend retreat with Amanda. Out in nature. Birdies singing, trees popping with blossoms, leaves still light green, an image of hope. And Amanda, even with allergies out the wazoo, still wants to do it. No interruptions. Just them for most of the day, and Caldwell's sessions from four to six, a pre-dinner ritual.

He's supposed to go back to Nina on Saturday, but if he says yes to the retreat he won't see her until Monday morning. Amanda, holding her hands tensely, said, "You could make it up to her. You could stay until the next Monday. I would accept a shortened week next week—if you'll do the retreat." And he had said, yes, probably, that would work.

284

Finally he gets into his car and goes home.

The rewards: The boys hanging off him. The smiles. What's so great about him, he doesn't know. Amanda is wearing shorts, very cute pink ones with a sweater. She looks uptight and young. Her legs are so thin that she usually makes excuses about wearing shorts, but today, there those legs are—not coltish, no, more plain vulnerable.

She kisses him lightly. The boys watch. He waits for her to say, "You're late," but she doesn't say it. He waits for her to say, "I smell booze," but she doesn't say that either. Lessons. She's learned 'em. Maybe from Aunt Mel who has strong opinions about everything.

He lets himself flop on the sofa. "We're having paaasta," Zach says.

"With chicken in it," Bryson adds.

"Sounds good."

"It's already made. It's in the oven."

"When you're ready," Amanda says.

EIGHT O'CLOCK, no dinner and she's still at the library—at the Pitt library now. The nice skinny, tall man at the reference desk is helping her. "What's this for?" he asked.

"A series I'm doing next year."

And yet, when the articles and books start to appear before her, Nina feels glum and once again foolish. There was a movie a couple of years ago! She never saw it but she must have heard about it—the idea that twins separated at birth find each other. Is this what has unconsciously nudged her along?

No wonder she's afraid Ben will scoff.

She keeps reading. Even the scholar she's reading acknowledges the attraction to stories of twins reunited. Shakespeare knew it. There are the twins in *Twelfth Night* and in *The Comedy of Errors*.

The thing is, the strange thing is, the thing that fascinates her the most as she reads accounts, is the likenesses in the lives of separated twins. In one case, two sets of new adoptive parents both named their girls Emily! In another, two boys both grew up to be doctors and both married and had two sons. Well, some of that had to be plain genetics.

Nina starts to pen paragraphs. What if she did a feature on twins? Perhaps it isn't a lie, what she told the reference librarian. She begins to recount stories from the journal articles. Children from a Catholic

285

orphanage in Chicago—one ends up in Chicago, the other in Davis, California. Both of them say they badgered their parents about having a sister. Did they? Or did they only believe in a sister after the fact?

No, it must be true. Twin after twin insists he or she *knew* there was another self. How strange.

She writes for another hour, case histories, ideas, putting everything into the stew: pop movies, Shakespeare, sitcomy misunderstandings.

Nina wishes again she were not an only child. To have another self. What would her other self tell her to do? Write the article, says the imaginary sister, write it now. Take a pause from Ben. Let it be. Have yourself some dinner.

She's had only a candy bar on the way in.

She could write the whole thing as conjecture. Would Hal go for that? She could write "What would have happened to Mary if Mary had lived?"

She checks herself out at nine thirty and on impulse goes to the Murray Avenue Grill for something to eat. Soup might do it, she tells herself before getting there, but when she's there, she orders the whole trout dinner, adding a glass of wine.

Man, it feels good to be out among people, to watch the baseball game on TV with chatter all around her, to order up a decent meal for herself.

CHAPTER

13

Anna and Ellen
July 1925

■ THE THINGS he led her to: baseball, why she hadn't paid much attention but the way he talked about it, then took her to a game the whole way over in Homestead—and it turned out she liked it. Once he took her and Ned to a Pirates' game at Forbes Field, and she liked the baseball fine (Ned loved it, which was wonderful to see), but she had to witness the way Will pulled up his dignity from his work boots and took them to sit where the ticket sellers told him to go.

Will was good to Ned, introduced him to things, fly fishing, of course, being one of the first things, baseball soon after that. And swimming. This was the summer just before the Pirates' and Senators' game of 1925, when Ned was eight. One day they took a holiday and rode the trolley to the end of the line where the big park was, Kennywood. They had heard about it plenty but had not been there.

"Two of you or three?" The ticket seller thought perhaps Will was a servant, supposed to wait outside the park for them.

"Three," he said. She saw that slight movement of his jaw backward as if to stuff words back, forward again to bring the machine that was his body back to normal.

Oh, she was used to it by now, people believing they were protecting her. She was a scandal at work and a part of her enjoyed the

Cambria City butcher shop, circa 1920s. Courtesy of Johnstown Area Heritage Association.

small revenge against the rabbity way people looked when they disapproved of something. Certain emotions flattered the face. Love did. She thought so.

Kennywood was marvelous. There were brightly painted rides every hundred yards. Children clamored to go on them and parents took them. "I can manage the Ferris wheel," she told Will. "The others, maybe you could take him."

He bought the tickets. She and Ned got into their car, she holding on tight to her son's shoulders.

"I'm not scared," Ned said, trembling.

"Well, I am! A little. I'm just not so used to going up high. It will be . . . different." In front of them two teenagers were rocking their car as wildly as they could. "Don't rock us," she warned her son. "I won't like that." He didn't. He was as eager as she for stability. The music started. Her breath caught. They went backward maybe a foot or so and then suddenly forward. She thought, "Oh, what good am I, so afraid of a ride." She could face a stomach wound, she could remove a bullet; blood didn't scare her. Just this height, this looking down, this movement she couldn't control. Her eyes sought out Will and found him. Smiling and waving, he nodded up at her as if to say, "You see, it's fine."

People stared at them. At Kennywood. Everywhere. This negative attention was something she was completely used to. Will said it used to be worse. He said when his grandparents first came to town, there were awful things, waiters putting salt in their coffee so they would never dare to enter a particular restaurant again. The waste of money was sad in itself—they had little, wanted to treat themselves, and then lost that little bit in ugliness. "They got charged more for everything. They had to take the freight elevators," he told her one night as they lay together. "Now what sense is there in that?"

Separation. It was always about separation. She saw all the tricks whites did to separate. Togetherness, especially of genders, made them very nervous. Ned was totally accepting of his mother and Will. He had sloughed off the attitudes of his grandmother who now no longer spoke to him. When the Ferris wheel ride ended, Anna goose-stepped to get her bearings, while Ned ran to Will and threw his arms around him. He was a naturally loving boy and she was glad of it.

Will loved showing her things. She had spent so much of her life working that she hadn't explored very much of what would be called fun. He'd wanted her to bring a swimming suit to the park but she didn't have one. Neither did Ned at this point in his young life. "Let's go buy them, then," Will had said yesterday.

"Wait," she said. "Not just yet. Maybe later in the summer. For now, let's just go see the park."

Of course she knew he wouldn't be allowed in the pool at Kennywood. He knew it too. He wanted her to go in with Ned, renting suits, and Ned was eager enough, but she didn't want to go in without Will. They stood at the gate, looking though the linked fence at dolphin-like men and children leaping and splashing, at modest women getting their legs wet and flinging finger-propelled spray at each other.

She didn't want to *own* a bathing suit or ever play in the water. It didn't appeal to her. "Let's go," she said. "Let's look at other things."

"I'm going to teach both of you to swim."

"Not here."

"Not here. We'll go to the municipal."

Her breath caught much worse than it had on the Ferris wheel. "Oh, maybe someday," she said, but Ned was saying, "Yes, yes, yes."

About two weeks later Will presented her with a bathing suit. "When I was a student nurse, we had to go to a pool. We rented suits there. They were just awful. Everybody looked terrible."

"And you swam?'

"No, I had the influenza. They sent me back to the residence. I missed that lesson."

A week after that, they went to the municipal pool, the one for Negroes. Across much of the country for every four or five white pools, there would be one for Negroes. Once more there were happy human dolphins and little children like fishes leaping through the water. She changed into her bathing dress, shaking uncontrollably. Oh, please no, not illness again. She couldn't afford it. She had work the next day.

"Just a simple first lesson," he instructed both her and Ned, "is to put your face in the water."

She watched Ned go first. He not only put his face in, he lifted his legs and tried to kick them.

"Excellent. Excellent. Let's give your mother a try."

"Don't make me do this."

He laughed.

She began hitting him. She'd never hit him before, ever; she couldn't remember ever hitting anyone. "Don't make me do this. I'm telling you—"

Ned was aghast. Will looked momentarily angry, even embarrassed at the way people cast glances at them. After a while he escorted her to the side of the pool and worked with Ned. That night as she lay rigidly beside him, he said, "There must have been something."

"Must have been," she said tightly.

"Can you tell me?"

"No. I don't know a why. I just know I hate it. And I can't do it."

He reached for her hand. She couldn't respond. Finally he rolled to his side and put his arm around her. She started to cry. "I'm sorry I'm crazy," she said.

"Oh, well," he teased, "you have some awfully good points. If ever you fall into a river, I'd better be around to fetch you out."

ONE DAY that summer, Bill Emerson said, "I miss going to Coney Island. We should take a vacation; we could take Rosemary there."

Ellen was all for it. She loved seeing where Bill had grown up, loved imagining him as a boy. They'd visited his Brooklyn home once. He'd worked from the youngest age (as had his brother) in the butcher shop as well as delivering papers and milk. He'd always worked, first in Maspeth, where they opened the first butcher shop and lived, and later in Brooklyn, where they settled after that with a second store that they expanded after they gave up the first. All this before the clerking job. Ellen had visited both places before she left New York with Bill. Once, during her graduate student days, she had attended a picnic near the Brooklyn house where she met his then wife, a frail and perhaps insistently innocent creature. But those were the days when she had worked hard at falling out of love with Bill. The two of them hadn't been back—and that was unfair to Bill who could savor things past as well as present.

So they went.

They took a train from Johnstown to Manhattan and a subway train from Manhattan to Brooklyn. Rosemary liked the trains.

Embraces with Bill's family, Ellen remembers, held a slight formality and the feeling they were studying her. They had loved Bill's first wife. Ellen tried to get the parents to come to the beach with them the next morning, but they could not imagine taking a day off work.

And so Ellen went with her family on the Brighton line to Stillwell Avenue on a hot July day, her birthday, but she didn't want to make too much of it. In fact she was fairly sure Bill had forgotten it. Bill swam all day and he lured Rosemary into the water with playful antics until the child got comfortable. But Ellen saw strain on his face, which she later thought of as premonition.

Ellen didn't go into the water.

Maybe seven times she told herself she was going to, but she didn't. Instead she sat on their blanket and read, covering her fair skin as well as she could. Water. She couldn't love it as recreation. Yes, she understood perfectly well that she was made up of water and that it was the source of life. She was reasonable in most things, and she could be logical about why she feared water, but even so her resistance won out.

Very sunburnt, all of them, they lugged their things to the train and off. By the time they walked the block to Bill's parents' house, they knew something was wrong. A man and a woman with sober faces stood outside the door, waiting for them. Bill dropped everything and ran to them, then into the house. "His father," the woman told Ellen. "I'm sorry."

She had never seen Bill this way. He wept openly and deeply. His mother kept smoothing his hair and telling him his father had been glad to see him again. All around them were neighbors bringing contributions of food—the delicious foods she had smelled and eaten when she was a tiny girl growing up: pierogies, stuffed peppers, kielbasa. Bill had to retire to the back bedroom to compose himself.

Ellen explained what she could to Rosemary and read to her and put her to bed. Once Rosemary was asleep, and the neighbors gone for the night, and Bill's mother given something to make her sleep, Bill and Ellen sat with two of his childhood friends and a bottle of whiskey and they talked.

"He was proud of you."

"Oh, he always said so in letters, but . . . he never said anything about himself."

"No. He never talked about himself, only the business or politics, things like that."

"I should have visited."

"He would have liked that. But hey, you took another path, right? Success." He saw envy in their eyes along with the love that came with their shared boyhoods.

"Your mother talks about you and your brother all the time," they told him. "Always tells us how you two are doing."

Early the next morning his brother, Stan, arrived, red-eyed. He'd become an engineer. He lived in Connecticut. He'd visited more often than Bill had.

But nobody ever had enough time.

"We were so close at one time," Bill whispered to Ellen when they were alone in the bedroom. "I knew his every move. How did we let ourselves go?"

Ellen had been fascinated by the boundaryless life of the immigrant families. But she saw clearly that opportunity changed people and they lost some of the closeness.

Bill worked to visit his mother more often after that summer. They sat in her Brooklyn backyard, drinking beer, an indulgence she loved guiltily, and she told him never to blame himself for anything. He often quoted that in jest when he and Ellen squabbled about something.

And then when Bill's mother was gone, there was only his brother. Bill and Ellen managed once to get to Connecticut. His brother came to Johnstown once and marveled at the changes in their lives.

"Remember summers? Coney Island?" his brother asked.

"The best. We were lucky. A wonderful childhood."

Once Bill and Ellen took a vacation to Stone Harbor, New Jersey. It was beautiful and she loved looking at the way the sun sparkled on the sea, but she managed, what with preparing food, reading, and dealing with weather, never to play in the water.

Josh Gibson of the Homestead Grays and children. Courtesy of Frank Ceresi and FC Associates

CHAPTER 14

Tuesday, May 9–
Friday, May 12, 1989

"LET ME GET THIS OLD. Just doing my thing, a nice, peaceful death."

"It isn't going to be that peaceful."

"What if the antibiotics bring her around?"

"They won't. Not at her age."

"Will she be happy or sad is what I meant. If she comes around."

"She'd be dazed, probably."

"We hardly ever see them this old. Look at her skin. It's not bad. I wonder what she used. Good genes, right? If I got this old, mine would be all pocked and horrible."

"I'd be demented. My whole family gets demented at sixty."

"That's kind of young to lose it."

"They lose it, all right. Don't know their toes from their nose. And when they go, they go kicking and screaming. You see that article in the paper about that woman who lived through that flood—a couple of floods. She was old, too, and looked damned good. What is it with these people who get the good genes?"

"I always heard it was meanness that keeps people going."

"Oh, I don't know. That's not the only thing. But something puts gas in their car. If meanness did it, my family would live forever. Temp is down a notch. Just a notch. Let's go get some coffee."

"Coffee puts gas in my car."

"Does Amanda think you're coming back?"

"She probably does."

All around them other journalists move back and forth, one crashes into a wastebasket, cursing, and two are shouting something or other to each other. Most of them are probably trying to listen in, but they keep moving, out of civility.

"Do *you* think you are? Going back?"

"No. I see that I *could* and I see that I don't want to. As much as I hate this experiment, I can see that it clarifies things."

"Okay."

"I like being with the kids, but I can't wait to get here in the morning, to see you."

"And to work. You always wanted to get here to work. I definitely get that you like work better than you like suburban life."

"And you're here."

"I'm here. Mostly. Until they send me somewhere."

"Like to a fire." He looks hard at her.

"I didn't call him."

"Look. I have to tell you one thing. I won't be back right away this weekend. It's the last big thing I have to do for this therapy I signed on for. It's a real retreat. Away. And I mean away from it all. For the weekend. We go to some woods. No interruptions. Except for the therapy sessions. I go Friday night. I get back Monday morning. I have to do it. Amanda will sign the divorce papers, no contest, if I do it. That's the deal."

"A weekend in the woods. Sounds wonderful."

"Don't be angry. You told me to do it. You sent me to the program."

Pagerina is looking at them, a kind of delight on his face, the shit. And then Barry comes to her and says, "Shooting in Homewood. Twelve-year-old on the way to the hospital. They say the perp is hiding in some basement somewhere."

"I'm there," Nina says. She turns back. "It's not anger at you. It's just . . . feeling dumb and undecided and fucked up."

"Exactly. I couldn't have said it better."

She waves goodbye.

Soon she is in her car. Soon she is on her way to Homewood. The kids there have been shooting each other and—is it anger at the other that motivates them or just feeling dumb and undecided and fucked up? How's that for a headline?

When she gets to Homewood, she can count seven police cars, lights flashing, all parked at hasty angles. And there are her pals from WPXI, KDKA, and WTAE. The disaster squad. There is Pete's tech guy, lugging the heavy camera. WTAE is down to a two-man team but KDKA still uses three. The techies have it hard, lugging around twenty-five to thirty pounds of cameras and batteries and cords. Then those tripods. And it's hot today. The teams are busy lining up interviews with people on the street—neighbors—three crying, two shouting, many looking just plain sad. She exits her car and begins to line up interviews.

The funny thing—it's a little like a bigger Johnstown here in Pittsburgh; it's the other Friendly City. In New York, the news teams won't talk to each other, she's heard, they elbow each other out of the way to get the best coverage, but here they say hello. KDKA even gave her a ride to the hospital when there was that fire. She's seen KDKA lend WTAE a battery, saying, "No problem."

She sets up interviews of her own. Oh, it's a terrible story, anger over a comment, a perceived insult, right out of the story of the Montagues and the Capulets, only this time fueled by drugs, and the revenge appears to be the shooting of the younger brother of the offender as a warning. What was the offense? A word, a gesture? *Do you bite your thumb at me? I bite my thumb, sir. But do you bite your thumb at me?* She probably won't be able to link in her article what happened here on the street to what happened in Shakespeare's play. It's like Verona, all right, but she's not supposed to say so. Those are the ways of newspaper journalism.

Nina talks to several neighbors of the boy. "Does anybody know how the shooter could hide for so long?" she asks.

"He had a lotta lotta friends," she is told. "He could be most anywhere."

The police are going door to door. After a while there is a pause, a lag in the interviews and she buddies up to the KDKA team.

"How's your firefighter?" Pete asks.

"Um, what are you asking?"

"I saw some sparks there. A little fire, I thought. I was hoping you two would—sorry, I'm out of line. Really, I'm sorry."

"No, I'm seeing someone. Sort of." So lame.

"Really, forgive me. I just . . . ought to keep my mouth shut."

"It's okay. No offense." She makes her way over to one of the cops. "Can you tell me how the search is going?"

"It's still going."

"Are you assuming he's on the loose, dangerous, or that someone is hiding him."

"My assumption—just me—is the latter. This is a tight community."

"Your job right now?"

"Stick with the car." He answers her in a brief way, but he's totally pleasant.

"Do you get bored?"

"Not bored exactly. Itchy for action. I want to make detective in time. I have an instinct. I think I do." He puts out a hand. "Richard Christie."

She takes his hand. "Nina Collins."

"You? You like your beat at the paper?"

"Yes, no, somewhat. I have my eye on something else. I have an instinct. I *think* I do." She laughs.

"Yeah, well, we might be fooling ourselves."

"You want to play detective, I'll give you a problem."

He frowns. "How do you mean?"

"Suppose I wanted to trace someone that was . . . kidnapped or otherwise taken a long time ago. Very young. No memory of it perhaps . . ."

"Sure." He doesn't seem surprised. "Start with the parents, the relatives."

"This is more or less confidential. Okay?"

"Okay."

"What I'm looking into is a long time ago and everyone is gone."

"How long ago?"

"Say, 1889."

He whistles. "Where? Because we have a guy at the office who keeps all the old clippings and files, but I don't think they go back before turn of the century. In Pittsburgh?"

"No. But in Pennsylvania. I do need for you to keep this under your hat."

He taps his hat.

"If this happened in 1889 and if I wanted to survey women of a hundred and four who report being born in Pennsylvania—say I wanted to—is there a way?"

"There's no family left?"

"Maybe . . . there's a sibling living."

"Who knows nothing?"

"Next to nothing. Except she wonders about what happened to the other one."

"I can't think of anything except massive manpower. Visiting every person who gets to that age and taking a blood sample. And people lie about their ages. You'd need to do a range. Census Bureau might help, but they'd need reasons to help."

"Blood sample?"

"Run that new DNA test."

Blood, saliva. She's read about it of course. "It's reliable?"

"Takes a while."

"But I'd have to find the person first." She smiles.

"Wish I could help. You've got me going."

"Please—"

"I know. I can shut up."

It was not until late afternoon when something starts to happen, when the police radios set up a racket, and everybody moves to a new position. Three police drag a handcuffed guy toward the cruiser and press him into it. Minutes later, she hears the boy from inside the cruiser cry, "No, no!"

She looks to the cop named Richard. "What happened?"

"We probably told the shooter the kid in the hospital died."

"Did he?"

Pursed lips. "Yeah."

She has a story to write. No Montague and Capulet references. Just the facts.

NANCY HAS nobody to ask, no women friends who aren't married and home for dinner, and so she goes alone, taking herself out. The whole idea makes her feel wild and spendthrift. Why, there at home is her orderly refrigerator full of food, but Nina said to do it, Nina said it was a liberating feeling. Wasteful! Wildly wasteful. She has chosen Johnny's downtown because she knows they have a bar and that's where men congregate.

"Order something expensive," Nina told her.

But she can't do it.

The waiter is trying to say, "Tonight's special is—"

But she says, "Please, just a burger. Oh, and a beer."

"On tap we have Budweiser, Heineken, Iron City—"

"Heineken would be fine."

She's on assignment to watch the men at the bar, to exercise her imagination. Just see what you feel, Nina told her.

She's early. There are only four men at the bar. For a moment she is in the imaginary embrace of the rotund man with the quiet voice and in that embrace she remembers her father, the thick cushion of him, the endless softness of a hug. When he turns slightly, she studies the aquiline nose, sad eyes. Of course she's just playing. He's married surely, everybody is, it seems. Talking to him in a loud voice is a tidy dark-haired man, younger. Nina has told her she should ignore age, that this is just an investigation into types. Ha, easy for her to say.

The small man with the loud voice bothers her. She cannot imagine being touched by him.

The other two men at the bar are young, posers, with a whole repertoire of things they do with their drink glasses. She can't ignore age even in a game of imagination—they're babies and she can't begin to imagine going to a movie or dinner with either of them even if she mentally adds thirty years. What makes you feel some spark? Nina asked.

It's going to be a long assignment, looking for an image. That's all she promised Nina she would do, that she would find an idea she could believe in. Nancy's heart begins to hurt—surely there is great disappointment in letting the mind play. Yet, oddly, it feels good to take orders from someone else.

Her beer arrives. "Here you go."

The two young men turn around to look at her and they quickly dismiss her. "Mutual," she thinks.

She watches each man as he comes in, a few with dates, wives perhaps, several more alone, their girlfriends or wives probably waiting for

300

them, wondering why the workday demands liquid debriefing. Women handle the stresses of work much better.

Her burger, medium, is delicious—somehow much better than anything she would make in the name of a burger at home. The bun is sinfully thick, the onions caramelized, the fries hot.

She told her daughter, "Your inheritance will disappear if I live like that, going out."

"I want it to disappear."

"All this time I've been saving for you."

"Listen, buy me a pair of shoes and we're square."

"What shoes?"

"Well . . . I've been looking at a pair of sexy shoes but I tell myself I shouldn't. You buy those for me and I won't fight it. It will feel like I should simply have them. Then you start spending on yourself."

"How much are the shoes?" Nancy took out forty dollars, but she caught an amused expression flitting across her daughter's face. "More?"

"Afraid so."

"These must be some shoes."

Still she wants to put a healthy down payment on a home when Nina gets married. And have something left over to start a children's college fund. Surely that's what Nina wants. Isn't it?

The evening ends with the best act of imagination being an embrace from the big fellow with the sad face. As she's paying her bill, he turns to leave, smiles at her, and says, "Good evening." It's insane how foolish she feels. Surely he is going home to a wife, but his voice—yes, that she could love, just the right tone and timbre, just the right volume. Good evening.

NINA EXAMINES everything this way and that for the whole of Tuesday evening. One: the fact that Ben was not at work when she got back—though he might have stayed late, just messing around, given Amanda any sort of excuse, but no he's not there. Two: the fact that she told him to go live at home, to try the therapy. Three: he has shown no signs of looking for an apartment for himself. So what will happen when she reminds him she wants her place to herself, for no matter what they decide between them, she does want her own space. She plays with the facts as if playing with a deck of cards.

She examines her heart. Physical love, yes. She wants to put her fingers through Ben's hair, to run her hands over his shoulders. It's easy to imagine kissing him again. She wants to watch him think, work. And more than that, she wants to comfort him, to make him laugh, light up. She likes being the person that pulled him out of his gloom.

A movie plays in her mind of her, say, a year from now playing games with his two boys. What will it be? Catch on the street? Frisbee in one of the city parks? Or going to the zoo. We can all make movies these days. All right, the zoo, close to her house. That would be a good excursion. The fantasy gets frayed, like film degrading. Then it disappears in seconds.

Ben wants permission to go back to his wife. She's the permission-giver. Otherwise he will wear down her capacity for joy. He needs permission. And she's been granting it, little by little, in dribs and drabs.

Tricky fellow.

She'd rather cry, a good long bath of a cry, but it's irritability she's feeling.

She goes down to knock at Michelle's door. "Let's go for an ice cream."

"Okay!"

When she gets home from the drive to Squirrel Hill, from the wondrous cone of chocolate ice cream crammed with almonds, she listens to her mother's report on the answering machine. Her mother *did* her assignment. Her little mother, poking her head up out of the sand.

"SHE MIGHT make it."

"Get out!"

"Look at her. She talked a minute ago. She was trying to say something. Her temp is down again."

"Still, I don't believe it. An old body like that? How much strength can there be?"

"No, I saw it in her eye. She wants something."

"Maybe somebody coming to visit. I saw one guy, he hung on through everything until his son got there."

"Shh. She's listening."

"I doubt it."

"Mrs. Hoffman. Mrs. Hoffman. How are you doing? How do you feel?"

They wait. "Her lips moved."

"Yes, they did. I'm listening. Mrs. Hoffman?"

A whisper. She's trying. "How . . . long have I been here?"

"Two days. It's Wednesday."

"Pneumonia?" she manages to get out.

"Yes."

Her voice is so weak. Can they hear? And she needs to take her time. "Antibiotics."

"You got 'em. You're getting them."

"I'll . . . need food."

"We're pumping it in."

"More? Can I?"

"We can try. What else—since you're handling your own care? You sound like a doctor!" A laugh.

"I'm . . . a nurse."

"Oh."

"Need . . . movement." She tries, can't.

"Holy cow. You are serious. Look, I'm contacting your doctor. I'm going to do what you're asking, all right?"

"She *is* serious," whispers the other.

"When . . . ?" She gestures backward.

"Not today, Mrs. Hoffman. If you have a visitor coming, I can send a message."

No visitor, she gestures. That's not it. It's something. Something she needs to do, but she doesn't know what it is. Soup, pureed, cereal, mashed potatoes, fruit juice, pudding, they should bring her those lists she is supposed to check off and tomorrow she should have meat, eggs; she has to eat. And move.

ON WEDNESDAY NIGHT, Nina takes herself to the movies at the Denis. They've still got *Field of Dreams*, which is a good guaranteed cry plus a nod to the feel-good mothering that movies provide when you can't go crying to mother any more.

Does magic happen more than once? She's curious.

The whole movie plays and no handsome stranger sits beside her. When she leaves the theater at nine thirty or so, there is, no surprise, a bit of a crowd from another movie that has just let out, too. Up ahead she sees the unmistakable figure of Douglas. It's not just that she's looking for him; he stands out—posture, energy. Maybe even a counter rhythm to those moving around him.

He's walking with a woman who looks from her profile, as she turns to speak to him, like everything he should want. Healthy, lively, good looking, animated.

Nina reverses direction and goes back to the ladies' room where she messes around for ten minutes—hair, lipstick, hand washing—thinking, "Good, good for him." She shouldn't have come here anyway, jostling fate or chance or whatever it is. She could have called him, of course, but that would be false because she still has one foot stuck in the relationship with Ben and she's going to need a lot of aloneness to undo it. She's going to need that *via negativa* state, that down-to-nothing emptiness that teaches.

ON THURSDAY NIGHT, she takes herself to a ball game by walking to Three Rivers from her downtown office. It's going to be scary when she goes back for her car, late at night, but that can't be helped. She'll do that thing with her keys between her fingers as weapons.

"Only one?" the huge wheezing guy behind the ticket counter asks.

"Yes."

She concentrates on the game. Bonilla is running hot and so is Bonds. Oh, how she wants to win against those damned Braves with their stupid song.

A family sitting next to her passes her their popcorn. She takes a few kernels so as not to insult them. Their reaching out to her makes her feel like a . . . child, no, the governess she would be if she were living in Russia, coming up from the peasant class. The Pirates are playing well tonight. When Andy Van Slyke hits a home run, she stands up with the rest and shouts, her voice rising up with an unfamiliar sound. At the seventh-inning stretch, she stands and sings with the crowd, again surprising herself.

ON FRIDAY NIGHT, she decides to stay home. To that end, she studies the paper for evening television, which she rarely watches. Hmmm.

Sitcoms. Well, she ought to know what America finds funny, but she'd rather read or watch baseball. She is noodling lazily through her pasta when the phone rings and she reaches to pick it up.

It's Hal's night man, saying, "Need to talk to Ben Bragdon."

"He's not here." She is about to say, "This is not his phone number right now," but she hesitates because she knows that no phone number is the right one for him this weekend while he's at the couples retreat. He's unreachable. As she hesitates, her caller, Tate, Tate Shefflin, who does assignments on weekends, says, "Sorry, someone needed to ask me something. I'm back now. Have him call me. We have a contact he needs to follow up. Some nurse at an old folks home says she has a woman who needs to talk to him."

Nina's heart thumps once, a large drumbeat. "I can get him the message right away," she says. "Can you give me the full message?"

"It's probably cornmeal. The nurse was kind of apologetic, doing her duty. She called because she has a woman who insists she was the child on the bed that Ben wrote about."

Nina says, "I've got it. I'm writing it down. Where is the nursing home?"

"Manor Care, Banksville Road."

"Okay, got it. Nurse's name?"

"Kelly is the last name. Melissa Kelly."

"And patient's name."

"Resident. She's a resident. Anna Hoffman."

"How old?"

"Doesn't say. You're getting this message to Bragdon, right? I tried the other number we have—"

"I'm on it. I'll get hold of him. He's just out of the house."

She sits for a full minute after hanging up. Damn. This story *cannot* go to anyone else. Caldwell is the name of the shrink who's doing the retreat. She finds a number and dials, cursing. She could have been honest, said she'd do it, but she didn't trust Tate to give it to her.

"I will retrieve messages on Monday. In cases of an emergency, there is another therapist on call. If you need to speak with someone, please call Eliot Graham. At the tone, leave a message."

She puts down the phone.

It's eight at night. She picks up her car keys and rattles down the stairs. When she's in her car, the whole way downtown, almost on the parkway, she realizes she should have called first to give her name, to win trust from Kelly and whomever she will have to talk to, but she simply drives faster. It's too late to patch it up. She's going to have to wing it.

Her heart is pounding so hard, she feels it in her neck. What if this is it?

The Manor Care place is just next to Marshalls. Probably the old folks go on shopping excursions. She sits in her car for a moment, trying to get hold of her breathing before she walks across the lot to that revolving door.

Inside the lobby with its softly upholstered chairs—the fabric all small pink flowers, unthreatening—is an open door with a sign that says, "Administrative Office." A woman sits behind the desk listening to a man, who is asking about his mother's diet. A small TV is playing in the corner of that office, but the sound is down so low, it might as well be muted. The actors pause at various points for canned laughter. *Family Matters, Perfect Strangers*, something like that, one of those programs Nina has not paid much attention to.

"She never did like bran," the man is saying.

"I promise I will look into it. And I'll call you. It's just that our dietician has gone home. Friday nights she's not here. And it's a weekend, but I'll get to it as soon as I can."

Finally, the man, scowling, leaves.

Nina enters.

"Name?"

"Mine?"

"Who do you have in here? Never mind. Go ahead, sign in."

"I don't have anyone here but I am here to see someone." She thinks quickly. There must be rules of all sorts. "But I'd like to talk to Nurse Melissa Kelly first. Then to visit my friend."

"You're not family?"

"No, I'm not."

"Let me see if Kelly is on." The woman turns the sign-in sheet around and recites, "Nina Collins."

"Yes."

"What is this about?"

"Could I explain to Ms. Kelly?"

The receptionist considers this request for a terrifyingly long time before calling someone and saying into the phone, "I'll let her explain," and then handing the phone over.

Nina says, "Melissa Kelly? I'm here for Ben Bragdon. Following up on your call about Anna Hoffman."

Kelly tells her, "I'm putting a couple of people to bed. I'll be down as soon as I can."

Waiting. The hardest thing.

"You can wait in the lobby," says her unkind host.

"How long has Anna Hoffman been here?"

Cautious. "I'm not sure. I think about ten years. You don't know her?"

"No." She starts out the door to the lobby and turns back. "How old is she?"

"That I know. She just turned a hundred and three. We had a party for her and she collapsed on us. We thought she was a goner."

"When was this?'

"Couple of days ago."

Nina goes to the lobby. A hundred and three. She wants to see the chart with date of birth and place of birth. But she doesn't want to push the receptionist too hard. After a torturous five minutes, she goes back in. "How's her mind been?"

"Dementia? They all have some of that at that age."

Not Ellen Emerson.

Nina smiles as nicely as she can and goes back to the lobby. Every once in a while a visitor heads for the front door. Otherwise it's quiet and there are no patients in sight.

And finally, Nurse Kelly, a woman with a yearning, smiling face, comes and sits next to her in the lobby.

"I took the call for Ben Bragdon. I'm also a journalist at the *PG*. He's away until Monday, so I'm gathering the preliminary information for him."

"Well, I feel a bit foolish. The woman is wonderful. I have a fondness for her. And she's always been more or less clear-headed. But she's been sick—well, we almost lost her—and she just got back from the hospital today. She saves newspapers. She got into the article that that Bragdon guy did about the girl on the bed who was in the flood and . . ."

"I know the article."

"And she seems to think she was that girl. I tried to talk her out of it. She begged me to call the paper. So I did."

"Let me say, first of all, that I need to keep this confidential. Think of it as a kind of investigation. Then . . . let me follow up carefully on a few facts, just in case—"

"Do you have an ID?"

Nina pulls out her press card. "Of course. Here it is."

"Are you saying it's possible?"

"Maybe. I'm eager to go see her."

"She's asleep. She got so excited we were sure she wouldn't sleep and she mostly refuses medication, but even she agreed. To rest. She needs rest. She's been very sick."

"How sick?"

"Pneumonia. She might be bouncing back. Nobody thought so."

"Tomorrow morning? How early can I come by?"

"She's usually pretty lively at seven."

"I'll be here. Meanwhile, let's take it a step at a time. Can you get me her birth date and her place of birth?"

Kelly goes into the office where Nina watches her and tries to interpret a quiet conversation between her and the receptionist. The receptionist finally opens a file drawer and takes out a folder.

The answers are May 8, 1886. That would make her a hundred and three years old all right. And the place of birth is listed simply as Indiana County. Next of kin, none. But there it is. Indiana County. Next to Westmoreland County.

The parents might have made her younger . . . as a dodge. "You say she had a good mind up until this illness?"

"Yes, she'd been a nurse. She was still sharp all along. Read the papers religiously every day."

"No family?"

"None left that any of us know about. None listed."

"Will you be here in the morning?" She knew the answer before she heard it.

"No. I could leave a note. I could pave the way."

"Would you?"

"Yes. Yes, I'll do that."

ELLEN IS HAVING her fourth rough night in a row. She keeps waking at midnight, unable to get back to sleep. Yesterday—oh, it was glorious—Ruth took her out for a walk around the block and they made it around three times. The only thing is, she really does need to sleep through the night. For four days she has taken more substantial naps in the middle of the day. So, she is awake. Again. Stirred up. Again.

Anna Karenina helps. Right now Anna is reckless, adding a note to Vronsky to the bottom of the princess's letter to him. Poor Anna, poor everyone. Ellen can remember seeing Garbo do the role on film with her mixture of Russian passion, moodiness, willfulness. And hope. Even innocence. For transgressors are sometimes innocents. She told Nina to get the Garbo film and watch it, but young people have such chaotic lives, she doubts if that will happen.

Nina was sad during the last visit. Putting on a brave face. Hmph.

Ellen reads for as long as she can without heeding the call of her bladder. Why now, why tonight? Slowly she peels off the blankets, remembering Ruth's admonition about not rushing, not moving fast, putting on enough light, using the walker—just to be sure. She does all of these things, making her way to the bathroom. Oh, she wants to be free, to run like the child she once was, or like the young woman she was when she broke decorum and ran for a train.

These restless nights! Using the walker, she goes to the kitchen, which is so clean from Ruth's care that she can smell the solution used to clean the counters. Outside the kitchen window are the lined-up trees that border her apartment building and through them the slice of a moon. The window is open a little, enough that she can feel a bit of breeze coming at her. These are the best days of the year, what Bill called baseball weather.

"It's spring," he would say, "and we need to celebrate it." A couple of times they took trips to Pittsburgh to Forbes Field. But mostly they had to make do with AAABA games at the Point Stadium in Johnstown. But it was exciting! There was that exhibition game early on when Babe Ruth and Lou Gehrig came to town. And she went with him to see Jackie Robinson and Satchel Paige when the Negro leagues came to town. Bill loved the game so much and she loved it through his eyes.

There are cookies beside her bed, but she's . . . restless, her word again. She takes a loaf of bread from the refrigerator and puts two slices in the toaster, finds the butter and the apple butter. Yes, that's what she wants. Her mother used to make apple butter and peach butter in autumn. She and Mary would lean over the table waiting to taste it. They had to wear their oldest frocks because they were likely to spill—she more likely to spill than Mary. They ate it on hot bread, with butter, and it was wonderful.

Tonight she tastes that memory, standing in the kitchen, looking out at the moon.

ANNA WAKES AT MIDNIGHT. Why? It's not even that bright out; there's just the thin moon slipping through her blinds.

Ah, she remembers. They want her to sleep, sleep, sleep, and so they gave her a pill, but here she is, awake again. They think she's nuts. Embarrassed that she didn't die, more embarrassed that she didn't want to, that she didn't want to give up her portions of oatmeal, farina, birthday cakes, memory lessons, she tried to behave herself when they allowed her to come back to her room, oh, she tried to be the sane model resident. But they think the pneumonia triggered a crazy bout in her.

Her newspapers. The miracle was they had kept them—well, Nurse Kelly had squirreled them away when others tried to throw them out. So somebody anyway thought she might live.

She got back at four in the afternoon. She kept demanding food. The nurses and aides kept sneaking worried looks at each other, but she knew she needed to build herself up. After she'd eaten, she took up the papers, looking for the article she had heard about—where had she heard? She wondered as she leafed through the papers if she had dreamt it—but finally there it was, an article about a woman who had survived long ago by floating on a mattress.

A line at a time, like a child who can't eat bananas being desensitized, a bite at a time, a bite one week, a single bite another week, like that, she read. And soon, though the old things happened, her breath catching, her heart tossing about in the canoe of her body, she managed to read the whole thing. A woman who lived. Ellen. She studied the face of this Ellen Emerson. And once more she began to cry.

Nurse Kelly had come on duty, looked happy to see her and then distressed that she was crying, and so she tried to take the newspaper away.

"No, no, I need to read this."

"All right. All right. But not if it upsets you."

Her heart was pounding so hard she thought the nurse would see the upheaval in her and send her back to the hospital. "I'm all right. Just let me read."

And then . . . the part about Bibles on a cart. She knows that. She saw that. Bibles with a mattress on top. People walking through water and her, safe, on a bed in the rain, moving. She *knows* this scene. The cousin who pushes, who climbs into a window—was it in a film? She saw this, too, somewhere. And then she turned a page to find two faded photographs reprinted. And for a while she didn't breathe. Are these the people who gave me away, she wonders? They don't look at all like the deadbeats she has always imagined.

She turned back to read line by line. And still it was her life. A sister. A twin. A twin who called out to save her. And then movement. Water.

"This is about me," she told Nurse Kelly.

"My dear, it can't be."

"I am the other child. The one they talk about."

"How can that be?"

"I know you think I was born somewhere else and adopted—I *was* adopted. I don't know how or what happened, but I was in that flood. I need to talk to someone." By then she was crying again, but it was different, almost angry.

Nurse Kelly hesitated, saying, "Well, I could call the paper."

"Will that . . . ? Is that . . ." Fear overtook her and she didn't say, "Can't we call the woman in the article?"

"I will contact the paper if you will take a small something to calm you. There is no good in rushing. If we rush, you may get sick again. I'll phone them and get things rolling. But you have to rest. Promise?"

311

"Yes."

A part of her doesn't want to ask. A part of her doesn't want to dig up anything that jolts her back into life like a giant defibrillator, back to where she can feel risk and pain and loss again. "You *will* call?"

"Yes."

She heard them in the hallway. They murmured about how erratic her behavior was, how she was finally letting those feathers fly all over the place, that change usually signaled the end. This phone call she wanted . . . they didn't want to take away her dignity totally.

And now she's up at midnight. Waiting.

She knows about desensitizing. She's helped diabetics get used to shots. And so she takes up the paper and reads a little bit, stops, a little more, stops, until she's finished the article once more. Then she does it again, fewer stops. She studies her sister's face, touches it. She dreams her way into the embrace of her mother and father. She knows those faces. They were good and they loved her. Once upon a time, they were all happy and had no idea they would be parted from each other.

CHAPTER 15

Saturday, May 13– Sunday, May 14, 1989

■ Nina hardly slept at all and now it's only six thirty in the morning and she is in her car, almost there. After a while, she decided the tossing was a silly way to spend her time. She got up and wrote a bunch of paragraphs—about twins, about the secret language of twins, and then conjectural paragraphs about a twin seeing an article and knowing—that part could turn out to be fiction, that part could be all about wishing. But she used her time last night and hardly thought about herself, which felt wonderful. She quoted Ellen about time—the short time of an event and the long time of the life after it. Which do you use to take the measure of a person? The latter of course. Why even a murderer might be better measured by the period of paying, how he paid for the act.

A new woman hunkers over the reception desk like a bulldog, like a junkyard bulldog, whose job it is to scare Nina away. "Yes, I was told about you," the woman says. "There is no law that you can't come in here, but it's disruptive of course. You may harm our resident. She's overexcited. I've been asking everyone who was on duty yesterday. So I have to caution you to do nothing to overexcite her fancy. Meanwhile when she's ready, I'll go with you."

This one has her name on the desk. Hilda Matvay. Protector.

"That's fine," Nina says as calmly as she can. "I'm interested to see this place. It looks lovely."

"Well, yes. We keep it lovely."

Billie Holiday singing. William P. Gottlieb Collection at the Library of Congress. Courtesy of the Maryland State Archives Collection.

"Those chairs are wonderfully soft." Nina points backward to the waiting area.

"Those, yes. They're too soft for the residents who have trouble getting up out of them. We do a different chair in their meeting area."

Nina says, "That makes good sense." She leaves the office to sit down in the soft chairs, wanting to sleep to make up for the short night she had, but also because she fears disappointment.

Eventually Matvay comes for her. They pass through an area with at least twenty wingback chairs in dark blue upholstery with a small diamond shape to pattern it. "These are better for the residents," Matvay says.

Nina touches the seating cushion of one of them. Foam, not the old classic stuffing of club chairs, but comfortable, probably, and firm enough to provide a hoist upward. There is a slightly flowery smell in the atmosphere, but not a chemical smell or the insistent smell of urine—these she knows from when her grandmother needed a retirement home.

They turn two corners and stop in front of a room. "You will be wise," Matvay says. Nina almost laughs to feel like she's in first grade again, being told how to be. *We will all be thoughtful today.* They enter the room.

Anna Hoffman sits propped up in a bed, supported by both the elevated mattress and several white starchy pillows. She's looking down at her gnarled hands, which rest on the turned-over flap of her sheet. Her hair is white, wavier and thicker than Ellen's, not long but almost stylishly bobbed.

Another nurse, not Kelly, stands as soon as they enter the room. "She's doing well and she says she's not sleepy."

Hilda Matvay says in a low voice, "Just remember her age. Go slowly. She may—" She makes a face to surely mean *make no sense at all.*

Nina has been hungrily studying Anna Hoffman's face, eager for a quick sign. Old ladies are like babies, similar. The eyes behind the metal-rimmed glasses are blue as Ellen's are. The nose, not quite the same, is perhaps a bit smaller.

Anna's lips tremble. "I wanted them to call the woman, Ellen. They told me they called the man who wrote the article. Who are you?"

"I'm a colleague of the man who wrote it. I don't want to be a disappointment to you. I'm here to try to help you."

"I am the other girl on the mattress."

"I need to go back to Ellen Emerson to tell her about you. And I will. But I want to give her some specifics. I don't want to frighten her either with—" She can't say "false hope."

"I remembered the flood when I read about it."

"I understand. If we could talk for a moment about things you remember that aren't about the flood? Something that wasn't in the newspaper. Like first memories."

Anna seems to be interested in the question. "I don't know. I remember growing up. Being given clothes to wear. Feeling lonely. And sad."

"Where was this?"

"It was here in Pittsburgh, on the South Side where I lived . . . but also before that, on a farm. I remember the farm a little. I tried to find it once. I mean, I did, but other people owned it."

"Oh. Wonderful. Where was that?"

"Down the Conemaugh River. Near Ninevah."

Ninevah. *Ninevah.* "Very good." Nina writes it down with a shaking hand as if this is just plain factual information. "Tell me about your parents."

"Which?"

"In Pittsburgh, on the farm. Those."

"Catholics. German. Tough on sin. Workers. I was a Burkhardt. That was their name. Are you here in place of Bragdon?"

No, this one doesn't sound crazy either. "Yes. Yes, I am. Did they ever . . . suggest to you that you were adopted?"

"My mother told me when I was sixteen. Did you ever see this woman, Ellen?"

"Yes. I visited her several times. Please, tell me what you know of your adoption. Did . . . your mother talk about your parents."

"I knew something was . . . wrong. There was always . . . a lot of silence about the early years. When my mother knew she was dying, she told me a poor couple had brought me to them. It sounded like I was sold to them, you know, not wanted by my real parents. I believed that for a long time. Now I don't believe it."

Nina wonders if she will ever be able to breathe. She wants to shout. Instead she asks in a level voice, "Do you have photos?"

"Not of early years. Not at all. Of later times."

"May I look at them?"

"In the bottom drawer."

The nurse who stands by hurries to the drawer and begins to bring things out.

There is a silence as Nina looks. There are newspaper clippings, award certifications for Anna as a nurse. And an envelope of photos. And right, nothing of her, as a young girl. That alone—the youngest photo she sees is of a lovely dark-haired girl of about thirteen. "Is this you?"

"Yes, a photographer came by. I should have just found a way to call information myself, to call Ellen," she frets.

Nina nods. "I'll go to her as soon as I leave here. Tell me what I should tell her."

Her lips begin to tremble again. "That I remember the cart and the house with the windows."

"Did you ever remember them before you read the paper?"

"No. But I dreamt about a flood. All my life. Why would I dream about a flood?"

"I don't know."

"You want me to prove it?" She begins to cry. "I don't know how to prove it."

"In your dream . . . what else is in your dream?"

"Water and mud. In the dream, I'm drowning. And a cow. The cow is already drowned."

Nina's breath catches again though the cow was in the article, but still. "Do you remember the name Mary?"

"Not . . . as mine. You don't believe me."

The thing is, Nina does believe her. "Is this your son?"

"My son. Ned we called him."

Light haired. He looks a little like young pictures of Ellen. But maybe hope is coloring those pictures. "And this man?"

"My second husband. That's Will."

Will. Bill. Of all of the things that might be signs, this one gives Nina some hope. Again and again, twins found ways of living parallel lives. Nina believes Anna Hoffman might have been the child in the flood. But Hal is going to ask for proof and Ellen deserves proof and the timing— Ben being away—is horrible. A mess. There simply must be other proof. "Are you willing to give a blood sample—so we can work on proving this."

"Anything. I want to see this woman, Ellen."

"I know. I want that, too. I'll go see her now and try to bring her here—"

"You could take me there. I could go with you."

"No, absolutely not," Matvay interrupts. "You are not strong enough yet."

It's ten in the morning when Nina takes her leave of Anna. She halts Matvay in the hallway. "Can I ask you to keep this confidential? It's very important to me that you not talk about it or leak it."

"You don't have to persuade me. I won't talk. But I have to tell you I don't think you know much about the elderly. Their minds do some pretty funny tricks."

"Anna is very sure of what she's saying."

"Today, yes. I've seen a lot. Almost every patient here delights us with something that passes for memory. Something that sounds good. And is completely false. One woman who never drove a car according to her family told me she ferried children on a school bus. Another person had the idea, insisted, she played golf. Her husband told us they'd never *been* on a golf course."

"Maybe she was remembering miniature golf, sort of inflating it—"

"It's not the same thing. This woman I'm talking about thought she'd been a champion golfer."

"Has Anna ever seemed to have this sort of fertile imagination before?"

Matvay thinks. "Once she was ill and I believe she thought her son was alive and in the room with her."

"Ill with what?"

"Fever."

"It was a dream."

"Maybe. I'll grant you, that is a classic dream."

"Does Melissa Kelly come on duty later?"

"Yes, at three."

Good. She's sympathetic. "I need a payphone."

"You can use the office phone."

Though Nina doesn't want Matvay to see her crying, she accepts the offer of a phone. She tells Ruth to put Ellen on. She tells Ellen in the most careful tones she can muster that there is someone who wants to meet her. "Do you think you could handle ninety minutes in my car?"

She tells Ruth to pack a bag in case Ellen is too tired or distraught to make the return trip. She has lives in her hands. She hadn't counted on that. And she hasn't had anything that could be called sleep.

THE DAY is becoming misty with rain. They have been walking in the woods—nice, who wouldn't fall in love here, good food, excellent scenery, those are Caldwell's pills for saving a marriage.

"Bryson was wetting the bed all last month. Not this last week though."

"Oh. You never said. Messy and depressing for you."

"Laundry every day. I did it. Mostly I worried about him. He was ashamed."

He hears her. If he can stand her at all, love her a little, which he can, there are two children whose lives, whose minds, might be the better for it.

"We should go inside," she says.

"Yeah. Caldwell couldn't persuade the weather." He winces at the bitterness that sneaked into his tone. "She's picked a good place. It's beautiful here." As she said, if people don't get back together, the gift she hopes they will take away is an absence of rancor.

"Do you miss work?"

"I do." It's the only time he really feels rooted. He has another big article coming on Monday about the centennial. This one is mainly about the reconstruction, the rebuilding in 1889, but mostly about the celebration of a tough spirit in the town, people who believe in work and just keep getting back to it.

"There's a church service tomorrow. Optional. Will you go?"

"Sure." Talk to God, see if he has any advice about how Ben can love Nina and want her and let her go. Well, he tells himself, taking on God's role, the fireman is probably a better fellow than he is. Indecision, which permeates him, is his default state. How fluid things are. "Noon already," he says. "I wonder what's for lunch."

"I read the chart. It's rare tuna with sesame and roasted potatoes on a salad. Crusty bread. Basically a Nicoise."

Caldwell keeps them well fed. He likes tuna, he'll probably have it. "What's the backup option?"

"I think chicken vegetable soup and a Panini. Or for vegetarians a gourmet bean burrito and sides of rice and avocado."

He likes most of the other couples. One is in their seventies and the woman wants out. Three couples are younger than he and Amanda, two without children, one with little kids of five and four. They tend to eat with the couple that has the kids. He wonders what the odds are, how many will get back together only to fall apart (without rancor, preferably) in the future. How many have fallen in love again? And how many will say, "Thanks but no thanks. We are splitting!"

A retreat by definition is apart from everything. Ben misses his computer, his phone, misses being able to hop over to the office to see what's happening. He hopes Amanda will show some interest in his next article and that he won't have to prompt her as he did for his last one. Before he left, he sent the draft to Hal and to Nina, so it's done. He's feeling pretty good about it—his linking of the aftermath of the flood in 1889 with the centennial celebration coming up in two weeks—the biggest event is actually a sort of town meeting in two and a half weeks.

There are cloth table settings in the restaurant. Caldwell sits at a table apart, reading a book, smiling benevolently as each of them enter, washed of ego, in someone else's hands. For a time.

ELLEN IS WEARING a navy blue dress with a white cardigan. Her shoes have a slight heel; her stockings are cloth. On her lap is a large package of some sort and a purse.

Nina sinks to the chair in front of her, saying words like *maybe, possibility, long shot, just to check it out.* She is afraid Ellen will faint. "You look wonderful."

"Oh," she waves away the compliment. "I can't do much with my hair these days and there's not much I can do with the rest of it." She's beautiful and doesn't know it.

"If I get to be eighty, I hope I can look as good as you do now."

"What do you think? Is it Mary?"

"I think it's possible. We're relying on some . . . something, a memory. But also, I want to order DNA testing. That's—the way it's often used is—"

"Criminals and renegade fathers." Ellen manages a smile.

"Oh, God, I want to be like you. You know everything."

"Not everything. I . . . do read, though. A lot."

"Will you be okay with the car trip?"

"Yes."

"If you think not, I can tell my editor what we're up to. It might take a little longer to order some other sort of transport."

"I can handle the car."

Ruth brings a glass of water. "Have a little," she says. She looks like a heartbroken mother whose child is leaving home.

Ellen insists on going to the elevator without using the walker, but Nina carries it along in case it's needed later, and she allows Ruth to be the one walking along with Ellen, hands near the elbows, ready to catch her if she wavers.

As the elevator descends, dizziness washes over Nina. Hold *me* up, she thinks. She and Ruth work to tuck Ellen into the front seat of the Civic. Should she have rented a car? Probably. "My car isn't much . . ."

"What is it?" Ellen touches the dash lightly.

"Civic. Honda. What ever happened to bench seats, huh?"

"I always liked bench seats. Kept my old car because it had them."

"When did you stop driving?"

"Not so terribly long ago," she says smiling. Ruth hugs and kisses her while Nina hurries to the driver's side, and a minute later they are off.

"Tell me everything," Ellen says.

Nina first explains why she ended up with the call instead of Ben. When she glances over she can see Ellen has taken in the information about Ben and her, but of course she needs to know about Anna. Or Mary. "She's been ill this week. She had a birthday celebration on Monday and was weak then—"

"Why on Monday? Why that date?"

"It's the date her parents celebrated. She doesn't have another date. Or an original birth certificate. She does say she was adopted and didn't know it until she was sixteen and her mother was dying. It was a sort of dying confession. But the mother never mentioned the flood. She told her some ragged couple gave her up, said they couldn't care for her."

They both go quiet. Ellen's shoulders sag for a moment.

Nina explains about her calls to the flood experts to ask about the water patterns. She admits that Anna's parents' farm was close to one of the places debris ended up. And Ellen's body straightens again.

"Debris," she whispers.

"Yes."

"Did you like her?"

"Very much."

"And she had been a nurse?"

"Worked for sixty plus years as a nurse. Yes."

"That's good. That makes sense."

"In what way?"

"It's how Mary was. It would suit." But they're both terrified of disappointment, afraid to shout for joy.

The Civic purrs along. Ellen says, "I drove only in town the last years. It's been thirteen years since I've been out of town. I figured it up this morning after you called. I remember all this though." The Conemaugh Gap is to her right, a big sweeping green canyon. "Pretty isn't it? My husband and I used to drive this road when we went to Pittsburgh."

"For what?"

"Symphony. Ball games. Doctor."

"Whatever we do by the way, we have to be sure not to put ideas in Anna Hoffman's head. Or Mary. We have to hold back a little. Test her."

"That's going to be hard."

Rain again. It begins to mist the windshield. "How will you feel if after everything, we don't think she's your sister?"

She stares at the rain for a while. "Oh. Disappointed. Devastated. I'll still believe my sister, wherever she ended up, lived after the flood. I felt it so strongly."

"And now?"

"I don't know. And I don't know why I don't know."

When they are a quarter mile from the Corner Restaurant, the halfway point, Nina offers a stop, a bathroom.

"No, I want to get on with it."

What a day. It's not yet two in the afternoon. And then the rain begins to come down more steadily—decisive sleek straight needles of water. With the windshield wipers on high, Nina leans forward to see, thinking, "I cannot have an accident now. Cannot."

"I always hated to drive in the rain," Ellen offers as if to calm her.

"I'll just go slowly."

The trip takes an hour and forty-five minutes.

"Here?" Ellen looks at the building of the Manor Care home as they drive onto the grounds, and right up to the door.

"Yes. I'm getting you inside, then I'll park. Ready to stretch your legs?" She reaches to the back seat for the emergency umbrella, which opens poorly and has a hole, but . . . it's something.

"I hope I can unbend them. I don't want the walker."

She does unbend her legs and they walk slowly at one-eighth the pace of Nina's heartbeat to the glass doors of the lobby. Once inside, Ellen supports herself by holding on to a chair back while Nina goes out to park the car and to wonder if she should fetch the walker—though they probably have plenty of walkers in this place. When she gets back (without it), Matvay has already come up to Ellen to greet her and now an aide hurries to her, offering a wheelchair. Ellen looks horrified, but she says politely, "I'd like to go in strong."

She allows Nina to put an arm around her waist, and Nina manages to hold onto Ellen's left arm. As they walk Nina can feel what it is to be old. "Just this last corner and then we're there," she whispers.

And then they are there.

Anna Hoffman wears a mauve dressing gown that is tailored enough to look almost like a dress. She sits, almost comically like an Edwardian hostess at a small table that has been brought in and that holds a teapot, cups, sugar, cream, and a plate of sweet rolls and muffins. She rises unsteadily. "You're here."

For a moment the women study each other as Edwardian women must have—why they might be in some old play. They might be in the tea scene of *The Importance of Being Earnest*.

"Yes, I'm Ellen." She supports herself with a hand to the table.

Anna looks at Ellen's hand resting on the table and she reaches out to touch it as a child examines the skin of a new babysitter.

"You think you might be Mary."

"I think so. I've been called Anna for a long time. I'm trying to study your face."

"Me, too." Ellen smiles.

Hilda Matvay interrupts them. "There are chairs. Please sit down."

"I've brought my tape recorder—Ben's tape recorder," Nina says. "I know it's a bother, but we'll be glad we have it later."

Ellen sits down and accepts a cup of tea. "Can you remember the name, Mary, being called that?"

"No. I wish I remembered."

"Ah, well, something else then. How was it where you grew up? Later, when you were five or six."

"Oh. It was here in Pittsburgh, a small house on the South Side. My parents were quiet people and they were old, too, older than other parents. He worked in the mills and she worked at home for a while, then as a clerk. Is that what you meant?"

"Were there other children around? Did you play games?"

"Things with dolls. Pretending. Ordinary games. Yes."

Ellen takes a sip of tea. "I so want you to be Mary. Did you ever play 'The Cow Jumped Over the Moon?'"

Anna's eyes tear up. "I don't know what that is."

"Tell *me* what it was," Nina says.

"Well, it was silly. I used to jump over my sister when I said 'The cow jumped over the moon,' and then the two of us would roll around on the ground, laughing, and she got to be the dog that laughed to see such sport. And I would pick her up and lead her by the hand, saying, 'The dish ran away with the spoon.' We made our own entertainments. We liked it."

"Do you remember, Anna?"

She shakes her head no, clearly distraught.

"Memory is tricky," Nina says. "Don't worry." But inside she is worrying Anna won't be able to access the usual long-term memory of old people who supposedly can recall which board was chipped on the floor of the dining room, the names of long-dead neighbors. "We can work on medical proof. I'll need two blood samples. I know you both know that. It's okay?"

"Of course," Anna says.

Nina doesn't worry them with the fact that it will take two weeks to process the DNA. "Good. Until then, just . . . talk."

"I don't remember the flood, but I remember dreaming about a flood. It came back when I read the article."

"Just talk," Ellen says. "My heart is pounding still. It's hard to be patient."

"The pictures in the paper," Anna offers. "I thought I knew them."

Ellen keeps looking at her hopefully.

For the next hour, they exchange photo albums. "This was her hair color, darker than mine," Ellen says happily. "And it was wavy."

Nina's brain is whirling. Is this enough? "What about personalities. Who was the initiator?"

"I don't think I was," Anna says, puzzled.

Ellen asks, "Do you remember: *I love the sun, I love the moon, I love the holiday coming soon.* And the rhyme was goofy. *I love the lunch we get at noon,*" Ellen finishes. "Dumb!"

"You would have been the initiator," Anna agrees. "But the verse . . ." She recites the first two lines again. "I got excited. I thought I knew it, but I would have said something about rain. That's what I thought it was."

Ellen cries out. "That's right! It's right. That was the third line. *I play in the rain, I don't complain—*"

"That's it. Rain!"

"But I made those verses up. For us."

Oh, my God.

Nina stands up. Ellen stands. "Only for some reason you had trouble when you were little with pronouncing the *n* sound and so you said, oh, do you *remember*, you said, *I love the raim, I don't complaim.* Even my name. You had your own way of—"

"Alum, Alum," Anna whispers. "They told me all I would say was 'Alum' for a long time. They thought I wanted cereal. They thought I was trying to say pablum. They said I kept calling for Alum."

Both women are crying. Nina is crying. Even Matvay is crying. Sure, they'll get the DNA. That will make for a finished story someday. But now they are wiping their tears and laughing and falling all over themselves to hug each other and that sure makes them look like sisters.

Oh, it's a glorious day. Glorious. Melissa Kelly comes into the room, having come on duty. Her hands go to her face. "Is it true?"

They don't need to answer her.

"I can't go back today," Ellen declares. "We need to talk. We need to catch up."

AFTER LUNCH, Ben digs in his overnight case and hands three pages to Amanda. "I need for you to read what I write. I mean, I just need that."

"Of course. I've been very bad about reading anything."

Not just anything. His. He waits till she has finished and then takes it back. She says, "I'd like to go to that—the main event. Will you be going?"

"If they spring me."

"Of course they will."

He shrugs. "Was it interesting to you?"

"Very. I never doubted your abilities for a moment. I admire them."

Hardly the cheerleading he hopes for. He sits in a chair in their cozy room and reads it to himself. No headline as yet. Just his working title, "Centennial Celebration Planned." And his note to Hal. *Here it is. For Monday.*

HAL IS IN THE OFFICE. He's always there. Always. He checks the article for Monday, ticking off corrections. He's kept Ben's working title, sort of. It reads okay, ready for Monday.

Centennial Celebration of 1889 Flood Planned

Spirit of Johnstown Credited with Strong Work Ethic 100 Years Ago

BY BEN BRAGDON

Volunteers were needed in 1889 when the South Fork Dam broke and the Johnstown Flood destroyed the city of Johnstown. In the wide world the town is still known for that disaster. In the city itself, people are more likely to talk about current unemployment, the demise of the steel mills, the devastation that the most recent flood, in 1977, wreaked upon the town. But now, one hundred years after the great flood, the talk has turned again to that day in 1889 and the weeks thereafter when the town's immigrant population showed an indomitable spirit in recovering and rebuilding.

A day after the flood, men trudged through muddy water, hauling out bodies and carrying them to where they might be identified. They laid the bodies out in the pews of a church. Women searched for dry clothing and edibles for survivors. Anyone who could manage the climb went into the hills for water and other supplies. Reverend David Beale was in charge of the temporary morgue, and Arthur Moxham took over flood relief until others relieved him.

Those who had carpentry skills were busy making pine boxes.

In spite of the enormity of the recovery job, the Cambria Iron Works had men back to work in a week.

This is the spirit that will be celebrated at the centennial.

Johnstown is one of the areas that is being supported by the National Park Service as a historic site and a draw for a new sort of economy—tourism. The Flood Site and the Flood Museum as well as the Inclined Plane have been the recipients of funds from America's Industrial Heritage Project. The Flood Site is the South Fork Dam itself with a new building that houses an exhibit that includes a model of the dam and the valley. Inside there is also a theater where a film about the flood plays on a loop.

The Flood Museum, under reconstruction in the old Carnegie Library building, is now temporarily housed in the former Penn Traffic Department Store. The exhibit is growing daily. It features newspaper clippings, diaries and other personal journals, household goods, and clothing recovered from the flood. A new film by Charles Guggenhiem, *The Johnstown Flood*, plays here.

The Inclined Plane, the local terminology for a funicular, is the steepest vehicular incline in the world. It was built after the 1889 flood to connect the town with higher areas and it helped to save lives in 1936 and was used during the recovery efforts in 1977.

Events on the anniversary include performances by the Duquesne University Tamburitzans, the River City Brass Band, the Coal City Cloggers, and the Johnstown Symphony Orchestra. There will be marches through the neighborhoods that saw the worst flooding as well as a huge city center festival on May 31 with dignitaries attending and a fireworks finale. "This is just a small part of what we are doing," says Heritage Association director Michael Morelli. "Mostly we want to let the world know this is a place of history and a place to visit to understand more about our country and specifically about the immigrant populations that made this country strong."

Those interested in attending the festivities are encouraged to call the Heritage Association for the final schedule.

"You want to know what's happening now, two weeks before the event?" Morelli asked. "Excitement. And work. Everybody here is a busy beaver. That's who we are. That's who we always were. Workers. We're no-nonsense workers."

HAL PUTS IT DOWN. It isn't Ben's best. Not his worst. Not quite the capper, but that's life. He'll come in and muck with it tomorrow.

NO STOPPING THEM NOW. Nina has to put in a new tape. But she has to get home to type this up eventually. And it's torture leaving them.

"I once had dinner with Lena Horne," Anna says.

"No!"

"It was nothing. We weren't important. But Will had done some work for her father and we were big fans and so when there was this big dinner one night, we were invited."

"Wow."

"Don't get too excited. I don't think she'd remember me. She's not going to invite us to her next concert. I didn't push myself. I just watched her . . . glitter."

"She's amazing."

"Amazing. Full of everything. Alert, you know. Still sounds good, too. Still looks good."

"You were courageous, marrying Will."

"Courage didn't come into it. It just was. The thing that was sad about Will's life was that he never had a chance at the better jobs. He didn't insist on the chance. His mind was such that he could have been, had he been schooled, a doctor or lawyer or businessman. He got great pleasure from helping people. But he was also stubbornly . . ."

"Unassuming?"

"Unassuming. Yes. He did his work at the hospital; that was the stable income. Then everything else, the gardening, the building, was what he wanted to do. He was a pretty good writer. He wrote a number of letters to the *Pittsburgh Courier* about all kinds of issues. He would sit at the kitchen table and work over those letters. One of them was about us, about intermarriage. For years there was a long series of correspondences about relationships with white people, all sorts of relationships. I was embarrassed to read them, the way some white people talked. Will wrote something, oh, sort of like, 'Sometimes you are going about your business and you see a person and something happens to your whole mind and body so that everything in you waits to see that person again. Love has its own way with us. It's a powerful force and it cannot be denied without doing more ruinous things to the soul. When love happens between Negroes and whites, it needs to be respected, as all love does. It hardly needs to be said here, but it's what we live for.' He said something wonderful like that."

"I wish I'd known him. Mary. Anna. I don't know what to call you."

"Both till we get used to it. I mean either. Did you really move heaven and earth to try to find me?"

"Oh! You can't imagine." Nina has to go out to the hallway to consult with Matvay and a doctor about the blood draw while Ellen tells about talking to flood survivors on the street, in the shelter, insisting on going to the morgue as a little kid. She tells about the detective Sklar who insisted Mary died in Idaho, in a house fire. Nina comes back in with the doctor and nurse and Matvay as Ellen is saying, "And all the while you were so close. Sixty-five miles away. We went to Pittsburgh fairly often. We might have been in Forbes Field on the same day. Or passed on the street. It could have happened."

"It could have."

All of them stop to listen. Ellen, always good with an audience, addresses them. "Pittsburgh was where Johnstown people came when we wanted something the hometown couldn't provide. Sports, music. Once Bill and I came to hear Eartha Kitt." She looks to her sister.

"Liked her. Very much. Went once to hear her. We had all the great jazz artists."

"In Johnstown, we just had their records."

They laugh. Anna says, mostly to her sister, "Pearl Bailey, Duke El-lington, Billie Eckstein, everybody, all of them came to Pittsburgh, but some of them started out here. Billy Strayhorn. You know about him? A boy in high school, writing great music."

Ellen says, "I could be a little jealous that you had all that."

"Oh!"

"Not mean jealous. Just wanting to be in your shoes."

"The one I wanted to see most was Billie Holiday. Never could catch her."

"Brillliant. And sad."

"Sad. Yes." Suddenly Anna looked distressed. "I forgot. What hap-pened to the boy who saved you?"

"He lived. He had a good long life. Became a bank clerk."

"That's right, that's right. Oh. Do you remember anything about a big can? With a picture of a girl on it?"

"A flour can. Picture of a girl eating an apple?" The medical staff is ready and they come in to do their thing. The women have to stop talk-ing while they get their blood drawn.

"Sorry," says the nurse, both times, as she pokes them.

"Old veins," Anna says. "They don't bounce back. Shouldn't we have done saliva?"

"We're taking saliva, too. To be absolutely sure. Of everything."

After the medical staff has left and things have settled down once more, Anna says, "I played with that can."

Ellen says, "We both did. Listen, I could consider moving here . . . but I would lose a lot. I have a wonderful place and all the help I need. If you come to stay with me for a while, we could see if you might want to turn that into a permanent arrangement."

"Oh. I'd want some independence."

"There are other apartments in the building. It could work. Think about it."

"We both need to walk more. To exercise."

"I agree. Funny, I just started the other day, pushing myself to do more."

"We have a lot to talk about. I want to know about your Bill. And . . . can you remember our parents?"

"A little. I think I do."

"And—"

And they talk and talk, long into the night.

THE NEXT MORNING she calls Hal at home. "Mr. Carson, Hal, I need to talk to you. I can come to your house if necessary. It's . . . important, crucial."

"I was on my way in."

"Good, I'll be there."

She's done everything she knows to do. She's written all night except for four hours of sleep. And she can only hope nobody has leaked the story.

A mirror in the lobby alerts her to the fact that she looks awful. She leans on the wall of the elevator as she rides up. Onward, she urges herself. Can't back out now.

Hal scowls at her. "What?"

"Some things have happened very fast. A good story, a really good story. Ben is away at a retreat with his wife, unreachable, so . . . I wrote it."

"Huh?"

She hands it over as she explains the phone call from Tate Shefflin, and he reads a few lines, looks up, and goes back to it.

The time that Hal takes to read the rest of her pages feels like two hours. She stands there sweating, dead on her feet. He slaps her pages down. "Damn."

"I need a photographer," she says.

"Lady, I think you've earned one."

The Inclined Plane. Courtesy of Johnstown Area Heritage Association.

16

Wednesday, May 31, 1989

■ THERE ARE THREE of them on the stage: Nina, Ellen, and Mary. Sitting in the audience of hundreds is Ruth in the front row, Nancy, tearing up, a few rows back and only two rows from Bobby's mother, and in the back, standing, as if cheering, Douglas. It's a big day. The centennial planners have asked all three women to sit on the stage, symbols of tenaciousness, survival. Nina is very nervous. She plans to keep her remarks brief because she's not the feature, the sisters are. "Heroes," the mayor is calling all three of them. Heroes. Funny to think of herself that way.

"Our favorite teacher, a citizen to be proud of, Ellen Emerson," says the mayor, with an arm out to beckon Ellen to the podium.

Nina watches as Ellen makes her way to the microphone. Ellen waits out the applause, looking back briefly to Nina and her sister. "They told us there would be champagne later," she tells the audience. "We had to come."

The audience is appreciative. Practically anything Ellen said would go over well. "Oh, dear," Ellen says. "I think it was my stubbornness that kept me alive. I hope I have some of that left because now I have my sister and the truth is, I feel . . . younger, quite a bit younger, ready to rock."

Lots of people applaud that line.

"I'd like to thank all the students I had over the years. I'd like to thank

Ruth Hannon who was one of those students and who takes care of me on a daily basis, and I want to thank the journalist, Nina Collins, who helped make this reunion possible. I don't have much to say, except that I'm very lucky. Very lucky." She turned around and looked at Mary. "I'm supposed to introduce my sister to you. I know you've seen her sitting with me. She grew up most of her life as Anna. I keep calling her Mary and she lets me. She's going to say a thank-you next." But then Ellen leaves the podium to give an arm to her sister and they walk back up together.

What Nina saw in the first hours when the sisters met at the nursing home was timelessness. Time simply stopped behaving in the ordinary way. When Nina watched them together then and as she watches them walking together now—why they are everything at once, two years old, just learning to walk steadily. In the blink of a second, teenagers, one following the other, trying to warn her of something. And a second later, Nina feels she sees Ellen supporting the pregnant widowed Mary and in another second it's as if the two of them are walking to a restaurant to have a light snack on an ordinary day. They're fitting it all in. Whole lifetimes are being condensed and lived in whatever order they can grab.

"We have a lot to catch up on," Mary says into the microphone now. "We plan to speak very, very slowly. For one thing, I have to get used to my name."

The audience gives a continued and somewhat sober chuckle at her idea of speaking slowly.

"Plus, I'm a nurse. I can watch out for signs of trouble in my big sister." Mary's attempt at humor lights Ellen's face. "We get to have a little time together. Sometimes miracles happen."

There are going to be fireworks and a big party with champagne. And the sisters plan to drink the bubbly, too. Nina can see them blinking away the lights from the cameras now as they wait out the applause.

They are for sure sisters, scientifically proven. Nina's second article was just in yesterday, cataloguing the DNA test. She managed to make a comparison with the other strands of their lives that matched.

Nina's first article about them was the one she wrote all through the night, starting with the hospital meeting between the sisters. When Ben came into the office on Monday morning expecting to see his piece on reconstruction, and when he found instead a huge photograph of two women holding onto each other and an article by Nina, she rushed to explain. He put up a hand and stood there, reading it. At the end he said, "Well done. Beautifully done. You deserve every bit of it."

And then the phone rang and Douglas said, "I think maybe you save lives, too."

What a day. What a day that was.

The mayor is calling Nina to come up to the podium to speak.

Ellen and Mary look at her encouragingly. And in the audience, there are wonderful people cheering her on. She must speak.

She has a sort of dumb speech ready about how we can only begin to guess at the inventions and changes our lives will hold, how we cannot guess at the surprises and disasters the world will see. If we think about it, we know there will be disasters both natural and man-made. We can only, like the Burrell twins, hope to hang on and to continue to be decent. She wants to say something about what it means to be a Johnstown woman or man—headstrong, patient, determined, dumb in the best possible way—full of youthful wishing. That kind of person, whether they come from here or not, seems to describe everybody she ever loved. She can hardly explain it to a huge audience waiting for the fireworks and champagne. She'd better stick to a couple of thank-yous.

Elsie and Jessie Canan, circa 1880s. Both lived through the flood. Courtesy of Johnstown Area Heritage Association.

Selected Recommendations for Further Reading and Viewing

Cambor, Kathleen. *In Sunlight, In a Beautiful Garden*. New York: Farrar, Straus and Giroux, 2001.

Cordón, Ingrid M., Margaret-Ellen Pipe, Liat Sayfan, Annika Melinder, and Gail S. Goodman. "Memory for Traumatic Experiences in Early Childhood." *Developmental Review* 24 (2004): 101–32.

Crouch, Stanley. *One Shot Harris: The Photographs of Charles "Teenie" Harris*. New York: Harry N. Abrams, 2002.

Duncan, Anthony. "On Intermarriage," *Pittsburgh Courier* (city edition). 24 August 1935, 10.

"Flood '77: A Commemorative Edition." *Johnstown Tribune Democrat*, 19 August 1977, 1.

Guggenheim, Charles. *The Johnstown Flood*. Charles Guggenheim Productions, video recording, Johnstown Flood Museum Association, 1989.

Hahner, David P. *Kennywood*. Portsmouth, NH: Arcadia, 2004.

Mattiace, Peter. "She Recalls 1889 Disaster." *Pittsburgh Post-Gazette*, 22 May 1989, 19.

McCullough, David. *The Johnstown Flood*. New York: Simon and Schuster, 1968.

Miller, Donald. "Fair Steeped in History." *Pittsburgh Post-Gazette*, 22 May 1989, 19.

Peterson, Carole. "Children's Long-Term Memory for Autobiographical Events." *Developmental Review* 22 (2002): 370–402.

Pitz, Marylynne. "National Park Service to Acquire South Fork Club, Which Was at Heart of Johnstown Disaster." *Pittsburgh Post-Gazette*, 18 July 2006. http://www.post-gazette.com/stories/sectionfront/life/national-park-service-to-acquire-south-fork-club-which-was-at-heart-of-johnstown-disaster-442456/.

———. "Minister's Diaries Offer Eye-Witness Account of 1889 Johnstown Flood." *Pittsburgh Post-Gazette*, 7 May 2007. http://www.post-gazette.com/stories/sectionfront/life/ministers-diaries-offer-eyewitness-account-of-1889-johnstown-flood-484240/.

Schoor, Thema M. *100 Years of American Nursing: Celebrating a Century of Caring*. Philadelphia: Lippincott Williams and Wilkins, 1999.

Simic, Andrei, and Maria Simic. *The Children of Lazo's Grove*. Produced and directed by Andrei Simic and Maria Simic. Byzantine Production, video documentary, 95 minutes, 2004.

Slattery, Gertrude Quinn. *Johnstown and Its Flood*. Philadelphia: Dorrance Press, 1936.

Stack, Barbara White. "Flood's Centennial Banks on Tourism." *Pittsburgh Post-Gazette*, 22 May 1989, 19.

Stark, Sharon Sheehe. "The Johnstown Polka." In *The Dealer's Yard and Other Stories*. New York: William Morrow and Company, 1985.

Stewart, Elizabeth A. *Exploring Twins: Towards a Social Analysis of Twinship*. New York: St. Martin's, 2000.

Witse, Jeff. *Contested Waters: A Social History of Swimming Pools in America*. Chapel Hill: University of North Carolina Press, 2007.J204

For a complete bibliography, visit www.kathleengeorge.com.